MURDER ON THE YUKON QUEST

SUE HENRY

SPEAKING VOLUMES, LLC
NAPLES, FLORIDA
2015

Murder on the Yukon Quest

Copyright © 1999 by Sue Henry
Map by Vanessa Summers

ISBN 978-1-62815-261-6

For more exciting
Books, eBooks, Audiobooks and more visit us at
www.speakingvolumes.us

MURDER
ON THE
YUKON QUEST

AN ALASKA MYSTERY

Books by Sue Henry

Murder on the Iditarod Trail
Termination Dust
Sleeping Lady
Death Takes Passage
Deadfall
Murder on the Yukon Quest
Beneath the Ashes
Dead North

For Dominick Abel
Absolute treasure of an agent.
No one does his job better,
or with more style.

"A health to the man on trail this night; may his grub hold out; may his dogs keep their legs; may his matches never miss fire."
    —Jack London, "To the Man on the Trail"

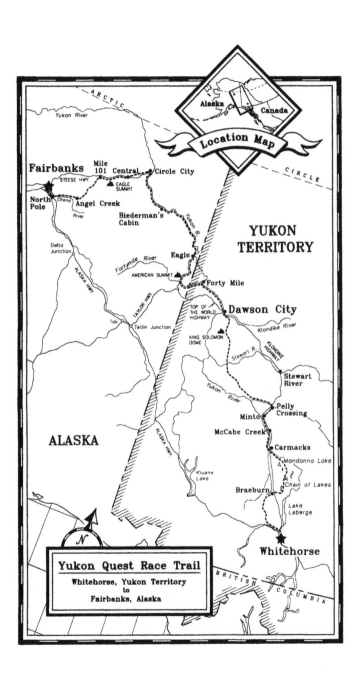

Yukon Quest Race Trail

Whitehorse, Yukon Territory
to
Fairbanks, Alaska

CHAPTER ONE

"It was clear and cold. The aurora borealis painted palpitating color revels on the sky. Rosy waves of cold brilliancy swept across the zenith, while great coruscating bars of greenish white blotted out the stars."
— Jack London, "A Daughter of the Aurora"

JESSIE ARNOLD HALTED HER TEAM AND STOMPED IN THE SNOW hook to secure the sled, though as far as they had come and this late on a chill mid-January night there was little chance that her dogs would proceed without an encouraging word from their driver. They had traveled almost two hundred miles in two days and nights of regular alternating stages—four hours of travel, four hours of rest—with one longer, six-hour camp and a few short pauses. With an important distance race—the Yukon Quest, from Whitehorse, Yukon, to Fairbanks, Alaska—coming up the next month, she was scheduling her training to adjust both the dogs and herself to the extended rotations of running that would be required.

The Yukon Quest was Alaska's second most important distance race and Jessie had decided to try it for the first time, forgoing her usual participation in the Iditarod, for the two were very close together on the calendar and it would have been difficult to run them both.

She was looking forward to testing herself on a new race, and the Quest had established a reputation as the

1

toughest sled dog race in the world, because of the extremes in temperature and terrain experienced by its participants. The route would take Jessie and the rest of the racers over more than a thousand miles of the most remote, inhospitable region of North America in the heart of winter, measuring their ability, raw courage, and sheer will with temperatures that often fell between -30° and -50°.

Jessie was particularly interested in traveling this race route because the relentless, demanding trail would trace the same trails used during the Alaskan and Yukon gold rushes, which had been natural and vital links for mail and freight mushers between communities during this era. The race would also be a challenge because the participants were only allowed to use one sled for the trip, like the mushers who had traveled the early mail routes and repaired their own sleds, if damaged. The Quest would therefore also test the self-sufficiency of each modern musher, leaving some cursing the unrepairable fragments and splinters of their transportation, often nursing their own injuries.

The trail Jessie and her team would run passed through fewer checkpoints than the Iditarod, with greater distances between them, and would include long stretches on the unforgiving Yukon River, the "Highway of the North," its icy surface often repeatedly broken and refrozen into a jumble of ice blocks the size of boxcars as it settled into winter immobility. Three extreme summits higher than any on the Iditarod would have to be crossed, and as she paused with her team on this training run, she was thinking about confronting the physical and mental challenges of this new race.

From his place at the front of the team, Tank, her lead dog, looked back as if wondering why they were stopping so close to home, then lay down in the snow. Two of the young dogs in the team remained on their feet for a minute or two, but, like the veterans, soon relaxed in their places, taking advantage of the pause to rest.

They're adapting fast, Jessie thought, generally pleased

with the response of these twelve huskies to the extended training run they were about to complete. Opening the sled bag, she retrieved a large insulated container of warm water mixed with vitamins, electrolytes, and the food scraps left from a feeding at the last four-hour rest stop. When each dog had been given a metal pan of this tempting liquid, she watched to be sure they were all drinking thirstily, then took a bag of high-energy dog snacks and moved along the line to give some to each, along with a minute or two of individual attention.

"Good dog, Bliss. Good girl. Hey, Sunny. You hungry, Wart? Oh . . . just want that magic spot behind your ears scratched, yes? Okay. All right, Darryl, I'm coming. How about your other brother, Darryl? Here you go, pups."

The two wheel dogs, who ran closest to the sled, were littermates named for the pair of Darryls on the old Bob Newhart television show, and were often referred to simply as One and Two. They looked so much alike it was hard to tell which was which, though Jessie knew that Darryl Two had darker ears and was more inclined to wolf his food. Very much a people dog, he greeted her with an affectionate lick on the hand as she presented his snack.

"Kisses for the pack leader? Thanks. Good job today, guys. Good dogs."

Replacing the supplies, she pulled the big fur mittens that reached almost to her elbows over a thinner pair of wool gloves that protected her fingers when the mittens weren't on. Nothing was as warm as fur, and they hung on an idiot string around the neck of her parka, where they would not be accidentally, disastrously lost. With the dark, which came in midafternoon this time of year, the temperature had dropped below zero and was still falling. Jessie was extremely careful to keep her hands warm, exposing them as little as necessary, but much of the work of caring for the dogs and herself could not be done in the clumsy mitts. Wiggling her fingers to encourage circulation, she left the team and turned to look around her.

The headlamp she wore revealed a trail well packed by

the many mushers in the Knik area who used it for training, all of whom did their part to keep it groomed. Beyond
her light the ghostly white trunks of the tall birches that
lined the trail faded into the dark on either side, branches
bereft of leaves until spring.

Pushing back the hood of the heavy down parka that
hung to her knees, Jessie took a deep breath of the cold
night air and sighed, placed her hands on the small of her
back, and stretched to ease the weary ache between her
shoulders. She knew a couple of mushers who had back
problems and wondered how they stood the jouncing of
the sled for over a thousand miles during a race, or the
hundreds of everyday training miles, for that matter. Almost immediately she forgot her minor physical discom-
forts as she became aware of a spectacular light show
above. Reaching up, she switched off the headlamp and
waited for her night vision to return.

Low on the horizon she could see the glow of the city
of Anchorage, but overhead was a completely different
story. In the subzero temperature and clear air, hundreds
of stars sparkled bright as diamonds against the inky blackness of the sky. Across them, swirling, shimmering curtains of the aurora borealis appeared to have snared their
brilliance in a gauzy net, the brightest of the greenish
white bands so vivid they almost obscured the glittering
points of light beyond them. Along the northern edges of
the aurora were pale hints of rose that pulsed, grew, and
spread, only to wane and slowly vanish as another part of
the moving splendor increased in intensity.

Silent and motionless, Jessie stood gazing attentively
upward as she almost held her breath in wonder. How
many hundred times have I seen the northern lights? she
mused. And I am still arrested and awed by them—en-
thralled as a child at a fireworks show.

Watching the ribbons undulate and gradually elongate
across the dark sky, she remembered seeing photographs
from space probes of the rings of similar auroras above
the poles of Jupiter and Saturn. It made her feel somehow

closer to and more accepting of the two distant planets to know that they shared such extraordinary and inexplicable phenomena.

Time to go, she told herself. With one last look at the splendor of the heavens, she turned and went to fasten the sled bag and whistle up her team. When they were trotting rhythmically along the trail again, the reflective tape on their harnesses winking as it caught the light from her headlamp, Jessie was glad to be almost home and began to consider what awaited her back at the cabin on Knik Road.

Her snug log cabin would be empty, but not cold, for Billy Steward, the dependable young handler who cared for the rest of her kennel in her absence, would have maintained at least a small fire in the potbellied stove to keep the house from freezing. A couple of chunks of wood would soon have its cast iron cheerfully glowing and would quickly spread comfortable warmth through the small living space. In the refrigerator she had left enough of a large kettle of stew for one meal, knowing she would be tired and in no mood to cook when she returned. The rest of the stew had gone with her on the training run, but after eating it for two days, she now found that the idea of more did not appeal in the slightest to her growing appetite. Another lesson relearned, she realized, and began to mentally revise the menu she would prepare and have shipped to checkpoints for her first attempt at the Yukon Quest in February.

From several years of running Alaska's most famous distance race, the Iditarod, between Anchorage and Nome, she had noticed that having a variety of foods perked up her appetite and gave her something to satisfy the hunger produced in the strenuous physical requirements of a thousand-mile race. Long days of racing with little rest drained mushers and exhausted their bodily reserves, necessitating a calorie-rich, high-energy diet. But an exhausted musher could lose all desire for food, or crave certain things she had forgotten to include in her supplies. It was too easy to concentrate on planning just the right food for the dogs and ignore the human athlete in the equation. A well-balanced, successful team required both.

So . . . what do I want for dinner tonight? The thought made her tired, knowing that caring for her team would continue to demand her undivided attention when they reached the dog yard. Ready for a long rest, the dogs must still be watered and fed before they settled for the night. With the handler gone home for the night, it would be up to Jessie to feed and carefully check each animal for small injuries or strains, though this would also give her the opportunity to pet and congratulate each on a job well done. But with these chores ahead it would be at least an hour before she even went through the door of the cabin.

She wished that someone else would be there when she arrived. Not to care for the dogs—she liked doing that herself—but someone who had already put wood in the stove, someone with dinner waiting. More than anything, she wanted a shower and not to have to make decisions. It would be wonderful to have a plate—of anything but stew—put in front of her on the table when she was clean. How nice it would be to curl up warm and stationary on the big sofa by the stove, wrapped in a cozy afghan, with a mug of hot peppermint tea that someone else had made for her. However much she loved running with her dogs, she also loved coming home and relaxing into the comfortable fatigue that resulted from long, successful days on the trail.

"Oh, wouldn't it be loverly?" she sang out.

The dogs pricked up their ears at the sound of her voice and trotted a little faster down the trail.

Alex, where are you when I want you? she thought, feeling, not for the first time, the absence of her friend, housemate, and lover, Alaska State Trooper Alex Jensen, and wondering again just how long he would be away.

It had been after eight o'clock, at the end of a training run much like this, when she had arrived at home to find him tossing clothes hurriedly into a suitcase. Just a week before Christmas.

"Hey, trooper, where're you off to?"

Tall and rawboned, he turned from his packing, handle-bar mustache askew, light hair with just a touch of silver at the temples standing up from where he had run his fingers through it, a grin replacing the frown on his face. Gathering her into a hug, he kissed each of her wind-burned cheeks and her chapped lips, tousled her short honey-blond curls, and looked down into her wide gray questioning eyes.

"You're home, but you're still cold. Must have been a lot of flying snow today," he said.

"Yeah, it was blowing a bit and piling up drifts out there. Where're you going? Out-of-town case?"

He stepped back to hold her at arm's length, his expression once again serious.

"Not this time. My mom called an hour ago, Jess. Dad had a stroke last night. He's in the hospital and I have to go down."

"Oh, no, Alex. How bad was it? Is he going to be all right?"

Jessie had never met Alex's parents, who lived on a ranch a few miles outside Salmon, Idaho, but she had grown quite fond of Keara Lacey Jensen through frequent letters and phone calls. For Alex's father she felt a warmth and respect, gleaned mainly from his son's affectionate comments, for, after a reserved greeting, the reticent Nels Jensen invariably passed the phone to his more loquacious wife.

"It was evidently pretty bad. They medevaced him up to the big hospital in Missoula and the doctors say they won't know much for a few days yet. For now it's one of those wait-and-see things."

"How's your mom?"

"Mom's doing okay, I guess, considering, but she sounded frightened and sort of fragile. I've never heard her sound like she was just barely hanging on. Wish it wouldn't take me till sometime tomorrow to get there."

"Shall I come with you?"

"There just isn't time, Jess. Besides, you need to be here to take care of the dogs and get ready for the race. I'll see how things are and let you know, okay?"

"Sure. Whatever works best. I could come later, if you need me."

"Right."

"What can I do to help, then? When does your plane leave?"

"I have a reservation on the red-eye to Seattle, where I can catch a Horizon flight to Missoula at six-thirty tomorrow morning."

"I'll drive you in. Just let me grab a shower and something to eat. There's time, right?"

"You won't have to, Jess. Caswell's already on his way here. I didn't know for sure when you'd be home, so I called him as soon as I'd made the reservations. Don't know how long I'll be gone, so I've got to stop by the office and get the paperwork on my cases in some kind of order to turn over to Becker. He and Ivan are meeting me there."

Jessie knew that if Ivan Swift, the post commander, was showing up, it definitely meant Alex might be gone for quite some time. Jessie, typically, swung into action mode.

"Okay. What else can I do? Have you had dinner?"

"Yeah, I ate a little, but I'm not really hungry. There's a roast chicken keeping warm for you in the oven. You could make me a couple of sandwiches to take on the plane—mayo, mustard, maybe some of that sharp cheddar. I can't eat that plastic food."

"You've got it. What else?"

"An orange? Maybe a couple of your Snickers." He smiled, knowing Jessie bought Snickers by the box as high-energy trail food and that they both ate oranges for the vitamin C.

"There's a load of laundry in the drier. You could fold it when it's dry. I'll need to pack some of it. Socks. Long underwear. Won't be any warmer there than here."

"Sure."

In less than an hour fellow trooper Ben Caswell had come hurrying into the cabin, said, "No, thanks," to a drumstick, and efficiently swept up Jensen and his duffel.

"I'll call you when I get there," Alex told her at the door. "As soon as I know . . . whatever."

"Let me know if you need anything. Give your mom my love."

"You know I will."

Looking up at his face after he kissed her good-bye, she assessed the distraction in his eyes, the lines of concern that framed the mouth below his handlebar mustache, and laid a palm on his cheek.

"I'll be here. Better call me late. I'll be running the mutts almost every day."

His focus shifted to her and he smiled. "Do good work, musher. That race is coming up fast. I love you."

She nodded. "Too."

He turned, clattered down the front steps, and climbed into his friend's waiting pickup, which was quickly swallowed up in the dark as it turned onto the road from the long driveway. Red taillights flashed momentarily between distant tree trunks and he was gone.

Jessie had closed the door, enveloped by a silence that seemed loud after the clamor of unexpected departure.

On this late evening in January, when Alex had been in Idaho almost three weeks, Jessie changed her mind and went into her empty cabin as soon as she arrived. She pulled up by the front steps, stomped in the snow hook, and dashed inside, where she added wood to the still-glowing coals in the stove and left it to warm the house while she went back out to the yard to take care of her team.

More than an hour later she took a long steaming shower, ate a cold tuna sandwich with a hot bowl of canned tomato soup, went directly to bed, and slept for eight hours, uninterrupted, except once when she woke to hear several of her dogs barking in the yard.

For several nights a moose had wandered close to the cabin, exciting the dogs and provoking them to vocalize loudly at what their tethers prevented them from chasing. Jessie had grinned to herself at the tracks she found in the snow, for the huge ungulate seemed to exhibit a sense of humor in coming exactly close enough to cause a ruckus without actually challenging so many canines. Its passing had left large divided hoofprints at the bottom of holes in the deep snow as it moved easily around the circumference of the yard on long gangly legs, munching on the willows that grew by the drive, even lying down to rest in a stand of birch and spruce to the north, pointedly ignoring the protests of the restless dogs.

Now, as she heard them barking again, Jessie smiled drowsily, rolled onto her left side, and drifted back to sleep in the middle of the big brass bed she usually shared with Alex. There would undoubtedly be more tracks to be found in the morning, but they were really nothing to worry about. A bear might have been different, for some bears would kill and eat dogs, especially those that could not escape. But, thankfully, all the bears, plump from a long summer banquet, were elsewhere, tucked up securely into their dens, keeping warm in their heavy fur, contentedly slumbering the winter away.

Though the dogs barked once or twice after that, Jessie did not wake again. She was unaware that, after the cabin had been dark for over an hour, a dark figure had slipped stealthily into the dog yard from between two large spruce trees; that he had watched Jessie come home from her training run, care for her dogs, and go inside. Walking slowly between the straw-filled dog boxes, he picked one, knelt, and silenced the dog by petting its head, rubbing its ears, and speaking in a low voice.

When he stood up and moved on to another, the first dog followed to where its tether should have stopped it, but found that it was unexpectedly free of restraint. It stopped, not used to being without impediment, then moved on, pursuing the man. When it found a running mate was also loose, the two decided it was time to play, and enthusiastically accompanied the provider of their liberty as he quietly made his way out of the yard and down the long driveway to Knik Road. Reaching the truck he had parked a bend or two away, they willingly jumped up into the cab at his invitation and rode away with him into the night.

"No. I won't do that. Who do you think you're talking to? And they would find out—somehow. I have to sign the papers that say those dogs can . . ."

"You'll do it. I'll destroy you if you don't . . . and here's how."

The voice behind the threat was low, but sharp, cold, and as full of menace as the handsome face of the man who made it. The grin that bared his perfect teeth held no hint of humor as he flipped a yellowed newspaper clipping onto the desk behind which his victim sat angrily protesting.

The sight of the headline and picture included in the article caught the man for whom it was intended like a blow. His anger leaked away like the air from a punctured balloon, leaving him pale and sweaty, feeling as if something slimy had landed on the desk in front of him.

"Oh, Jesus. Where the hell—"

"Shut it, dummy, and listen up. The goddamned things move—don't they?"

Almost beyond listening, the seated man had recoiled in his chair and was glancing desperately around the room for an escape that didn't exist, mentally scrabbling for safety.

"*Don't* they?"

The ominous tone of the question yanked him back to the edge of panic. He shrank into the chair, focused his horror on the yellowing scrap of newsprint, and panted out an answer without looking up.

"Yes. They can, if they're not placed right."

"So, they'll just think this one moved when they can't find it. They won't know the difference. Pretty good chance of that, huh? Still, they'll be unwilling to let it slide through, right? Now, be a good boy.''

''Yes . . . they'll expect some of them to move, so they'll look thoroughly—carefully. If they can't find it anywhere, they'll have to . . . Where . . . how did you get this?''

The shaking finger he pointed at the clipping and its accompanying photograph was ignored by his assailant, who placed both hands on the desk, leaned forward until his face was less than a foot away, and hissed, ''And you'll fix it so *you* do the searching when necessary, won't you? Then *you* can find it. *You* can report it. By the time somebody else takes a look, it'll be too damn late, won't it?''

''But how—''

''Goddammit, you son of a bitch, I don't care how. You'll just *do* it, right?''

''But why? And why me?''

''You don't need to know why. And it's you because I have . . . this, you pervert. Because I say so. Right?''

''Right.''

Strangled by frustration and fear, his resignation was expelled on a breath, barely above a whisper.

''Louder.''

''Right.''

''If you screw up—''

''I won't.'' It was almost a sob, as he covered his face with both hands.

There was silence, the soft sound of a door closing gently, and when he looked up the office was empty. The repugnant newspaper clipping lay where it had been tossed on the desk.

He did not look at it directly again, but after a minute or two struck a match taken from a desk drawer and held it to one corner of the paper. Obsessed with the burning, he watched it blacken and curl until it scorched his fingers, forcing him to stomp out the last scrap where it had fallen to the floor, leaving a narrow black scorch on his office carpet.

CHAPTER TWO

*"They had dropped out of the world. . . . They had come
and gone, some said this way, and some that, and still
others that they had gone to the country of the Yukon."*
—Jack London, "An Odyssey of the North"

JESSIE WAS FRANTIC THE NEXT MORNING WHEN SHE FOUND
two of her dogs, Bliss and Pete, missing from the yard;
she had been planning to use both of them in the upcoming
race. She wondered if, tired from the long run, she could
have somehow missed securing them to the chains
attached to the top of the metal posts planted firmly in the
ground beside their boxes. The tethers lay slack, with no
sign of damaged links in the chains or broken swivels.

Pete was a reliable older dog. She could even turn him
loose when they ended a run, for he always went straight
to his box and lay down in the straw to wait for food and
water. She might have forgotten to clip his collar to the
tether, but would not have expected him to leave the yard
or get himself in trouble with the others.

Bliss was another question. A bit skittish and inclined
to squabble over food, she might roam, given the opportunity, so Jessie was always careful to keep tight hold of
her collar, walk her across the yard to her place, and assure
herself that this dog was well fastened. Even though, hungry and glad to be home, she had been running on automatic pilot the night before, she was convinced she had

13

fastened Bliss as usual. So where was she? And where was Pete?

It was impossible to follow tracks. The dog yard was full of them, the snow flattened by thousands of canine prints and those of Jessie and her handlers. She called and whistled down several trails that led out of the yard into the surrounding woods, but neither of them responded.

While she worried about finding them, she set about feeding and watering the rest of the dogs. She had just finished with this chore when a bark drew her attention to the trees just south of the cabin and Pete came trotting into the yard. Going directly to his own box, he immediately thrust his nose into the water pan she had just hopefully filled.

Jessie crossed to where he was drinking thirstily and set down the bucket that still held a little food.

"Pete, you good old mutt. Where have you been?"

She rubbed his head and shoulders affectionately and he looked into her face, tongue hanging out, panting as if he had been running hard for a long ways. He flopped down in a little straw that was scattered in front of his box and sighed as he laid his head down on his front paws, slowly wagging his tail as she examined his collar to see if it might be the problem, but it was fine.

"Hey, buddy. How'd you get loose? Why'd you take off? Where's Bliss? You two been chasing that moose?"

I *must* have forgotten to tether him, Jessie thought, frowning at her mistake. Got to be more careful.

At least now she would only have to find Bliss. And if Bliss had gone with Pete, she might still come back on her own. Jessie decided to wait awhile to see. If not, after a planned trip to the vet, Jessie decided she would take a few dogs and the sled, and make a quick search of the surrounding area, before expanding the hunt to kennels up and down Knik Road.

She fed Pete and gave him more water, both of which he consumed in record time before going to sleep, and went into the cabin to get her own breakfast, keeping an eye on the dog yard from the large window that faced in that direction.

Still watching for Bliss, Jessie enjoyed a third cup of her favorite morning coffee and considered names for the puppies she had brought inside for a bit of socialization. It was important to establish relationships with puppies while they were still young and imprintable. Becoming a positive, normal part of their lives as early as possible made their training easier and helped them develop skills for working with people and other dogs as a team. Since dogs, like wolves, are naturally members of a pack, she made herself the alpha leader of her pack, automatically accepted by them all as dominant—the boss.

On the braided rug on the floor before the sofa lay Rosie, a young first-time mother, with four pups of her almost month-new litter. Three of these were attentively enjoying a liquid breakfast provided by their patiently re-clining mom. The other, darkest and most active of the gang, had climbed to her shoulder and was licking one of her ears. Jessie had named her Daisy for the single white spot that surrounded one eye like a flower. A fifth, a min-iature edition of his father, Tank, wriggled in Jessie's lap as she scratched his round, milk-taut belly and smiled at his baby growls and repeated attempts to gnaw her fingers.

"What a clown you are," she told him. "If you've inherited any of your daddy's dignity, it doesn't show yet. Maybe you've got his smarts—make another good leader someday."

When the phone rang she put him back on the floor with a pat and a push in Rosie's direction and went to the desk.

"Arnold Kennels."

"Jess? It's me."

"Hi, you! How's everything down there? How's your dad doing? I just got back from two days out with the guys. Made it almost to Skwentna before—"

"I tried to call last night."

"You didn't leave a message so I could call you back."

"I wanted to talk to *you,* not that blasted machine."

There was something in his voice that warned her, a tension she recognized—stiff upper lip sound.

"What's wrong, Alex?"

But she already knew what he would say.

"My dad . . . died . . . night before last."

For a minute she couldn't answer. "When?"

Dumb, she thought . . . stupid, unfeeling question, then realized the word was an attempt to keep him talking while she regained her balance.

"About two in the morning. He just went . . . while he was asleep. Breathing . . . everything . . . got slower and slower . . . and he was gone. It took a minute before I knew he wasn't there anymore."

A deep breath. Then, "Oh, Alex. I'm so sorry."

"Me, too."

"Your mom?"

"Not so good. She was expecting to have to spend a long time nursing him, but not . . . She's in shock, Jess. Needs time. This really turns her safe world upside down."

"Was she there with you when . . . ?"

"No. We—my brother, Ned, Mom, and I—have been . . . had been . . . taking turns staying with him, so he . . . wasn't alone. I had to call the motel and wake them up. She'll be okay in a while, but this makes everything different . . . hard for her."

The thick sound of his voice, the pauses in what he was saying, told her more than his words.

"And you?"

Focused on the voice in her ear, she tried to ignore Tank's small double as he dauntlessly followed her across the room to attack the tempting dangle of her boot laces.

Jeep. I think I'll call him Jeep, Jessie thought. That works.

"I'm . . . okay for now. You know. There's a lot to do. We'll take him home . . . to Salmon . . . tomorrow.

Back on the ranch it'll be better, I think . . . for mom . . .
for all of us. The funeral's Tuesday.''

"Alex . . . I'll be there as soon as I can.''

The race? A year of planning? Were they really so
important? She knew they shouldn't be, but . . . Was she
actually holding her breath?

"Ah . . . Jess. You're good to offer, but no . . . I don't
think so. There's all the . . . arrangements . . . Mom . . .
Ned. The whole community in Salmon to . . . I just can't
divide myself right now . . .''

Divide himself? What the hell did that mean? How—
and when—had she become a *division* to him?

Disconcerted, she moved her foot abruptly and the pup
scampered back to his mother, where he flopped down
with his littermates.

". . . If you'd ever been here—knew people . . . ah . . .''
He sputtered into an embarrassed pause. "I'm sorry, Jessie. I didn't mean that the way it came out. Can you
understand? You know that feeling of going home that
makes everything else seem unreal . . . ?''

Unreal?

For a moment she hesitated, awash in and trying to rid
herself of a combination of exasperation and guilty relief—a small silence to which he immediately applied his
own interpretation.

"Oh, shit . . . Jess. I've said it all wrong. It's just
that—''

She interrupted, speaking too fast, heard the tense false-
ness in her voice, and couldn't explain guilt born of feeling
hurt and . . . guilty.

"It's all right, Alex. I understand. You've got a lot to
take care of now. You should do what is best for
yourself . . . and your . . . family. It's okay.''

There was an awkward, uncomfortable stillness filled
with misplaced feelings of fault and contrition on both
sides.

"I think maybe we—at least I—should go back and
start over,'' Alex said, finally.

"No, really. You don't need this kind of hassle at the moment. Believe me when I tell you that it is okay—it'll be fine. I understand and you're right. We'll talk about it later . . . or not."

Grateful that her voice sounded somewhat close to normal, sincere and sympathetic, she heard him sigh.

"Thanks, Jess. I miss you."

"I miss you, too. Take great good care. Okay?"

"Yes. I'll talk to you very soon."

"I'm here—whenever—well, part of the time. You know my kind of schedule. Don't worry. Oh, Alex—I almost forgot. I'm taking the dogs to Whitehorse two weeks before the race. We'll get settled and rested from the trip, stay with Fred, and do some Yukon runs, get them a little more used to the colder temperatures. Gotta get their prerace vet check there, too."

"Okay. I'll get a number from you before you leave."

"Sure. . . ."

"Later, love."

"Bye."

She stood staring at the receiver in her hand for a long moment before replacing it in its cradle with exaggerated gentleness and returning to the sofa, where she sat down and leaned back into a pile of pillows. There was a lump of tension under her breastbone, a clenched fist that ached and forced her to take shallow breaths. Feeling as if someone had wrung out her thoughts and emotions like a wet washcloth, she tried to sort her scrambled mind into some kind of order, but something howled painfully in bruised reaction.

I should go.

You don't really want to go.

He didn't want me . . . need me!

Oh, stop it. You're overreacting. His dad just died.

But I'd want him!

You don't know what you'd want in similar circumstances. You're the one who doesn't want to get married, remember?

I never said . . . never.

Same thing.

Not at all. I wanted more time . . . to think.

Nonsense! You kept putting it off. Maybe too long.

I was considering . . .

Yeah?

You're right. I've been satisfied with what we had— had?—and ignored it.

Avoided it.

Yeah. Oh, hell . . . okay . . . avoided.

Uneasy, depressed, confused, she stood up and went to the kitchen, where she splashed coffee into her mug, spilling half on the counter. Angrily, she mopped at it with a sponge, as if she could smear away the unsettling hurt and regret as well.

How many times did we talk of going to Idaho to visit his folks, but never went?

Not all my fault. We were both busy.

Yes, but going seemed like a commitment you didn't want to make.

True. I knew they'd make assumptions . . . and so would Alex.

You think he didn't? Well, now he won't. Mollified?

"No! Dammit . . . I'm not!"

Rosie raised her head at the sound of her human's voice, stood up, and shook herself. Greedy pups, including small newly named Jeep and Daisy, dropped to the braided rug in an indignant heap of yips and whines, which their mother ignored.

Jessie had to smile at their protests as she went to give the bitch a few appeasing pats.

"It's okay, girl, but time for you guys to go back to the nursery shed. I've got a full day ahead that doesn't include your family—just the team I'm taking to Whitehorse and some ID chips at the vet's. I've also got to find where Bliss has gone."

Putting on her boots, parka, and gathering the squirming gang of five into an armful, Jessie held the door open for

Rosie, who was attentively watching her brood, and led the way to the shed that she kept warm for new mothers and pups born during the winter months. Securing them in the comfortable shelter, she turned to implement her plans for the day, and her conscience gave her a parting shot.

What're you going to do about all this?

I don't know. And right now there's not much I can do. I'll think about it, okay . . . later?

Okay, Scarlett O'Hara, but . . .

Swearing mentally, Jessie went to work.

Purposely considering her reasons for choosing each one, she began to move the dogs that would make up her Yukon Quest team into the compartments of the dog box on the back of her pickup. The Darryls, her best wheel dogs; Mitts, a beautiful female with a longer than usual white ruff and the determined self-confidence of a Vegas showgirl; dependable Pete, who sometimes alternated lead with Tank, though the latter hated to run anywhere but at the head of the string. Goofy was an energetic, perpetual pup who would always rather lope than trot.

By this time the whole yard of more than forty were yelping, barking, and straining at their tethers, eager to be selected to go wherever Jessie was going, hoping for a run. Tank, tethered nearest to the truck, sat watching like a supervisor, too dignified to make such a fuss, knowing he wouldn't be left. She ignored them and loaded another thirteen dogs, the team she had selected and four alternates, in case any of her first-choice racers had to be replaced at the last minute. The four not put into harness for the start of the race would be brought back from Canada by her handlers along with any she dropped before the halfway point.

The compartments in the dog box, two high and six wide, faced outward on each side of the truck, with holes in the doors to allow the dogs to look out and fresh air to get in. Large enough to let the dog stand up, lie down, turn, and move around in safety, each compartment was lined with straw for individual comfort and warmth. An entire box would hold twenty-four dogs at once in their compartments, a traveling doggie motel of sorts. Boxes of this type, designed by and for mushers, were arranged to carry not only the team, but a sled or two secured to the top and, in a space accessed from the rear between the two outer lines of dog compartments, harness, gang lines, dog food, and other equipment the musher or animals may need.

"Come on, Tank. You last, buddy," Jessie said, lifting her leader to the lower compartment just behind the driver's seat. "You've already been chipped, but it won't hurt to make sure it's still okay since the last race."

The drive to the veterinarian in Palmer took half an hour from her Knik cabin and she arrived to find three more trucks with dog boxes ahead of her in the parking lot. Vets all over Alaska were putting computer chips into sled dogs for next month's Yukon Quest and the Iditarod, which was annually held in March. The chips, introduced with a large needle under the skin between the shoulder blades, were the size of a grain of rice and held recorded identification information that could be read with a scanner at race time, ensuring that no dog had been substituted and all were approved to run. It also ensured the identification of any dog that wandered or was lost on the thousand-mile race, aiding in a quick reunion with its owner. Though this did not happen often, periodically a dog would vanish and be found miles from where it disappeared, sometimes even far away from the race route. Since a racer could not continue until the dog was found and returned to the team, it could be an important factor to a frustrated musher.

Jessie had never lost a dog during a race and had no intention of doing so now: She was careful to teach hers not to take off if they found themselves loose from the line. Still, there could always be a moose or a snowshoe hare they couldn't resist chasing, so it was comforting to know that each member of her team could be so easily identified.

As she waited for her turn with the vet, Jessie was surprised when he came out to the truck. She had already unloaded Tank and Pete, who greeted him with wagging tails. Her dogs were not afraid of Bob Spenser, who always treated them with gentle friendship and even remembered the names of those he had seen most often.

He knelt in the snow to greet the two affectionately.

"Hey there, Tank. You're looking fit, as usual. Good boy, Pete. Going to win Jessie another race, are you?"

The older dog cocked his head attentively, recognizing the word *race,* and seemed to smile, making Jessie smile as well.

Spenser looked up.

"Hey, Jessie. You missing a dog?"

"Yes, I sure am. A couple of them played hookey from the yard last night. Pete's back, but I'm going looking for Bliss as soon as we're through here. Why? You hear about someone seeing her?" she asked eagerly.

"Better. She was tied with a rope to the handle of the front door when I came in this morning. Someone must have found her and thought I'd be able to give you a call. I tried, but you didn't answer; then the line was busy. It's Bliss, all right—her name and yours are on the collar. She's out back in the kennel."

Warm relief spread through Jessie. "Is she okay?"

"Fine—happy and rested. Ate a good breakfast and seemed pleased to see me." He grinned. "She one of those you want chipped?"

"Yeah. I'll get her when it's our turn."

"I'm ready now. Might as well start with these two."

How had Bliss made it all the way to Palmer? Jessie wondered. Maybe whoever found her had brought her in from somewhere along Knik Road. Pete had looked as if he'd been running a long time. So how could Bliss be rested? Perhaps he had escaped capture and run home instead of riding in style to the vet's. She'd love to know where they had been, but probably never would.

Truants, she thought, amused. They're just like a couple of kids skipping school. Now that they were both safe and found, she hoped they'd had a good time. If they *had* been chasing the moose, it wouldn't be back anytime soon.

I've got to be more conscientious about tethering them, she told herself. It must have been my sloppy mistake that let them get away in the first place.

Late that afternoon, with her team all chipped and a few errands done in town, she was home again, had returned her dogs, including Bliss, to their individual spaces in the yard, fed and watered them all. She was in the process of packaging frozen trail meat in the storage shed, which made a good winter refrigerator, when a truck turned off the highway into her drive. Wiping grubby hands on the thighs of her jeans, she went to greet Linda and Ben Caswell, whom everyone called Cas, as they got out carrying grocery sacks and a large baking pan.

"Hi. We brought dinner," Linda called.

"I *love* you!" Jessie returned with a grin, remembering last night's soup-and-sandwich dinner. "I'm so sick of my own food I'd eat dog food if someone else cooked it."

"We can do better than that. Lasagna okay?"

"Better than okay. Superb! Garlic bread? Salad? I'm dying for greens."

"Oh, yeah. We've got all the trimmings," Cas chimed in. "Even an apple pie and ice cream. But don't let us interrupt. Finish what you're doing. We'll just go on in and get it ready."

"Oh, no," Jessie cautioned, laughing as she headed up the front steps to open the door and usher them in. "Whatever I'm doing can wait. I'm not letting you out of my sight with the goodies."

"Golly, dern. And I thought it was our sterling company you'd appreciate."

"Well, that, too, but first things first. I'll appreciate your company much more *after* we've eaten."

Over the course of several years, Cas and Linda had grown to be good friends with Alex and Jessie, and the two couples often spent time together playing bridge, going to movies, or out to dinner. Alex and Cas, who both worked for the troopers, often on cases together, were fishing addicts, so camping trips to the Kenai Peninsula were always part of the summer activities for all. Though the women seldom joined the hook-and-line activity, they both liked to garden and had numerous gardening and sewing projects they shared, as well as shopping trips to Anchorage, fifty miles away.

Cas and Linda had already heard about the death of Alex's father from a quick phone call Jessie had made before going to the vet's office. Now she knew that part of Cas's clowning was intended to cheer her, and was grateful for the extension of his sympathy for Alex.

Inside, Jessie went to clean herself up while Linda headed immediately for the kitchen to put the lasagna and bread in the oven to warm while she finished making a salad. As Jessie washed off the evidence of her day's work with the dogs and changed her clothes, it seemed strange that Alex was missing from his usual place in the quartet. An unsettling memory of their morning's phone conversation rose in her mind, but she dismissed it for the moment and returned to the front of the house, where she added wood to the stove and gratefully accepted the beer Cas handed her.

"Thanks. You're a lifesaver. I'll set the table."

"Already done, but you can let Don in before he does some structural damage."

A thundering tattoo on Jessie's handmade door was immediately followed by a long-haired Paul Bunyan of a man with huge shoulders. Don Graham, sure of his welcome, had opened it himself and stood grinning benevolently at them through his beard.

"Something smells awfully good in here," he boomed

in a voice that all but rattled glassware. "Linda's been spending time in the kitchen again. The Julia Child of the north, God bless her."

"Come on in, Don, and shut the barn door," Jessie directed, cheered by his irrepressible presence. "You're heating up the whole outdoors."

He moved inside and allowed them to see that he was not alone. Close behind him came Billy Steward, the enthusiastic young junior musher who was Jessie's daily handler. Gangly, all elbows and knees, he appeared small next to Don, though he was actually close to six lanky feet tall and still growing.

"Hi, Billy. Thanks for changing the straw in the nursery shed while I was gone this afternoon."

"That's okay. Gave me a chance to bond with the pups. Have you named them all yet?"

"Not all, just Daisy and the male that looks like Tank. I'm going to call him Jeep. You pick one yet? Any but that one. I've decided to keep him."

"Naw, I'll wait till they're a little bigger, thanks."

"Good idea. Just let me know when you're ready."

Divesting themselves of coats and boots, Don and Billy crossed the room to join the others at the table and the conversation grew slightly less animated as all five made appreciative inroads into Linda's lasagna. By the time they reached pie and coffee, the subject had switched to their plans for the upcoming Yukon Quest.

These four friends would be Jessie's support team for the race from Whitehorse to Fairbanks the following month. When he heard she was planning to enter the race, Don had called to volunteer, surprising and pleasing Jessie because he had past Yukon Quest experience as a handler. The four would be driving two trucks: Jessie's, with its space for extra dogs and equipment, and Don's, which was fitted with a camper in which they could rest, cook, and wait for her to arrive at checkpoints. They would provide whatever assistance was allowed by the race rules and pick up any dogs dropped from her team at accessible checkpoints.

At least half the route of the Yukon Quest was run through checkpoints in the Yukon and Alaska that could be reached by road. Though the first half did not follow the highway from Whitehorse, wandering instead farther west through the wilderness, it met the road at the Carmacks checkpoint and again at the famous gold rush community of Dawson City, where the racers would have to take a thirty-six-hour mandatory rest stop.

North of Dawson the graveled Top of the World Highway was drifted closed in the winter and dog teams took off into wild country, crossed the vast American Summit to reach the isolated town of Eagle, Alaska, on the banks of the Yukon River, and followed it to Circle, which was connected to Fairbanks by another long road. Support teams had to return 333 miles south to Whitehorse, turn northwest, and drive 602 miles to Fairbanks, then east another 162 miles to Circle, the historic mining community at the end of the road that was only 50 miles south of the Arctic Circle itself.

The eleven hundred miles of driving took at least two days to reach the site where the Quest racers came off the river, and had to be done in all kinds of winter weather conditions, at times frustrating support teams as thoroughly as mushers. In February it was always cold in the interior of Alaska and the Yukon, but on clear sunny days the trip was pleasant enough, if wearing. If a storm swept in, it could be a nightmare of blowing snow and howling wind that rocked and shook trucks carrying loads of dogs, equipment, and tired handlers, adding hours, sometimes days to the journey.

Since Jessie planned to drive herself, the team, and Billy to Fairbanks, then on to Whitehorse two weeks before the race, the group now at her table decided that Cas would fly Linda in his Maule M-4 on skis, to meet them there four days before the race. While the three finished last-minute preparations, he would return to Palmer and join

Don in his truck for the trip to Canada. After the start of the race, the four handlers would drive the two trucks to Dawson, meet Jessie, and, when she had rested and checked out on her way to Eagle, would take turns driving the long road back to Fairbanks in one long run, and stop there overnight before continuing on to Circle.

"This would be a whole lot easier if we lived in either Whitehorse or Fairbanks," Billy commented, when they had finally worked out the details of the trip, the packing and shipping of food and equipment Jessie would need for the race, and some of the hundred other details that would need to be taken care of before she left Knik.

"Would you rather stay here and take care of the rest of the dogs?" Jessie asked with assumed innocence. "I could get somebody else to—"

"No!" His response was loud and definite enough to make them all smile, knowing how much he was looking forward to the whole experience. "You wouldn't. Would you?"

"No, Billy. Don't panic. I was just teasing. Ron Franks has already agreed to stay here at the kennel."

By the time everyone had gone home, it was after nine o'clock and had been a long day. While Jessie went out on another training run the next day, Don and Billy would finish packing the food she wanted to ship for the dogs. Jessie felt good about the plans they had made and was glad to have friends who were willing to carve time from their busy lives to help with such a massive undertaking. But, as the rumble of the Caswell truck going down the driveway faded, she once again found herself alone and thinking of Alex, who had intended to be part of it. He seemed farther away than ever after their unsatisfactory conversation that morning. He had wanted to be on the support crew. Would he possibly make it back in time?

She doubted it.

CHAPTER THREE

"They were men, penetrating the land of desolation and mockery and silence, puny adventurers bent on colossal adventure, pitting themselves against the might of a world as remote and alien and pulseless as the abysses of space."
—Jack London, White Fang

FOR ANYONE WHO DID NOT CARE FOR CROWDS, FIRST AVE-nue in Whitehorse, Yukon Territory, Canada, was the last place to be on the first Sunday in February, packed as it was with a huge, excited, milling throng of people who lined the street to watch the start of the Yukon Quest sled dog race. The noise level was enough to induce auditory overload with an all but deafening combination of the race announcer's blaring loudspeaker, mushers, handlers, race officials, and spectators shouting to each other, and the yelping and barking of hundreds of dogs ready and yearning to run—to get out on the trail in the beginning of the annual thousand-mile trip to Fairbanks, Alaska, through some of the wildest, most isolated country imaginable.

Though the dogs that made up the forty-seven teams of racers that registered for this race had no way of knowing where they were headed or how far, they had learned from past experience that they were about to go somewhere, and that was enough. Going was what they were trained for, eager for, what they and the mushers who owned and

managed them liked to do best. Leaping against their tethers and barking, the dogs expressed their anticipation
enthusiastically.

Among the mushers, last-minute tension manifested itself in checking and rechecking equipment and supplies
as they eyed each other's dogs in an attempt to figure out
who had the fastest, most dependable teams that might
become front-runners in the race. Psychology played a
large part in racing strategy, some striving to convincingly
sell the idea that their dogs would be among the finest on
the trail, others trying to keep a low profile, dismissing
the idea that they might possibly have a strong team, or
that anyone should be at all interested or concerned with
keeping track of them.

Drivers new to distance racing were understandably
more nervous than the veterans who were familiar with
what would be required of them. While the rookies
couldn't stand still and continually fidgeted with their dogs
and gear, former Quest racers went competently, confi-
dently about the tasks that were essential to getting themselves out of Whitehorse, or stood casually conversing
with other old hands, at least outwardly calm as they
waited their turn at the starting gate.

The trailbreakers, members of the Canadian Rangers,
were already long gone. Much earlier, they had headed
north into the wilderness, towing sleds filled with equipment and survival gear behind their whining snowmachines, to create a trail that would lead the mushers and their
teams 175 miles to Carmacks, first in a series of seven
checkpoints between the start and finish of the race that
each team would have to pass through on their way
through parts of two countries in the next two weeks. From
Carmacks the Rangers would proceed in stages ahead of
the racers as far as the border between Canada and Alaska,
near Forty Mile on the Yukon River, where they would
be met by American military counterparts, who would continue to break the trail to its eventual end on the frozen
Chena River in downtown Fairbanks.

At a banquet two nights before the race, the mushers had drawn numbers for starting positions. Now those who would leave Whitehorse first were harnessing their teams and rechecking the contents of their sled bags, fearful of forgetting some essential item. Most rookies carried more than they should, unfamiliar with the trail and its exacting requirements, afraid of needing something they had left behind. But even the sleds of the veterans could weigh in at over three hundred pounds, for checkpoints in this race were farther apart than other distance races, and mandatory gear added to the food and equipment necessary to cover the miles between them made up a sizable load.

Trucks with dog boxes, some large, some small, were strung out for blocks on the sides of the street behind the starting line in reverse order, those who would leave last parked closest to the gate. This allowed crews to pack up and leave as soon as the racer they supported had gone, without the risk of driving through teams still waiting to start.

The week before the race had seemed more than usually fraught with problems for several of the mushers, starting the rumor of a jinx among the handlers and volunteers.

Two of Jessie's dogs had eaten something that made them sick and forced them to be isolated; she could only hope it was not something that would spread to the rest of the team, taking her out of the race completely. Their energy suppressed by the illness, the two would be unable to race, and would be transported back to Fairbanks with the support crew. Tux, a sweet, willing young dog, injured a paw on one of the last training runs and came close to being left out of the racing team as well.

Several dogs owned by another Alaskan musher had somehow broken loose, disappeared from their tethers in a local kennel, and hadn't been found, though one of them had been sighted loping along the bank of the Yukon River near Whitehorse. A whole team had canceled out at the last possible minute, all the dogs sick with some kind of virus or poisoning. A crew of handlers quit, leaving the

racer frantically making phone calls to find someone—
anyone—to drive his truck and provide support. Another
lost the brakes on his truck coming down a hill into town,
putting him in the hospital and out of the race in the
resulting crash with an eighteen-wheeler headed for Alaska
with a load of freight.

In spite of all the trouble, the race would start as sched-
uled, with two fewer teams, as the musher without handlers had managed to recruit a replacement crew of young
Canadian would-be racers. How well they would perform
was something to be discovered as the race progressed.

Just before one o'clock, an official called the first team
to the line. Like many who would follow, a handler rode
a second, or *drag* sled immediately behind the first to slow
the excited dogs that leaped, barked, and howled in a
frenzy to be off. Others might leave with only a handler
balanced atop the heavy sled, which, with an attentive
driver and a team accustomed to spectators, as some were,
would probably be enough to keep the dogs under control
in such distracting conditions. An out-of-control team and
sled could be dangerous to themselves and the spectators
that were crowded along the temporary fences set up to
keep them off the street. Hopefully none of those watching
would have been inconsiderate enough to bring a canine
pet to watch the start—a practice that made mushers growl
derogatory remarks about "Fifi" and "pampered poo-
dles"—for if any nonracing fido escaped into the path of
an outgoing sled, it could ruin a smooth start, often resulting in a team thoroughly tangled in their traces and a
totally panicked pet, not to mention possible injuries to
animals or people.

Sled at the starting point, gang line taut from the com-
bined energy of the eager dogs connected to it by their
tug lines, the first musher stopped in place and dug in the
snow hook to await the official countdown. The announcer
shouted out the name, where the musher was from, past
history of other races, and whether or not this was a first

attempt at the Yukon Quest. He then counted down the last ten seconds.

It took almost as many handlers as there were dogs to keep the team from false starts, and the minute the word "Go!" echoed from the loudspeaker and they were released, the team sprang away full of energy and adrenaline, loping enthusiastically down the snowy street. They were always so hyped that if a driver was not careful and vigilant the dogs could wear themselves out from the simple joy of running in the first day or two of the race. Experienced racers knew how to carefully restrain them without dampening their spirits until the team settled into a normal distance-covering trot, falling back on what they had learned over hundreds of training miles.

As soon as the sled had cleared the line, another group of handlers moved the second team forward, held it in place, and the announcing began again. For the next hour and a half, racers would regularly leave the gate every two minutes until all forty-five were on their way. The uproar would lessen slightly with every team that cleared the gate, until the last would finally go out, leaving an odd silence in its wake. The difference in the starting times would be adjusted in Dawson, where the teams would make the longest mandatory rest stop.

Officials and some of the spectators would then quickly turn their attention to heading for Carmacks, the first checkpoint. Others would go home to watch the progress of the race on their television sets, videotaped by reporters who covered it, always trying to be one jump ahead of the mushers, which wasn't too difficult considering that the teams seldom traveled faster than six to eight miles an hour.

Some of the media crews, like the support crews, would drive the only available miles of road, making the long journey to Dawson, then to Fairbanks, and Circle. Others would fly in small chartered ski planes from one checkpoint to the next, making it possible to reach those inaccessible by road. Like the handlers, none would get much sleep, however they traveled. Arriving in checkpoints, they might have to wait hours for the race leaders to appear, so they would catch naps wherever they could find an out-of-the-way corner in a roadhouse or a vehicle, wear the same clothes for days, and eat whatever they could buy, beg, or carry along. But at the start, fresh and ready to go, Canadian and American cameramen and reporters surrounded the starting line, recording each and every musher and team to begin the toughest race on record.

The morning of Jessie's rookie attempt, Quest racers and their handlers, as usual, had arrived early at the starting area, before it grew light and long before all but the most die-hard of spectators, knowing there was still much to accomplish and prepare before they were ready to go. Nerves frayed ragged for many as they worked to complete their preparations and account for everything they would need in the next thousand miles.

As the race got under way, far down the street, sixteenth in order of start, with twenty-nine similar trucks between herself and the line, Jessie had already unloaded fourteen of her dogs, hooked their tethers to the bumpers and sides of her truck, and given them water. The four she would not use in the team stuck their heads through the holes in the doors of their dog box compartments and watched the activity around them with interest and a growing sense of disappointment, knowing they were about to be abandoned in favor of their kennelmates.

These dogs were only alternates until the race started. During the race neither Jessie nor the other racers would be allowed to add dogs to their teams. Dogs might be dropped at designated locations along the route, but a racer must start with no fewer than eight and no more than fourteen dogs. The racers had to finish with no fewer than six dogs, and all dogs must be either on the towline or hauled in the sled.

Early on, without the blaring loudspeaker to encourage excitement, most of the dogs around the truck lay down calmly. Dependable Pete even snoozed, head on paws, but the rest alertly eyed the activity, while Billy watched them and put booties on all fifty-six of their feet. As straining, yelping teams in harness began to pass on their way to the line, Jessie gave the last four in their compartments an apologetic pat or two and focused on the fourteen who were all up and moving restlessly, infected by the desire to go that was sparked by their awareness that a race was imminent.

Don and Cas had lifted the heavy sled down from the top of the truck and Linda had checked all the necessary items off on a list as Jessie identified them in the sled bag, and moved a few, taking care to balance it as well as possible. She had also attentively examined the sled itself one last time, for it was different from sleds she had used to run Iditarods past. Not allowed to change sleds, participants had to drive the same one throughout, hoping it would survive the entire race. It was, therefore, stronger, heavier, and "capable of safely negotiating a 1000 mile trail, and of hauling any injured or fatigued dogs and the required food, materials, and equipment," as stated in the Yukon Quest Rules.

The last thing she had done was recheck the mandatory gear that each driver must have in his or her possession at all times during the race, which included a good cold-weather sleeping bag, a hand ax at least twenty-two inches long, a pair of snowshoes with an area of at least twenty-two square inches, her veterinary records for each dog in the team, and a packet of mail that each racer must carry to Fairbanks for the Quest committee. The limited-edition envelopes in the packet, with stamps that were canceled in both Fairbanks and Whitehorse, would be sold later as collectibles. All these things were of supreme importance, for in the event that any item was missing at a checkpoint, the driver would be required to acquire or replace it before being allowed to check in and continue, and would be assessed a time penalty of thirty minutes per item at the last mandatory checkpoint in the race.

In addition to this mandatory gear, each musher was required to have eight booties to protect each of the dogs' feet, either in the sled, or worn by the dogs at check-in. Dozens of booties were used between checkpoints in the Quest, but this rule ensured that there would always be some extras available. Not mandatory, but recommended by the race committee, was a compass, a map, flares, and dog blankets, all of which Jessie had packed in her sled along with items of her own choice, including food for herself and her dogs, extra clothes and mittens, two disposable cameras, a first-aid kit, buckets, her cooker and fuel, feeding pans, water bottles, an insulated cooler that she would use to keep food and fluids from freezing—and an assortment of odds and ends of personal gear. She usually included her Smith and Wesson .44 and ammunition for it, but, because handguns are not allowed in Canada, she had not packed it and would run without a weapon.

Carrying a rifle or a handgun was not unusual for distance mushers; many routinely took them along even on training runs in case of a threatening tangle with a moose. Bears hibernated during the winter months, but hundreds of hungry moose roamed the north country and could be a problem. They grew cranky with little to eat and found the trail packed for and by racing teams easier to negotiate than deep soft snow. Met on a trail, they often refused to move away from it and sometimes attacked, viciously, kicking with their powerful sharp hooves, devastating sled dogs that were trapped by their harness to the gang line, unable to escape. Small planes flying over the race route periodically identified the track of a sled that had made a wide half circle, detouring away from and returning to the trail, to go around a moose that stubbornly declined to clear the way.

Fortunately, Jessie did not have to carry supplies for the entire trip. Food and other necessaries for later in the race had already been sorted and packed in bags of no more than sixty pounds, clearly marked with her name and a designated checkpoint. Two or three of these had been flown out to each of the checkpoints, where they would be waiting for her along with bales of straw to be spread on the snow to provide warmer resting places for her dogs. Jessie, trailwise from past Iditarods, knew what was essential and what was unnecessary, thereby lightening her load and shipping costs considerably.

"I sort out everything I might need," she had explained to Linda, as they had worked together in Knik to bag the things to be shipped. "Then I take out at least a third of it, more if I can."

Though a rookie in this race, she was nonetheless a veteran musher. Still, as always before a race, Jessie could feel a tension in the pit of her stomach and across her shoulders; she was as anxious as her team to be gone. With everything packed, wearing her favorite, as well as warmest, red parka and the rest of her cold-weather gear, all she could do now was wait until it was time to hitch her dogs' tug lines to the gang line and head for the starting line.

Satisfied that she was as ready as possible, she was pouring a last cup of coffee from Caswell's oversized thermos when a familiar voice hailed her.

"Jessie Arnold. How the hell are you?"

"Jim Ryan!" She stepped forward to give an old friend a bear hug. "Haven't seen you since the fall after you tangled with that moose in the Iditarod and I had to haul you to Ophir with your head sliced open."

"Right. Thanks again. And those dogs you sold me that fall are doing great. Got three in this team."

"Darn it." She grinned. "I probably gave you good ones I should have kept. If you beat me to the finish I'll be sorry. But it's still good to see you back in the game. I saw your name on the mushers list and was hoping to have a chance to say hello. I missed you at the drawing Friday night."

"Yeah, I saw you, but there was a whole roomful of people in the way, so I decided to wait and catch you later. So, you're running the Quest this year . . . back to being a rookie, huh?''

"Right, and looking forward to it."

"Got your *really* cold-weather gear? It was forty below for almost the whole damned race last year."

"That's what I heard, but it hasn't been so bad yet. I just hope it stays below zero. Any warmer will be tough on the dogs. But if the thermometer decides to take a plunge, I've got everything I need and will wear it all at once if I have to. Come and meet my support team."

She introduced the compact musher with the cheerful face to the Caswells and Billy Steward. She was glad to know he was in the race, for they had started racing sled dogs about the same time and had run many miles together in past competitions. Turning to the last member of her crew, she found that Ryan already knew Don Graham, who had been handler for two other Yukon Quest racers.

"You helped me repair my sled in Dawson last year. Good to see you, Don."

The big man grinned, offered his hand. "You, too, Jim. Got a stronger one this year?"

"You better believe it. We almost didn't make it to the finish line last year. Say, Jessie, you got a minute? There's somebody I'd like you to meet."

"Sure, if we're quick. It won't be long till I need to hitch up."

He led her past three trucks in the direction of the starting line and across the street.

"What number'd you draw?"

"Sixteen. You?"

"Twenty-seven. But don't worry, I'll catch you before Carmacks."

"Well, we'll see. I've got a pretty good team."

"So do I. It took a while to replace the team that moose stomped so bad. I really miss those dogs, especially Mike, the leader I lost. I took a couple of years off before I got back into the racing game with this race last year, but I'm back up to speed, so watch out."

Jessie grinned, knowing how mushers worked to psyche each other out before and during a race. You never knew how much was real and what part of their bragging was just hot air. Almost everyone had their *best team ever* before a race began. After that they soon sorted themselves out in terms of potential winners.

As they approached a green truck with a LELAND KENNELS sign painted on the side, a musher wearing a red knit hat who was helping the crew hitch dogs to the gang line of a sled glanced up and saw them coming.

"Leland?" Jessie questioned, reading the sign. "I didn't know Jake was in this one."

"He's not." Ryan grinned.

As they drew nearer, they could hear a female voice admonishing a dog that was barking at a passing team.

"Stuff it, Squirt. Your turn will come soon enough."

The woman—girl, really, of nineteen or twenty—finished what she was doing, stood up, and gave them a smile touched with a hint of shy respect. She was shorter than Jessie and her face, framed in strands of coppery hair escaping from under the hat, was bright with excitement and anticipation. Like Jessie and Jim Ryan, she wore a race bib of two rectangles that hung over her shoulders, tied around the waist with tapes on both sides, and displayed her starting number—ten.

"Jessie, this is Deborah Todd, Jake Leland's stepdaughter and a real rookie. This is her first long race."

Jessie held out her hand and smiled. "I'm Jessie Arnold."

"Oh . . . I definitely know who *you* are," Debbie said. "I thought you'd be running in the Iditarod, though."

"Well, I decided to try something new. I'm glad to meet you, Debbie."

As Jessie spoke, a handler in a well-worn black snowmachine suit came around the back of the truck leading two dogs, a collar in each hand.

"Hey, Jake. You been demoted to crew? Outclassed, huh?" Ryan needled his good friend.

Jake Leland, dark as his stepdaughter was fair, was one of the state's best-known sled dog racers, had earned his reputation with participation in many distance events, once won the Iditarod and twice the Yukon Quest. The dogs from his kennel were the best in the business—strong and dependable, painstakingly bred and trained. Though sizable, the prize money he won annually was small compared to amounts commanded by the dogs he was willing to sell. The kennel definitely brought in a substantial living for him and his family, and allowed him to afford the best in equipment for the races he entered and several assistants in his dog yard. He carefully screened young mushers, who were eager to learn his methods and secrets, and who paid Leland for the experience of working and training with him.

He grinned, pointedly ignored Ryan's jibe, and greeted Jessie instead as he clipped the dogs into place on the line.

"Hi, Jessie. You're keeping questionable company hanging out with this Ryan wannabe. See you've met Deb."

"Yes, thanks. You starting a dynasty of winners here? I know what to expect if you taught her all you know and she's driving some of your dogs."

"Oh, well—I don't know. She'll run her own race, won't you, Deb? Can't teach 'em much at that age."

"Wait a minute," Debbie contradicted him indignantly. "I *listen* . . . most of the time, anyway." They grinned at each other and Jessie noted their easy affection: evidently a good alliance for step-relations.

The girl shifted her attention. "Hey. There goes number eight. We'd better get moving. Nice to meet you, Jessie."

"You, too. Good luck. See you later."

She and Ryan watched as the crew, plus a few official Quest handlers, walked the eagerly straining team, with its beaming driver riding the back runners of the sled, into line behind racer number nine and headed for the starting line. Debbie looked back once to wave, then focused her

attention on what lay ahead. Jake Leland rode a drag sled
behind her, clearly proud and looking slightly amused.

"Well, I'd better see about getting my own mutts in
line," Jessie told Ryan, turning back toward the truck,
where she could see that Billy and Don had begun to
move dogs to the gang line of her sled. "See you in
Dawson—if you make it that far."

"Oh, yeah. But you'll see me before that, if my guys
have anything to do with it."

Half an hour later, she had pulled her sled into position
at the line and was walking along her team, checking
harness and gear, lifting Sunny, who had leaped over in
his excitement, back across the gang line to his regular
place. Each husky looked up as she spoke to it and laid
a mittened hand on its shoulder or head, attentive to the
familiar sound of her one voice among the many from
the crowd.

"Wart, you ready to go? Good boy, Two. Hey, Mitts."

On one knee in front of her leader Jessie rubbed his
ears and crooned affection. "Good old Tank. Time to go.
You ready to take us to Fairbanks? Good boy. Steady,
now. You're my main man."

"Ten seconds," the loudspeaker blared.

A last pat, as even Tank began to bark and strain
forward, and she stood up to begin the walk back to her
sled.

"Five . . . four . . . three . . ."

She stepped onto the runners and reached down, ready
to pull the snow hook.

". . . two . . . one . . . *GO!* And she's off, folks. Jessie
Arnold, top Iditarod finisher, on her first Yukon Quest.
Good luck, Jessie."

She barely heard the announcer as she yanked and
stowed the hook, the handlers released her dogs, and they
leaped forward against harness and line to jerk the weighty
sled into motion.

"Hang on," she called to Billy, who sat grinning
proudly atop the bag of supplies and equipment. "They're
gonna take us out of here like a rocket."

CHAPTER FOUR

"The bleak vastness stretched away on every side to the horizon. The snow, which was really frost, flung its mantle over the land and buried everything in the silence of death."
—Jack London, "The Story of Jees Uck"

IN FEBRUARY, A MONTH AND A HALF PAST THE WINTER SOL-stice, the sun still rose late and set early in the far northern latitudes where the Yukon Quest was run. On the Sunday this race started it came up at almost nine in the morning and went down at approximately five in the afternoon, a gain of approximately seven minutes of daylight over the day before. By June, it would be light until after midnight and grow light again by four in the morning.

From the starting gate in downtown Whitehorse Jessie trotted her team through a series of streets, concentrating on keeping her dogs on the right course while avoiding spectators, parking meters, kids, and other distractions be-fore passing out into the more open country the team was used to. All along the route, people waved and cheered as she went, some standing around fires or barbecues, en-joying winter cookouts and keeping warm. Several recog-nized her and called out her name along with their encouragement.

At the end of town, where the trail went down onto the

41

ice of the Yukon River, she found her support crew waiting with the trucks and paused to let Billy off her sled.

"Hey, good luck, Jessie," he told her with a grin. "We'll see you in Carmacks."

"You sure you don't want us to stop in Braeburn, just to check?" Linda Caswell asked.

"No, it's only a rest stop, not a checkpoint. I'll be fine. The trail's supposed to be pretty reasonable as far as Carmacks."

"Okay. We'll be waiting when you get there."

She drove over the bank and onto the river to join the other mushers, still running close together, some singly, some in groups or trains, one after the other. The two-minute gaps between them widened or narrowed as some went faster than others. The teams followed the bends in the river on the track established by the trailbreakers until it was joined by the Takhini River, which flowed in from the west. By the time Jessie reached this confluence and turned to run up the winding Takhini for a few miles, she had passed, and been passed by, several teams.

The trail was good and easy running and on the rivers she could often see other racers as much as a mile ahead or behind her. With lots of room to pass, there was much jockeying for position as they began to sort out the order of running.

Beginning to relax and enjoy being out and away from civilization, she watched the shadows slowly begin to lengthen as the afternoon progressed. A stiff breeze sweeping down the river was chilly, but fresh with hints of wood smoke from cabins near the riverbanks, and there were sunny spaces that presented at least the illusion of warmth, with welcome brightness. Overhead several ravens danced on the wind, effortlessly revolving on the thermals in swoops and dives, like kites anchored to strings. Jessie liked ravens. The all-black tricksters of the Arctic, they defied the snow and ice, and lingered, expressing contempt in raucous croaks and cries for their less hardy brethren who migrated south to escape the cold.

*   *   *

On a road that ran along the banks of the Takhini River, interested spectators had pulled off to watch the teams and drivers pass below, or to slide almost a hundred feet down the bluff onto the river ice to be closer to the trail itself. They stood, shuffling their feet to keep warm, as they waited for the racers to appear.

As the sun began to set behind the hills of the Miners Range, laying long blue fingers of shadow between the ridges and across the river ice, and tinting the snow-covered hills with a rosy glow, about three dozen people, some family members or handlers taking a quick detour on their way up the highway toward Dawson, stood watching the sleds and dogs slip past.

To those unfamiliar with sled dog racing or travel by dog sled, it seemed almost eerily silent for such an active sport, especially compared with the noisy confusion at the Whitehorse starting gate. Except for encouraging shouts to racers by friends or fans, the jingle of small bells from the harness of one team, and a short word or two of direction from a musher to his dogs, there was only the soft shush or scrape of runners across the snow and ice of the Takhini, the panting sounds of working dogs that seldom bark when they run, or the faint creak of a sled flexing over an uneven spot in the track.

A little apart from the cluster of ten or so at the top of the bank who had not clambered down onto the river ice, one man stood alone, aloof from the conversation and anticipation. Most of the spectators were eagerly awaiting the arrival of specific teams and paid little or no attention to the still figure who stood in silhouette against the sunset, almost as dark as the hills beyond. If they had examined him more closely, they might have considered his behavior a little odd and his attitude disconcerting, for he exhibited no enthusiasm or pleasure in watching, but stood quite expressionless and still. Interested in this first part of the race, those people who even glanced his way simply dismissed him with a mental shrug and redirected their observation to what was passing below.

He was a little above average height, but it was hard to discern his build, for he was dressed for the cold weather in a heavy, much-worn green parka, a tear patched on one sleeve with a strip of duct tape to keep the down from escaping. Insulated pants and black Sorrel boots were visible beneath it. Heavy snowmachine gloves with extended cuffs protected his hands. A cap of some questionable dark color left little of his face exposed, for above his upturned collar its bill was pulled low over his eyes and its flaps hung down over his ears. His only visible features were thin lips pulled back over even, white teeth, and a straight, slender nose that seemed to suggest an attractive shape to his face.

Clearly solitary, unsociable, unapproachable, he had neither spoken to nor made eye contact with anyone, did not even bother to respond to a woman who asked him if he had the time. Ignoring her as if he had not heard or did not wish to hear her question, he continued to stare down at the sleds gliding silently over the ice until she gave him a confused, angry frown and moved away to question someone else. Then, without turning his head, he cast a contemptuous glance after her with eyes of a curious golden brown.

Carefully, he inspected each passing racer until he was satisfied enough with that person's identity to nod almost imperceptibly to himself, turn his attention away, and wait for the next.

One after another an even dozen teams glided by and disappeared around the next bend in the frozen river.

The man on the bank paid particular notice to the thirteenth racer, a woman. His lips narrowed slightly in what was almost a smile of satisfaction along with his consistent nod of recognition. When she had gone, the ice was vacant for close to five minutes before the fourteenth came into sight, drew even, and moved away. Again he waited before the empty river. In ten minutes, a musher in a red parka appeared and once more he focused intense interest as the driver came near enough to identify.

"Good luck, Jessie," someone called from the bluff.

She looked up, smiled, and waved as her dogs, trotting steadily along, drew her heavy sled smoothly past the viewpoint.

Close behind her another musher in a blue and yellow parka passed, and once again the watcher's attention was caught. He remained motionless until the man riding the back of the sled looked up as if searching the top of the bluff for someone. Then, for the first time, the watcher raised an arm, not in a wave, but clearly a gesture intended to attract the musher's notice. The driver lifted one gloved hand from the handles of his sled, just high enough to indicate that he had seen the motion, and continued on up the river.

As soon as the musher had departed, the watcher's concentrated interest evaporated completely. He walked swiftly from the riverbank to a pickup parked at the side of the road, climbed in, turned it around, and drove east, the way he had come, toward the highway.

The woman whose question he had ignored was the only person to note his exit.

"Bastard," she commented under her breath as she watched him go. Then she turned back to wait for her cousin to drive his team into view below.

CHAPTER FIVE

*"The white woods, and earth, and moonlight. . . . Over
the whiteness and silence brooded a ghostly calm. There
was not the faintest whisper of air—nothing moved, not a
leaf quivered, the visible breaths of the dogs rising slowly
and lingering in the frosty air."*
   —Jack London, "The Dominant Primordial Beast"

JESSIE TRULY LOVED HER DOGS. THEY WERE A LARGE PART
of the reason she raced and ran a kennel. The rest fell
somewhere between her competitive spirit and a deep appreciation of the Alaskan wilderness. With a team of sled
dogs it was possible to get away from towns, roads, and
people, and come close to being a part of the vast uninhabited northern country unsullied by the disturbing racket
and pollution of an engine. She liked traveling quietly
through stillness broken only by the soft susurrus of runners over snow and the unobtrusive, natural animal sounds
of the dogs.

   In the early days, dog teams had been the only option
for winter travel between villages and mining communities. Modern Alaskans in rural areas had for the most part
given up their dogs and sleds for snowmachines, a faster,
easier way to cross country. Their howling engines, however, destroyed the great silence in the same way that
those of planes or power boats drowned out all other
sound. Jessie favored her sled for the same reason she

preferred gliders and sailboats: It intruded less on the environment.

Long after dropping Billy where the trail ran over the railroad tracks and dropped onto the Yukon River for the first leg of the race, she was loosening up, relieved that she was finally on her way, glad to be almost alone in the peaceful ivory monotone of winter for the first time in days.

The strong, rolling country of this part of the Yukon Territory spread out around her in a world that retained only its shape, for its colors had shifted from lush summer greens and blues, and the brilliant golds and scarlets of fall, to a crystal white that softened the lines of everything it blanketed. The hills and valleys, like some of the northern animals—the hare, the ermine, the ptarmigan that traded their hues for a white to match the snow—flowed away: a pale, colorless world. Though at first impression the country might seem bleached, careful attention revealed it to be a setting of stark contrasts between snow and the black of spruce, the deep blues and purples of the long shadows cast by a sun that hung low in the sky even at its highest point. An ever-changing panorama of silhouettes, of line and contour, it was an environment that never failed to raise Jessie's spirits along with an appreciation of the surroundings and circumstances she had chosen for herself.

She came by her choices naturally, for her parents had always encouraged independence in both their daughters. Her father had always loved the outdoors and much of Jessie's childhood had been spent on hikes and camping trips.

"People make noise," he had often told her. "Nature makes music, if you listen."

She had been listening for as long as she could remember.

"You can pretty much figure out who you are—or who you want to be—if you get away from the civilized racket," she remembered him saying, and smiled as she

glided along the track of the mushers who were running
ahead of her. It felt so good to be *away from the civilized
racket* of the last few days.

Several teams had gone past her on the Yukon and
Takhini rivers, as racers reshuffled themselves into a more
reasonable running order, fastest teams moving forward,
slower ones falling behind. The luck of the draw did not
take into account the experience or speed of individual
mushers, but randomly cast them out upon the trail, leaving them to sort out the swift from the tardy. Though she
had politely requested the trail to pass some slower teams
and would continue to catch up with more before reaching
the first official checkpoint at Carmacks, she had not had
a problem holding her dogs to a steady, comfortable,
ground-covering trot. She was pleased and proud of this
team, knowing they were in their prime, perfectly condi-
tioned and ready for the race.

After a long run up the Takhini, the trail turned right
and up the bank onto a cat trail someone had graded out
to run a trapline. It wound back and forth through an aspen
forest, a change from the frozen surface of the river, but
snow in this area had been light and there were spaces
with little cover that forced the team to run on partial dirt
and rocks that scraped the sled and made Jessie glad she
had chosen the heaviest plastic runners for this first part
of the race. Besides the trees, there were stumps that had
to be carefully avoided to keep from high-centering her
toboggan-style sled, or banging it or a dog against them
in a turn. Mostly, this was just a bush trail, a minimal
track, and not well kept. She was glad to be running it in
the last of the dying light to be able to see quickly what
came up ahead. When it finally ended in a wider road,
she was relieved to be out in a more open area.

It was an old road, originally part of the old Dawson-
Whitehorse Overland Trail, the winter stage route between
the two communities. She thought about the sleds that
had traveled it, sometimes carrying passengers, who, less
important than mail and freight, often had to walk to

lighten the load for the dogs. Leading to Braeburn, a small lake with a lodge, this route had added perhaps thirty miles to the race and eliminated a previous one which had included Lake Laberge, made famous by Robert Service in his humorous poem, "The Cremation of Sam McGee." Crossing the ice of Laberge had not been appreciated by some of the mushers, who did not like running ice over deep water, and who said they grew as bored as their dogs at going in a straight, flat line for sixty miles. Others were disappointed that the lake was now only a part of Yukon Quest history; they'd enjoyed the open country and smooth running of the well-maintained and traditional trail. In certain weather conditions, however, there had been occasional sections of open water and fog on the lake, a hazardous combination.

Daylight faded and was gone by the time Jessie left the bush trail for the road, so she had paused to put on her headlamp and switch it on. The tunnel of light that resulted allowed her to see her team stretched out ahead of her sled, but the bright artificial light destroyed her night vision. She was sorry to lose sight of the country through which she was traveling, but glad enough to be running through a variety of trail conditions. Though changing conditions made the run more interesting for the musher, she had initially been a little disappointed not to run across the famous lake and, before the race, had taken one training run over part of its expanse just out of curiosity.

Now, as she cruised along between low berms at the side of the road, recalling the lake's broad expanse of flat ice, Jessie glanced back to see if anyone was close, gave in to temptation, and loudly recited the opening of Service's well-known verse.

> " 'There are strange things done in the midnight sun
>   By the men who moil for gold;
> The Arctic trails have their secret tales
>   That would make your blood run cold;
> The Northern Lights have seen queer sights,

> *But the queerest they ever did see*
> *Was that night on the marge of Lake Lebarge*
> *I cremated Sam McGee.' ''*

Tank turned his head to glance back at the sound of her voice, but did not hesitate, used to Jessie's habit of talking to herself or singing as they traveled. She laughed as he returned to his task as leader, accepting her recitation as normal, if curious behavior. Alex would be proud of me, she thought, as the sound of the poem reminded her once again of her absent companion, who loved to soliloquize and knew scraps of dozens of poems. The glaring errors he included in most of his repertoire were part of the charm of hearing him expound, but as far as she could remember she had quoted this correctly.

In the rush and confusion of last-minute preparation for the Quest, she had had several short telephone conversations with him, none more than adequate, and a couple of which had left her decidedly dissatisfied. The funeral in Idaho was over and he seemed disinclined to discuss it or the situation there, except to say that he would be staying awhile longer and his mother was growing a little more reconciled to living without her husband, though still taking it hard.

Late on the evening before the race, he had called to wish Jessie luck. Unfortunately, dealing with a dozen last-minute decisions, caring for two sick dogs and Tux, the black and white two-year-old who had developed a sore paw on a training run, had narrowed Jessie's attention and limited its span. At Alex's suggestion, she had gone back out to treat the dog, leaving Cas to finish the call. Now, with time to consider, it gnawed at her, and she remembered that Cas had answered a subsequent question about their chat almost too quickly with, "Just trooper stuff."

"What do you mean, *trooper stuff?*"

"Oh, nothing big. Said he's helping the local deputy sheriff with a sticky assault case. Keeping his hand in, I guess."

"Where's the sheriff?"

"Just retired."

"Oh, well . . ."

Something about his tone had bothered her. As she was turning the memory over in her mind, she became aware of something ahead—another team, halted in the old road. As she approached, she could see that the musher was switching the order of the dogs on the gang line, changing leaders. Instead of pulling out to pass, she drew up behind the stationary sled, set the snow hook, and walked forward to greet Deborah Todd.

"How's it going, Debbie?"

"Great." The girl looked up with a smile. "Just stopped to snack my dogs and put Spunky in the lead for a while."

"I was just about to snack mine, take a quick break, then go a little farther before I give them a long rest. Want to share some peppermint tea?"

"Sure. I'll pull my rig over a little."

Though there was plenty of room on the road, they both moved their teams to the side of the track to allow following mushers plenty of room to pass, lining them up side by side. As Jessie gave each of her dogs a snack, she had a chance to take a good look at the strong team of dogs the girl was driving. Debbie brought an insulated mug and they settled on top of Jessie's sled to sip the tea she poured still hot from her large thermos.

Knowing from past experience the dehydrating effects of traveling in subzero temperatures, Jessie was careful to include lots of liquid in her racing diet. Mushers were always drinking something and carried it close at hand in unbreakable thermoses to keep it from freezing. Dehydration was a condition encouraged by cold weather, both for drivers and dogs, a thing to be guarded against at all costs.

"Did you notice the pine trees back there?" Debbie asked.

"Sure did. They make the spruce we have in Knik seem stunted. I forget how tall trees can be."

"They're even more stunted in Fairbanks. I wish we had some this tall. They make me feel at home."

"Where was home before you moved to Alaska?"

"Montana, just outside of Billings. But I really like it up here. I wouldn't move back now."

Jessie returned to examining the younger woman's dogs.

"Looks like you've got a couple of Jake's mutts in your string," Jessie commented. "Isn't that Royal?" She indicated a cream-colored dog harnessed in swing position, second in line, that she recognized from media photos of Leland. It was not unusual for members of a racing family to share a few of the same dogs. But Jessie thought Jake must respect his stepdaughter's ability as a musher if he was willing to offer her one of his best as a backup leader.

"Yeah, it sure is. He loaned me Royal and three of his younger ones that need some distance experience. Spunky's mine, though."

The lead dog she had just replaced looked up and cocked his head at the sound of his name, revealing eyes of two different colors, one blue, one the brown color of the tea they were drinking. Tradition, or consistent rumor, indicated the odd combination meant that somehow in his history he was related to some of the fine racing dogs bred by George Attla, a talented musher famous in the earlier days of modern sled dog racing. Jessie had always wondered if it was true.

"How long have you been racing, Debbie?"

"Ever since I was little. I had one old dog and a beat-up sled when I was nine, the year Mom and Jake got married. Greaser was really past racing, but he hated to be left in the yard, so Jake gave him to me and I learned a lot from him. But I've never done a big race like this before."

"It's not much different than a lot of training runs when you stay out for a night or two. You just don't get to go home, clean up in between, and eat a meal your mom cooked." Jessie smiled to herself, remembering how it had seemed that her first Iditarod was never going to end. "Do you like going by yourself? You haven't hooked up with any of the other younger rookies.''

The idea made Jessie suddenly aware of the considerable difference in their ages.

"Yeah, well"—Debbie frowned slightly—"I know some of them from junior races and may do that later, when it gets tougher. But Jake said I'd be better off to run my own race, at least as far as Carmacks. Get settled into it at my own speed.''

"Good advice.''

So she *was* listening to her stepfather, Jessie thought with approval.

They were both bare-handed, warming their fingers on the mugs of tea. Jessie saw that, in addition to her heavy outer mitts, Debbie wore a pair of bright, hand-knitted mittens around her neck on an idiot string.

Noticing the girl's free hand in motion, she glanced down to see what Debbie was doing with the cord meant to tighten the bottom of her parka. It wasn't idle fiddling. Without looking, she was tying specific, useful knots in the end of the cord she had pulled through to be longer on one side, practicing. As Jessie watched, she tied a quick bowline one-handed, then loosened it and did two running eights.

"You're pretty good at that.''

"Oh. Thanks. I still get bowlines wrong sometimes. I want to be able to do them without thinking, even in the dark, and when I've got to hold on to something else with the other hand.'' She grinned. "I woke up in the middle of the night last week trying to tie an end loop in the lamp cord by my bed.''

They looked up as another team come into view and watched as the musher passed them with a wave.

"Who was that?'' Debbie asked.

Jessie shook her head and shrugged. "I haven't a clue. Seems odd, though, not to know most of the drivers. I do on the Iditarod.''

"Bet you know more than I do.''

"Oh, I doubt it. You must meet a lot of them through Jake."

Debbie drained the last of the tea from her mug and stood up, leaving the last running eight still tied in the cord of her parka. Hesitantly, she turned to Jessie with a question.

"Would you mind . . . I mean, if there's something I don't understand, could I ask you?"

"Sure, Debbie. I hope you will . . . if I'm around."

"Right. You're probably gonna go faster than I will, but . . . thanks. And thanks for the tea, it was great. Never had peppermint before."

"My favorite. More?"

"No, thanks. Think I'll get back on the road."

"Better dig out your headlamp. It's pretty dark."

"I already did." She grinned. "I just took it off when I stopped."

She started toward her sled, then turned back. "Do the trailbreakers turn around for some reason?"

"Turn around?"

"Yeah. Head back to Whitehorse? Do they only go part of the way—then let another one take over?"

"No. Especially not this close to the start. They might trade off later, but I don't think so. Why?"

"Nothing, really, except I kept hearing a snowmachine about an hour ago. It wasn't going very fast, but it was a long time before the sound stopped. I was just wondering."

"Probably someone out for a Sunday run, or to watch the first part of the race. They're not supposed to get close enough to bother the dogs, but we're still close to town."

"I hope they stay a long ways away. I hate snowmachines." She paused, hunching her shoulders in a shiver. "One ran head-on into my team three years ago. Killed one of my dogs . . . a good one . . . and hurt two more. They still scare me—especially the sound of one I can't see and can't tell where it is."

Jessie frowned and bit her lip in sympathy. It was a

musher's worst nightmare: Some egotistical snowmachine drivers, overcome with the power of the machines they rode, roared along too fast to avoid a team they couldn't hear or see over the sound of their transportation, on trails too narrow to avoid disastrous collisions.

"Oh, I'm sorry, Debbie. I wouldn't worry too much during a race like this, though. It's been posted and they know which trails not to use. It was off somewhere else, I think."

"Yeah, that's probably what it was."

"Don't worry. There'll be plenty of trail broken just for us, unless it decides to dump snow. Then you just follow the markers. They're not usually more than a mile apart and they mark troublesome spots with two markers crossed in an X. You'll be just fine."

Jessie pointed to one of the stakes with its distinctive reflector. The Quest race committee worked diligently each year to be sure the trail was clearly marked with the thousands of stakes made by the inmates of Fairbanks and Whitehorse prisons.

Debbie smiled, cheering up.

"Okay. See you. Thanks again for the tea."

Calling up her dogs, she was soon pulling away.

Jessie watched her go as she put the thermos back in her sled bag before turning her own team back onto the trail. Half an hour later she passed Debbie with a wave, as the girl moved her team off the track on request.

"See you in Braeburn," she called out as Jessie went by.

She had almost forgotten the young woman's query about the snowmachine, but would recall Debbie's question later, with good reason.

CHAPTER SIX

"After that all the world began to flock into the north. I was a poor man: I sold myself to be a driver of dogs."
—Jack London, "An Odyssey of the North"

NOT LONG AFTER HER MEETING WITH DEBBIE TODD, JESSIE pulled off the trail and settled her team for the long rest she had planned. Most mushers follow a racing schedule of equal hours of rest for hours of travel, giving the dogs plenty of time to recover before going on. She was no exception, knowing that rest, along with good nutrition, was essential to making good, steady time in a race. When she found she was yawning and hungry, it was time to take care of herself as well.

First-time rookies, and some veterans who should have known better, would go too far, too fast the first day, wearing out their dogs and themselves in enthusiasm and adrenaline left over from the start, with its unusual conditions that included many more teams and people, both racers and spectators, than they were used to. It was an easy mistake, but one that Jessie was too experienced and trail-savvy to make.

Almost automatically, adept with much practice, she found her cooker in the sled bag, filled it with snow, and started her propane stove. As the snow began to melt, she got out the rich mix of frozen chicken, beef, lamb, and some dry food that was her tried-and-true working diet for

56

the dogs. Several times she added more snow to the cooker and, when sufficient water finally boiled, dropped in the meat to thaw and cook slightly.

Mitts was on her feet, attentively watching Jessie's every move. Though this female always seemed excessively proud of her own long-legged, white-ruffed appearance, she was a gobbler when it came time for dinner. If she wasn't monitored closely, she would gulp her own, then finish Goofy's and anyone else's that she could reach. Easygoing and undefensive, Goofy was often inclined to let her.

"Give it up, greedy," Jessie admonished her. "You're not getting more than your share this time. Lie down and take a rest."

Mitts obediently lay down, but continued to concentrate on the mechanics of food preparation.

Walking down the line of resting dogs, Jessie put a familiar, battered aluminum feeding pan next to each one. Before carrying the cooking kettle along the line to fill their pans, she watered them from what she had put in the cooler before the start of the race. In short order they were all eating hungrily, contentedly settling down to snooze as soon as they had licked their bowls clean.

Refilling the cooker with snow for water to carry along, Jessie tossed in a sealed plastic package of frozen spaghetti for her own meal. When it was hot, she poured the water from the cooker into the insulated container to keep it from refreezing, and sat down on her sled to enjoy her dinner.

As soon as she had finished, she checked each of her dogs for sore feet, gave them a little attention and praise as they curled up to rest, got out her sleeping bag, and found a semi-comfortable spot on top of her sled to spread it out. The two Darryls watched her closely from their position nearest the sled, ready to go again at the slightest suggestion. When she crawled in without removing her cold-weather clothing, they put their heads down, resigned to the fact that she didn't intend to resume the trip anytime soon.

Shutting off her headlamp, she lay listening to the silence of the night. It was utterly still. Nothing rustled the underbrush or chirped from the trees. Most of the birds had flown south and many of the squirrels and other small animals were curled up in their cozy dens to snooze fitfully until spring. Though the ravens hung around all winter— a stark contrast of black on white—even they flew away to a secret roost in the wilderness night, the last echoes of their raucous cries disappearing with them on the cold air.

For a few minutes it was quiet. Then, just as she was drifting into a light sleep, vaguely aware of a team that had quietly passed on the nearby trail, Jessie heard the call of an owl not far away, then the soft *whir-r-r* of its wings, and the *whump* of its landing. It had heard a mouse moving under the snow and, with its uncanny sense of hearing and direction, glided swiftly and silently to the kill, for there was one tiny squeak that betrayed the successful capture of the tiny rodent.

You should have stayed in your nest, mouse, Jessie thought, and sank into a temporary hibernation of her own, sleeping bag pulled up to her ears.

In just over three hours, rejuvenated, she was back on the trail, passing other racers who had also wisely opted to rest their dogs.

The country she traveled through on either side of the dark road felt open at first, having been burned and cleared for homesteads and hay fields. It rolled gently along, easy trotting for the team.

This ended when the trail left the road and became tight and winding, more like a snowmachine track, constantly changing direction. Things happened quickly as the team swung around turns and made several portages between creeks and a number of small lakes. Somewhere on this part of the trail Jessie came to a cabin where a trapper had opened his small living space to racers. Three other teams had stopped there to rest.

"Hi, there," a voice greeted her as she stepped in and closed the door, thermos in hand.

"Gail. How're you?"

It pleased Jessie to see another distance racer that she already knew, especially one she recognized as a caring, friendly person, as well as an extremely competent professional. Gail Murray had once reduced her own chances for placing high in the Iditarod standings to help transport an injured racer back over a storm-blown trail to the last checkpoint for medical attention.

"How's your first Quest so far?"

"Good. It's fun to be on a trail that's new. I don't know almost every foot of it, like the Iditarod."

Gail grimaced and shook her head. "Maybe too new. I hear there's a bad stretch coming up between Braeburn and Coghlan Lake—that new section of trail. Supposed to be a wild bumper-car ride through the trees."

"I'll be sure to watch it and slow the mutts down. You ran the Rocky Mountain Stage Stop last year, didn't you?"

"Sure did."

"Like it?"

"Yeah, I did. It was a lot of fun and a really different kind of race—more of a sprint, really. Running just thirty to seventy miles a day turns it into more of a speed race than the real distance ones where you're traveling all the time. It's only four hundred miles, but it takes nine or ten days, so you run the day's quota and stop for the night, and wherever you stop they feed you like it was the last meal you were ever going to have. I actually gained three pounds, and I usually lose." She grinned. "Won't happen here."

A fairly new race, the Rocky Mountain Stage Stop annually went through a series of towns in western Wyoming and, like the Tour de France bicycle race, was run in daily timed stages. The communities through which it passed all had celebrations for the day the teams came in. Banquets, pig roasts, dances—all kept the residents and racers well fed and entertained. It was definitely not an endurance race like the Quest, where an important part of the concept was for the mushers to be almost totally self-sufficient and able to handle whatever the trail and weather threw at them. Still, it was extremely competitive and required much of both dogs and drivers, who burned up calories almost as fast as they could ingest them, and clearly there were plenty of opportunities to ingest them.

Jessie and Gail talked racing while Jessie refilled her thermos. The friendly trapper who owned the cabin was keeping plenty of water hot for the mushers, which Jessie welcomed, though she already had the water in the thermal container for her dogs. She washed her hands and face, brushed her teeth, and, feeling reasonably clean and more awake, drove on.

As she pulled away from the cabin, another racer in a blue and yellow parka pulled in. She didn't recognize him, but remembered that he had been behind her on the Takhini River most of the way to the bush trail turnoff. Well, she thought, time enough to find out who it is later.

"Let's go, guys. Next stop we'll rest again."

For the remainder of the night she traveled steadily, passing only one other team. As it was growing light in the east, she saw a power line ahead, ran under it, up a small hill, and was suddenly coming into Braeburn, startlingly full of dog teams, vehicles, and people; strange to see, 110 miles from Whitehorse.

Though not an official checkpoint, Braeburn was an official dog drop, where drivers could leave an animal they felt, for one reason or another, should not continue the race. A dog or two had already been dropped—one for a sprained wrist, one that wasn't eating well and could be coming down with some virus that the musher was probably praying it hadn't already passed on to the rest of the team. Other mushers would be hoping so as well; because dogs came in close contact with other dogs during races, viruses were easily passed from team to team.

Time altered for participants in distance sled dog races, spun out in long threads of seemingly endless running, then knit itself together into hours that appeared to pass instantly. Racers stopped measuring time in terms of day or night and, instead, calculated it in terms of running and resting, whatever the clock might say. Obviously, this also became true for the handlers and those concerned with the operation and reporting of the race. Vets, checkers, volunteers, cooks, pilots, media people, even fans—all accommodated themselves to the coming and going of the teams and the schedules of their passing along the trail, just as the mushers, if they were wise and savvy racers, accommodated themselves to the needs of their dogs for rest, food, and water.

For these reasons, Braeburn was a busy place, full of teams still running fairly close together, constantly coming in and stopping, or going on through, and the parking lot was crowded with the vehicles of handlers and a number of hardy spectators. Those who elected not to stay long usually at least halted for coffee in the bustling restaurant, since the lodge was famous for its much-anticipated plate-sized cinnamon rolls.

Still feeling the relief of being by herself and appreciating Debbie's idea of settling into her own race, Jessie found the hubbub frustrating and irritatingly noisy. But she took a long, six-hour break, for there was a good fenced area for the dogs to rest, and a cabin in back of the lodge for mushers to sleep mostly undisturbed by the activities and enthusiasm of those who were not racing.

By the time Jessie woke and readied her team to start the fifty-mile run from Braeburn to Carmacks, the first official race checkpoint, it was well after noon, the place was twice as crowded as it had been when she had arrived, and the fenced holding area was jammed full of dog teams.

Watering her dogs and moving them back into harness on the gang line, she took a few minutes in the restaurant for a quick lunch. As she ate a sandwich and bowl of soup, nodding to people who stopped to speak encouragement and recognition, she found herself listening to a conversation that was going on at the table next to hers, her attention caught by the surprising rancor of its tone.

An older Alaskan, into what sounded like a well-worn

gripe, was haranguing a younger woman with a pile of camera equipment, probably a photographer for some newspaper, who was forced to listen, clearly unable to insert more than a few words into pauses in the ongoing tirade.

"Nope. Not gonna get back into the racing game. Never again. Got rid of all but six of my dogs two years ago and that's enough for anything I want to do, but it won't ever be these big races."

"But you even ran the Iditarod at least once, didn't you, Cal?"

"Yeah, more than once, back when it was a *race,* not a commercial media event. The Quest, too—first three— same thing. That's what burns *me.* After the Iditarod got so big and expensive—when they started using all the name boots and clothes made out of that *whore-tex* stuff to accommodate the demands of their big corporate sponsors, and got all involved in that uncalled-for gear and sleds that cost a fortune—a few people organized *this* race so it was tougher and supposed to be for *real* mushers. They kept the entry fee low enough so that Canadians, who don't usually have that kind of money or sponsorship, and some of us Americans who could race with the best but finished in the middle of the pack out of the prize money, could still run it and not go bankrupt in the process. Now it's the same old rotten story. If you can afford it with all the fancy trimmings, that's fine—you're in. Otherwise, you're a second-class citizen and nobody gives a good goddamn. They've even raised the entry fee. Now *it* costs what we used to spend on the whole race."

"But doesn't it cost a lot more now to put this race on than it did in 1984?"

"Aw . . . well, maybe it does, Linda. So? I still think they forced out a lot of good racers—let it get out of hand. They forced me out, that's for damn sure. I had to quit so my family would have food on the table. Guy shouldn't have to make that kind of choice to do something as basic as driving dogs. Is that fair? Put that in your newspaper column.''

Cal? Jessie glanced over her shoulder to get a look at the musher with the bitter attitude, while searching her memory of the Iditarod for someone named Cal. He was a rugged-looking individual in jeans and a brown flannel shirt, his skin as tanned and creased as old leather. Dry skin and frostbite had always laid distinguishing fingerprints on the faces of those who ran dog teams in the far north, marks as unmistakable to other mushers as the scars from injuries sustained on hands and fingers numb and awkward from the cold. They willingly suffered the ravages of cold weather and resigned themselves to having character rather than handsomeness, counting it an acceptable exchange.

As the older man raised his head to look out the window at something in the parking lot, Jessie got a look at his profile—battered nose and sharp chin—and suddenly recognized him though they had never met. Cal "Hoo-Doo" Wilson. He had run the Iditarod back in the days when it was still building its reputation and strength—long before she had found her way into the racing circuit.

He, like others, had dropped out during its rise to fame and all but disappeared. Only their names remained on the old lists, like those who fought their way into the Klondike during the gold rush, the freight and mail carriers, and earliest of sled dog racers in Alaska—the Leonard Seppalas, Charlie Biedermans, Scotty Allans. The Mushers Hall of Fame was also filled with names that had a familiar ring in the history of the sport—Joe Reddington, George Attla, Dr. Roland Lombard, John "Iron Man" Johnson, Earl and Natalie Norris, Herbie Nayokpuk—but not the also-rans.

Wilson was correct in his assessment that the entry fees and the equipment and gear required to successfully run modern races had become too expensive for many. Sponsors tended to put their money on winners, or high finishers who might win, not on those who simply ran and had no chance of winning. The latter were the ones who, sooner or later, vanished from the scene, and some were more than a little bitter about it. Wilson's argument was one Jessie had heard before, from more than one musher who no longer entered the big races, but his upset seemed more deep-seated and unsettling than most, more virulent in a way she couldn't quite define.

He raised his right hand to rub his temple and she saw that it was missing the little finger.

"One of these days someone's going to do something about it," she heard him bluster. "There's got to be some kind of equality and somebody'll take just so much of it before they get mad enough to stand up for the rights of the little guy. And it may be sooner than you think. You just wait and see."

That was an approach that Jessie *hadn't* heard before—one that gave her an even more uneasy shiver. What could he mean? What could a *little guy* do? Racing had gone beyond *doing* anything, she decided before determinedly shrugging it away. There was no way to make the sport run backward in time. His anger was understandable, but he would simply have to learn to live with it—probably had, mostly. But once or twice a year, when the annual running of the famous races made the papers, he would be reminded and his resentment would flame up for a few days. The rest of the year it would be only a pilot light that claimed a hot spot in his memory now and then. The best thing to *do* would be nothing—to leave it alone until it faded into a repetitious garrulousness that expressed his disappointment but contained no fire.

But why did he come to watch, if it bothered him so much? No, she shook her head slightly, answering her own question, knowing that the love of sled dog racing would not easily disappear if *she* stopped running these events. It got into your blood and became part of how you defined yourself. Next month when the Iditarod started, she knew she would yearn to be out on the trail heading north to Nome, though forgoing the Iditarod was a choice she had made in order to try this new race.

When she glanced back once more, "Hoo-Doo" Wilson was looking straight at her, having caught the movement as she turned her head, and clearly knew she was listening to his complaints. He scowled resentfully and stared, as if daring her to butt in, or object to his point of view, though perhaps he had merely taken offense at the fact that she could afford to run the race and he could not. When she found her temper rising slightly in response to his un-called-for rudeness, she knew it was time to leave.

Laying down her spoon by the empty bowl, she finished the last of her coffee and, slipping a tip for the waitress under the edge of the plate, made her way through the crowd into the cooler air outside, ready to get back on the trail and leave all such arguments behind. There might come a day when she could not afford to enter the races, either, but for now all she wanted was to get back on the trail as soon as possible, munch a cinnamon roll as she drove, and be glad she had arranged to meet her support team in Carmacks instead of Braeburn. She hoped for more peace and quiet at the next stop, which would give her dogs and herself a better quality of rest without interruptions.

Nevertheless, his angry words still bothered her and slipped back into her mind for the next few hours. She did not at all like the last threatening concept he had expressed, "One of these days someone's going to do something about it. . . . Somebody'll take just so much . . . before they get mad enough to stand up for the rights of the little guy. And it may be sooner than you think."

It gave her a shudder. "Someone walking over your grave," her grandmother had often said of the feeling. But chances were slim that it was anything but talk, she decided, and purposely began to think about something else. He was probably just getting it out of his system.

As she had pulled out of Braeburn, she had seen Debbie Todd working with her team and waved, but hadn't stopped for conversation. The younger woman hadn't seemed to notice the wave, possibly hadn't seen it, for she seemed to have acquired an interested fan or reporter, a male figure in a green jacket patched on one sleeve with silver tape. Clearly not a musher, he had stood leaning on the fence with his back toward outgoing teams, his attention focused on Debbie as she repacked her sled. Remembering, Jessie smiled to herself and turned her attention toward crossing the highway and taking her team up the long hill from the lodge in the valley. She soon found herself heading east through another aspen forest.

The change in the route had not helped racing conditions on this section of trail, which had not been well cleared or worked. Very narrow and tight, it wound around trees and brush in steep short runs that yanked the sled back and forth dangerously; this kind of track made it very easy to damage sleds and injure dogs. Paws could drop into holes, spraining wrists or shoulders, sharp turns might pull a team dog that worked in the middle of the string into a stump or tree as the line tightened between leaders and sled.

Big timber had forced the trailbreakers to put in sharp turns and switchbacks that swung sharply around to almost meet themselves coming back and Jessie was soon thoroughly tired of wrestling the heavy sled to get through them. Hot and sweaty, her clothing grew damp and she hoped the temperature wouldn't drop suddenly with the coming dark before they dried. She unzipped her red parka and tossed back its hood, cooling herself as much as possible.

Suddenly there was a huge downhill drop and things were a little smoother for a while, but the team was soon back into trees that seemed to go on and on through low rolling hills. Eventually, when her shoulders ached with the strain and she thought it would never end, she reached Coghlan Lake: first in the Chain of Lakes that ran south to north between Lake Laberge and Carmacks. Far to the west lay the highway she had crossed and the Yukon River swung to the east in a huge bend. Between them the trail snaked its way through the trees to rejoin the old route of the Yukon Quest and she dropped down onto the smoother lake ice with a deep sense of relief that she had neither damaged her sled nor any of the dogs, glad to have run this part in the daylight.

Ahead of her the race leaders would reach the Carmacks checkpoint, fifty miles beyond Braeburn, approximately thirty hours after leaving Whitehorse. In the clear, cold weather, temperatures hovering between five and ten degrees below zero, perfect for running dogs, they would cover the distance quickly.

She had packed extra wool socks, knowing that the weather near Whitehorse tended to be warmer than that of the rest of the race and that the lakes in the chain often had slushy, if not wet, surfaces. The temperature had dipped and stayed cool, however, and Coghlan Lake, first in the series, was solid and dry when her team dropped onto it after the harrowing wooded trip from Braeburn.

The Chain of Lakes country was beautiful to travel through. Between the lakes, the portages took Jessie and her team through heavily forested spaces where the trail once again wound back and forth among the trees, but the ice on the lakes themselves made for easier traveling. They were approximately a mile wide and six or seven miles long and she enjoyed gliding quickly over the hard, snowy surfaces. Large outcroppings of granite went down to the lakes between forested parts of the banks, and here and there small creeks ran into them, frozen now. There was overflow in some parts where the portages began or ended on the lakes, where the dogs' feet found little purchase and both team and sled slid along the slippery spots. Thankfully those parts were short, but Jessie had learned to listen for the toenails of her dogs scratching at the ice, as a warning.

In the portages between lakes the trail writhed like a snake and she found herself growing tired of stepping on and off the brake. She tried to anticipate the turns and, though physically challenging, the trail was pleasant enough to travel through.

The team was as tired as she was, however, and not even Goofy was inclined to lope. By the time they reached Mandana Lake, last and northernmost in the chain, it was time to take a rest. It was a big lake, full of bays and inlets, with a small cabin on the east bank. She pulled up at the cabin, passing a musher who was in the process of feeding his team. Another team of dogs was resting beside the building, nose to tail in the cold, with no driver in sight. The purr of a generator broke the stillness.

As she stopped and set the hook, the door opened and a short, heavyset figure shrugging on a down parka stepped out, closed it quickly behind him, and approached Jessie's sled.

"Hi, I'm Wayne, unofficial checker at this unofficial stop. How's it going? Need a place to get some Z's?"

"Yes," she told him. "I definitely need to get over the last few miles."

"Everybody says that. The part before the lakes is new trail that hasn't been finished yet. It needs attention before somebody gets hurt. The portages between the lakes are older, but still take it out of you, don't they?"

Jessie agreed and stepped gratefully off her sled. A break was definitely in order before running the last leg to Carmacks.

"There's plenty of room for your dogs, some back there"—he pointed to the trees behind the cabin—"if you want to get a little away from teams coming through."

Knowing it was good advice, she drove the team in that direction and found a good space to tie off her gang line, spacing the dogs out in a line under the trees.

In a little while, she had gone through the routine of caring for and feeding her dogs. All were uninjured and healthy, eating and drinking well. She pinched up the skin on the back of each dog's neck and watched to see if it retained the pinch or quickly sprang back to its normal position. Retaining the pinch would tell her a dog was dehydrating and in need of fluids. All seemed fine, and soon lay down to sleep.

From the smoky scent of a wood fire that drifted from a metal chimney on the roof, she knew it would be warm inside, so as soon as she had taken care of the dogs and checked each one over thoroughly to make sure no hidden injuries had been suffered on the hazardous run, she headed for the cabin with her sleeping bag under her arm to warm it up before climbing in for her own nap.

A blast of heat from a wood-burning stove hit her as she went in and closed the door. It was so warm that she immediately peeled off her hat, gloves, and parka, before she sat down on a handmade bench to have her snack. Frozen soup, heavy with vegetables and beef, soon thawed in a pan on the cabin's wood stove and went down well with some garlic bread, toasted close to the glowing stove. It all disappeared quickly, interspersed with two Snickers bars and some conversation with the "unofficial."

He informed her that thirteen teams, counting the two outside, had already passed through on their way to Carmacks. She was now fourteenth. Though Jessie had not been keeping close count of those she passed and that passed her, she was pleased to note that she had moved up a couple of places. She had been glad to start in the front half of the forty-seven racers. The snow of the trail softened as hundreds of dog feet and sled runners passed over it, making it punchy and more difficult for those who followed. In below-zero temperatures, this was less of a problem, but it might warm up.

Finished eating, and yawning in the heat, she made more tea in her thermos, adding a generous amount of sugar—instant energy—and gave up the idea of sleeping in such a small space. It was crowded with even three people in it, including a bearded musher who was snoring with his hat over his face on a bench across the room, and more were definitely on their way. When she heard the yips of a dog or two as another team pulled to a halt outside, she could tell it would be much better to retreat to her sled and snooze a little next to her dogs.

Four hours after she stopped, she had shut off the alarm, watered the dogs, packed up, and was ready to pull back onto the ice of Mandana Lake. From here, she would go all the way into Carmacks, where a two-hour layover would be mandatory and welcome. Stress as well as the poor trail had been catching up to her, but sleep had cured her attack of the yawns. The team was also more than ready to go, full of energy and sass, straining at their harnesses.

A question to the unofficial checker told her Debbie Todd had not stopped in or passed the cabin while she snoozed. Too bad, she thought. It would have been nice to see her and she couldn't have been far behind. She would probably catch up at Carmacks or soon after. Maybe even Dawson, if Jessie's team continued to make good time and stayed ahead.

"Okay, Tank. Take us out, boy. Good dogs."

Stowing the snow hook, she let her dependable leader guide the string of fourteen back onto the trail, once again passing the unknown musher in the blue and yellow parka, who was bent over, working on his tug lines. Must be pacing me, she thought. Likes the speed of my team.

Some mushers found it easier to follow another that was traveling at a comfortable pace. Keeping them in sight was a good way to let someone else do the thinking and, if it was an experienced musher, make the decisions that can be more difficult for a rookie. It was also a good way to learn from someone who knew just when to run and when to rest.

She was not surprised, therefore, when she noticed that he had followed her out onto the ice of Mandana Lake and wasn't making any attempt to catch up, seeming content to follow along at the same speed.

CHAPTER SEVEN

"The trail, packed down fully a foot by the traffic, was like a gutter. On either side spread the blanket of soft snow crystals. If a man turned into this in an endeavor to pass, his dogs would wallow perforce to their bellies and slow down to a snail's pace. So the men lay close to their leaping sleds and waited."
    —Jack London, "A Daughter of the Aurora"

IT WAS DARK AGAIN ON MONDAY BY THE TIME JESSIE REACHED Carmacks, the first official checkpoint in the race.

The trail after the Chain of Lakes had not improved, it had been worse, and running it in the dark, which made it impossible to see beyond the reach of her headlamp, had added to the tension. Though parts of it were fairly smooth and fast, hard-packed where the trailbreakers had passed, to either side deep soft snow made for difficult going if the dogs for any reason moved from the track. The heavy sled would slide into the drifts and force a musher to struggle to get it back on the more solid surface.

The area was heavily forested with lots of willow and alder that had forced the trailbreakers on their snowmachines to set a track that took teams up and down banks, and back and forth among the trees in ninety-degree turns that made them feel as if they had been propelled from paddles—a section some racers wearily referred to as Pinball Alley.

71

If it had been wide enough for their machines, the trail-breakers had hoped it would be wide enough for the sleds that followed, though even without considering a line of dogs in front, the heavily weighted sleds were significantly longer than the machines. Mushers shook their heads and widened their eyes at the concept as they later recounted incidents of lines hung up in the willows, broken brakes, smashed brush bows, crushed stanchions and side rails, ripped sled bags, and sometimes bruised and battered dogs and drivers. Wild survival stories circulated among trail-shocked rookies, sweatily angry about shoving sleds, coming around tight turns to find themselves staring down the light from their headlamps on eighty to a hundred feet of Yukon River bank as they swung perilously past it.

"Saw more crossed stakes in a few miles than I thought were possible. Thought about stopping at a couple to add a skull to the crossbones."

One Alaskan rookie racer, who slowly limped his team in to scratch from the race in Carmacks, related a collision that had wedged his sled so firmly between two small trees he was compelled to hack one of them down with an ax before he could remove the splintered remains and duct tape enough of them together to hold while he cautiously traversed the remaining fifteen miles. On arrival, he disgustedly tossed the worst parts into the first fire he came across, loaded his dogs, sled bag, and anything salvageable into his truck, and hit the road back to Whitehorse and points west.

Another caught a branch across the face that blacked an eye and broke his nose, but decided to continue at least as far as Dawson.

"I'll just take it like I always do—one checkpoint at a time. If it gets so I can't breathe, or hurts too bad, I'll bag it there. I been damaged worse'n this a time or two and still made it to the finish line. Cold air's a convenient ice pack for the swelling."

After listening quietly to a few of the comments, a veteran dog driver leaned back in his chair and smiled serenely. "Aw," he told the younger, less experienced group, "we haven't even got to the *good* parts yet."

Before reaching Carmacks the trail left the quick little downhills, tight turns, wicked brush, and thirty-foot-straight-down, and once again dropped onto the Yukon River. The switch onto ice was more than welcome to Jessie, though this ice was rougher than the smooth surface of the lakes she had crossed.

As the upper, narrower part of the Yukon freezes each fall, it does not do so all at once or over still water like the lakes. Ice forms slowly, creeping outward from the banks as the temperature fluctuates above and below freezing. Above freezing, what has already solidified breaks up easily into chunks and is conveyed by the still rapidly flowing water of a young river into piles of ice rubble, producing an irregular, uneven surface that is too rugged in places to be successfully traversed by dog sled and must be avoided. Between the chunks and blocks, there are often sections of open water—black steaming water—dangerous water. The trailbreakers attempt to pick the smoothest route through such sections, but at times they are forced up onto the banks in order to create a passable track away from these holes in the rough ice.

Hundreds of miles away, across Alaska, where the Iditarod is run, unlike the narrow upper part that grows slowly deeper and wider as it is joined by many other creeks and streams, the lower part of the more than fifteen-hundred-mile river is a mile wide and moves much more slowly. For this reason it freezes to a more smooth and level plane without forming an impassable obstacle course of random irregularities, blocks, and black-water holes.

It was just after midnight, after little more than an hour along the river's ice and banks, having covered the last ten miles in the dark with no problems by carefully following the trail, when Jessie ran under the bridge and pulled up the bank into Carmacks, a town of nearly four hundred inhabitants, where for the first time she was required to go through the official check-in procedure.

"Hi, Jessie. Everything going okay?"

She did not recognize the checker, a Canadian wearing a Quest jacket and carrying a clipboard, but appreciated his cheerful welcome. Through several years of running the Iditarod she had become acquainted with many along the route who annually donated their time and effort, so it seemed odd that most of the volunteers in this race were strangers. She assisted him in locating all the required gear in her sled bag and signed the check-in sheet. He established that she had the packet of promotional material every driver carried for the race committee and took a quick look at her veterinary record book.

"You're legal," he told her with a grin, and waved a hand toward a building she could just see in the dark, though lights danced around it from people coming and going with headlamps and flashlights. "Find your dogs a space over there behind the community center and I'll let the vet know you're here. They're checking heart rates and will want to have a look at your guys as soon as they can. Your bags of food and straw for the dogs are right next door."

She pulled away from the checkpoint and circled the Carmacks community building to find the holding area where she along with the rest of the racers would settle their dogs. She found a place for her team at one end of a group of five others, all resting quietly except one that had obviously come in just ahead of her, for the musher was still spreading straw for his dogs. Locating the three white poly-bags that bore her name, Jessie dragged them to a space beside her sled. Their contents would replenish the supplies she would carry in the sled for the next part of the run, including her own food, and she was ready for something new on the menu. Breaking open a bale of straw, she spread out a patch of it for each dog, providing insulation between dog and snow. While their food heated in the cooker, she took the booties off each one and carefully checked their feet, a never-ending concern that was more important than ever after the grueling run they had just completed. She rubbed foot ointment into many of their paws, but even Tux was doing well, his sore spot completely healed.

"Good feet," she told him. "You have such good feet, Tux."

As she was completing this chore with a sigh of relief, two veterinarians appeared out of the dark, headlamps bobbing, to check her team.

"Hey, Doc," she greeted the taller of the two—her own vet from Palmer, who was head veterinarian for this race. "I wondered when and where I'd see you."

Spenser nodded and smiled, a reserved man with friendly eyes behind a pair of glasses with dark frames. Jessie knew him to be knowledgeable, conscientious to a fault, and it was to him that she trusted the health of all her dogs.

"How's it going? Your bunch doing well?"

"Great. All healthy and happy. No thanks to that last section of trail."

"I know. It's been pretty hard on teams this year. You're lucky yours came through okay. Checked them all over?"

"You better believe it. Can't afford to miss anything that'll get worse going on."

They watched as his partner began her examination of the dogs. Kneeling in the straw, the vet held her stethoscope to the chest of each dog, listening carefully to the heartbeat for any sign of abnormalities. As she worked, she murmured individual compliments to them for good behavior, reading their names from their collars. Used to the procedure from past examinations, the dogs cooperated easily, affectionate Darryl Two even giving her a sloppy lick under the chin as she leaned within reach to pinch up his skin, checking, as Jessie had, for dehydration.

"You've got some real lovers here," she told Jessie with a grin, and gave Two several extra pats. "They're fine and will be better once they're fed and watered. You giving them vitamin supplements?"

"With every meal and watering."

"Good. You're aware that Pete has a heart murmur? Athletic heart?"

"Right. It's been checked and disappears with two or three weeks' rest—just the usual enlargement from strenuous exercise."

"Makes sense. Ten years ago they might have cut him from your team, but we keep learning a lot with every race."

"That would have been too bad; he's one of my best performers."

"Usually are, like human athletes. We'll be back in a while to get their resting rates. I'll remember to check him once again before you leave, but it's only a slight swoosh anyway. Bob, you want to scan this pack?"

"Sure, but I've known these guys for years. Chipped them all in Palmer a month ago. You're taking good care of them, Jessie. Keep it up."

The taller vet, likewise headlamped, stepped forward with a scanner and began by running it between the shoulders of Darryl One till he located and ascertained the number of the identification chip. As he moved down the line, he checked each number it showed against a list of dogs he was carrying on another clipboard. Twice he paused, having a little trouble locating the chip, moving the scanner back and forth over the dog in question until it evidently read out correctly, giving him the information he needed, though he frowned and seemed a bit irritated.

"They were scanned in Whitehorse before the race," Jessie asked the other vet. "Why are you doing it again?"

"Oh, we're doing it at all the checkpoints. The vet committee just wants to cross all the T's. Might as well make use of all the new technology. We've even got portable EKG machines again this year."

Spenser finished his monitoring with Tank, who, recognizing him as a friend, rose attentively to his feet as the man approached, but lay down again as soon as he turned away.

"All present and accounted for, Jessie," he told her. "Ready for a good rest."

"Great."

"See you in Dawson."

"You going on up?"

"Yeah, gotta play head vet there, too. Sharon will take over here until the rest come through."

"Thanks."

They left.

Jessie fed and watered her dogs and left them curled up on the straw to rest like the other teams around them. The checkpoint was as busy as Braeburn, but the mushers who came and went regularly all tried to cause as little disturbance as possible for each other's sleeping dogs, knowing they expected the same courtesy in return. It was less hectic, partly because the race was now well under way, but also because of the required layover and careful preparations for it.

Since Carmacks was located on the highway between Whitehorse and Dawson, it was accessible to those following the race. Cars, vans, and trucks crowded the parking lot around the lodge at the south end of the bridge that crossed the river at this point. Handlers and support crews met the teams here, but were not allowed to assist in any physical way. They shared information and strategy with the musher they supported, but could only watch while the work was accomplished by the racer alone. Once the team had cleared the checkpoint, they could load up any leftover food and straw, already collected and bagged by the musher before leaving, but not until the team had gone on up the trail.

Jessie had seen and spoken with her handlers when she arrived, but at her request they had left her alone to take care of her team. Now she was glad to find them where her truck and Don's were parked among others in the lot, and to be free to compare notes with her crew of four.

"Hey, Jessie. You've moved up four places," Billy told her with a grin. "You going to win this one?"

"Can't tell yet." She smiled back. "It would be a long shot, but I always give it a try. Finish in the top ten, maybe. That last section was a bitch, but we haven't hit the hardest parts yet."

Don and Cas had questions about the shelter they were allowed to put up for the dogs at the Dawson checkpoint, where each musher must wait thirty-six hours before continuing. It had been constructed of poles and a large blue plastic tarp in Knik and hauled along on top of Don's camper.

"Can we put it up and have it ready when you get in?" Cas asked.

"You could, I think, but why don't you wait till I get there," Jessie told him. "I'd like to have a look at the space and pick out a good one for the team. It won't take long, since we already know exactly how it goes together—ten, fifteen minutes, maybe."

"Okay. That makes sense. We'll get it off the camper, anyway."

"How's your sled holding up?" Don questioned.

"Great so far. I want to check and tighten everything and change runners in Dawson, before going over the summit to Eagle. There's one stanchion that got a little loose between here and the lakes that I want to take a good look at. I tightened it and it's fine now, but I want to make sure before we start over American Summit. I've got a roll of duct tape if I need it."

"I'll go take a look—"

"No, Don. You can't help me here or I'll be disqualified."

"Just a look. I won't touch. Okay?"

"Okay, but if you've got ideas, just tell me and I'll take care of it."

"You've got it. Which kind of runners do you want in Dawson?"

"The yellow. These are a little beat, but they'll hold till then. I think I'll just replace them with the same hard plastic. They'll be fine, especially if it stays cold."

"Right. I'll have them out and ready. Anything else you'll need?"

"Just the usual stuff. Let's go find something to eat in the lodge and talk about it. I'm starving. Have you guys had dinner?"

"So long ago I'm about ready again. You need some rest soon."

"Yeah, but I want to eat first. Then I'll try for about four hours. I'm pooped after that last run—it was murder in a place or two. I'll plan to leave about seven."

As they crossed the parking lot a musher Jessie didn't recognize came out the lodge door and, catching sight of her in the bright outside lights, turned in her direction with a wide grin, holding out a hand when he was close enough.

"You're Jessie Arnold, aren't you? I'm Lynn Ehlers. I've been reading about your Iditarod and looking forward to meeting you for months, ever since I found out we'd both be running the Quest."

Jessie detected the hint of an accent in his voice that gave her a clue.

"And you're the musher from Minnesota, right?"

"That's me."

"Hey, I was born there."

"I think I read that somewhere."

"My folks are still there, but they lived in Anchorage when my dad was stationed there for a couple of years in the Air Force."

"They must miss you. Go back often?"

"Not very often, but they have a motor home and drive up the highway to Alaska for a couple of months almost every summer. My dad's a photographer and thinks he's gone to heaven up here."

"Are they here for the race?"

"Not this one. I couldn't compete with my sister and her husband, who're about to give Mom and Dad their first grandchild. Besides, they've seen me race before."

"You should come down for our race—the Bear Grease."

"Maybe I will sometime."

"Great."

"Did I hear correctly that you *drove* all the way up here towing your dogs and equipment in a trailer?" Jessie asked.

"Yup. Left six weeks ago and drove for three. Caught a blizzard in Montana. I've been staying with Sally Philips out on Chena Hot Springs Road outside of Fairbanks."

"Hey, Sally's great. Sorry she isn't running this year."

"Yeah, she helped me out a lot. Went over the whole route with me on paper and told me what to look out for. She's playing handler for me, along with two of her friends."

A little older, but about the same height as Jessie, the Minnesota musher seemed taller in a long parka over shoulders broadened from years of wrestling a sled. The creases around his mouth and eyes spoke of time spent squinting into the glare of sun on snow, though they fell attractively enough into a frame for an infectious smile. The lower part of his face was covered with a neatly trimmed dark beard, enlivened with a sprinkling of gray.

There *was* something attractive about outdoor people, Jessie thought, especially mushers, though maybe that was just a natural personal preference.

Introducing him to her support crew, Jessie was impressed with the ease of his friendly interest in them.

"Wow!" Billy exclaimed. "Minnesota's really a long ways away."

"Farther than it looks on the map, for sure," Ehlers agreed. "But the Alaska Highway and this race make it worth the drive."

"Come and eat with us?" Cas invited.

"Thanks, but I just finished. It's crowded in there anyway and I need to get some stuff done here and catch some sleep before I'm ready to leave. See you in Dawson, Jessie? Maybe we'll have time to share war stories."

"Sure. Have a good run. Come on, guys, what I want is breakfast for dinner. Think they'll do it for me?"

The restaurant in the lodge, as Lynn had warned, was full of noise, packed with mushers, handlers, race officials, media people, and spectators who lived there, or had driven up from Whitehorse. Racers, it seemed, were being given priority, for a group of handlers who had finished eating immediately offered Jessie and her group their table, so it wasn't long before she was focused on getting on the outside of the huge plate of ham, eggs, and country-fried potatoes the kitchen had had no trouble supplying. Smothering three pieces of toast with extra butter and jam, she washed them down with heavily sugared coffee, supplied by a waitress who hovered close with refills, clearly protective of her service provision for this particular musher.

As Jessie took her last bite of toast and sighed happily, a television reporter, who had been lurking nearby with a cameraman in tow waiting for her to finish, politely asked for a quick interview for a Fairbanks station, so they moved outside where he could find a background that included some of the resting dogs.

"Instant celebrity." Don grinned. "You don't need us. We'll be in the camper when you're through, okay?"

Greeting three more mushers that she knew took another few minutes. The third was Jake Leland, questioning the absence of his stepdaughter.

"But you haven't seen her since yesterday evening, right?"

"On the trail, then again in the morning as I was leaving Braeburn," Jessie replied. "She was doing fine, running alone and still pretty keyed up about it all. You must be proud of her, Jake."

"Oh, I am. But right now I'm a little concerned that she's not here yet. Hope she's not having some kind of trouble."

"I wouldn't worry. She seemed to be taking good care of herself—and those mutts of yours," she teased. "This last part of the trail was pretty nasty. She's smart enough so she's probably just going slow enough to keep from beating up her team and sled. She knows it's gotta last for the rest of the race. No replacements.''

"But it's not—"

"I know, but it's early on, Jake. There's less than twenty teams in so far. She'll be along soon. Wait and see. Don't be a mother hen.''

He grinned, slightly chagrined. "You're right. Don't tell her I was fussing, okay?''

"I wouldn't dream of it.''

Heedless of the congestion of the checkpoint, Jessie found a place to sleep in the community center's section reserved for drivers' rest and was sound asleep in minutes, alarm clock next to her ear.

Later, as she was getting ready to put her team back in line and hitched up to leave, the vet Sharon returned to check Pete's heart.

"He's good to go.''

"Thanks, Sharon.''

"Have a good trip.''

Linda Caswell gave her a hug. "We'll be waiting for you in Dawson.''

"Don't gamble away all your money at Diamond Tooth Gertie's while you wait.''

"We haven't got enough to make a difference,'' Linda said.

At just after seven, the four handlers watched her pull away, go through the check-out procedure, and waved till she had vanished into the dark that was just beginning to turn gray, and all they could see was the light from her headlight bobbing along for a minute or two.

The race was definitely under way. Besides the musher with the fractured sled, only one other had scratched in Carmacks, because of sick dogs. The other rookies had bucked up their courage and decided the veteran couldn't be serious about the "*good* parts" yet to come. Twenty-one dogs had been dropped and collected by support crews. Jessie was satisfied to have her whole team still healthy and ready to make good time to Pelly Crossing, the next official checkpoint, and pleased to find that, although she wasn't in the front-running group, her dogs were clocking times between checkpoints very close to those of the race leaders.

Things were looking up. So far, so good.

But where, she wondered, was Debbie Todd?

CHAPTER EIGHT

"There was a great silence, and in each man's eyes many pictures came and went."
—Jack London, "An Odyssey of the North"

JESSIE LEFT CARMACKS AT THE FIRST HINT OF APPROACHING dawn, her breath steaming in the cold air as she ran down the road past the headlights of the cars and trucks of people driving to work and taking their children to school. As she came to an intersection, a pickup stopped and the driver waved her on through. Two grade school children riding next to their dad climbed over each other in excitement to see her go by and flapped their mittened hands rigorously.

"Good luck," they called out the window they had cranked down, not caring that they had let out all the heat from the cab.

The team ran along for fifteen miles on a road well packed by vehicles. It was blissfully easy running compared to the night before: up and down low hills, a quick, smooth trail. As the sun rose—just before nine—the gray half-light gave way to the deep blue shadows only possible in a world of white. The bright sunshine sparkled on each tiny crystal of snow and glittered from the crest of each drift, creating a million points of light as if the sunshine scattered diamond dust over everything it touched.

The wind had been at work along the sides of the road,

carving graceful loops and curves in the snow cliffs that had been cut sharply vertical by the steel blades that opened the way for travel. Here and there it had blown the suggestion of an arced line across the hard surface of the track: the wind's subtle reminder that it had not yet finished with its creative sculpting, and could return powerfully at any moment to reshape the world with its own vision, obliterating that of men who drove plows. Jessie looked back and almost regretted the disruption her dogs' feet and her sled's runners had made in the smooth, natural, lovely shape of it.

An hour out of Carmacks, Jim Ryan caught up and settled his team into a companionable trot just behind her, gesturing her to go ahead when she offered to give him room to pass. She wondered if she had lost the racer in the blue and yellow parka at the checkpoint. Perhaps he had gone out ahead of her, or was still back at the checkpoint, resting.

It was good to see Ryan, for Jessie had had little time to visit with him when he took her to meet Debbie Todd before the start of the race. They were old friends, had run together before, and enjoyed each other's company.

The trail followed the gently sloping plowed road for the next hour, but soon gave the pair of mushers a taste of more rugged country as it dropped back and forth onto the Yukon several times with steep descents and climbs through small gullies. Traveling in the daylight made it possible to see what lay ahead, but going downhill they struggled to keep their heavy sleds from catching up with the wheel dogs and they added their weight and energy to push the sled when going up the banks. Once they found it easier to join forces in pushing the sleds one at a time to the top of a particularly steep rise.

The country in this part of the Yukon Territory was heavily forested, with more impressive hills and valleys, and the swift river cut a deeper gorge through much of it, twisting and winding through canyons, with a few rapids that had frustrated Klondike stampeders in boats a hundred years earlier. Frozen, these rapids were no threat to the travelers on sleds, except for the uneven surface of the thawed and refrozen ice. The banks were crowded with heavy willow, brush, and stands of birch and a few poplar thrusting bare limbs skyward like skeleton fingers.

The ice of the Yukon was rough, and the wind had blown the snow from much of the brilliant broken surface that glistened in the sunlight. Sharp as shards of glass, the ice was not easy on the dogs' feet and both Jessie and Ryan stopped more than once to check them and replace booties that had been lost or worn through on the abrasive shards.

Dog booties are made of a variety of materials—fleece, Cordura, and nylon pack cloth—and protect the feet of the dogs from sharp ice and snow, providing insulation for feet that are extremely vulnerable and can easily become sore or damaged, with cracks in the pads, chafing, or blisters. Used in combination with foot creams or ointments, the booties help to keep the dogs' feet as clean and dry as possible. They must fit well, must not be too tight or have too much excess material flapping to accumulate snow and ice. Velcro strips fasten them around the dogs' legs and some dogs who do not care for wearing them quickly become experts at stripping them off with their teeth. Since foot care is vital to the success of any racer, hundreds of booties are used—and lost—in any distance race.

Jessie welcomed Ryan's company. It reminded pleasantly of miles they had run together in past Iditarods. He had always been an easy friend with whom to travel, because he didn't talk his head off, gave her personal space, and respected her abilities as a musher, lacking the women-are-less-able nonsense that a few male mushers still occasionally exhibited. For another hour they ran together until pulling off the trail to give their dogs a snack, then spent a little time by the fire he built to make coffee, as they caught up on each other's lives.

"You lost your head and got married, I hear," Jessie

teased as she tossed him one of her Snickers bars to go with his coffee. "Poor baby. Bachelor days all gone now."

"Okay—okay. You can give me grief, but I should have done it years ago. I was too damned focused on this." He gestured toward his team and sled. "It kind of takes you over—addiction—obsession—whatever. Gets in the way of some other important things, you know. Life isn't all dogs and trails to somewhere."

She nodded slowly. "I know. You're preaching to the choir, Jim."

"I understand you've still got a good thing going with that trooper we met the year of my moose disaster."

Jessie took a sip of coffee and bit her lip before answering.

"Yes . . . well."

Ryan gave her a quick questioning look. "*Not* a good thing?"

When she hesitated, considering, he backpedaled. "Hey, I'm just being nosy. Ignore me, okay?"

"That's all right, Jim. I don't mind—I just don't really know how to explain it."

Telling him about Alex's father's death and the extended trip to Idaho gave her a chance to examine out loud some of the things she had been feeling and thinking.

"There's something uncomfortable about it right now. We're off our usual wavelength."

"Well, he's pretty concerned about some other things, right?"

"Right, but it's more than that, and we both know it. We just haven't talked about it. Whatever. We'll work it out when he comes back, I think. How's married life treating you?"

"Good—very good. Better than that, really. It's great. Anne is . . ."

As she listened to him share his positive feelings about his new wife and the contentment of their wedded state, Jessie found herself comparing it to her own relationship and finding that what she and Alex had between them was similar in honesty, trust, and respect, mixed with a warm affection and sense of humor. Though Alex had never crowded her intentionally, she knew he would be happier if she agreed to a wedding. Wasn't it traditionally supposed to be the man who was reluctant? What made her so disinclined? Was her hesitation responsible for what felt out of key between them?

". . . so I just keep her in a box in the closet and feed her angleworms once a week," Jim continued in a serious tone.

"You *what?*"

"You were nodding at the right places, but I didn't think you were really listening." He grinned. "Gotcha."

They ran on, through an area that had been burned several years before and was full of stumps and a tangle of timber. Thankfully it was short, only ten or fifteen minutes of ugly trail that soon came out onto a slough of willows and alder. Then they were back onto the Yukon, where there were large cracks and steps in the ice.

In some places the river water had frozen solidly to the bank, but there was a drop onto ice that had broken loose and fallen, to refreeze on a lower level. As Tank led the dogs carefully down this step, Jessie watched closely and halted the team quickly when Bliss slipped and fell into a dangerous crack between the two levels that the others had successfully jumped across. Hauling Bliss out uninjured, she drove the rest slowly and carefully over the hazard and several more that followed. Having crossed similar obstacles in training, the dogs all did well, but Jessie was not sorry to leave this section behind her and proceed on smoother ice.

Nine of the front-runners in the race reached McCabe Creek between noon and two-thirty on Tuesday, having run just over forty miles from Carmacks with no long rest stops. Jessie and Jim Ryan pulled in at a quarter to four, happy to find themselves in tenth and eleventh positions for the moment. After a reasonable stay, they set out together for Pelly Crossing, thirty-five miles away, planning an extended rest there for both humans and dogs.

Crossing the highway in the lead, Jessie was pleased as her team trotted steadily along beside it for a ways before following the race markers off onto a trapline. Soon she stopped to shift the position of two of her dogs, only to hear Ryan swearing as, passing her, his team hit a patch of overflow that sent his sled sliding wildly to knock into a tree with a teeth-jarring thump. A small frozen lake gave them a quick break before more of the same, and more of Ryan's curses, but the trail then smoothed out along with his temper.

Pelly Crossing had been added to the race route as a checkpoint for the 1996 Yukon Quest and the people of the small community had worked hard and successfully to make their section of the trail the best of the run. It was wide and even, with the foliage trimmed back, giving the grateful racers a pleasant and stressless trip to the tall bluff that told them they were only three short miles from the checkpoint.

The next 250 miles, from Pelly to Dawson, would be the longest of any section of the Yukon Quest, and would include two formidable climbs; one over the 3,550-foot Eureka Dome, the other up King Solomon's Dome, at 3,800 feet, the highest point in the race, just before reaching Dawson City. They both knew it would be wise to start for Dawson in good shape, with well-rested, well-fed, and energized teams.

Jim Ryan checked in first and drove off to find a good space to settle his team. As Jessie finished going through the routine examination of required equipment and food with the checkpoint official, she noticed an impatient Jake Leland waiting to speak to her. He said nothing until she had driven clear of the checkpoint area to allow the next musher to pull in, but followed close beside her with long strides and a worried look on his face. Fifty yards from the checkpoint, Jessie stopped the team, punched in the snow hook, and turned to see what was wrong.

Jake looked ten years older than when she had seen him in Carmacks, tired and tormented.

"What's up, Jake? Still no word on Debbie? She must have—"

"Jessie, please—I need your help. Someone's got her."

"Got her?"

"Taken her—kidnapped her—snatched her right off the trail."

Confused, Jessie frowned and shook her head, thinking she'd misunderstood.

"You must be mistaken, Jake. She's just late and . . . you're worried. It's harder to wait for mushers, especially rookies, than to run yourself. She'll be—"

He huffed impatience, scowled, and didn't let her finish, frustration drawing deep lines in his forehead as he waved a gloved hand to erase her words.

"You're not *listening*. I said someone's *taken* her."

Jessie *was* listening now. This was not the calm, take-things-as-they-come, confident, handle-anything dog musher she had known for years. She had never seen Jake Leland so distracted or incensed. There was both rage and fear in his voice.

She held up one mittened hand to slow him down. "Whoa. How can you know that?"

He nodded, recognizing that he had her complete attention. "Okay, here's the deal. She never made it to Carmacks. Left Braeburn an hour after you did, with two teams between and the next one forty minutes behind. No one passed her after that. She didn't stop at the cabin on Mandana Lake, went right through, though the volunteer there thinks he might have seen her going down onto the lake. He said you were sleeping out back."

Jessie agreed, remembering the tiny crowded cabin.

"I must have been, the timing's right, but he said she hadn't come through. I asked him."

"Yeah, well . . . all he remembered was someone's back and the description fit, even if he didn't get a good look or a name. I waited hours longer than it should have taken her to get to Carmacks. She didn't come in.''

''But, Jake, she's got to be there somewhere. Where the hell . . . ? Someone must have seen—''

He went on, ignoring her comment, the words pouring out in a torrent of concern and growing anger.

''I asked *everyone*. Nobody'd seen her. When I decided that nobody in Carmacks knew where she was, I borrowed a snowmachine and ran the trail all the way back to Braeburn, turned around, and ran back again. She wasn't there. But halfway back, on Mandana Lake—you know, the last one of the Chain of Lakes—I found a place where a single sled seemed to have stopped and the driver thrashed around it in the snow some, then drove away from there, off to the east. There were snowmachine tracks, too; looked like it had passed the sled on the trail and circled around after it. I tried to follow the sled track, but it went off the lake into the trees and some more snowmachine tracks covered it over, went back and forth across the sled track until it was impossible to find.''

''But why would she take off away from the marked trail, Jake? It doesn't make sense.''

''I don't know. The snowmachine might have scared her. She ran into one a while back and hates them.''

''She told me about it.''

''That's possible, but she's not the kind to panic. It might not even have been her sled. But it was the only thing I found that was a possibility. It was a clean, clear track of just one sled and team. Went in a straight line across the lake surface and disappeared. I drove circles for half an hour, but couldn't locate it again. I was about to go ask one of the pilots to search—''

''But that doesn't tell you she's been grabbed by anyone,'' Jessie interjected. ''She may just be lost. It happens.''

''Well, you can't tell from looking at the track just how fast the team was going. If someone on a snowmachine was chasing her, she might have been going flat-out, trying to get away from it. It was totally confusing and I was hoping she was just lost—until I got back here and the checker handed me this.''

He held out a sheet with a few words on plain white paper that had originally been folded and sealed into an envelope with Leland's name on it.

Jessie stripped off her mittens and took it to read. The words had been printed in large square capital letters with a black ballpoint pen.

LELAND. WE HAVE YOUR DAUGHTER. IF YOU WANT HER BACK IN ONE PIECE KEEP YOUR MOUTH SHUT AND DON'T DO ANYTHING STUPID. DON'T TELL ANYONE BUT JESSIE ARNOLD— ESPECIALLY THE POLICE. WE WANT $100,000. YOU'VE GOT MORE THAN TWO DAYS TO GET IT. YOU'LL HEAR FROM US AFTER ARNOLD GETS INTO DAWSON ON FRIDAY. BE SMART AND DO WHAT YOU'RE TOLD OR ELSE.

"Jesus, Jake. Who gave this to the checker?''

"He says he found it on his clipboard. Didn't see who put it there.''

"Why would they want you to tell me?''

"I don't know. I thought you might have some ideas.''

She shook her head, stunned, as she stared at the message in her hand, then up at him, speechless, trying to take it in. Debbie. This note meant Debbie, the young woman she had met, shared tea with, and liked, was in trouble. Who . . . ? And why me? she wondered. Leland held out a hand for the paper and folded it back into the envelope before he put it carefully into an interior pocket of his jacket.

"Don't let that get away from you, Jake, and don't handle it any more than you have to. A forensics lab might be able to get something from it.''

"Dammit, Jessie. They said *no police*. I'm not about to do anything *stupid,* as they said. Someone left the thing. They may still be here watching—me—you—whatever.''

"I meant later, Jake—later. And you're right, of course.

With the highway running through here it could be any-body—someone passing through—handler, race people, spectators—someone connected with the race—vet, offi-cial, the checker who says someone left that note, even a musher. Dozens of people coming and going, and two hundred and fifty or three hundred people who live here. And there is an RCMP unit, I think.''

"No. I won't *do* that. Jessie, why Debbie? What the hell am I going to tell her mom? Jill wasn't real hot on her running the Quest this year to begin with. She's going to have—''

"Hey, Jake. Don't start—okay? Better concentrate on what you can come up with—not what you can't change. It's not *your* fault.''

"You wanna tell that to Jill?''

"Nope. But . . . what're you going to do? What are *we* going to do? I'm obviously involved somehow, from what that note says.''

"What *can* I do? Try to round up a hundred thousand dollars somewhere—I hope. I'm going to *hate* the phone call home that I've got to make.''

"While I go to Dawson?''

"Yes. You've got to get to Dawson, Jessie. They said they wouldn't contact me until *after* you get to Dawson. So you've got to get there. The sooner, the better. I can't stand this.''

CHAPTER NINE

"And when, on the still cold nights, he pointed his nose at a star and howled long and wolflike, it was his ancestors, dead and dust, pointing nose at star and howling down through the centuries and through him. And his cadences were their cadences, the cadences which voiced their woe and what to them was the meaning of the stillness, and the cold, and dark."
    —Jack London, "The Law of Club and Fang"

AS SHE PARKED HER DOGS AND SLED IN THE FENCED AREA reserved for teams in Pelly Crossing and, almost on automatic pilot, went about the chores of taking care of them, Jessie wondered how and where Jake Leland intended to collect $100,000 in two days, and if she could stand the anxiety she was feeling for the time it would take to get to Dawson City.

If the kidnappers were watching him, they were probably also watching her. She found herself taking careful glances at the people she saw, assessing them as possible threats or conspirators. Suddenly she felt completely alone and isolated, knowing she trusted no one, and that there were a lot of people involved with and following this race that she did not know.

Who were these kidnappers? How many of them were there? From the ''we'' and ''us'' in the note there was obviously more than one, or that was the desired impression. How could they be identified? How dangerous were they? There was a lot of wilderness country out there for any musher to disappear into. If it could happen to Debbie, it could happen to Jessie as well.

It frightened and incensed her to feel observed, a feeling that took her back to the preceding fall, when she had been the object of a stalker who, for a while, had made her life a misery. She knew the events surrounding that situation had forever changed her perspective on the people she knew, or met, and had taken for granted; had stolen not only her personal space and time, but her sense of trust in the world around her, which still made her angry and resentful. Now it all came flooding back again, for herself and for Debbie. Where was the girl, and more important, *how* was she? How were her captors, whoever they were, treating her? Knowing what she had faced herself, Jessie felt she could anticipate or guess some of what the girl would be going through—the offense and insult, the fear.

Was there anything that could be done other than just go on to Dawson, leaving Leland to collect the cash? More than anything Jessie could imagine, she wished Alex were there with suggestions, not still in Idaho. But there was Cas, his partner in solving many crimes in the past. Could he help? The letter had been very specific: "If you want her back in one piece keep your mouth shut. . . . Don't tell anyone . . . especially the police." Cas was definitely one of those Jake had been warned against telling. But would they know he was an Alaska State Trooper, or think of him as a part of her support crew? Was it worth the risk? If the kidnappers were Alaskan, they might know of his law enforcement connection, but Canadians might not. Which were they—or could they be both? She knew that if she told Cas what was going on, it would be impossible to keep him from doing something—asking questions, doing his job—even though this was not his country or jurisdiction.

Concentrating hard on the problem, she didn't hear the

approach of the veterinarian who had come to check her dogs. She jumped and gulped air as though she had had an electric shock when he said hello and laid a hand on her shoulder.

"Sorry. Didn't mean to put you off."

It was a moment before Jessie could catch her breath to speak.

"That's okay. I wasn't paying attention."

"Your pups doing okay? Anything you'd like me to look at, besides the usual?"

"Oh . . . ah . . . yes," she said, distractedly. "Ah . . . Bliss . . . she seemed to be favoring her right shoulder . . . after some of the rubble on the river."

"Right. No problem. Which one's Bliss?"

As he proceeded to go through his routine checks and to examine the dog in question, Jessie looked after him with a frown. There was something about the way he spoke, clearly western Canadian, that made her stop and realize that it was apparent, not only from his accent but from the words he used, that he was not Alaskan. "Didn't mean to put you off." An Alaskan—an American—would probably have said, *didn't mean to scare you*, or *didn't mean to startle you*. Not *didn't mean to put you off*. It was a small thing, but small things sometimes mattered more than large ones.

Was there anything in the note to let them know the nationality of its author? She tried to think, but couldn't remember the exact phrasing. Hurriedly putting on more snow to melt for later use, she left the vet at his job and went to find Jake Leland to have another look at the note.

"I'll scan your dogs for chips when you go out," the vet called after her.

"HERE—'ESPECIALLY THE POLICE.' HE SAYS *POLICE.* Wouldn't a Canadian say *constable* or the *RCMP?* And the phrasing. I think this person's an Alaskan—at least an American."

Leland shook his head at her suggestion. "You can't know that, Jessie."

"Read it out loud and guess, Jake. It sounds more Alaskan than Canadian. 'Keep your mouth shut . . . don't do anything stupid . . . police . . . or else.' "

He did as she said, read it aloud, slowly, and finally agreed.

"You could be right. But where does that get us? Doesn't tell us which Alaskan, or if they're all Alaskan. Just that whoever wrote this damned thing is probably Alaskan."

"Yeah, I know. But it's a start. Whatever happens, they can't just be allowed to get away with this. Listen, Jake. I really think we need some professional help here. I know some people—"

"No!"

Leland responded as she had expected he would, with absolute and utter refusal, to the idea of any assistance.

"I told you. I won't do *anything* that might jeopardize Debbie's chances. I'm scared enough for her already."

"Jake. We don't even know what those chances are. It may be worse to do nothing—to do just what they tell us. They're probably keeping us both busy worrying to complicate the matter—you trying to get the money, me out of touch with just about everything for two hundred and fifty miles between here and Dawson. How can we just go meekly along? We need someone to be doing something else—looking for Debbie, figuring out what happened and where they may have taken her."

Stubbornly, he shook his head. "Absolutely not, Jessie. No. Not."

She stared at him, understanding his obstinate attitude, feeling helpless against it, feeling he was wrong in action, right in sentiment.

"Okay, Jake, okay. I just hope we're doing the right thing by doing nothing."

"Believe me, finding that much money on short notice is not nothing."

She had all but promised silence. So much for Cas. But if Alex had been available, she knew she wouldn't have hesitated to tell him, whether Leland agreed or not. And Alex wouldn't have been willing to follow the guidelines they had laid down. He would have done something—would have contacted . . . *Delafosse!*

He would have immediately contacted his Canadian friend, RCMP Inspector Charles "Del" Delafosse. She knew without a doubt that it would have been his first move—and that she *could* do the same with assurance of discretion, but should she?

Wisely, Jessie kept this particular insight to herself. She needed to think it over and it was definitely not something she wanted Leland to veto before she had the chance to do so. What he didn't know couldn't upset him.

"I'll see you before you leave, okay? I'll let you know . . . well, whatever, but don't go without seeing me," he was saying.

She agreed.

Turning to go back to her team, where the water she had left was probably hot by now, she saw the racer who had been following her for the last day or so pulling into the checkpoint in his blue and yellow parka. She kept seeing him. Was he following, not just keeping pace with her? Could he be part of this? Who the hell was he anyway? Was she just paranoid? It was time to find out.

"Rick Roney. Rookie in his second year, because he didn't make it to Dawson last year, but he's run enough middle-distance races to qualify," the checker told her.

"But who is he? What does he do? Does he have his own kennel? Work with someone who does? What?"

"Don't know. I just do the checking here. The Quest committee would know. They registered him. Find Ned Bishop. He's around here somewhere managing the race, unless he's already taken off for Stepping Stone. He'll know. Why'd you want to know all this stuff anyway, Jessie? He's just another young musher."

"Oh, just curious. I keep seeing him and wondered."

"Well, Ned's the best one here to ask."

"Thanks."

Jessie found Ned Bishop, race marshal, by an incoming sled and team that were involved in a penalty dispute because the racer had lost his ax somewhere on the trail between Carmacks and Pelly Crossing.

"I don't have time to argue with you, Charlie. You know the rule on mandatory gear. You have it, fine. You lose it, there's a thirty-minute penalty in Angel Creek. I'd suggest that you stop griping and go find another one, or you're going to catch hell from checkers from here to Fairbanks. That saw you've got won't cut it, if you'll excuse the pun."

"But I hardly ever use an ax. Don't see why it should be so damned important."

"I don't make the rules. You can protest if you want. I'll give you the paperwork to fill out. But I can tell you that if it's on the list you gotta have it, just like everybody else. You know that. Sorry."

The musher turned away, frowning and shaking his head. Bishop turned to Jessie.

"Ned, there was a driver came in just before Charlie. He had on a blue and yellow parka. You know anything about him?"

"Ah . . . hold on." Bishop turned to call out to the checker, who was walking away toward the dog yard. "Hey, Bob. Who came in before Charlie?"

"Rick Roney."

"Oh, yeah. Thanks."

"Rick Roney," he repeated for Jessie. "Rookie from Atlin."

"You know anything about him?"

"Not really. He's pretty new. Moved up there a couple of years ago—maybe five. Just got his first team together last year and ran some smaller races, but hasn't won any.

Met him a time or two. Pretty quiet . . . keeps to himself. Why?''

''He's been behind me almost all the way from the start. I just wondered who he was and why he's following me—a little information.''

''Well, that's about all I can tell you. Probably likes your speed and doesn't have anyone specific to run with. Your reputation precedes you, Jessie. There's some rumors flying about that you've got a good team ahead of you. That you're one to watch.''

''Oh, *really?* Anything makes good gossip, I guess.'' She had to smile. Through her worry, it was good to know that people—other mushers—respected her ability enough to consider her a contender in a race she had never run before. ''You're probably right that Roney's just playing follow the leader. I'll just have to make sure I stay in front of him. Thanks, Ned.''

''Hey, no problem. Sorry I don't know more. He's kind of a standoffish sort. Anyway, glad to have you in the race, Jessie.''

Paranoia, she told herself, walking away. Just paranoia.

But something about it wasn't that simple to explain and still made her uneasy. She shrugged her shoulders to alleviate a shiver that ran down her back, and headed back to her dogs.

Now the decision had to be made—should she, or should she not try to get in touch with Delafosse?

''Dammit, Alex Jensen. Where are you when I really need you?'' she muttered, frowning.

Without warning a new reality swept into her mind, stopping her in the middle of the busy Pelly Crossing checkpoint to stare at nothing with a painfully sick feeling.

He's not coming back, she thought. He's going to stay in Idaho and not come back at all.

And, without question, she knew that she believed it.

''Get that thing down quick before someone drives by or another musher shows up. The trail crosses the highway here and we're really exposed. I wanna get away fast.''

"I'm moving as fast as I can, goddammit. This thing's heavy as hell.''

"Full of fancy trimmings and expensive food. She's a rookie—has no idea what to take, so she takes everything. Must weigh three hundred pounds. Just get it far enough off the truck so I can reach it.''

"How the hell'd we get it up here?''

"There were four of us, remember?''

"Oh, yeah—well, we should have known we'd have to get it down. Ouch. Shit. Got my thumb under the runner.''

The two men were struggling to move a racing sled from the top of a dog box on the back of a pickup. Fully loaded, the sled was unwieldy and all but impossible to handle. As they wrestled with it, another truck rounded a bend in the road and drove toward them.

"Dammit to hell. Here comes someone, and there's a box on that truck—it's some racer's support.''

"There's only one guy.''

Seeing the difficulty the two were having with the sled, the driver of the approaching truck pulled up and stopped behind the parked pickup, climbed out, and came to do a friendly good deed.

"Looks like you guys need a hand.''

"Ah . . . oh, shit . . . sure. Thanks.''

Behind the newcomer's back the two men gave each other long significant looks. One frowned and shook his head. The other shrugged.

Together, the three managed to move the sled far enough so that it finally overbalanced, began to slide from the top of the dog box so fast that all they could do was try to break its fall to the snow at the side of the road.

"Is it broke?''

"Doesn't seem to be. Lucky, I guess.''

"Good thing nobody was under it. Heavy enough to mash you.''

"Yeah, thanks for the help.''

"No problem. Glad to. Whose sled is it?"

The newcomer frowned slightly, beginning to assess what he was seeing and confused by the irregularity of it. Why were these two removing a sled from a truck anyway? Assistance was not allowed in this part of the race. And where was the driver? Neither of these two was dressed for distance racing. Were they waiting for a racer? Did they intend to switch sleds—another racing no-no?

"Hey, I know you, don't I?" he suddenly said to the man nearest him.

"Don't think so. Who're you?"

"B. J. Lowery. I handle for Rick Roney. Yeah, I *do* know you. You ran this race back a few years. You're . . . ah . . . Wait a minute—I'll get it. You're . . ."

"Shit."

Another meaningful glance between the first two men. Then the near one took a handgun from under his jacket and trained it on their volunteer helper.

"Move," he said. "Over there, off the road."

Stunned, Lowery hesitated, trying to comprehend what was happening.

"You deaf? I said move—now. Hold your hands away from yourself and get over there." He gestured threateningly with the gun.

Slowly, Lowery, hands carefully held up in front of him, casting anxious glances behind him, walked off the road into the snow, the two following close behind him.

"Aw, you're not gonna—" began the gunman's partner.

"He can recognize us. What the hell do you think I should do?"

As the three approached the tree to which the dog team was tethered, Lowery suddenly threw himself to the right in an attempt to put the tree between himself and the other two. The man with the gun instantly fired, hitting him high in the center of his back. He crashed forward, sprawling face-first into the snow, injured but not dead. Still trying for the tree, he thrashed one arm—the other seemed paralyzed—striving to reach some kind of protection.

The dogs went crazy, barking and scrambling nervously at the startling sound of the gun and the metallic scent of fresh blood, knowing something was wrong.

The second bullet hit Lowery in the head from close range and he was abruptly motionless, bright red soaking into the frozen white beside him in a shocking contrast.

A dog howled, starting a chain reaction among the others that were now repeatedly hurling themselves against their restraints.

"Fuck. Now what're we gonna do? Did you have to—"

"Yeah, I *had* to. He knew me. Would have got my name in another couple of minutes. Come on, let's get him back into that brush before he bleeds any more. Help me, you shit. Don't just stand there whining."

Between the two of them, they dragged Lowery's body farther from the road and buried it with snow. Carefully they kicked more snow over the stains that had left a crimson trail to the place where they had left him.

When they had finished their hurried cover-up, climbed in their truck, and gone, the team was still howling—the mournful, unsettling sound floating on the wind to the ears of a racer approaching the highway from the east, raising the hair on the back of his neck and setting his own dogs howling in instinctive sympathetic response.

CHAPTER TEN

*"There is a magic in the Northland night which steals in
on one like fevers from malarial marches. You are clutched
and downed before you are aware."*
     —Jack London, "A Relic of the Pliocene"

JESSIE WAS VERY CAREFUL—SO CAREFUL THAT SHE ALMOST,
but not quite, felt ridiculous in the extent of her own
caution. But she reasoned that if the kidnappers *were*
watching Jake Leland, they could just as easily and anony-
mously be watching her and would know if she made any
attempt to locate RCMP Inspector Delafosse.

With painstaking prudence, she considered her options.

Billy Steward, she felt, was too young and inexperi-
enced to entirely understand and respect the seriousness
of the situation. Afraid he might already be suspicious of
her distracted attitude, she feared that Cas would be sure
something was up and demand more of an explanation
than she was willing to give, considering her unspoken
promise of silence to Jake Leland. It wasn't that she didn't
trust Cas. She did. He had proved himself more than once
when her life was a stake, and Alex trusted him like a
brother. But she couldn't be sure that the people he would
feel obliged to trust with the information would be as
cautious with it. So, shoving aside her small guilt, she
went instead to Don Graham for help.

"I need you to do something for me, Don, and to not

104

ask me any questions about it. And, whatever you do, you must not tell anyone—not *anyone*. It's not about me, and I can't tell you any more, except that if you so much as mention what I want you to do, it could be disastrous— very dangerous for someone else. Will you promise? Will you do what I ask you to do, the way I ask you to do it?''

"Of course, Jessie." The big man stared at her, eyes wide, seeing how serious and intense she was. "You know I will. But if something's wrong, can't you tell me—"

"No, Don. I can't. You have to trust me on this— I can't."

There was a long moment of silence as he considered this, with no real possibility of refusal, only concern to do the right thing.

He's very loyal, Jessie thought.

"Okay," he agreed. "What do you want me to do?"

She told him.

Jessie's dogs were reenergized and ready for the run to Dawson when she and Jim Ryan left Pelly Crossing that night, but she was tired and irritable, having had no rest and little to eat. She was also tense, worried, and so angry she could hardly speak until they'd been on the trail for more than half an hour.

The vet had showed up as promised to scan her dogs at the checkpoint when she pulled up with her heavy sled filled with supplies and equipment she had shipped to Pelly for this long section of the race. Running the monitor over each dog in turn, he had paused at Sunny and Wart, harnessed across the gang line from each other in the middle of the team. Four or five times he ran the scanner over the shoulders of the two dogs, read the result, then tried again. Flipping through the records of identification numbers he carried in his other mittened hand, he had finally turned to Jessie with an apologetic frown.

"Arnold, right?"

"That's right."

"Well—these aren't your dogs."

She stared at him, confounded. "Say that again."

"They're not yours—have different numbers. This one dog's supposed to be in Debbie Todd's team—name of Royal. The other one's not on the list at all."

"That's not possible. Don't you think I know my own dogs? That dog's name is Sunny and he's been in my kennel since he was born. The other one's Wart and he's definitely *on* the list—you must have an incomplete list. I don't make those kinds of mistakes."

"Well, that's what the chips say."

"Let me see that board."

He showed her the number for Sunny that the scanner revealed, then laid his finger on the same number on the pages of his list. The name of the dog it belonged to *was* Jake Leland's Royal. The number by Sunny's name was totally different. Flipping through the rest of the list, Jessie couldn't find Wart's number anywhere.

"This is wrong. You've got the numbers mixed somehow. Read their collars. See? This one says his name is Sunny and that one's Wart and they're mine."

"But the chips say—"

"Look. This is crazy. Both these dogs' chips were scanned at the start and again in Carmacks. Both times they checked out fine. Bob Spenser did it himself, both times."

"I don't know, Ms. Arnold. All I know is that they're not right here."

"Jessie. It's Jessie, please. Let me get Jake Leland. He'll know Sunny's not his dog."

He did.

"Not a chance. I know Royal and that dog's not him," Leland told the vet in no uncertain terms. "I don't care what your damned scanner reads, it's wrong."

"Okay?" Jessie asked. "Satisfied?"

The vet bit his lip, shook his head, and frowned stubbornly. "Can't just *say* it's okay. The numbers are wrong. Both dogs."

"What the hell's going on here?"

Jim Ryan, who had pulled his team up behind Jessie's, set his snow hook and trotted up to see what was causing the furious, determined expression he could see developing like a thundercloud on her face.

"He says Sunny and Wart are not my dogs," she snapped.

The vet turned red to his ears and began to equivocate. "Now, I didn't say that. I said the numbers of the chips—"

"What? Oh, hell. I'll get Ned Bishop."

Ryan stomped off through the snow in search of the race marshal.

But Bishop, regretful and sympathetic, was no more help than the vet, though he was obviously uncomfortable with the decision he felt forced to make.

"I can't explain it or let it go, Jessie. All I can do is let you drop the dogs," he told her. "There's no way I believe you'd purposely run a string with illegal dogs in it, or that Jake would lie about this not being his dog, but I can't break the rules for one musher. The reason we have these chips is identification. We all agreed to rely on them and it's the best and only method we have. I don't know why it reads what it reads, but I can't let you go on with these dogs in your team."

"Dammit, Ned. There's something way the hell wrong here. It's not fair and you know it. I think Bob Spenser—"

"Jessie—hold on. I can't check with Bob, because he's not here, he's gone on up to Dawson. I'll let you go on, but only without the dogs. I won't penalize you and we'll work it out later. It's the best I can do.

"You can protest if you want," he added, as she had heard him tell the musher concerning his lost ax.

"You better believe I *will*."

In the end, white-faced with anger and frustration, she took Sunny and Wart off the line and allowed the vet to lead them away to be given the complete physicals required of every dog dropped. They would then be picked up by her support team for transport in the dog truck.

"I'm really sorry, Jessie," Bishop told her, as she pulled away from the checkpoint with twelve dogs left in her team and Tank glancing in confusion at the empty space where his teammates usually ran. Jessie would adjust the length of the gang line later.

"Yes," she said between clenched teeth. *"So am I."*

Jake Leland raised a hand in farewell and his eyes spoke volumes of anxiety and determination.

"See you in Dawson," was all he said.

Angry about Sunny and Wart, worried about Debbie Todd, distinctly numb over her thoughts of Alex, Jessie now began to be concerned about the race as well.

Running a distance race with any prayer of finishing well took a number of things working well together. Giving the dogs the best possible care was first, making sure they were eating and drinking the right things and enough of them, that they were rested, healthy, and uninjured. Taking care of yourself came next. But the main ingredient in successful racing was total concentration on the job at hand. Besides the dog and musher care, this included paying strict attention to what the other racers were doing, where they were, and how fast they were traveling compared to your own place and speed. Being aware of conditions, weather, temperature, and rate of travel, anticipating what was coming next and what you would need, all were extremely important.

Jessie knew that the last thing she had going for her was anything approaching total concentration, that her whole frame of reference had shifted and only half her focus was directed to the race and her part in it. There was little she could do about that, but just being aware of it was good and somewhat helpful. She had to make conscious choices about it, the best ones she could, and accept the fact that the race was no longer of primary significance—the most important thing was Debbie Todd's safety and rescue. It was, however, still a race and she intended to do her best.

It was too early to give up her own goals unless she was forced to make a choice.

After five miles of travel on a plowed road, Jessie and Ryan dropped down onto the Pelly River, and her flagging spirits began to lift slightly. This section of trail was much better than previous stints on rivers, for the people of Pelly had worked the jumbled blocks and cracks in the ice to make them safe for dogs and mushers, filling in when necessary, cutting off sharp frozen edges, and widening the track wherever possible.

A full moon relieved the dark with a beautiful, ghostly light that was reflected from the surface of the ice, the luminescence broken by deep intermittent shadows. Winter had silenced the river's voice and the utter stillness that filled the night was broken only by the soft sound of the sled on snow and slight scrapes as it passed over icy irregularities. The riverbanks rose in tall cliffs on either side, forming the walls of a canyon with a frozen passage between them. The moonlight poured in, filling it with silver.

Anger fading, Jessie found herself responding to the peace of this part of the trail, took a deep breath, and let go some of her exasperation, knowing it would accomplish nothing constructive to rage over what couldn't be changed and that she needed to center all her energies and concentration on the problems at hand. But for a little while she let herself simply enjoy the power of her team and the wonder of the softly illuminated night, remembering once again just what it was that she loved best about dog mushing.

They ran four hours on, four hours off all night. It was full daylight at just after ten in the morning, and they were a little more than two hours into the third four-hour period when they reached Stepping Stone, an unofficial stop for many racers, made up of a cluster of buildings: main house, cookhouse, sheds, and cabins. Pausing briefly for water and to snack their dogs took only half an hour, but before she left, Jessie, needing to feel connected, approached the ham radio operator to put in a call for her back to Pelly Crossing.

When Jake Leland was found and brought to the line, his voice was cautious, though she had told them to make sure he knew who was calling, afraid he might assume the worst.

"Jessie. It's Jake. What?"

"Nothing. Just had a feeling I should keep in touch."

"Glad you did. Is anyone listening to you up there?"

She glanced around. The radio operator had thoughtfully absented himself after putting the call through. There was no one within hearing distance, if she spoke quietly.

"No, why?"

"I need to tell you a couple of things. Radio's not the best way to do it, but . . . I was trying to figure out how to let you know that Eulie Caulder brought in Debbie's team behind her own about three hours ago. Found it tied to a tree where the trail crosses the highway between McCabe Creek and Pelly."

"Debbie?"

"No. Nothing, and the word is out that she's missing, but . . . ah . . ." He paused, clearly working out how to tell her something else.

"What, Jake?"

"Ah . . . Ned Bishop and an RCMP constable went back to take a look at the spot where Eulie picked up the team. They found a body, Jessie. A dead man that had been dragged off and buried in the deeper snow. He'd been shot, twice: once in the back and once in the head."

"Oh, God, Jake. Who?"

"Guy named Lowery—B. J. Lowery—he was handler for one of the Canadian mushers, Rick Roney."

Roney? *Again?*

"The guy from Atlin," Jessie sighed.

"You know him?"

"Roney? No. But he's been behind me most of the way from the start. Wears a blue and yellow parka. I know Lowery, though. He's been around the racing circuit for years, usually as a volunteer or handler. Helpful, friendly sort. He plays—well, *played* a banjo that he carried along sometimes. Nice guy. It doesn't make much sense, does it? Why would someone kill him?''

''Well, the RCMP is speculating that he might have seen whoever left Debbie's team at that location, stopped to help, or to find out what they were doing, and could identify whoever it was. There were boot prints of three people—including Lowery's—but none small enough to be Debbie's. So they now know she's missing. Who knows? Lowery might have been part of a disagreement between two other guys. His truck with two dogs in the box and all Roney's equipment were missing, but turned up here at Pelly, parked in the lot, and no one knows how it got here.

''Jessie, they even wondered if Debbie might have shot Lowery, but there was no indication she was ever there.''

Jessie paused for a moment, thinking. Leland sounded more than just a little desperate.

''Does she carry a gun, Jake?''

''Oh, come on, Jessie. Handguns are illegal in Canada. She had a rifle of mine on the sled, but it was strictly for emergencies—moose—you know. She hated it. I made her carry it, but she buried it pretty deep. She wouldn't shoot someone.''

''Unless there was a good reason that we have no way of knowing?''

''It would have to be a damn good one.''

''Well, someone trying to kidnap her would be a good one, right?''

He thought about it, then disagreed. ''No, it was still in the sled when Eulie brought it in and hadn't been fired. Listen. Roney's somewhere between here and where you are at Stepping Stone, and they're looking for him. If you see him, have him get in touch with Bishop real quick, okay?''

''I understand. I mean I understand to tell him if he

shows up while I'm here. But I don't understand about Lowery getting killed at all.''

"Neither do I, but it certainly ups the ante. They've got nothing to lose now, Jessie. It terrifies me. But I'm following . . . ah . . . the directions. You understand?''

"Yes, Jake. But I think you're wrong. Especially now, with the RCMP already involved.''

"Can't risk it. That's how I want to play it, Jessie. Okay?''

"Okay.''

It was not okay, and was becoming less okay by the moment. Whoever was responsible for the situation was clearly not concerned about taking drastic action. So it was common knowledge that the young woman was gone, but still unknown to the authorities that she had been abducted, though there must be some suspicions at this point.

"Another really odd thing,'' Leland was saying, "is that Royal is missing, too. That doesn't make much sense, either.''

"Well, I can assure you he's not in my team, number or not.''

"Yeah, I know. Sorry about that, Jessie. Ah . . . they're going to do a search for Debbie—air and ground.''

"Right. They would, of course. Jake—''

"No. It'll be all right, Jessie. There's nothing you can do but . . . So, keep your schedule for now. Get on to Dawson.''

Nothing had changed, except that the Yukon Quest committee was now on a wild-goose chase of a search around the Chain of Lakes area that would result in nothing, which, Jessie was sure, would please and satisfy whoever was responsible. The abduction of Debbie Todd seemed well planned, not just a spur-of-the-moment opportunity taken. That feeling frightened her even more. But the worst was having someone found dead and not knowing why. Well, at least this would bring in law enforcement, though Leland seemed determined to go on trying to keep the abduction of his stepdaughter and the demand for her ransom quiet.

Feeling distracted and discouraged, she was going out the door of the checkpoint when she met Minnesota musher Lynn Ehlers, about to go in.

"Hey, Jessie. Leaving?"

"Just about to."

"How's it going?"

"Oh . . . okay . . . fine."

"What's this I hear about a musher being lost somewhere below Carmacks?"

Damn. So the word was out even here, Jessie thought as she answered. But he hadn't asked about the dead handler, so maybe he didn't know everything.

"Yeah, I guess so. Debbie Todd, Jake Leland's stepdaughter."

"First race?"

"Yes, but she's an experienced dog handler—has been running for years."

"You know her?"

"Met her just before I left Whitehorse."

There was a pause as he looked at her serious face. "Something wrong, Jessie?"

God, she thought, I'm such a mirror of my emotions.

Shrugging her shoulders in a small shiver, she shook her head and forced a ghost of a smile.

"No. Just tired, I guess."

"Why don't you stop for a while. Shake it out. You might go better with a little rest. Is that Jim Ryan you're running with?"

Was it her imagination working overtime, or was he watching her just a little too closely? And what was it with all the questions?

"Yeah, that's Ryan—he's an old friend—and I think we'll get on up the trail. We want to get to Dawson as soon as possible."

"Don't we all?" He laughed. "Okay. See you there. Take care, Jessie."

"Thanks, I will. You, too."

Shaking her head, she returned to her waiting sled.

Ehlers was probably just being friendly, making an effort to relate to other people in the race, make himself more at home. He seemed a nice person, attractive, and, for some most likely innocent reason, interested in her, she admitted to herself. Well, he interested her a little, too. Any other time or situation, she would have liked to be able to focus on him and find out what he was like, ask him about mushing where he lived. Most sled dog people felt a kind of immediate bond, because of their similar interests and experience. On the other hand, why should he single her out, make an effort to approach her? And how did he find out about Debbie being lost and miss Lowery's being found dead? There was no checkpoint or stopping place with race communications between Pelly Crossing and Stepping Stone and Ehlers had to have been on the trail between the two to come in so close behind her and Ryan. How could he have heard? Could he be . . . ?

Oh, what the hell is wrong with me? she asked herself. Is there going to be a boogie man around every corner now?

Well, maybe there really was, perhaps more than one. Best to get on promptly, keep moving, reach Dawson, and get it over with. Away from the checkpoints, official and unofficial, there would be less chance of observation. She could feel more secure, knowing it was only herself and Ryan, whom she knew well and trusted.

At Jessie's urging, they left Stepping Stone quickly and went on into the huge aspen forest that followed. Crossing the river, they passed several homesteads with cleared fields and pastures, and soon found themselves on an old logging road with ancient log buildings gradually falling into total disrepair as they succumbed to the lure of gravity in returning to the earth.

Climbing a hill, they were suddenly on infamous Scroggy Creek Road, a section of the trail abhorred by mushers because there was almost always road-building machinery on it in February, working to open it up for traffic to and from a mine farther north. Caterpillar tractors, bulldozers, and fuel trucks made it difficult for mushers and frightened their dogs as they struggled to pass equipment on the single lane that was just one cat wide, with no extra space for racing teams. Alarmed and flinchy, the dogs shied away from the roaring engines and usually had to be led past by the musher.

Ryan was in the lead when they turned a corner and met a bulldozer coming straight at them. Both machine and teams stopped, facing each other, and the driver of the 'dozer waved in acknowledgment. While they waited, he backed up a few feet and swung the huge blade so that it formed a V with the roadside bank.

Filled with apprehension, Jessie watched as, following hand signals, Ryan led his team into the V and stopped, dogs bunched together, sled barely leaving room for the driver to turn the blade again so the other end rested against the bank and opened a way for the team to pull forward, out of the reverse V and onto the road beyond. As she nervously took her turn, she hoped the driver was as good at handling the enormous blade as he seemed, but again it worked and she was quickly past and ready to continue, with a thank-you wave to the 'dozer operator.

Feeling as flinchy as the dogs, she tried her best to concentrate and stop her thoughts from skittering randomly from one problem to another like a panicked mouse in a livetrap. Had Debbie been taken from near the highway, where her team was found? No. She had disappeared earlier, from all they knew. Then why had the team been moved, or left there at all? A diversion? To avoid the inconvenience and risk of retaining it? People would be more likely to notice anyone with a dog team. Why had they taken Royal, too? The dog was valuable, as a racing dog and as stud, yet they had not mentioned him in the note left for Leland. Had taking him been a last-minute idea? Would they include him in their ransom demands?

And why had Lowery been murdered? Had he been part of the plot, or not?

Who were these people? Were any of them connected with the race in any way? Or had they picked it as a good opportunity for getting a sizable piece of money? How ruthless were they? Would they really release Debbie Todd safely, or . . . ?

Her stomach turned at the thought of the alternative.

None of the questions that ricocheted through Jessie's mind had answers, though they suggested possibilities. The small shreds of guilt she had felt over her request to Don Graham melted away and she was glad she had asked for his assistance. Still, she would have to wait until she reached Dawson to find out if he had had any success in achieving the objective she had given him.

Running ahead of Ryan at the moment, she clucked to her team and they responded by immediately increasing their speed slightly. Taking a deep breath, Jessie tried for patience and turned her attention back to the cat road on which they were still traveling. It did no good to play what-if. There was nothing she could do that she was not already doing. Gritting her teeth, she also refused to contemplate the issue of her shaky relationship. Instead, she forced herself to begin a mental reorganization of her kennel and dog yard, a reassessment of her training schedule for the spring, and a plan for an addition she had been considering to her log cabin back in Knik.

Traveling at a steady seven or eight miles an hour, the pair of teams ran up and down rolling hills for six and a half hours on this long road and made good time, meeting only one other machine, a truck, which was easier to pass, as it simply stopped and let them make their way around it. Crossing several small creeks, the dogs and sleds slid around on the overflow—water that escapes from under solid ice, having nowhere to go but up and over it. The dogs had trouble finding purchase on the slippery surface, which felt more fluid as the thin winter sun slightly warmed the day.

The temperatures had so far been warm for February, but not unreasonably so, hovering around zero. Nevertheless, giving the dogs a break from pulling the heavy sleds, Jessie and Ryan rested them, and themselves, all afternoon, through the warmest part of the day, and ran on again into the cold of the night. While they rested, they had been passed by two or three other racers. Now they in turn passed those racers, who were taking their own breaks in temporary camping spaces beside the trail, their dogs curled up with their noses tucked into tails for warmth. One or two dogs raised their heads to watch as Jessie and Ryan sped quietly past, then lay back down again.

Jessie had not seen the blue and yellow parka since Pelly Crossing. Roney from Atlin would have to be told by someone else to call Bishop at the checkpoint when he reached it.

It was a night filled with northern lights that spread themselves across the sky in luminous bands, curtains of whitish green that moved and swayed as if blown by some powerful wind of the upper atmosphere, though the air on the trail the mushers traveled was still. The lights seemed to add to the glow of the bright moonlight, the combination dimming the stars. As she rode along, standing on the extensions of the runners of her sled, Jessie could see a clear shadow of herself, the sled, and some of her team, cast by the light onto the snow beside the trail. The temperature had suddenly plummeted to ten below and she was glad there was no breeze to add a windchill factor to it. When they paused, she found a small fire welcome for light as well as heat.

As they awkwardly fed themselves with mittened hands, dogs sleeping all around them, Jessie and Ryan talked temperatures.

"I'd like it to stay just about how it is now," Jessie said. "We won't get it—it'll get windy on the summits— but this is perfect for me and the mutts both."

"A little colder wouldn't hurt my feelings any," Ryan decided. "Remember how cold it was that year on the

Iditarod when we hit Norton Sound? Thought I'd freeze my buns off.''

"Hey, we could be above the Arctic Circle, or in Siberia, where it gets *really* cold."

She reached to move the coffeepot farther off the fire, to stop the coffee from getting any stronger.

"Did you know," Ryan asked, "that in Siberia it can average in the minus-fifties in January?"

"That's more than I'd be willing to live with."

"Me, too. They've got a neat word there though. *Zvyozd*. It means the 'whispering of the stars' and it's the name for the tiny tinkling sound that your breath makes when it freezes at that temperature. As you breath out, the moisture in it drops to the ground in very tiny crystals. Can you imagine hearing your own breath hit the ground? Weird."

"I do remember how cold it was out on the sound that year. I thought I'd never be warm again. And the wind was howling so loud you couldn't hear anything—almost had to lip-read someone standing next to you and shouting in your ear."

They were quiet for a few minutes, Ryan finishing a bowl of some kind of stew, Jessie once again worrying the question of Debbie Todd's abduction and wondering what was happening as she traveled in such splendid isolation, with no way of finding out. Wondered just what happened to kill Lowery, too. She hoped Jake Leland was finding the money he needed and would, perhaps, have something new to tell her by the time she reached Dawson. Had Don Graham done what he said he would? She wouldn't know that, either, until they made Dawson.

The whole thing made her impatient to get back on the trail and get there, but that would be imprudent. Running too far, too fast, could easily burn out the team and she'd never make it at all. Hurry up and wait, hurry up and wait, she thought, chafing at the necessary delay. Frowning, she didn't realize she had huffed in frustration until Jim Ryan spoke suddenly.

"Okay, Jessie. What's wrong? Something's going on. You've been somewhere else ever since we left Pelly. Not still worrying about that screw-up with the chips, are you?"

Startled at his question and insight, she looked across the fire at him and shook her head, realizing that she had actually forgotten all about Sunny and Wart. Remembering brought another flash of anger, but she quickly let it go again.

"No. It burns me, but it's history. I'll take care of it later, after . . . the race."

"After . . . what? You started to say something else. Jensen?"

She knew she hadn't given Alex much thought, either, but recognized her own tendency to shy away from considering what was becoming extremely painful.

"Not that, either, Jim. I'm deferring all thought of it until this is done. I'm playing Cleopatra—queen of denial." She tried to grin at the terrible pun and did it poorly.

Ryan scowled, then gave her a half-sympathetic, half-quizzical look.

"Jessie—look. Maybe I'm dumb, but I'm not stupid, and I know you pretty well—at least as far as your abilities as a musher, and a little more as a friend. You're one of the most focused people I know. It's what wins races for you. But I've never seen you so intent on anything but the race you're in. Since that call to Leland—even before—you've been pushing us along as fast as you can, taking the minimal amount of time in stops, rushing through the chores. What the hell is going on that makes you want to get to Dawson so soon? Not just the race. Something's wrong, isn't it?"

She stared at him, astonished into silence, having had no indication that he was paying such close attention to her, or that her feelings and actions could give her away so easily.

"Jim, I . . ."

He waited.

She felt her eyes fill with tears that she did not allow to spill over.

"I . . . It's not . . . I can't . . ."

Good, dependable, undemanding friend. He shook his head, got up and came across to where she was sitting on her thermal container, hunkered down in front of her so they were on the same level, and gave her a long serious look.

"It's okay, Jess. You don't have to tell me. But I'll try to help if you'll let me. I can be very good at keeping my own counsel."

She broke her promise and told him.

CHAPTER ELEVEN

"The sleds came to a halt where the trail crossed the mouth of Stuart River. An unbroken sea of frost, its wide expanse stretched away into the unknown east. . . . We saw no men; only the sleeping river, the moveless forest, and the White Silence of the North."
     —Jack London, "An Odyssey of the North"

STEWART RIVER, LIKE STEPPING STONE, WAS NOT AN OFFI-cial checkpoint, but a site along the river where dogs could be dropped. There was no real community, just some wall tents brought in for the race, with a race veterinarian and some volunteers to take care of the dogs mushers found it necessary to leave behind.

Dropping a dog does not always mean that it is sick or injured. Sometimes mushers take along a dog or two that have never been involved in a distance race, knowing they need the experience, intending to drop them part of the way along the trail and go on with their solid experienced team the rest of the way.

This was the case with the dog Ryan dropped at this point. Once again between regular timed rest stops, he and Jessie paused at Stewart River only briefly early Thursday morning after running all night, and each dropped a dog before going on. Ryan's was a young female that he had planned to drop in Dawson, but he was not unhappy to leave her at Stewart, when she began to refuse to drink and exhibited initial symptoms of dehydration.

121

Perhaps Digger was lonely without Sunny and Wart. Perhaps the balance of the line was off slightly, though Jessie had moved dogs to compensate for this and didn't think so. Most likely he had stepped into an invisible hole somewhere on the trail, but five miles from Stewart River the peppy black and white dog stopped pulling his share of the weight and began to drag back against his neck line, favoring one leg. Jessie stopped, took him off the line, and put him in the sled bag, head sticking out to see what was going on—he could never stand to be left out of anything—and carried him on to the stop in the basket. The vet diagnosed a sore left wrist and strained shoulder, and agreed that he should be dropped before it grew worse.

Down to eleven dogs, the same number as Ryan's team, Jessie followed him directly onto the Stewart River for about a mile, then up onto the trail that ran away from the other bank. There they followed another cat trail for about five miles through homesteads and cleared spaces with abandoned buildings, watching the country change as they passed through it.

They had begun to travel through hard-core mining country. Not only had gold been found in this area in the 1890s, but more recent twentieth century dredges had reduced to bare earth what had once been scenic rolling hills covered here and there with trees and brush. Everywhere there were long lines of snow-covered tailing piles from the dredges, rusted-out trucks and mining equipment, broken flume and sluice box parts, and other scattered evidence of radical mining activity. It was discouraging to see what the machines of man could do in response to his obsession with the precious yellow metal.

Apocalyptic was the word that came to Jessie's mind, and she was grateful that snow blanketed the worst of the blasted area through which they passed. Exhausted with concern and lack of rest, she was not sorry to be able to sleep through most of the long break they took in the center of this devastation, and to be back on the trail without lingering. But she ached all over with fatigue and had begun to feel this part of the trail would never end. For one of the first times in her racing career, she was not enjoying the running of it and the country she was passing through.

"I feel like a horse that was 'rode hard and put away wet,' as my grandmother used say," she said, as she stretched to relieve muscle tension and rubbed at a sore spot in one shoulder, wishing she could rub at the sore spots in her mind and nerves as well.

Now understanding her concerns and impatience, Ryan was amenable to crossing through this country as quickly as possible, while keeping close track of the condition and needs of the dogs and not taking any chance of burning them out. These dogs *must* get them at least to Dawson, after all, and could not be risked in doing so, whatever the crisis. The two mushers were caring dog handlers and would not under any circumstances have sacrificed their animals willingly. They were now running in the eighth and ninth positions, having left two more teams behind them, one that had slowed down considerably and one that had scratched from the race in Stepping Stone.

"Hell of a reason to make great time," Ryan said with a wry smile, as they paused along a bald ridge above tree line.

They had just finished a half-hour climb up a huge hill so steep that the trailbreakers had put in intense sweeping switchbacks to help the teams make it to the top. The sun was just rising, with the full moon low in the sky, and from where they had paused on top they could see for miles in all directions, ridge after ridge that fell away like a rumpled blanket across the landscape—the Black Hills around Black Hills Creek.

The temperature had dropped another two or three degrees. The sun would shortly disappear into a bank of clouds that stretched out overhead, leaving only a rapidly narrowing band of clear sky to the east, through which a beam of early sunshine cast a glow on the snow-covered summits of the ridges.

"If this cloud cover's as full of snow as it looks, it could get nasty on American Summit," Jessie speculated.

"It could get nasty before that," Ryan answered. "I'd rather do King Solomon's Dome without it, if possible, and get on into Dawson for my thirty-six, where I can sleep indoors and for at least one night be away from mushers who snore."

"I beg your pardon," she objected haughtily.

"Oh, I didn't mean you, of course." He grinned. "Your snores are the very appealing, gentle kind."

She threw a Snickers bar at him that she had been about to eat, which he neatly fielded and pocketed.

"Don't you ever run out of these? I'll wait to eat it when I can thaw it out. About broke a tooth on the last one."

For fifteen miles they ran over the ridges before dropping down along a frozen creek that ran down a valley filled with more ugly evidence of strip-mining. Old equipment, oil drums, and tailing piles littered the snow-covered ground.

Coming up out of the creek, Jessie clung to the drive bow of her sled, letting it help to lift her over the edge of the bank. Suddenly the rear stanchion that she had checked in Carmacks gave way, leaving her drive bow unsupported on one side. With a cry, she let go and tumbled back down, banging an elbow on the ice as she rolled over in the snow.

"Whoa, Tank. Whoa," she called to her leader, but, well trained, he had already brought the team to a halt at the sound of her first yell.

Ryan, running ahead, also stopped, set his snow hook, and came back to give her a hand up the bank and make sure she was okay.

They examined the loose stanchion.

"Damn. I checked that again in Pelly Crossing and it seemed fine."

"Well, it's just the one end that's broken. We should

be able to tape it up enough to make it into Dawson with no trouble.''

"Yeah, I think so, too.''

Jessie opened her sled bag to get out the duct tape she always carried for repairs of all kinds. She was sure that half of Alaska was held together with it—she'd seen everything from air mattresses to airplanes sporting the sticky silvery stuff.

The tape was not where she expected it to be. Ten minutes later, having searched through all her equipment and supplies, she had to admit it was missing.

"Accidentally leave it somewhere?'' Ryan asked.

"Must have. But I haven't used it—haven't even taken it out of my tool bag. There was a whole new roll.''

"You're sure you put it in?''

"Yes, absolutely. I double-checked the list the night before the race. Besides, I saw it in Carmacks, when I took out a toggle.''

"No problem. I have some.''

"I can't use yours.''

"Yes, you can. It's allowed when it's an emergency. I can't leave you sitting here in the wilds.''

"You're right. Okay. Let's get on with it.''

In half an hour they were back on the trail, Jessie's sled solid enough to run again. Still, the incident troubled her as they ran along the creek and began to head up out of the valley. Never once in a race—or a training run, for that matter—had she ever neglected to carry any essential item with her. Thinking back, she recalled the question in her mind of forgetting to secure Bliss and Pete the night they ran off to play hooky from the dog yard. Now she wondered if this might be another such oversight.

Am I getting too confident of my own abilities? she speculated. No. I *know* I packed that tape.

But you could have moved it to reach the toggle, or not noticed when it fell out.

Possible, of course, but I don't think so.

Does it really matter?

Not really. It's just irritating. I'm not losing my mind—
I hope. Just my concentration—maybe.

She shrugged it off and continued to follow Ryan up
the hill that rose ahead of them.

Far in the distance, when they had climbed again, they
could see the south side of King Solomon's Dome and the
hills around Dawson. It was still a long ways away and
there would be hours of traveling through the night before
they even came close, but at last it was possible to see
where they were headed.

The area they crossed seemed an unending series of
mines, hills, mountains, valleys, and creeks—of going up
one ridge only to come down the other side and start up
again, ceaselessly, for hours. Still much of it looked better
cared for than the mining country on the other side of the
ridges, and they found a small abandoned cabin in a big
empty valley for one rest stop among several. It was welcome, for it offered some protection from the wind that
had begun to keen along the heights where there was little
to break it in the vast rolling ocean of all-but-treeless hills.

In the morning dark that was only an hour or two from
growing light again, they finally began the five- or six-
mile climb up the back of King Solomon's Dome on a
snow-covered dirt road swept bare to the gravel and frozen
ground by the gale that blew flying snow down their necks
and into their faces in the total exposure of empty space.
Jessie led the way; there was no communication with Ryan
but gestures because the gusts whipped sound away almost
before it was made, and flying crystals of snow worked
like sandpaper on any bare, unprotected skin and drummed
on their parka hoods. The windchill factor took the temperature to a low of close to thirty below zero, stiffening
scoured flesh and tired bodies in its relentless attempts to
slip icy fingers into small openings between parkas and
gloves, hoods and collars.

As the blowing white grew thinner, an anxious and exhausted Jessie could sporadically glimpse the lights of
Dawson far below and, with relief, knew it would soon

be daylight and they would be running through the town's streets.

At long last they came out onto the Klondike River, which empties into the Yukon at Dawson City, famous gold rush center. Then, in the early light of dawn, they were gliding down the long main street, past the riverboat *Keno* with its huge paddle wheel, to pull up at the Dawson Visitors Center, halfway checkpoint in the thousand-mile Yukon Quest, hearing the Dawson City Fire Department siren wailing to let the residents know another musher had come into town. In Jessie's case it also signaled that she was no longer a rookie, for making it as far as Dawson canceled her first-timer status, even if, for any reason, she didn't finish the race.

Hungry and so weary she felt drained and found it hard to concentrate, Jessie preceded Ryan to a halt in the bright lights of the waiting video crews, caught sight of her support crew waiting, and, nearby, an anxiety-ridden Jake Leland, eyes dark-circled from lack of sleep, his face lined with tension.

Strange, she thought, securing the snow hook and stepping stiffly forward to help the checkpoint official search for her required gear. Except for Jake they all still think it's a normal race from Whitehorse to Fairbanks.

The stop in Dawson City, Yukon, was different from any other in the race. There, teams were required to take a thirty-six-hour layover and allowed to accept major assistance from their support crews. It was permissible for the musher to sleep in a hotel or accept the hospitality of a resident, rather than stay in an area designated for racers only, or with their dogs. With time to spend, they could sleep for hours, and did, catching up on rest, allowing their bodies and minds to repair the damage of overextension and bone-deep fatigue. In the cafes and restaurants, they consumed enormous amounts of protein and carbohydrates for the same reason.

Some racers were convinced the Quest was really two

races, one from Whitehorse to Dawson City and the other one from Dawson to Fairbanks. They believed, with good reason, that the success of the latter was based on how well a team and driver were able to rebound from the former, to come back from the first half of the run and begin the second half, to more or less start over at this point.

Though mushers were always more comfortable caring for their own dogs, in Dawson the support crews were allowed to relieve them of much of the work. While the drivers replenished their own flagging energies and calorie levels, at least one of the crew was always with the team, which was bedded down across the river from downtown Dawson, in an area that was a public campground during the summer months.

The mushers, however, carefully checked each animal entirely, looking for any small injury or stress indicator that could be missed by anyone else, even the veterinarians, who did not know them as well. Every paw was examined and massaged with ointment, every muscle fingered, every joint palpitated with instinctive knowledgeable hands. Crew members walked the dogs several times during their long rest to keep them from stiffening in the cold, encouraged them to eat and, especially, drink as much as they would, to rebuild reserves of energy and stamina.

A local service station opened its big bays day and night to racers who needed to repair their sleds, offering assistance, tools, warmth to work indoors, and bright light to see and carefully check every inch of wood, metal, canvas, line, and piece of hardware. Every bolt was tightened, anything worn, reinforced or replaced. Some sleds that had suffered massive damage along the trail and had been held together with prayers and pieces of duct tape and wire, were practically rebuilt from the runners up.

As the official checked off the gear in her sled, Jessie carefully but casually examined the watching crowd and soon met the expectant eyes of the red-haired woman she had hoped to see. Giving no sign she had noticed, she smiled and spoke to a reporter that she knew, and turned back to answer a question from the checker. When she looked up again, the woman had disappeared and the space where she had stood was occupied by a television cameraman.

When the necessary ritual at the checkpoint was complete, Jessie drove her team across the frozen river to the campground where they would be bedded down for their long rest in Dawson. It was far enough from the noise of the checkpoint—and a town celebrating a break in the winter to welcome the Yukon Quest—for the dogs to sleep peacefully, without interruptions. Except for the officials, veterinarians, mushers, and support crews, no one was allowed near them. Nevertheless, she and her crew would take turns staying with them at all times, especially now, although Jessie was the only one who really knew why it was so important.

She picked a spot between two trees and, with the assistance of Billy and Linda, began the chores of feeding and caring for the dogs, while Don and Cas put up the shelter that had been carried from Knik on the top of Jessie's truck. Though the dogs could not be kept in a heated shelter, and no musher would want them to, they would be protected from wind and snow while they slept on their straw beds.

"Good dogs," Jessie told them, as she removed their booties and checked their feet and legs, as their food heated.

"Hey, Tux. How you doin', lover? Bliss, you hungry, girl? Food coming soon. Here's Billy with your water, Pete."

"You have an accident?" Cas asked, examining the stanchion she had duct-taped into reliability.

"The blasted thing gave way late yesterday," she told him. "I'll have to replace it. Sure glad I brought an extra along with the gear in the truck."

Don Graham stopped to take a look and frowned thoughtfully.

"Shouldn't be too hard to fix, Jessie. Don't worry about it. I'll run it down to the shop at the station this afternoon and get it taken care of, okay?"

"Thanks, Don. I'll probably come with you to check out the rest of the sled. It's got to last me a long ways yet. How's the shelter working out?"

"Great."

Behind the shelter, as she walked around to check its stability, she had a chance to give Don Graham a questioning look.

He said nothing, but gave her a nod, indicating that he had accomplished the task she had given him in Pelly Crossing. It was comforting, but she already knew his mission had been successful when she located the woman in the crowd at the checkpoint.

"Thanks, Don," she told him.

"No problem. You okay?"

"Fine, or will be."

"Why don't you go and get something to eat," Linda suggested. "We'll take care of what needs to be done here. You need food and then a lot of sleep."

"I think I'll do just that," Jessie told her, thinking, What I need as much as food is to talk to Jake Leland.

The water on her cooker was hot enough for her to wash her face and hands in some of it, getting rid of a couple of days' worth of grime and dog food. Feeling much better with at least part of herself clean, she applied a soothing cream to her cheeks and nose, reddened from the cold and flying snow on King Solomon's Dome, then took the time to brush her teeth and comb her hair.

"Getting fancied up for civilized company?" Cas teased, taking Bliss off the gang line, removing her harness, and fastening her to a resting tether near her bed of straw.

"Don't want to scare 'em to death," she said with a yawn.

"You go on ahead," Linda instructed. "I'll bring the stuff you need for a shower and your clean clothes to the hotel room in a little while."

"Thanks, guys," Jessie told them. "I really—"

"Get outta here," Don interrupted. "Think we can't do our job, huh?"

She gave him a tired grin and headed for the river, across which, in the flat white light of the cloudy morning, she could see Leland pacing the bank, waiting for her. Seriously hungry, she hoped he would be willing to talk over breakfast, but doubted that anything he had to tell her would go down easily.

CHAPTER TWELVE

*"His face . . . was fair, honest, and open . . . the lines . . .
firmly traced . . . the blue eyes gave promise of the hard
steel-glitter which comes when called into action, especially
against odds. The heavy jaw and square-cut chin demon-
strated rugged pertinacity and indomitability of purpose."*
—Jack London, "To the Man on the Trail"

MUCH LATER, JESSIE SLOWLY BECAME AWARE OF A PILLOW
under her head and the cozy, blanketed warmth of a real
bed beneath her in the dark. She felt stiff and headachy,
as if she had slept heavily and too long in one position.
Groggily, eyes still shut, she struggled for a moment to
remember where she was, for there was neither the homey
scent of a wood fire in the room, Alex's shaving cream
drifting in from the bathroom, nor that of the unfinished
logs of her own cabin, all slightly tinged with dog and
cooking smells.

The sound of distant voices, laughter, a shout, the thud
of feet on a boardwalk outside, and a vehicle passing
below the second-floor room, reminded her that this was
the Midnight Sun Hotel in the historic gold rush town of
Dawson. It felt decidedly strange and unreal, for she had
never slept in a hotel in the middle of a thousand-mile
race, much less in the center of a community full of cele-
brants out for a night on the town. Every restaurant and
saloon in Dawson, usually closed for the winter, must be

132

open and doing a thriving business from the sound of it, thanks to the Yukon Quest.

Yawning, she rolled over and sat up on the edge of the bed, reaching to switch on a small lamp and check the time. Eight o'clock. She had slept the day away, somewhat longer than she had planned, trusting her crew of handlers to care for the team and equipment. As she stood up and stretched to relieve the stiffness in her body, her stomach growled—hungry again. Time for another luxurious hot shower and some dinner, though it seemed like only a few minutes ago she had been reviewing the situation quietly with Jake Leland over breakfast in a semiprivate corner of the hotel dining room.

"So, you haven't heard anything yet?" Jessie had asked, pouring them both coffee from a thermal container the waitress had left on the table.

"No, but you just came in an hour ago."

"I know. I just thought maybe—"

"I don't even know where to be, where or how they'll contact me, or even *if* they will, considering this unexpected death. At least I have to suppose it was unexpected. Maybe not, but who knows? So I've just wandered around town to keep myself obvious . . . hoping. Damn. I hate this waiting—this *not knowing*."

"So do I. It sets me on edge. If there's something to be done, I want to get at it right now. But, as you said, I just got in, so let's assume that we'll hear soon. Did you get the money?"

He frowned and looked decidedly uneasy.

"Half of it. That's all I could get, and I don't know what to do about the rest. I couldn't get the fifty thousand without telling Jill, and she's terrified and as pissed off at me as she's ever been before. We're hardly speaking, but she's coming over here, with or without the rest of it."

"Oh, Jake, I am sorry. It wasn't your fault."

"Whatever. She'll get over it—or she won't. That's not the point right now anyway. I've got to find the rest of the cash somewhere, which seems impossible as an American in Canada, especially since I can't tell them why I need it so desperately. Jill's trying to borrow it in Fairbanks, but so far I haven't heard.''

"Well, surely you'll hear soon. Meanwhile, let's think more about it. There must be someone—somewhere.''

He gave her a desperate nod. "Yeah, right. Nothing happened for you on the way here?''

"No, nothing. Did the race committee find anything else in their search for Debbie?''

"Not a thing. Waste of time, but we knew that.''

The waitress appeared with a huge plate of food and Jessie waited until she set it down and disappeared before continuing their discussion. Before she spoke again, she leaned over to inhale the enticing aroma of the still-sizzling breakfast steak she had ordered and lifted a heaping forkful of the home fries that accompanied it.

"Um-m-m," she sighed, chewing slowly as she cut a slice from the steak and broke the first of three over-easy eggs to use as sauce before it quickly followed the bite of potatoes. When her mouth was empty, she could talk again, but it did not remain empty long.

"Sorry, I'm starving. Listen, Jake. I had to tell Jim Ryan—''

"Dammit, Jessie, I told you. The more people that know—''

A sip of coffee helped wash down the forkful she had taken as he interrupted.

"Whoa. Stop. I didn't have much choice. We were running together and he figured out that something was wrong after I talked to you in Stepping Stone. I was afraid he would say something somewhere at the wrong time, or ask questions somebody else couldn't answer and would be suspicious about, when he heard about them finding Lowery. And he was obviously going to hear about that, everyone's talking about it. He won't tell anyone the rest of it. I trust him completely and you can, too. Besides, he might be able to help somehow.''

"I don't like it," Leland growled, chin out, forehead a mass of worry lines.

"Well, it's done. There's nothing to worry about, so put it out of your mind unless you need him, okay?"

"For now . . . but, dammit, if anything else goes wrong—"

"If anything goes wrong it won't be Ryan's fault, I assure you."

"Where will you be? So that if I hear from these guys, or anything else happens, I can find you."

"Upstairs, sleeping for the better part of the day—as soon as I finish this. I'm really pooped, Jake. We ran as fast as we could to get here and the wind was blowing like a son-of-a-bitch on the dome. Then I'll either be across the river with my team, at the station making sure my sled is tight, or somewhere—probably here—eating or drinking something. Time to fill the tank. I've been running pretty close to empty and the body's starting to protest."

"Okay. Since the last message came in through the checkpoint official, I'll keep going back to this checker at least every hour or so, because they may repeat. I'm staying at the Downtown Hotel, a block toward the river. You could leave a message there if you had to."

Then he had left her to finish her meal alone, but she was soon joined by Linda Caswell with an armful of Jessie's personal items, soap, toothbrush, and clothing. By the time she had cleaned the plate, she was all but nodding over the last of her coffee. Within an hour she had showered, put on clean socks and the oversized T-shirt she liked to sleep in, and was already snoring gently when Linda went out the door of the hotel room and tried the knob to make sure it locked behind her.

A couple of hours later, the soft rattle of the doorknob didn't even slightly rouse her, as someone carefully tried the door.

Now, at almost nine, as she towel-dried her short honey-blond hair into its customary waves, the sound of a hand on the knob, followed by a soft knock, caught her attention immediately. She threw it open to find Billy Steward and Don Graham in the hall outside.

"Hey, you're awake," Billy said, grinning. "Thought you'd go on sleeping till tomorrow sometime."

"Not likely, Billy. I've got a lot of stuff to take care of before that."

"Not much," Don told her. "I already went over your sled from top to bottom. Took it up and fixed that stanchion that gave way. The rest was actually in great shape for coming all the way from Whitehorse. It'll last the rest of the race with no problem at all, unless you decide to drive it directly into something immovable."

"Thanks, Don, but I'm not planning on that. How're the mutts?"

"Doing just fine. We walked them all three hours ago and they've been fed again. You might as well go back to bed. The vet says they're in good shape."

"I want to check on them myself before they think they've been abandoned. Then I need something to eat—dinner in a big way."

"The dining room and bar next door are jammed with a big crowd of noisy, booze-happy folks having a great ol' time right now," Don warned. "You may want to avoid 'em, if you're tired."

This, Jessie thought suddenly, remembering what she had in mind for later that evening, could be used. For a moment, she considered it.

"I think you're right," she agreed. "Maybe I'll just go check the team, then find something to bring back up here, eat, and settle in for the night."

"I could get you some dinner while you're across the river, if you want," Billy volunteered.

Perfect. Jessie nodded. "Good idea. Got any suggestions?"

"They've got great burgers down the street a little—like homemade only better."

"Sounds terrific." She handed him money for the food and he turned to go.

"Wait," she called. "I won't be back here for at least an hour. Bring it then, and ask them to put on bacon and double cheese, will you? Lots of mayo. Do they have good french fries?"

"Awesome, and carrot cake."

"Large order of both, then. Milk shakes? Good. Chocolate, the biggest they have. You guys want anything?"

Don shook his head. "Naw, we ate already."

Billy, who was always hungry, grinned. "Vanilla shake?"

"Sure. Help yourself. Gotta keep my team stoked, too. Make sure they put the burger and fries in something to keep them warm, will you?"

"No problem." He was gone down the stairs in a clatter of boots.

Don chuckled. "He's having a really great time. It's all we can do to keep him from sleeping with those dogs of yours, Jessie. They're going to be spoiled rotten."

"More likely they'll spoil him rotten. He's turning into a very good handler—really treats them well. You watch, he'll be running this race in a year or two."

"I'd already got that figured."

"Be sure he gets a chance to see some of Dawson and doesn't spend all his time across the river, will you?"

"Sure."

Hair dry, Jessie put on her outdoor clothing and boots, shut the door, which automatically locked, and started down the stairs with Don, headed for the dog yard across the river.

As they passed the front desk, she glanced at the clock on the wall above it. Nine o'clock. By the time she came back and ate her dinner it would be time to take care of the rest of her business.

"You okay, Jessie?" Don asked suddenly, interrupting her train of thought, giving her a concerned look.

"Just fine. Thanks for your help, Don."

"No thanks necessary. I'd sure like to know what that's

all about, though—when you feel you can tell me sometime.''

"You got it. When this is over, okay?''

At eleven o'clock, Jessie was back in her room, having spent time with her dogs, carefully checking to be sure each of them was healthy and resting comfortably. But rather than resting herself—as she had deliberately told everyone she would when she made them promise not to disturb her for anything less than World War Three—she had quickly eaten dinner and was dressing to go out.

Her bright red parka would not do for this excursion. Instead she pulled on two heavy sweaters and dark snow pants over her thermal underwear, and added a dark blue down vest. To hide her light hair, she rolled up a knit face mask, usually used as protection from the cold, turning it into a stocking cap and pulling it on. Taking her gloves and thrusting the room key into a pocket, she cracked open the door for a careful look at the hallway outside. Empty.

Slipping out, she shut the door softly and went as quietly down the stairway as her heavy boots would allow. Pausing at the landing, she waited until a pair of intoxicated revelers crossed from the hotel bar toward the outside door, then hurried down into the lobby and fell in behind them as they went out, following closely, making it seem they were a threesome.

"Les go down to Gertie's.''

"Aw right.''

One of the two, a short, round man—Canadian, from his accent—noticed that they had gained company and started to turn back, stumbled, half-stepped, and wound up beside her, laying a casual arm across her shoulders to help regain his balance.

"Hey, babe. Where'd you come from? Wanna go with us to Gertie's?''

Let it ride, makes it look better, she told herself.

"Come on, Terry,'' his friend said, suddenly realizing

he had dropped back. Then he noticed the reason. "Hi, there. You here with the race?" he asked Jessie.

"Yeah," Jessie said, allowing Terry's arm to remain across her shoulders. "Sure, I'll go to Gertie's. Why not?"

Geez, he weighs a ton.

"Yeah . . . why the hell not?"

"Where you from?" the second man asked her.

Don't say Knik—somewhere else—anywhere.

"Ah . . . Nenana. Where you from?"

Ask them questions. Keep them talking.

"Whitehorse. I'm from Whitehorse with John. Ya know . . . Noble. He's a real good musher."

Terry staggered again as they stepped off the boardwalk into the street at the corner and turned left, headed for Diamond Tooth Gertie's a block away, one of Dawson's most famous gambling establishments. It was usually closed for the winter, but while the Quest was in town it was wide open, and in the bright lights over the entrance Jessie could see people coming and going. The block between it and the hotel was dark, and halfway along it she stopped suddenly, sliding from under Terry's friendly arm.

"Hey. Where you goin', babe?"

Oh, please, don't call me babe. I hate being called babe.

"Changed my mind," she told him. "You go on ahead. I'll join you in a few minutes."

"Oh, gotta take a pee, huh? Okay. See you there."

Drunk enough to be amenable to almost any suggestion, they rocked away from her toward the distant glitter and, without further hesitation, Jessie quickly crossed the street and slipped into a shadow, rolling the mask down over her face, as much for warmth as to avoid recognition. Once there, she stood still for a long few minutes, carefully watching the street, but saw nothing to make her think that anyone had noticed her exit from the hotel, or was following.

Still, she walked around two blocks in a direction away from where she was really headed and sidetracked through an alley before she felt securely alone in the night. Then, as quickly as she could walk, staying in what shadows she could find and avoiding busy streets, she headed for the southern edge of town.

Familiar with Dawson from a previous visit when Alex had been involved with a case that concerned both Canada and Alaska, Jessie knew her way around the grid of streets beside the Yukon River. This made it easier to watch out for anyone who might be curious about her late-night errand.

A short ten minutes later, she was standing at the front door of a snug log cabin that sat among several trees and spilled a warm glow from its windows into the dark, knocking quietly on the door as she pulled off the face mask. It was immediately opened by the attractive red-haired woman she had seen at the checkpoint that morning, who reached with eager hands to draw her into the soft light of the warm interior.

"Jessie. Finally. Oh, it's so good to see you. Come in. Del's here. Of course, he's always here, now."

"It's good to see you, too, Claire. Thanks for being so patient. I had to be sure I wasn't followed from the hotel."

"Hotel? You should be staying here with us."

"Thanks, but I think you'll understand why it's not a good idea when you hear what I've got to tell you. I can't have anyone know I've even been close to here."

"That critical, is it?" A square-shouldered, dark-complexioned man stepped forward from behind Claire to hold out a hand in greeting. There was an air of physical strength and the ability to move quickly about RCMP Inspector Delafosse, as well as the assurance of a competent intelligence.

"Yes, Del, I'm afraid so," she told him soberly.

"Take off your coat and . . . Oh, you're not wearing one. Jessie, you must be frozen. Come over here by the fire and get warm. How could you—"

"Don't worry, Claire. I've got on enough under this vest to brave a blizzard." She grinned and began to pull off layers of gloves, vest, and sweater. "I'm used to the cold anyway, and my red parka would have been a dead giveaway to anyone watching. Might as well stand in the middle of the street and shout my name.''

''Well, sit down and let me get you something. A glass of wine? A drink? What would you like? You drink something Irish . . . Jameson? Right?''

''That would be great, thanks.''

''Ice? Water?''

''Just a straight shot, with a glass of ice water, please, Claire.''

Settled in a comfortable armchair beside the fire that crackled in the stone fireplace, Jessie glanced around and sighed in the relief of being there.

Claire McSpadden's . . .

No, Jessie thought, it's Claire Delafosse—for her friend and the inspector had married since they had last seen each other.

Claire Delafosse's handmade house was enough like Jessie's own cabin in Knik, with its snug four rooms full of comfortable furniture, brightly colored curtains, and many books, to make her feel quite at home.

Claire returned with the Irish whiskey and a beer for Del, and settled on the sofa close to her new husband.

''Is it all right for me to stay?'' she asked.

''Yes, of course. I trust you as much as I do Del. And, by the way, congratulations, you two! Sorry we couldn't make it over for the wedding.''

Delafosse laid an affectionate hand on Claire's knee and smiled.

''It was a good party. We missed you. But now, how can I help, Jessie? Your friend Don Graham called me, but didn't say much—just relayed the message that you needed to talk to me about something seriously important and private.''

''He doesn't know any more than that,'' Jessie told him. ''I more or less promised I wouldn't tell. But I'm going to break that promise with you, because I think it's less important than a woman's life. I think we need help and are about to need more.''

Delafosse was immediately on alert, sitting up just a bit straighter than before and leaning slightly forward, listening intently.

Just like Alex, Jessie thought, and shoved that thought from her mind in favor of the subject at hand.

''Who did you promise?'' Del asked. ''Who's *we?* Just tell me everything. This concerns the race? What? Just start at the first and tell me all of it.''

She couldn't help smiling. ''You should have been a doctor, Del. Great bedside manner.''

For the next half hour, between sips of Jameson, she told him, including the murder of B. J. Lowery, the recovered team, the note Leland had received in Pelly Crossing, and everything she imagined could be even remotely important concerning Debbie Todd's abduction.

Inspector Delafosse listened intently, and only interrupted twice to clarify what she had told him. When she finished, he asked a few questions, then sighed and narrowed his eyes in thought.

''So, the searches—Leland's and the committee's—didn't turn up much.''

''Nothing useful.''

''Interesting that the note should emphasize *no police,* then they draw attention to Debbie Todd's absence by leaving the sled and team near the highway, to say nothing of the dead man. Clearly they wanted at least the team to be found. That dog of Leland's going missing as well is odd, though I wonder if it might not have got loose and run off. It might still be out there somewhere.''

''Doesn't make much sense.'' Jessie agreed. ''I didn't say so, but I wondered if they could have killed Royal for some reason, accidentally or otherwise.''

''Anything's possible, of course. Was the dog particularly protective of the girl?''

''No more than ordinary. These dogs are not watchdogs or trained for security. Jake sells some of his nonracing dogs for pets, so he wouldn't train them that way. But Royal's worth a lot—he's an Iditarod-winning lead dog.''

Delafosse was quiet for a minute, considering. "You know,'' he said finally, "by leaving the body, and that sled and team, they must have known that the RCMP would eventually be called. When they found Lowery and couldn't find anything in a search, they'd call us. We'd have to be involved. Whoever this is must have known that.''

"Maybe they're dumber than it seems.''

"Maybe—but they tried to hide the body, after all. It almost seems something they hadn't planned. The rest of this seems to have been well thought out ahead of time—premeditated. Another thing about that team occurs to me, though. By leaving it where they did, they guaranteed that any search would be focused on where it was found, or where she supposedly disappeared. That would be handy if they planned to be somewhere else, wouldn't it? And I'd be willing to bet that's exactly where they are—somewhere else. Now if we could only figure out where.''

"There's no way of knowing, and a lot of 'somewhere else' out there between where she disappeared and Fairbanks. If there's any chance of finding them—and Debbie—I think we need help. That's why I'm here, Del.''

"Where's Alex, Jessie?'' Claire asked suddenly. "Is he working on this, too?''

Jessie told them about Alex's father's death and his trip to Idaho.

"I can't ask him to come back now, for this. His mother needs him. Besides—''

The inspector nodded, turning his attention back to the problem at hand. "I have to agree, Jessie, that whether Jake Leland thinks so or not, you need help—lots of very expert help. But not the kind that would inspire whoever is responsible for this abduction into doing anything foolish to the girl.''

"You mean like *killing* her, don't you, Del?'' she said with brave honesty. "Might as well say what we're all thinking and what terrifies Jake and his wife. The kidnappers could kill her—easily. And may, no matter what we do, right? Could have already—afraid she could identify them."

"I doubt that. They probably know they might need her at some point. But that's part of what I mean, yes. There are lots of ways to kill someone. Just leaving them alone in this kind of cold, far from anywhere, will do it. In this country it's very easy to arrange it so they'll never be found, alive or dead—just disappear, leaving no evidence. There's a very large and unexplored wilderness out there, Jessie, thousands and thousands of miles of wilderness, much of which has never been touched by the foot of man. And there are other things to take into consideration.

"Right now, however, that's not the issue. Right now we need to figure out what can be done, and fast. And it'll have to involve both Leland and some very carefully selected law enforcement on both sides of the border. But it might be better to wait until just after you leave town and they are less likely to be watching Leland so closely, focusing more on you and the money. Let me think it over."

Jessie felt her breathing change and her chest tighten in a tense response, knowing he was right. It would be so easy for someone to make just one small mistake—and even the smallest slip could mean the life of Jake Leland's stepdaughter. She could only hope she had done the best thing in coming to Delafosse.

But the contact was made. It was out of her hands now.

CHAPTER THIRTEEN

"It is a simple matter to see the obvious, to do the expected. . . . When the unexpected does happen, however, and when it is of sufficiently grave import, the unfit perish. . . . On the other hand, there are those who make toward survival, the fit individuals who escape from the rule of the obvious and the expected and adjust their lives to no matter what strange grooves they may stray into or into which they may be forced."
—Jack London, "The Unexpected"

UNACCOMPANIED, JESSIE SLIPPED BACK INTO THE HOTEL much as she had slipped out of it, by waiting and following someone else through the door, then quickly disappeared up the stairs to her room.

As quietly as possible, she went in and, with a glance down the hall to make sure she had not been observed, closed the door. As she turned away, something crackled under her boot. In the soft glow of the light she had left turned on by the bed, she saw that she had stepped on an envelope that had apparently been slid in under the door.

"JAKE LELAND," it read in squared-off letters, as if it had been written with the assistance of a ruler, just like the first he had received.

So, the kidnappers not only had someone in Dawson, they knew where Jessie was staying and which room was hers. She hoped she had been careful enough that they did not know she had been away from it for the last hour or more, much less where she had been. Maybe this new note could tell her.

If it had not been addressed to Leland, she would have looked to see. But as much as she wanted to immediately rip open the sealed flap to get at the message, she resisted. First she must find Jake.

Clutching it, she started back out the door, remembered how she was dressed, and stopped. Pulling off the vest and one of the sweaters, she tossed the ski mask on the bed and grabbed her red parka.

Back to being musher Jessie Arnold, she thought. Whoever's watching needs to see me as myself. They might remember what I looked like coming back in here, even if they didn't recognize me, and I sincerely hope they didn't.

As she laid her hand on the doorknob, the phone on the bedside table rang, startling her so that she dropped the key she was holding, along with the envelope. Leaving them where they had fallen, she crossed the room and lifted the receiver.

If they knew where she was, it might be . . .

"Hello?"

"Hello, love."

Alex. It was only Alex. He had said he would call her in Dawson, and it had totally slipped her mind.

Only Alex?

"I tried to call earlier, but you weren't there. How's the race going?" he asked. "I've been following it when I can get a report. Not much on the news down here, though. How're you doing?"

"Oh," The race . . . oh, yes . . . the race. "Ah . . . fine. I'm doing fine so far. In the top ten . . . barely."

"Hey, that's great. Keep it up."

"Yeah, sure. I will. Yes."

"You don't sound very pleased about it."

The envelope lay on the floor, just out of reach, demanding her focus.

But this is Alex, she told herself. I need to talk to him.

Just being with Del and Claire—his friends, too—had brought him closer somehow. Still, right now he seemed not only incredibly far away, but almost from some other life.

How can I talk to him now? I've got to find Jake.

"Jessie? Are you okay?"

"Alex, I . . ."

"Is something wrong, Jess? What's going on? Tell me. I'm right here."

"I . . . Alex . . . I'm sorry, but I absolutely cannot talk to you now. There's something important that I *have* to take care of. Something . . ." She knew her voice sounded weak and distracted . . . confused.

"*Jessie.* You're scaring me. What's wrong?"

"Oh, God, Alex . . . everything. And I haven't got time to explain."

"Okay. We can talk later. I'll call you back, just tell me when. Or you can call me. . . . Jess? Are you in some kind of trouble?"

"No . . . yes . . . I need . . . I've got to . . ."

"Do you want me to come, Jess?"

"No, Alex. I've already talked to Delafosse and Claire. . . ."

"It sounds serious."

"It is, but not about me, and Del is working on it. There's so much . . . and I . . . well . . . I just can't divide my attention right now."

As she heard herself say the words, she remembered the other, earlier conversation with him, when she had offered to go to Idaho and felt hurt and guilty when he refused.

Divide . . . there was that word again, and this time she understood it, though the situation was much different. He had become a *part* rather than a whole.

Dammit.

"I'm sorry, Alex. I *have* to go. Call me later."

"Can I call Del?"

"Yes. Oh, yes, call *him*. He knows it all. He can explain. Sorry. Bye."

She grabbed the envelope and her key, and was on the

stairs before she realized she had hung up on his response. Guilt swept in, momentarily slowing her feet. Then she was once again hurrying down the steps, heading for the door. She would think about it later. Right now . . .

Where could she find Leland?

"I'll be around," he had said. "The checkpoint official . . . I'll keep going back . . . at least every hour or so."

It was a place to start, but Jessie realized now that *around* wasn't half good enough. They hadn't anticipated that the message might be delivered to her, had they? They had expected that it would come to Leland, then he would find *her*. All she could do was search him out—and it was almost one o'clock in the morning. Where the hell would he be?

A quick look in the bar of her hotel told her he wasn't there.

He was not in his room or the bar at the Downtown Hotel, on the corner of Second and Queen, a block from her own.

Three more noisy bars and a restaurant that was open late yielded nothing.

The big service station bay held only three racers and several support crew members engaged in repairing battered sleds.

Jessie checked them all, as she headed for the Yukon Quest Dawson checkpoint in the tourist information building at the north end of Front Street, the last place on her mental list and her best hope.

"He was here almost an hour ago," the checkpoint official told her. "He's been in and out all day. Said he'd be back."

"Do you know where he was going?"

"Nope. Could be just about anywhere, I guess."

Spinning abruptly away in frustration, she walked hard into the solid form of race marshal Ned Bishop, who had come up behind her.

"Ooph. Hey, take it easy, Jessie. Who you looking for?"

"Sorry, Ned. Jake. I'm trying to find Jake Leland. It's important. Very."

"Back there." He waved a hand with a mitten on it. "Talking to Connie Stocker in the office."

Jessie looked in the direction he indicated and saw a closed door with a window in it. Through the glass, she identified the back of Jake Leland's head, nodding, as he gestured with both hands, speaking to a woman she did not recognize, but who appeared to be listening intently from behind a desk.

"Thanks, Ned."

Swiftly, she headed for the door, heedless of Bishop's words from behind her. "I wouldn't—"

Leland turned as she came through the door and closed it behind her, then rose to his feet at the look on her face.

"What?"

"Here." She handed him the envelope.

"They left it for *you?*"

"Yeah. Found it on the floor of my room, where someone slipped it under the door."

He ripped it open and unfolded the single page it contained. They read it together silently.

DOUBLE WRAP THE MONEY, ALL $200,000, IN BLACK PLASTIC GARBAGE BAGS. CLOSE IT SECURELY WITH SOME KIND OF RED TAPE AND GIVE THE PACKAGE TO JESSIE ARNOLD. RUNNING BY HERSELF—NO ONE ELSE—SHE MUST CARRY IT IN HER SLED WHEN SHE LEAVES DAWSON. SOMEWHERE BETWEEN DAWSON AND EAGLE SHE WILL FIND OUT WHERE TO DROP IT. THIS IS FOR YOU AND ARNOLD ONLY. DON'T TELL ANYONE ELSE—NOT THE POLICE. WE KNOW THEY'RE INVOLVED NOW. BUT BE SMART LELAND. DO ANYTHING STUPID AND YOU'LL NEVER SEE YOUR DAUGHTER AGAIN.

"Goddammit."

"But that's more than . . ."

The woman behind the desk had risen and stood watching with concern on her face. "What is it?"

The door opened and closed again, with Ned Bishop just inside.

Jessie looked up, realizing that she and Jake Leland were anything but alone. Had she just made a bad mistake by bringing the envelope to him here, not waiting until she could catch him by himself somewhere?

"I'm Connie Stocker," the woman said, coming around the desk and holding out a hand. "I'm the Canadian YQI president."

"YQI? Oh . . . Yukon Quest . . . ?"

". . . International. Right. And you're Jessie Arnold. Now, what's up? Is that your instructions, Jake?"

Leland looked at her and nodded his head in frustration. "Exactly. And it says I can't let you see them, Connie."

Bishop had moved across the room to stand near Connie Stocker. "We can understand that," he said. "It's your call, Jake. They still want what they originally demanded, from you *and* us?"

"Yes. I have all of mine. Jill came in with it from Fairbanks late this afternoon—in cash. It's in the hotel safe."

"Wait," Jessie questioned. "*Us?* What do you mean, *us?*"

"The bastards sent a second note, Jessie. To the Quest committee—demanding another hundred thousand. So their price has doubled, with the same threats. If we or the committee tell anyone not named or directly involved, or anyone contacts the police, Debbie dies."

"But . . . how can the Quest—"

"We'll have to use the prize money from the race," Connie told her. "We've discussed it and decided we don't have a lot of choices here. The American half of the committee agrees. It's going to cause problems, but we'll work them out later. It's all we have, and I hope we have that. Pledges from sponsors were still coming in when I left Whitehorse."

"Can you get it by tonight? I came in this morning . . ." Jessie glanced at her watch. "Well . . . yesterday morning, now . . . so I'm supposed to leave at eight-forty this evening, including the fifty-eight-minute adjustment to my start time. If I'm supposed to carry this payoff, it'll have to go with me then.''

''And you shouldn't alter your schedule,'' Connie agreed. ''From what Jake tells me and what we've figured out on our own, someone must be keeping close track of us.''

''They slipped this note under my door, so they know where I'm staying. But they can't watch all of us all of the time, can they?''

''Maybe not,'' Connie replied. ''But how can we know who's being watched, and when?''

She was right. There was no way of knowing. They would simply have to go along, especially with Leland so adamant about it. What else could they do?

And she had already gone to Delafosse, Jessie remembered. How could she tell Leland, or the others, about that now? Del had said he would call her, or send Claire in an emergency, but she had no idea just what he was planning or would do about the situation. Would it fit in with these new instructions? She would have to get word to him somehow, but decided to keep her visit and conversation with him to herself for a while longer. There was no need to worry Jake Leland any further—he had enough on his plate at the moment. This news would make him crazy.

Guiltily, she knew she was also leaving the breaking of that news up to Delafosse, avoiding the unpleasantness she knew would result. But he had said it might be better to wait for her departure, so she held her peace, though she wondered just how this new piece of the puzzle would affect his plans.

As she left Connie Stocker's office with Leland a few minutes later, she was desperately hoping that the inspector would be able come up with some plan of action before she had to leave Dawson. Leaving without knowing what they would do would not add to her confidence, or give her any idea what to do in case something went differently than anticipated. She also heartily wished she had her familiar Smith and Wesson .44 tucked securely in the pocket of her parka—and not with moose in mind this time out.

CHAPTER FOURTEEN

"On either side the sun are sun-dogs, so that there are three suns in the sky. . . . And all about is the snow and the silence . . . and all the air is flashing with the dust of diamonds."
—Jack London, "The Sun-Dog Trail"

JESSIE DID NOT TALK AGAIN TO ALEX BEFORE DEPARTING from Dawson.

Leaving Jake Leland, she returned to her hotel room, went straight to the phone, and called Delafosse, reasoning—hoping—that whoever was watching was only *watching*, not listening. It was a calculated risk, but one that she and Del had agreed was probably safe, considering the odds that whoever had abducted Debbie Todd wouldn't bother with listening devices, relying instead on observation and intimidation. It was a better option than trying to meet Del again.

"They probably think they've got you sufficiently discouraged," he told her. "That you'll all be too afraid for Debbie Todd's safety to tell anyone, especially law enforcement."

Now she told him about the note she had found in her room and taken to Leland, about the demand that had been made to the Quest committee for another $100,000 and the role the note had demanded that she play in carrying the ransom money to a still-undisclosed drop. She also shared her frustration at not being able to carry her hand-gun on the Canadian part of the trail.

"What do you usually carry?" he asked, and when she told him, he said he would take care of it. "I think this situation merits a bending of the law a bit and I'll be responsible. I'll be more comfortable, and so will you, if you have some protection along that you're used to. I'll have someone uninvolved and safe take a firearm to Don Graham in the dog yard. That'll be better than trying to get it to you directly."

When they finished talking, she went to bed and—though she had thought she might not be able—slept soundly until Linda Caswell came knocking on the door at eight o'clock the next morning.

Alex did not call again, but had asked Del to tell her that he had heard the whole story and that she should be extremely careful, whatever she did. But he had talked to Delafosse *before* they knew the contents of the note that had been slipped under her door, before she knew she was to carry the ransom. Still, she made no attempt to call him, remaining focused on what she had to do in the next few hours and days.

It bothered her, in a distracted way, that she seemed to have no need to share the problem with him, felt tired at the thought of having to explain it all over again to some-one who was not, and could not be, involved, but the whole thing was beginning to wear her out emotionally and mentally. Perhaps this was how he had felt about his father's funeral, she thought—not up to *dividing* himself into too many pieces.

The idea of carrying the ransom was unsettling and there was little she could do except determine to make the best job she could of following the kidnappers' instruc-tions and hoping that would be enough for them to release Debbie Todd unharmed. The only thing she felt she could do ahead of time was prepare herself as well as possible physically, so she went to work on that, and, letting every-thing else go, including Alex, slept, then ate a huge breakfast and went out to get her team and equipment ready for the last half of the race.

Walking through the streets of Dawson toward the river made her feel that she had stepped back in time, for the town was lined with boxy, false-fronted buildings, some old, some new, constructed in the style that had been popular during the gold rush a hundred years earlier. Even the names of various establishments echoed the vernacular of stampeders intent on making a fortune: the Bonanza Shell Station, the Trail of 98 Restaurant, the Jack London Grill, the Eldorado Hotel, the Klondike River Lodge RV Park, the Gold Poke Gift Shop. On the bank of the river in the middle of town rested the sternwheeler SS *Keno,* one of the last majestic steamboats to ply the Yukon bearing greedy gold seekers. Now, refurbished, painted, and polished, its distinctive Victorian shape looking almost like new, it was a popular tourist attraction.

As she passed the riverboat, Jessie remembered being here before with Alex, after the earlier case he had worked with Delafosse had been solved. They had strolled past the boat through the quiet snowfall of an early winter evening and she recalled feeling that things were exactly right with her world, that there was nowhere she would rather be than where she was, knowing he felt the same satisfaction. The contrast with her feelings now was striking. She frowned, shook her head in dismissal, and hurried out onto the river ice toward the dog yard on the opposite bank.

Don Graham met her there with a worried look. "I have something for you, Jessie. A short guy with hair like steel wool, but bald on top, brought this and told me you'd be expecting it."

He handed her a brown paper grocery sack. Inside was a dozen of Claire's homemade oatmeal cookies in a plastic container and, underneath, another brown sack, wrapped around itself and secured with a heavy rubber band. Inside she could feel the hard outlines of the handgun Delafosse had promised her, and a box that could only be extra ammunition.

"Said his name was Robert Fitzgerald and that he was from the museum. Ah . . . ?"

Jessie had to smile. Fitzgerald was clearly as "safe" a person as Del would be able to find and one she already knew. Curator of the Dawson City Museum, he had been slightly involved, in a peripheral but important way, in the case Alex and Del had shared. Dedicated to, in fact almost buried in, the hundred-year-old world of gold rush history, he was one of the last people she could imagine who would ever be suspected of carrying a firearm—even for someone else.

"Don't ask, Don," she told him. "It's okay. Really. He's a friend."

"But, Jessie, if that's what I assume it is, it isn't legal."

"The cookies, you mean?" she asked with a wicked grin.

"No, the—"

"That's been taken care of. Don't worry."

"Why?"

"Don. You promised not to ask me any questions and I promised to tell you when I could. I can't yet. Please. Have a cookie."

He wasn't happy about it, and changed the topic to a discussion of the weight of her sled for this segment of the run, but he gave her suspicious sidelong glances and frowns throughout the rest of the day when he thought she wasn't looking.

The sun came out briefly in the afternoon, changing the flat gray day to a splendor of sparkling crystal and white as it touched each grain of wind-tossed snow with a tiny light till it seemed the very air was aglitter. Overhead, Jessie noticed a pair of sun dogs, one on either side of the sun, shimmering like spots of concentrated rainbow in the sky. The brightness of the sun itself was softened, slightly veiled in the snow the wind was scouring from the hilltops that surrounded Dawson.

"The weather's going to change," she commented, "and probably not for the better."

She was rechecking the list of what she was carefully packing in the sled bag, and smiling at the antics of a raven that was hopping cleverly just out of reach of Tank and Pete as it pecked at a scrap of spilled dog food, when Jim Ryan showed up late in the morning to find out her schedule for leaving Dawson.

The adjustments to each racer's time were made to compensate for the delay of two minutes between each start in Whitehorse. The team that had started last had no time added, because he had accumulated the most time waiting for his turn at the starting gate. In Dawson, the rest had time added to make up the difference between theirs and his, so that all were even when they left after their long rest. Jessie had started fifty-eight minutes before the last racer in Whitehorse, so she had that amount added to the thirty-six hours she was required to layover in Dawson. Ryan had thirty-six minutes added to his time, putting him ahead of her by twenty-one minutes on his way out of town, though he had come in just behind her.

"Boy, do I feel better," he told her with a grin. "I slept like a log, but I'm ready to get out of here. How about you? With the adjustment to my start time, I'll take off at eight-nineteen tonight. Hey, I told you I'd be ahead. What's your leave time?"

"Eight-forty."

"That's only twenty-one minutes. You want to do the summit together? I'll take it easy till you catch up, if you want, and we can help each other over the rough spots. They say it's blowing like a son of a bitch up there, with more bad weather on the way."

Here was a complication that, in her concern for the ransom problems, she had not considered. The kidnappers' instructions stressed that she must make the run from Dawson to Eagle alone, at least until she found out where she was to drop the package of money. But how should she tell Ryan she couldn't travel with him without explaining why? She knew him well enough to know that he would be resistant to letting her go alone if he knew she was carrying the ransom.

Glancing around at Ben and Linda Caswell, who were in the process of watering the dogs before Billy took them two by two for exercise, she hesitated.

"Let's walk," she suggested, and called to the crew. "Back in a while. I'm going to pick up whatever I've got left in the hotel room before noon check-out. Then I'm going to grab some lunch with this guy."

When they were far enough out on the river ice not to be overheard, she had considered the problem enough to decide that at least partial honesty would be best.

"Listen, Jim. I'm going to do this part of the run by myself. It has nothing to do with you—you know I like your company. I just need to do it that way, okay?"

He gave her a questioning look. "This have anything to do with what's going on with Leland's daughter? Has he heard from them yet?"

"Yes," she said, and stopped to turn and face him. "Yes, it does. And that's all I can say. Will you just accept that and trust me?"

"Of course, Jessie. But it makes me uneasy for you to be running alone. Can't we somehow—"

"Nope. Haven't got a choice. I've got to do it this way. I'm sorry, really, but I have to know that you won't do anything to put me at risk by holding back and sticking too close, okay? Promise?"

He didn't answer for a long minute of thought, conspicuously reluctant to do so.

"What if I—"

"*Jim.*"

"All right. But I don't like it. I'll be looking over my shoulder all the way to Eagle. And if you're not there in a reasonable amount of time . . ."

"Good. It'll make me feel better to know that someone's paying attention to where I'm supposed to be."

They walked on across the river and into Dawson in time to watch one of the late mushers arrive at the checkpoint looking windblown and tired. His dogs, however, looked great—rested and still ready to go. It was a fact that in distance racing it was the mushers who suffered— tired, sleep-deprived, tense with the strain of keeping everything operating smoothly. The dogs—who got lots of rest, food, and attention—usually gained weight, were at the top of their form, and could go on long after their drivers would have crashed from total exhaustion and stress.

"I've already eaten," Ryan told Jessie, when they had reached the middle of town, a block from her hotel. "And I've got to finish replacing the runners on my sled, so I'll take off for now. If you change your mind, let me know and I'll wait for you."

"I won't, Jim. I'm sorry, but I can't."

"Okay, but be careful, Jessie. I don't know what you're up to, but this doesn't seem very smart to me, especially when somebody's already died over this. These may not be people to take any chances with, right?"

"Right, and I won't. Don't worry. I won't do anything unnecessary or foolish, and, if it'll make you feel any better, I've been given permission to carry along some protection."

His eyes widened. "You've got a gu—"

"Yes," she swiftly cut him off. "That's not for publication."

"Right. Sorry. That does make me feel a little better. Also tells me you've talked to someone in authority, who's also keeping track. Still . . ."

"I'll be just fine." She hoped it would be true. "Just pretend you know nothing about any of this, okay? And I'll see you in Eagle."

COLLECTING THE FEW ITEMS SHE HAD LEFT IN HER HOTEL room that morning, Jessie went down to the restaurant to get some lunch. She had ordered a seafood pasta dish, with a salad and double garlic bread, and was waiting with anticipation for the high-carb-and-calorie lunch when Lynn Ehlers walked into the dining room. He saw her immediately and came across to her table by the window.

"Hey, Jessie. I thought I'd have to refuel alone. Okay if I join you? Or are you expecting the rest of your crew?"

"Nope. Got stood up, so I'm lunching alone. Make yourself at home," she invited, looking forward to some conversation that didn't center around the kidnapping.

But when he sat down his first comment dashed her hopes.

"Have they found Debbie Todd yet?"

"Not yet. But everybody's looking."

"Damn, that's so strange, don't you think? How could she just disappear like that?"

It was good to know that word of the abduction had not made its rounds of the notoriously gossipy racing group, but Jessie shook her head and tried to change the subject. "I have no idea. Are you ready to go out?"

"Just about. What time do you leave?"

"Eight-forty. You?"

"Eight-fifty-three."

He would be right behind her by thirteen minutes. It wasn't an unwelcome thought.

"What number did you start?" she asked him, a half-formed idea drifting through her mind.

"Eleven."

So—he had started between her and Debbie. But she didn't remember passing him before Braeburn, so he must have passed Debbie and been ahead of them both. Still, he had to have been running very close to the girl when she disappeared.

"Did you see Debbie between Braeburn and the Chain of Lakes?"

"No, but I think she left ahead of me. I was still taking it easy with the dogs, making sure they didn't run themselves into the ground."

Well, he *could* have missed her somewhere, passing without seeing her.

More paranoia, Jessie decided. Why can't I let it go, even long enough to eat lunch? She settled back in her chair and poured cream into her coffee.

"Well, what do you think of it so far?" she asked Ehlers. "Everything you imagined it would be?"

"And more. What great country. I've got to come back up here in the summer and spend some time exploring this gold rush country; it's fascinating. Have you been to Dawson before?"

"Yes, and it's great. Up and down the rivers all around here are historic locations—mines, discoveries, old log cabins. There's even a steamboat graveyard across the river. What kind of a kennel do you have in Minnesota?"

"Not as big as yours, I'll bet. I've got thirty-two dogs— maybe a few more when I get back, since I left a bitch about to have pups."

"Got someone good to take care of them while you're gone?"

"Yeah, another mushing buddy. We trade off when one of us wants to be away, racing, or whatever. I've never been gone this long or this far before, but then, I've never run a Quest, either."

"No family?"

"No. I'm afraid my obsession with racing finally got to be too much for my marriage three years ago." He frowned and a resigned expression flitted across his face. "No kids, which was good, I guess."

Another mushing casualty, Jessie thought. Some relationships survived, some didn't, and she shouldn't blame it all on running dogs, she supposed. Still, it was a time-intensive sport that also demanded most of the musher's energy, focus, and money, leaving too little for a family who did not always understand or agree with these expenditures. Some spouses, on the other hand, became as enthused as their partners, which could turn into a competition that might also be lethal to a marriage or relationship.

Once again, she refused to let herself dwell on an assessment of her own alliance with Alex. Turning her attention to her lunch companion, she realized that she was attracted to the man who sat across the table, and only partly because they shared an interest. He looked up at her and smiled in response to her reflective look.

"A penny?"

"Ah . . . what?"

"A penny for your thoughts. You looked a long ways away."

"Oh . . . that?" She smiled. "Not worth it." And pulled her concentration back to sled dog racing.

"Is this very different from racing at home?"

"Not much. Some slightly different rules, but mostly they're the ones that make this race unique and are required to make it run smoothly."

The lunch they had ordered arrived and their conversation drifted into sporadic comments as they both turned their attention to it. For the first waking moment since she had arrived in Dawson, Jessie relaxed and let herself simply enjoy the food. What would be, would be. All she could do was go along with whatever was required of her, and she didn't have to do it right now. She was glad Lynn Ehlers had appeared when he did. He was easy to be with, and as comfortable with silence as with talk. Just what she needed at the moment.

When Jessie drove her team through the dark to the checkpoint that evening at eight-thirty, Ryan had already left Dawson on his way across the summit to Eagle. Ehlers would soon be behind her on the trail.

She was not surprised to find Ned Bishop acting as checker, and Leland hovering nearby, clearly in sight.

"Here's your package, Jessie," Bishop told her, stepping close enough not to be overheard, and tucking it into her sled as he checked her required gear. It was wrapped in black plastic and, as required, taped securely with easily identifiable red duct tape.

"They've narrowed the field somewhat by giving us a broad clue of where they may make a try for it—where you'll be most isolated, up on top. Not much, but maybe some help, okay? Delafosse says to be extremely careful. These people are clearly not to be taken lightly. He thought about sending someone in your place, but is afraid you were picked because they know you and would see through a switch in a minute."

Startled, she tried not to show it. Anyone could be watching now, but that was the idea—that they could see but not hear what was said. Delafosse had evidently changed his mind about waiting until she had gone, which didn't make her unhappy.

"Del's talked to you? Does Jake Leland know?"

"Yeah, he knows. He's not too happy with you, Jessie. But he'll get over it. If you had to go to someone—and I personally think it was a good idea—you clearly went to the right person. The inspector evidently knows how and when to keep his mouth shut, from what I've seen so far—which is almost nothing of him, but a fair amount of a friend of his from the museum staff. It'll be all right."

Del was clearly making more use of Robert Fitzgerald than just delivering handguns.

"I hope so. I'm the one out there, if anything goes wrong. Don't let Leland get crazy and do anything to cause trouble. He must be pretty upset, and he's used to doing things his way."

"We won't. I don't think he'd risk it anyway, but it's Jill we'll be keeping an eye on. She's really not doing well with all this, furious with Jake, and terrified for Debbie. The minute you get to Eagle get in touch with us. We need to know that you're okay, and how and where the drop went down."

"Once they have it, I'll be making a fast run to Eagle, or wherever is the closest place I can call from. Tell Del I said thanks for the . . . protection."

"Yeah, we know about it." He grinned as he patted her on one shoulder, and said quietly, showing his teeth in a teasing grin that she knew was intended to lighten the exchange, "Try not to use it in Canada, Jessie. If you have to . . . ah . . . protect yourself, do it in Alaska. Less hassle for everybody that way."

"Ned, you turkey. If I need it, I'm not going to care, but I'll keep it in mind."

As she pulled away from the checkpoint, she caught a glimpse of the familiar blue and yellow parka she had seen earlier in the race. So, Rick Roney is here to watch me leave, she noted. Or maybe he's about to go out, too—minus Lowery. He wouldn't have anything to do with killing his own handler—would he? She had no way of knowing, but their leave time would be close. It was always possible that he could be her secret, silent observer. Anyone could. Best to be watchful and careful of anyone she did not know well enough to trust. She would keep an eye out for him on the trail, especially through this part of it.

Ten minutes later, she was alone and gliding through the night, the reflective tape on the harnesses of her thoroughly rested and rejuvenated dogs flashing in the light from her headlamp as they trotted eagerly along the river ice, settling into a run she hoped would result in the return of Debbie Todd. She had no idea how, where, or when she would find out about dropping the $200,000 she carried in the sled, but the handgun was securely zipped into a convenient pocket of her red parka, where she would be able to reach it quickly if necessary.

CHAPTER FIFTEEN

"There be places where there is a fall to the river, and the water is unruly, and the ice makes above and is eaten away beneath. In such a spot the sled I drove broke through, and the dogs."
    —Jack London, "An Odyssey of the North"

DAWSON CITY WAS LOCATED AT THE CONFLUENCE OF THE Yukon and Klondike rivers. The added water of the smaller river increased the flow and created rough and rugged winter ice, with huge blocks that had jumbled up in the freezing and refreezing—blocks as big as boxcars or small houses that the mushers were forced to run between on a winding track laid down by the trailbreakers on their snowmachines.

People from Dawson had worked hard with chain saws, sledgehammers, and axes to clear the way through this silent city of ice, making it as safe as possible for the dogs and drivers. But, after a mile or so of twists and turns, Jessie found herself once again forced off the ice for three or four portages onto the historic freight and mail route that had been used by mushers in the old days. It took complete concentration and quick reactions to avoid crashes, as she ran the team back and forth between this trail and the river track below it on the Yukon.

"Take a left, Tank—go gee. Up now, onto the bank. Good boy. Haw—go haw now. That's it. Good dogs."

Her leader gave her a glance over his shoulder that told her she needn't have bothered with instructions, that he was totally capable of negotiating the obstacle course on his own, as he moved with experienced confidence up the riverbank and along the trail.

After this demanding section, Jessie noticed that the land around the river had begun to widen, allowing its banks to spread farther apart, and the slowing of the current had made smoother ice as it froze in the autumn. Because of this, and also due to the many small rivers and creeks that poured into it during the warmer months of the year, the broadening Yukon showed the first signs of becoming a really big river.

Through the night, she ran alone, neither passing, nor being passed by, another musher. Once she thought she heard dogs barking a long ways behind her, and, going around a bend in the river more than two hours after leaving Dawson, saw a flash of light that might have been a musher's headlamp, but it did not reappear. For the first time in several years of mushing, she felt very much alone and vulnerable. It reminded her of the fear she had experienced during one Iditarod race when she had known there was a killer on the trail somewhere. Tension tightened her neck and shoulder muscles, and kept her awake and alert, on the lookout for anything unusual.

The temperature had dropped a little more and the sky was overcast, allowing no light from moon or aurora borealis to add definition to the trail with soft light and deep shadows. The dogs kept up a good pace, well rested and eager to run, as they always were when starting a new race. After the long layover in Dawson, this seemed like a new race, but she knew that the feeling was also because her objective in running had decidedly shifted. Now it was much more a race to deliver the ransom and less a race to Fairbanks. It no longer mattered so much to her where, or even if, she placed well in the Yukon Quest.

Where and when, she wondered, would she find out how to drop the money she carried? Who would pick it up? How would the kidnappers contact her? Was anyone keeping track of her progress? It would be difficult for anyone to come near her on the trail without her knowledge. But the kidnappers could certainly find out where she was at a couple of unofficial stopping places along the river between Dawson and Eagle.

A stiff and chilly breeze had come up, swirling dry grains of snow across the ice in ripples and waves, moaning enough to make it difficult for anyone at a distance to hear the scraping sounds of her runners over the ice and her infrequent commands to her dogs, though her headlamp would be a bright, moving point of light in the darkness. Her vision was limited to what fell within the circle of light from that lamp, so she saw very little of what she was passing.

Mushers, intent on winning a race, trying to keep other racers from knowing how fast they were traveling or exactly where they were, sometimes turned off their headlamps and ran in the dark, trusting their lead dog to keep the team on a trail other dogs had passed over before them. This could be misleading if the front-runner took a wrong turn, and it was not unheard-of for several racers to wind up lost together and retracing their own trail.

It was pleasant to run dark when the northern lights were putting on a show overhead, but in the inky blackness of this overcast, Jessie had no inclination to switch off her headlamp, for she found that even the single, narrow beam was a comfort compared to the immensity of the wilderness that surrounded her. This was a foreign feeling, for she often found it more comfortable to be out with her dogs in the wide, welcoming, open spaces of the north than confined inside walls and behind closed doors. Now she was constantly aware that anything, or anyone, could be out there, unseen. She felt observed, as if some threatening watcher knew exactly where she was and followed her every move from some hidden location. The feeling made her swallow hard and glance often behind her, though there was never anything to see, and if there had been, she could hardly have seen it anyway, light-blind as she was.

At one long curve of the river, high on a west bank that Jessie felt was there but could not make out, a figure *was* watching as she steadily moved past on the ice below. The bluff was not as high as that on the Takhini a few days earlier in the race, but it was farther from the track the racers followed, for the river here was much wider and the trailbreakers had found the smoothest ice near the center of it.

Secreted in the black silence of the night, a lone individual stood beside the snowmachine that had carried him to the spot an hour earlier. There he had waited, frequently moving to make sure his feet were warm in their insulated boots, swinging his arms and tucking his hands in their heavy mitts into his armpits a time or two—not because they *were* cold, but because it seemed that they should be, with the temperature hovering at less than twenty below. As the bobbing beam of Jessie's headlamp fell onto the scarlet bag of gear in her sled, it illuminated the white letters of the name painted on the side, ARNOLD KENNELS, and from his lookout the watcher knew this was indeed the musher for whom he had waited. He stood without moving near one of the trees that lined the banks of the river and waited until the dancing light disappeared around the next bend. Then he waited a while longer and, twenty minutes later, was rewarded by the appearance of another light following the same track.

He did not bother to ascertain the identity of this racer, wanting only to know how closely Jessie was being followed by the next team, but did not start up the engine of the snowmachine until this light had also vanished around the bend. Then the machine roared to life, shattering the peaceful stillness.

Another musher, still out of sight, heard it and raised her head from the standing doze she had fallen into on the runners of her sled, wondering what on earth anyone

could be doing out along an uninhabited section of the
Yukon in the frozen dark. The sound was faint, however,
and had ended by the time she rounded a curve and approached the location·where the watcher had stood, so she
shrugged it off and continued toward Forty Mile.

Running on the ice of a river, though rough at times,
was always essentially the same—flat. Flowing in broad
bends through a sweeping expanse of country, following
the path of least resistance, rivers lack sharp curves, and
do not give mushers and sleds the up-and-down motion of
a trail on solid ground. Adding to the sameness was an
odd feeling that Jessie was making no headway at all in
the total dark, that the forward motion of the team was
merely an illusion and she was remaining in the same
place—like a jogger on a treadmill.

Clouds overhead reflect light back to the earth, when
there is light to be reflected. In the enormous almost-
deserted wilderness between Canada and Alaska there is
seldom any light at all and what there is comes only from
the tiny fire a musher may build for warmth or food, or
the glow from a cabin's window that barely reaches the
snow-covered ground outside. Such slight gleams are easily snatched and swallowed up by the encroaching dark.

Traveling through the blackness on ice over water often
gave Jessie a sensation of being somehow suspended, that
she was floating, not really touching the earth, though the
surface, in most places frozen several feet deep, was more
than substantial. She had noticed the same feeling close
to the end of the Iditarod as she traveled across the sea
ice of Norton Sound near Nome.

Sometime before midnight she pulled up the bank and
stopped for a short rest at a tiny wilderness cabin that
belonged to a former Quest racer, then continued for another hour and took a long one in a spot on the riverbank
where she found Ryan bedding down his own team, cooker
already alight under a kettle of melting snow.

"Hey," he greeted her quietly, careful not to disturb

the team that was resting close to his, another musher soundly sleeping on a pile of straw near his dogs.

"Who's that?"

"Gail Murray. Glad you made it. Everything okay?"

"Just fine. It's pretty black out there, though. I didn't get to see much of the country."

"Like running in a tunnel, isn't it? I've made a daylight run through here before, going the other direction, and you didn't miss much but riverbank and miles of ice. The wind's picking up—it'll be howling down the channel soon. Guess you were right about the weather changing. We're supposed to catch some more snow on the summit."

"At least we'll be going over most of that in the daylight. I think I'd rather be blinded by snow than only be able to see what my headlamp hits and have to imagine the rest."

"Yeah, me, too," Ryan agreed. "Still, it could be a real struggle. This summit doesn't have a lot of switchbacks, just a couple of quick ones. It just goes up and up—straight up the mountain at an angle so steep you'll be pushing your sled to help the dogs keep it moving, when it's just about all you can do to move yourself. You think it's never going to end, then it goes on some more, and that's in good weather. In bad weather it can be a real bitch. There're always teams that quit and refuse to go on until they've rested and made up their minds to it, and there's no place to rest that's out of the wind and blowing snow."

"Sounds just peachy. I can hardly wait."

"I'm not fooling, Jessie. Be ready for it."

"I know. I will be. But right now I'm more concerned with getting these guys and myself fed. Then I'll crash until about six. There's still the rest of the run to Forty Mile and up that river before I have to start climbing."

Jessie did not sleep well; she woke up several times at small sounds in the dark that made her take long looks around their camp, finding nothing untoward. She was glad to be resting with someone else, but wondered if she should have found a solitary spot. What if the kidnappers had intended to approach her when she stopped, not, as she had been expecting, while she was traveling? Well, she decided, too late now. If that's their plan, they'll just have to wait. They can't expect me to begin to think the way they do. Though maybe I already have, she thought, and hated the idea that her racing strategy was being influenced.

When Jessie woke to the sound of her alarm, Gail Murray, the sleeping musher, had already departed with her team and Ryan was harnessing his dogs.

"Coffee's over there by the fire," he told her, as she rose from the sleeping bag she had placed atop her sled, stretched, and stomped around to help get her circulation going. "There's hot water in my cooker, if you want some before I mix it with kibble to take along for the dogs."

Jessie used some of it to wash her face, then poured coffee over powdered hot chocolate in her insulated mug, to which she added two heaping, calorie-loaded spoonfuls of sugar. As Ryan packed the rest of his gear, she moved a skillet from her sled bag onto the fire, tossed in a dozen frozen sausages and a handful of snow. They would steam themselves thawed and hot, then brown when the water evaporated. While she drank the hot chocolate and waited for her breakfast and the water for dog food to heat, she watched Ryan finish his preparations.

"Those sure smell good. Sure you don't want me to wait a bit?" he questioned, turning to her when he was ready to go.

She laughed. "Yes, if you mean you want more breakfast. There's enough, with some powdered eggs. Otherwise, no. I'll be okay by myself, Jim. You go on and make good time. Maybe I'll see you at Forty Mile for another break."

"If not, I'll be watching in Eagle to be sure you come in."

She gave him part of an hour before putting her own

team back on the Yukon River ice, taking even more seriously the instruction that she must run alone. After this, she would make sure she camped alone, too, unless the unofficial checkpoints came at a time when the team needed to rest.

Damned if I let these guys destroy my whole race for me, she thought, heading down the steep bank to the ice again.

The cabins at the tiny site of Forty Mile are the farthest west buildings in Canada, built even before the Klondike gold rush at a place where the Forty Mile River meets the Yukon that was believed to be forty miles from a trading post, Fort Reliance, near where Dawson City would later be established. In reality, it was closer to fifty miles between the two.

Jessie was perhaps five miles from the Forty Mile River when she was passed by a racer she had not encountered before in the front-runners. Slowly, he pulled up behind her with a team of eleven dogs, called for the trail, and went by as she pulled her dogs to one side of the track.

"Thanks," he called out, bringing a mitten to the band of a bright orange stocking cap in a jaunty salute as he passed.

She encouraged the team back into its normal seven- to eight-mile-an-hour trot, then slowed them slightly, ignoring Tank's tendency to race after anyone who got in front of him, talking him into a trot of about seven miles an hour. The ice was quite smooth and slick, easy running, so they cruised along, watching the distance slowly grow between them and the orange-capped musher, who seemed in a hurry to reach the next stop. He was still in sight, however, when he reached the place where the Forty Mile River ran into the Yukon.

The churning water at the meeting of the two rivers had resulted in rougher ice, with thick and thin spots that must be carefully negotiated, a dangerous situation for those traveling the frozen highway with heavy sleds. Jessie was just close enough to be able to see a large hole in the ice by the left-hand bank, where someone had broken through sometime earlier, when she heard a shout, accompanied by an ominous cracking, and the other driver was suddenly waist deep in icy water, his sled rapidly sinking, the wheel dogs and two more on the line were being yanked in with it.

Calling her team to a lope, Jessie quickly drove a wide circle to the right to be sure she was on solid ice, stopped the dogs, threw down the hook, which refused to dig into the hard surface, and ran across to grab at the team leaders of the sinking sled, trusting Tank to keep the dogs where she had left them.

The driver was now completely wet and struggling with the sled, which was partially afloat with air trapped in its bag. Still on firm ice, the dogs at the front of the stricken team were scrabbling, toenails scraping frantically to find a purchase on the slick surface, but being inexorably drawn back toward the hole by the weight of the team and sled. Jessie threw herself down and added her body weight to the front of the line, which helped stop their slow, steady backward slide toward the freezing water.

Someone on the bank was shouting in the dark and she had the impression of a light, but couldn't turn to see if help was coming without loosening her tenuous hold on the line. In the water the racer, headlamp still burning and in jerking motion, was gasping with the shock of the sudden cold, but kicking hard, trying to shove the sled onto the shelf of solid ice, which continued to break off in chunks. Finally, after long moments that resulted in burning pain to her arms and shoulders as Jessie pulled with all her strength yet felt that she was getting nowhere, the tension on the line eased a little and two of the drenched dogs managed to clamber out onto unbroken ice. Immediately she helped the rest of the team take up any slack and prayed the ice wouldn't break again. It held long enough for the wheel dogs to climb out as well, but she was distrustful, almost certain it would crack under the weight of the fully loaded sled, its weight increased with water and becoming more saturated by the second.

"Hup, boys. Pull, Silver," the half-drowned and frozen musher was calling through clenched teeth to his leader, the dog pulling beside Jessie's right shoulder.

With almost superhuman strength, the man managed a strong kick and gave the sled a giant shove that, along with the efforts of the whole team of dogs and Jessie, tipped it up and far enough onto the solid ice to keep it from sliding back. Remarkably, the ice held. Scrambling to her feet, still holding tightly to the line, Jessie carefully moved the dogs forward, giving thanks that most mushers have strong upper bodies from sled wrestling and weight training.

"Come, Silver . . . keep them coming," she encouraged the dog, talking her forward.

As the obedient leader threw her shoulders against the harness with all her weight and will, slowly the soaked figure of the musher was dragged out of the hole behind the sled, clinging desperately to a rear stanchion, dripping water that immediately began to freeze his clothing to the ice on which he collapsed, gasping. As he let go, rolled, and struggled to regain his footing, Jessie kept his team in motion until she had moved it away from any thin ice, closer to her own and in no danger. Leaving it, she went quickly back to do what she could for the musher, knowing the man was now in more danger than the dogs, though they would need help, too, or they could freeze, their undercoats clearly sodden.

Three men from the tiny settlement, watching for approaching mushers on the river, had seen the accident, climbed down the bank, and were hurrying across the ice, flashlight beams joggling as they ran. They carried a rope, which was now unnecessary, and a blanket, which was.

"Th-th-a-anks," the dripping racer, so cold he could hardly speak, managed to sputter at Jessie, as he was cocooned in the blanket and forcefully propelled toward the bank by one of his three would-be rescuers. "My t-t-team."

"Don't worry about it," he was told. "We'll take care of them. He's a vet." A hand was waved in the direction of the other two, one of whom was already getting set to drive the team toward some buildings Jessie could just make out on the edge of the dark river. "Let's get you inside, where it's warm, and out of those wet clothes."

"You okay?" one of them asked Jessie.

"Yes, fine."

"That was a good job you did. We'll see you up there, then."

And they were off, hastening to find life-giving warmth for the man and his dogs.

He was lucky to have gone through the ice in a place with assistance and a fire handy. Soaked and shivering mushers who had fallen through the ice far from any shelter were forced to build their own quick fires and hope for dry clothes to change into, stripping off their wet ones as fast as possible, sometimes hopping from one bare foot to the other in the snow. Most carried a complete set of extra clothing and outerwear carefully sealed in plastic for just such an emergency. Boots, even with felt liners, could be emptied of water and put back on, for their cold-repelling insulation usually kept feet warm even when they were damp. The dogs had to be rubbed as dry as possible, then kept near the fire like their driver.

Glad the accident had not resulted in serious problems, Jessie went back to her own team, which had remained standing where she'd left them.

"Good dogs. Oh, you are the very best dogs in the whole world," she told them, giving each one a pat or two.

When she looked back at the frightening hole in the ice, her headlamp caught the bright orange of the musher's hat, floating gently in water that had already developed a thin skin of ice. Leaving it to its fate, she drove on into the historic site of Forty Mile.

*   *   *

"I couldn't have got out without you," the musher, warm and dry, though still suffering a periodic shiver, told her later. "Thanks."

"You'd have done the same if I'd gone through," Jessie told him honestly. "Hey, do you have a name?"

He grinned. "You want to know who you're responsible for, now that you saved my life?"

"Nope, just want to be able to tell about it," she teased. "Can't tell credible tales without names. Besides, you saved your own skin. I was just an anchor."

"I'm John," he told her, holding out a hand. "John Noble."

His grip conveyed the temperature of the mug of hot soup he had been using as a hand-warmer between swallows.

"Oh, you're the guy your handlers were bragging about in Dawson, on their way to Gertie's. You're a very good musher, from what I was told."

"Terry, right? And Hank? Had to be the night they went out to party."

"Might have been just a bit sloshed, as I remember it." She grinned.

"And who are you?"

"Jessie Arnold."

"Yeah? Hey, wait a minute. I've got something for you."

He turned to the gear that was spread out to dry around the small trapper's cabin that a hundred years earlier had been a gold rush store, and dug into the wet pocket of the parka he had been wearing when he took his unexpected bath.

"Here," he said, handing her a soggy, folded envelope. "Sorry about the baptism, but it's probably still readable."

Stomach tightening as she recognized the squarely penciled letters that formed her name on the outside, Jessie sincerely hoped so.

CHAPTER SIXTEEN

"It's a cold night, boys,—a bitter cold night. . . . You've all traveled trail, and know what that stands for."
—Jack London, "To the Man on the Trail"

As soon as Jessie was well away from Dawson City on her way down the river to Forty Mile, Delafosse went directly to work on the case. Before her support crew could leave town on their long drive back to Alaska and Fairbanks, he found Ben Caswell and Don Graham in the dog yard across the river and enlisted their help.

Cas was angry and incredulous that he had not known what was going on almost in front of him.

"You *knew* and didn't *tell* me? Why not?" he demanded of Graham.

"Jessie made me promise not to tell anyone," the big man rumbled, embarrassed at Cas's pointed irritation. "Would you have told me?"

"Yeah, well . . . probably not, I guess. But still . . ."

"We've got too much to do to argue about it now," Delafosse told them both. "Done is done. Jessie did the best she could, considering. At least she came to me— though, from what I understand, Leland is very unhappy about it. Can't blame him. He's understandably concerned for his stepdaughter."

"Okay. What are we going to do?" Cas asked, shifting

176

into professional trooper gear and needing to get his thoughts together.

"First we need to talk to Jake Leland, and Ned Bishop, the race manager, and be sure we coordinate anything we decide to do. We need to review everything that anyone knows about the situation, including that murder back down the trail. I sent two of our men out this morning to take another look in a couple of places, and they'll be back soon. Then maybe we can come up with something that will help catch these guys without endangering either Debbie Todd or Jessie in the process. It could be extremely touchy, especially spread out all over the map, as this race is."

"Aren't you afraid there'll still be someone watching Leland?"

"*He* is. But I think that they were checking, knew exactly when the ransom went out with Jessie, and now will concentrate on following her progress until they get it. There's a slim chance that they'll leave someone here to spy on Jake, but the odds are in our favor that they won't, and taking them is better than doing nothing. Right?"

Cas nodded his agreement.

"Okay, let's go find Leland."

"Wait a minute." Cas frowned. "We should tell Alex what's happening up here that concerns Jessie. He'd want to know—I would, if it were Linda."

"He already does," Delafosse assured him. "I told him all about it last night on the phone and we discussed what should be done."

"Does Jessie know that?"

"No, but she knows that he called me and I told him what was going on. She's really focused on getting that money delivered, as she should be, and probably hasn't thought about anything else much."

Again, Cas nodded, satisfied. "Leland?"

"I think we'd better have someone bring him to us, rather than hunting him up. Just to be safe, in case there *is* someone tracking him."

*   *   *

Claire Delafosse was called into service as a messenger and shortly brought Jake Leland and Ned Bishop—making certain they were not followed—to the cabin on Dawson's south side where Cas, Don Graham, and her husband were waiting.

Leland glared at Delafosse, as they met in the living room of the cabin. "I don't like this. It's one hell of a risk to my stepdaughter's life, and Jessie Arnold promised to keep this to herself. Now half the race is involved, and who knows who else? The RCMP—obviously."

"Jessie was very careful about filling me in," Delafosse told the stressed and indignant stepfather. "No one knew she had talked with me. We made sure of that. Now that she's gone with the ransom, all we want to do is help. Your daughter's safety comes first, without question—and Jessie's, of course. But we can't just sit on our hands and do nothing to catch these people."

He paused, then, partly to shock Leland from his stubborn dismissal of assistance, said, "Do you really think that they are likely to just let Debbie go as easily as that? A hundred things could go wrong and we don't even know where she is or how they've treated her. If she could recognize any of them . . ."

What he didn't say hung in the minds of everyone in the room. Jake Leland abruptly sat down in a chair by the fireplace and stared at him without speaking for a long minute before dropping his face into his hands with a groan.

"Jesus. Her mother will never understand or forgive me if . . . Jill's practically hysterical now. I sure don't want to be the one to tell her that."

"Do you have to tell her? Where is she?"

Leland raised his head. "At the hotel. The doc gave her a shot—she's out, for the moment. Best thing to do."

"Jake, listen to me carefully."

Delafosse sat on the hearth beside him and laid a hand on his arm.

"You've been trying for days to hold this together by yourself—get the money, keep everything quiet—just the strain of waiting for these bastards to contact you has been enough to fell a weaker man. For God's sake, let us shoulder some of the weight. We've got some pretty experienced and smart people in this room—on your side. Let's use them. Right?"

Leland thought about it, then nodded reluctantly. "Okay. I'll have to admit I've just about come to the end of my gang line. Let's hear what you've got in mind. But I want your promise that nothing gets done that I don't know about."

"You've got it. We can't be working against each other, or something surely *will* go wrong."

An hour later some workable decisions had been made and they had arrived at a basic outline for a plan of action. Bishop had a race to continue managing and would be leaving shortly for Eagle, to watch the front-runners of the race pass through. Leland would continue to wait in Dawson, doing what he had been doing, hoping for word from the kidnappers and keeping in close telephone touch with Inspector Delafosse. Cas would stay in Dawson to assist Delafosse with the investigation and contact the state troopers for help on the Alaskan side of the border. Don Graham would start the long trip to Fairbanks with Billy Steward and Linda Caswell, for, after dropping the ransom money, Jessie would finish the run to Eagle, then continue the race down the Yukon to Circle, where she would expect and need to be met by her support crew.

Claire had just refilled everyone's coffee mugs and put out a plate of sandwiches, and Delafosse was having another look at the notes that had been left for Jake Leland and Jessie, when there was a knock at the door. Outside were the two constables who had gone to investigate the murder scene and the lake where Leland thought Debbie might have run into the snowmachine along the trail when she disappeared. They came through the door carrying a black plastic trash bag of what they had collected, both clearly enthused about the success of their discoveries.

"What have you got, Gene?" Delafosse asked.

"More than we expected," the tallest young constable, who held the bag, told him with a grin.

"We think we found where they took her," the shorter one with a mustache added.

"Where?"

Leland was on his feet. "You found—"

"No we didn't find her—"

The two constables interrupted each other in their eagerness to tell what they knew.

"They must have moved her again soon after . . . but look at these."

In the middle of Delafosse's living room carpet, carefully, the constable set down the bag and they spread it open to display the contents. Several candy wrappers and a greasy sandwich bag containing a few crumbs lay inside, along with an empty red plastic gasoline can, a black ballpoint pen, a piece of cord with a couple of knots in it, about a dozen cigarette butts, and an empty book of matches, partly burned. There were also some charred scraps of white paper, one of which had clearly had something written on it, for the edges of a few partial letters remained unscorched.

Leland reached to pick up something, but Caswell caught his arm.

"Don't touch anything that might have fingerprints, Jake."

Jake nodded agreement and pointed instead. "That," he said. "That's Debbie's."

"What?"

"That knotted cord. It's the cord from the parka her mother made for her. I'd know it anywhere. She was always practicing those knots. See—that's a running eight and the other one's an end loop—the two she was concentrating on just before the race."

"They were not too concerned with cleaning up after

themselves, were they? Where did you find this?'' Delafosse demanded of his men.

"Tucked down next to the log wall, where it could have
been overlooked. If she left it, she tried to hide it from
her captors."

"But where? You didn't just find this by the side of
the road somewhere."

"O-o-oh no. We found it in an abandoned cabin in
Minto."

"Minto? What the hell were you doing in Minto? There
was never anything that would have directed us to Minto."

"Yes, I know, but after we searched the murder site
again and found nothing, then took the snowmachines out
to Mandana Lake and still found nothing new at all, we
started trying to think of someplace that would be easy to
hide her in a hurry and still be accessible to the highway—
somewhere nobody would be likely to accidentally stumble onto them. Most of the communities along the road
between here and Whitehorse are involved in the race, but
no one lives in Minto and it seemed to fill the requirements, so we went to take a look—just to check it out on
the way back—and there was . . . this stuff."

"Where and what is Minto?'' Cas asked, unfamiliar
with the area, except for the race route.

"Abandoned—a ghost town," Delafosse explained.
"It's a little way off the highway between Carmacks and
Pelly Crossing and used to be a village that cut wood for
riverboats, back when they were still running the Yukon
on steam. It's close to, but not on, the Yukon Quest route.
There used to be a government campground there, but they
closed it four, maybe five years ago. There's an RV park
on the highway a little ways away, but nobody's lived in
the old Minto village area since . . ."

He paused and gave Jake Leland a quick, apprehensive
look, as if considering what his reaction might be.

"Since what?'' Don Graham asked, speaking up for the
first time since the constables had made their entrance.

"Ah, since . . . Minto is actually a pretty notorious place. Most people stay clear of it."

"Why?"

"It's known as the murder capital of the Yukon."

Leland sat up a little straighter. "What the hell do you mean?"

"Well . . . during the gold rush three people were killed at Hoochekoo Bluff, not far from Minto. Then, back in the 1960s, three more people died in the village itself, apparently a murder-suicide, but no one could ever figure out a cause of death for two of them, so it was never really solved. Supposedly everyone involved was dead, but about six months later, the woman who had found the three bodies was murdered—shot. After that, the few people that were still living out there packed up everything they owned and left. It's been gradually falling apart ever since, with no one in residence."

"But there's still empty cabins?"

"Yes, some derelict buildings and an emergency air strip. That's about all."

Jake Leland was sitting very still, staring at the items in the black plastic bag. He looked up as Delafosse finished his account.

"And you found these things in one of the cabins?"

"Yes, sir. There was the remains of a fire in an old wood stove, and what you see was scattered around the one room."

"Well, this tells *me* that Debbie was there. Is there anything here that can identify who took her, Inspector? You're the expert."

"We need forensics." Delafosse visually inspected the collection. "There could be fingerprints on the candy wrappers, the sandwich bag, the gas can, and the pen—maybe on the paper scraps. We might get some saliva to establish a DNA identity from the cigarette butts, but that would have to come from Vancouver and would take too long to help us now. Might be useful later. Even if we got something usable, we'd also have to have a print or DNA for comparison.

"What interests me now are those few partial bits of writing on the paper scraps and that empty matchbook."

He picked up the pencil he'd been using and turned the matchbook over.

"Braeburn Lodge. That's on the race route. If one of these guys was there before they took Debbie, we might be able to get someone down there to remember who picked it up, or was asking for matches. It's a long shot, but at least it's something.

"All of this does need to go to a local lab for testing—fast," Delafosse continued. "They'll see if that pen is the one that wrote the letters on the scraps *and* if they match the ransom notes you got, Leland. They should also be able to tell us what was in the sandwich bag. Not that that's important, probably, but you never know."

"Smells like ham and cheese, sir," the mustached constable spoke up.

"Really?" Delafosse's tone, widened eyes, and carefully controlled lips held a hint of suppressed humor.

"Yeah. Cheddar. My favorite. May also have had some mustard."

"Oh." His grin broke through. "Well, there's your expert, Jake. Good work, you two. I want you to take this all to the Whitehorse lab, please. Tell them I said to put a rush on it. Then, on your way back tomorrow morning, I want you to go to Braeburn and see if you can find out anything useful about that book of matches. Yes?"

"Yes, sir."

They collected the bag with its contents and were out the door before Claire could offer them food.

"Just as well," Delafosse teased her, gesturing at the empty plate on the table. "I think we've just eaten all the ham and cheese in the house, with or without mustard."

The group adjourned shortly thereafter, Caswell to retrieve a change of clothes from the camper and move into

Delafosse's spare bedroom. The rest of Jessie's support crew was anxious to get on their way to Fairbanks.

"All we can really do now is wait to hear from Jessie when she arrives in Eagle," the inspector told them. "Aside from keeping a lookout for anyone who appears to be following you, Jake, it's mostly a waiting game. If you see anyone suspicious, let me know immediately. I'd like to catch one of them before he could warn the others—there are clearly several involved. He might help answer some questions for us. It's too stormy on the summit to fly up there, and only Jessie will know where she delivered the ransom, when she does. She may then have some idea where they could be headed with it. That may tell us something, but we've got hours to wait for word. Meanwhile, we'll get started on help from Alaskan law enforcement."

"I'll check in with you when I get to Eagle tomorrow," Ned Bishop told him as he shrugged into his parka and headed out the door. "We're going to fly low to make it up the river. I'll be watching for Jessie and will see what she has to say. Catching these idiots and getting Debbie back would be great, if we can do it somehow. And we'd sure like to get the race's prize money back."

"I'm sure you would—as Jake would like to have what he put up. But Debbie and Jessie have to be the focus now. Having Jessie alone out there with all that cash doesn't do much to build my confidence in human nature. Have you got *any* ideas at all about who this might be, Ned? You know most of these racers, and past racers, pretty well from several years of race managing. Jessie had an idea that it could be someone connected with the race somehow."

Bishop shook his head regretfully. "I've thought about it till I'm going gray-headed, but nothing—well, no one—comes to mind."

"Keep in touch," Delafosse told him. "Especially if you think of anything. . . ."

"You bet I will."

CHAPTER SEVENTEEN

"Dark spruce forest frowned on either side the frozen waterway. The trees had been stripped by a recent wind of their white covering of frost, and they seemed to lean toward each other, black and ominous, in the fading light. A vast silence reigned over the land."
　　　　　　　—Jack London, White Fang

DON'T TAKE YOUR BREAKS OR REST STOPS WITH OTHER MUSHERS. STOP BY YOURSELF. YOU WILL BE CONTACTED.

THE DAMP NOTE IN HER HAND POINTEDLY CONFIRMED WHAT Jessie had wondered about camping with other racers after stopping to rest with Ryan. That it did not say *where* she would be contacted was frustrating, but it did let her know that somehow, someone was watching at least part of the time, and she had no way of knowing which part.

The person who wrote this has got to be a musher, she thought, or someone who knows sled dog racing very well. Everything they've written sounds like it somehow. She still thought the writer was American, not Canadian. She didn't know exactly *how* she knew, but she'd have been willing to bet on it.

"Who gave this to you?" she asked John Noble, the musher she had helped pull out of the hole in the ice.

"Some kid handed it to me in Dawson as I left town. When I said I didn't know if I'd see you, he said the *man*

185

said to give it to you *if* I saw you. I didn't ask who the *man* was.''

"But you got it in Dawson?"

"Right. Just before I pulled away from the gate."

Then how did they know she had stopped with Ryan the night before? Jessie wondered. Maybe they didn't. They might just be covering their bases and making sure she was alone so they could find her with no one else around. It made some kind of odd sense, but was also scary.

"Thanks," she told Noble, and went to get her team ready to travel.

Waiting. It was all waiting for something to happen—somewhere—sometime. She wished it would be soon so she could get it over with, and grew more and more tense as time wore on.

It was a relief to be off the Yukon and onto a smaller river for a change, where the channel was narrower and not so wide open to the wind, which had begun to build into a solid blow by the time Jessie left Forty Mile. It was not snowing, but, from the look of the blank white sky, soon could be. The sharp, clean smell of approaching snow was on the air. It would make little difference whether it snowed or not on the summit, however, where the howling wind would stir up enough from the ground to severely punish any racer daring its heights, sharp icy grains would grind away at any exposed flesh, and the icy fingers of the cold would brush pale patches of frostbite onto the cheeks and noses of the unwary. She did not look forward to the crossing at all.

Going up the Forty Mile River, however, was a pleasure that she let herself enjoy in spite of the wind, pushing her concern out of her mind. After the blind darkness of the night before, it was a relief to run up the small scenic stream with its rocky outcroppings and be able to see it. It had character, was much narrower than the broad expanse of the big river, and the spruce on the hillsides seemed inclined to lean together, almost supporting each other in holding their ground and not slipping off the steep slopes. Running in the tight winding channel through hilly country did not allow her to see out of the drainage, but every bend and turn brought some new and interesting view. Infrequently there was a small homestead or some old mining sheds huddled along the river's edge, some still occupied.

An old man with hair and beard that matched the snow came to the door of his cabin to watch as she passed, unmistakably glad to see some other human in the isolating depths of winter.

"Hello-o-o," he called, cupping his hands around his mouth.

"Hello-o-o," Jessie called back, and waved, tempted to stop and give him a little company, share the coffee she was sure he must be keeping hot on the stove. But her conscience and the wish to get on with her unpleasant errand sent her on up the river until she caught sight of the bridge she had been told to expect. Going up the bank, she crossed it and knew that she was now in Alaska.

Well, if I have to use the handgun, she thought, it will please Ned Bishop to know I've crossed the line and am legal. She patted the pocket of her parka and felt the shape of the weapon she carried.

Just off the Forty Mile she stopped to take a break, knowing she would soon need all her strength and that of the dogs in her team. She fed them a good meal and gave them all the water they would drink, then let them rest while she took her own nap, though it was hard to sleep with the wind howling past and she started up at every sound to see if it was someone who had come for the ransom she carried. If it was blowing this badly where she was, she knew it would be a terror on the summit. She thought about staying put and waiting to see if it would die down in late afternoon, but knew that this kind of storm was more likely to continue or get worse and that, whatever the weather, she'd better go on while she could

see and get across to Eagle, where she could take a good,
long rest indoors at the official checkpoint.

Besides, no one had contacted her, though she had expected it on the Yukon. The more she thought about it,
the more she was convinced that the contact would come
somewhere on the summit she was about to cross, where
it would be easy for them to pick up the ransom and get
away in a number of directions. She also thought they
must use a snowmachine, the only form of transportation
that made sense, for the roads were closed tightly until
spring, and a snowmachine could travel without roads,
moving much faster than a dog team through snow-
locked country.

From the top, whoever picked up the package of money,
in its black plastic and red tape, would be able to go back
into Canada by following the general route of the closed
and drifted Top of the World Highway, head back to Dawson, where he could easily disappear into the crowd of
race officials, mushers, residents, and handlers, and the
cheerful midwinter celebration that was going on there.
He might alternatively elect to go into Alaska, escaping
over the longer distance of the Taylor Highway, which,
also closed, ran west until it reached the Alaska Highway
at Tetlin Junction. It would also be possible to travel down
past Eagle and leave the area by the race route, which
went on down the Yukon River to Circle, where he could
pick up a plowed winter road that ran to Fairbanks, though
this was improbable with a race in progress, for dozens
of people might see and be able to identify him later.

Would the kidnappers bring Debbie to the drop point?
Jessie thought not. In fact, she agreed with Delafosse that
they had probably taken Debbie completely away from the
race area, fearing some kind of search. Though there were
many hiding places in gold rush country, most of the shel-
ters were near the rivers in this broad historic mining region. Because most of the gold had been found in the
valleys, washed down from above, and because water was
necessary to wash the dust from out of the earth that car-

ried it, its seekers had built their wooden tents close to their work. Much of the transportation was also there, along the river highway—water in summer, ice in winter. So, cabins and outbuildings to be found beside the rivers and streams were the easiest and most obvious place to search. For that reason, the kidnappers probably would not use them, inhabited or not.

But the girl could be anywhere. There had been plenty of time for the kidnappers to spirit her away in the days since she had disappeared. It was doubtful that they would bother to transport her to the drop site. "Take the money and run" would probably be more their style. Then, Jessie hoped, they would leave her somewhere else to be found, or to get herself out, unless . . . Jessie stopped her thoughts. There was no reason to start on the *unless*es. She was nervous enough without them, and things would go better if she maintained a positive outlook.

So, she positively got up from her catnap, put new booties on the feet of all her dogs and jackets with belly covers on three of those with the shortest hair, for the exposed and unprotected skin of a dog can freeze almost as easily as that of a human. Putting on her warmest and most windproof clothing, tucking her face mask into a pocket and her sleeves carefully into her big mittens, she snapped the front flap of her parka tight over the zipper, raised her fur-lined hood, and got back on the trail, anxious to put the summit, and the ransom drop she had convinced herself would be made somewhere on it, behind her.

Running past half a dozen cabins, she drove the team up toward American Summit. For a little more than an hour they ran through trees, passing O'Brien Creek, and stopped once again, just before they reached the tree line. For the last time before the hardest part of the climb, Jessie gave her dogs water and a snack, then they headed up into the stark landscape of the heights.

Just above that clear line where the shelter of the trees ended, a strong side wind hit, howling defiantly down upon them, making the dogs instinctively turn away from its fury. It was like walking into a wall of flying snow that instantly searched out every small opening in Jessie's warm clothing, sifting freezing crystals of snow, like fine sand, under the cuffs of her mittens onto her wrists, into the narrow gap between her face and parka hood, and down her neck, finding even the small holes for laces in her boots. In seconds her eyelashes were full of ice and frost that clung and stuck them together when she blinked. Her dogs had all but halted in their traces, tails between their legs, bodies hunched against the icy onslaught.

Tank and Pete both turned to give her looks that questioned her sanity at going up into such a maelstrom. You *really* sure about this? they seemed to ask. If you *are*, you're crazy. This is no fun and we'd just as soon not, but if you're sure . . .

It was almost impossible to hear the shouted command that was instantly snatched away by the wind, but Tank was familiar enough with her gestures to know that she really wanted forward motion and gave it, abandoning his initial reluctance. Here was a challenge. Throwing himself against his harness, he pulled the gang line tight and started the others uphill with the heavy sled. Though Jessie had packed carefully and emptied her sled bag of everything that was not absolutely essential in food and gear to get them to Eagle, it was still a considerable load to pull in such poor weather. Slowly but steadily, however, they moved up a grade that would have taxed their strength even on a calm, clear day, making Jessie proud.

The trailbreakers had placed the stakes with their distinctive reflectors that marked the trail carefully and more closely together, but many had been blown down and buried in the drifting snow that covered them almost as fast as it blew away the trail they had marked. Looking behind her, Jessie saw that the lines made by her sled runners were filling and disappearing almost as soon as she left them. She could see no recognizable sign of sleds passing ahead and would have to trust that Tank would be able to find the trail by his brand of scent radar whenever possible, knowing there wasn't another dog more capable of doing just that. He had proved it many times in the past when they were caught out in similar storms, and worse, but this track was steep and the blowing storm a torment.

She presently found herself, as Ryan had predicted, pushing behind her sled, working as hard as the dogs, but they seemed to be staying on the track. Periodically she watched a marker move slowly past as they progressed, yard by hard-won yard. She was soon exhausted, hot and sweaty with the effort she was making, and hoped her clothes wouldn't freeze when she was finally over the crest and on her way down.

The storm made it hard to breathe, for the wind seemed to steal away the very air, and with each breath it felt as if she took in as much ice as oxygen. Tense muscles were soon burning with the strain and her back and legs ached with lifting and shoving. It quickly seemed as if she couldn't make one more step in the cast-iron boots she was suddenly wearing, or force her lower body through one more drift after the sled, but somehow she did.

The hill grew steeper and the team slowed a little. There was absolutely nowhere to escape the brutal assault of the wind-driven ice. She could see that snow had begun to fall from the sky as well and the whole world became a blinding whirl of white. They would move for a few yards, stop to rest and regain their strength, then start again. Several times Jessie staggered forward to break off the ice that formed on the dogs' faces and brush away part of what had packed itself into their coats. They struggled on, ever upward, knowing that somewhere it *had* to end.

Jessie knew that there would be approximately ten miles of this punishment in a landscape as stark as the mountains of the moon, whether she could see it or not. The slow pace they were maintaining made it seem much longer, but at least they were making progress. Hell, she thought, would be a trail just like this that never did end, then smiled as she immediately contradicted herself and put it into perspective. No, hell would be *not* being allowed to do this once in a while, along with all the better parts of driving a team of dogs in this kind of country—being denied what she loved and had learned to do well. This kind of situation and misery were temporary. Driving a dog team was what defined her and what she couldn't imagine doing without, or doing in any other place, for she knew she loved the vast country of Alaska, whatever it had to offer her.

They reached the first switchback, which Jessie recognized only when she suddenly made out a shadow that was Tank turning to one side in the white curtain, and thought for a second that he had become disoriented. Panting to a stop just beyond the switchback, she once more cleaned ice from the dogs' faces. Her own cheeks burned, stung by the flying grains of ice. For a moment, she covered her face with her mittens and checked to be sure she could still feel her nose. It hurt, so it wasn't frozen, and felt slightly better for the brief time in the temporary shelter of the fur mitts. She thought of her mask, but didn't want to take off the mitts in order to put it on, so she snugged her hood up around her face and prepared to go on.

With no place to rest, the only solution to the situation was to continue to the top and go down the other side until the wind abated. She knew better than to expect any kind of shelter where no one would be foolish enough to build one; it could never succeed against the wind and weather, even for a spectacular view on the very few clear and windless days. From this summit, Jessie knew it was possible to see for what must be a hundred miles in several directions.

As she paused, the dogs had defensively curled into nose-to-tail balls of fur in the snow. She called them up, yelling to be heard, and up they came, still game to attempt the rest of the climb. What a great team. She would reward them handsomely with all their favorite treats the minute she had a chance in Eagle. But, for now, the trail upward went on and on, just as Ryan had predicted. They reached a point of exhaustion where everything seemed a perpetual purgatory of cold, wind, and driven snow, then, in starts and stops, it went farther.

They had just come to a second switchback, which Jessie recognized by a marker or two, before Tank abruptly halted the team. Through the driving haze of the blizzard, she could see no reason for her leader to stop and called out to get him going again. He looked back in response, but refused to move. Several of the dogs lay down and curled up. Dammit, she thought. Just when I was giving them mental trophies for endurance. What the hell is wrong? They can't be giving up on me. Not *this* team. She wallowed forward around the sled through a drift that came to her waist, and, as soon as she reached the head of the team, saw what had inspired the halt.

The switchback circled a slight rise in the ground that would cause a sled to tip precariously away from it, forcing the musher to work as a brace along that side to keep it from overbalancing. The sled traveling just ahead of her had done a disastrous job of negotiating this hazard. It lay on its side below the turn, where it had tumbled over as it fell, dragging the dogs after it to land in a jumble. They had somewhat sorted themselves out, and curled up to rest, burrowing into the loose snow for shelter. But the driver was nowhere to be seen.

Staring intently at the half-buried sled, Tank barked, a thing he seldom did, even in the yard at home, leaving the noisemaking to canines of lesser dignity. Now he barked, then barked again, focused on the pile-up, and over the moan of the wind, Jessie thought she heard a thin voice.

"Help," it called weakly. "I'm down here. Help . . . me."

CHAPTER EIGHTEEN

"It is not the way of the Wild to like movement. Life is an offence to it, for life is movement; and the Wild aims always to destroy movement. It freezes the water to prevent it running to the sea; it drives the sap out of the trees till they are frozen to their mighty hearts; and most ferociously and terribly of all does the Wild harry and crush into submission man—man, who is the most restless of life, ever in revolt against the dictum that all movement must in the end come to the cessation of movement."
—Jack London, White Fang

THERE IS NOTHING TO JUSTIFY THE ASSUMPTION THAT MEN make better sled dog racers than women, though the two have slightly different skills to contribute to the sport.

Men usually have more upper body strength, which makes it easier for them to wrestle heavy sleds, manhandling them around and over difficult sections of the trail. But women quickly learn to compensate for this by being agile and using their wits instead of muscle to conquer the same obstacles. They learn to think and move a little faster, keep their sleds lighter, choose their dogs with this in mind, and it sometimes works to their advantage. A lighter woman and her sled may not break through rotten ice that will dunk the extra weight of *man* and sled.

Though all good mushers are physically fit, being powerful is not necessarily a requirement for sled dog racing. A driver of either sex needs only enough strength to get the job done, not to win displays of muscular development and definition.

When the sled that Jessie discovered on the American Summit switchback had overbalanced, it had been an accident that could have happened as easily to a male musher as to the woman who lay under it in the snow. Acting as brace for the weight of the sled, she had been within the arc of its falling, unable to move away quickly enough to avoid it, awkwardly held in the grip of the deep drift of snow through which she was fighting and floundering. It had effectively pinned her to the ground and thereafter solidly resisted any attempt she made to move it or to dig herself out. Worse, it had fallen with the narrow edge of one sled runner directly across her legs, fracturing one of them just below the knee.

"Gail?" she yelled over the shriek of the wind. "Gail Murray, is that you?"

"Yes," the answer came back faintly. "Gotta get . . . this thing off me . . . I'm freezing under it."

The temperature had been steadily falling as Jessie went up the hill toward the summit. Now, figuring in the wind-chill factor, she knew it had to be more than fifty degrees below zero—a condition that would reward inactivity with frostbite in a very limited amount of time.

As she struggled through the snow around the sled to reach Murray, she kept up a constant shouted conversation against the wind, both to encourage the woman that she was coming to her aid, and to find out what she could that might aid in a rescue.

"How long have you been under there?" she called.

"Don't know. Knocked out for a bit. . . . I think . . . maybe half an hour. Ever since that damned . . . snow-machine came out of nowhere and startled me."

Bad. Half an hour was bad news. It didn't take long to freeze in this kind of cold and she'd already been under there for at least half an hour.

"Snowmachine? What was a snowmachine doing up here on this trail? Trailbreaker?"

Or could it have been the contact Jessie expected to meet?

"I don't know. It didn't . . . stop. It was gone as fast as it came, and I was under this damned . . . sled before I could . . . get out of the way."

Jessie stopped wondering about the cause of the accident and concentrated on Murray and what could be done quickly.

"Where're you hurt?"

"Head hurts. Leg hurt, too, like a son of a bitch, but it's gone numb . . . now. I'm afraid it's freezing . . . can't feel my feet."

Arriving at Murray's side, Jessie saw immediately why the woman's head was hurting. A stanchion had knocked her in the right temple, breaking the skin and, evidently, knocking her silly for at least a few minutes. Blood, now frozen, had run down the side of her head into her hair and the hood of her parka, which was twisted slightly to one side, exposing one side of her face. Pale patches on her cheek and nose signaled an initial touch of frostbite, but she was probably not aware that any part of her face was colder than another—didn't need to have another worry added right now.

Frostbite was as insidious as it was dangerous, and—Jessie had always imagined—that was the reason they had used the word *bite* in describing the condition. Quick as a snake, it could slip up and strike, if you were not vigilant. The only defense was to dress correctly, be sure you had the right gear, and keep moving.

So, the first thing she did was yank her own mask from her pocket and pull it over Murray's head, covering her face. Then she shifted the woman's hood so it fit correctly and fastened it securely with the Velcro strip at the throat, closing as many gaps as possible to keep out the cold and snow.

Through the eye holes, Murray looked up at her gratefully.

"Thanks, Jessie. God, it's good to see you. I was so afraid that I'd—"

"You'd have been glad to see anybody, Gail," Jessie interrupted the frightening thought. "And someone stronger might have been more helpful. It's going to be a bitch to move this sled off of you. May hurt some, too."

The lower half of Murray's body was hidden beneath the sled, mashed into the snow.

"I think my right leg's broken. It got sort of twisted over the other one as I fell and the runner came down on top."

"Well, let's see what we can do to get you out. I think if I unpack your sled I can get it off of you, hopefully without causing any more damage or hurting you too much. Right? We can't wait for someone else to come along. It could be . . . who knows how long?"

"Right. Like I said, the leg's numb . . . now, so just go ahead and . . . do whatever you have to . . . to get me loose. If it hurts . . . well, it'll just have to . . . hurt . . . so ignore any howls. I've been trying to unload the bag, but . . . couldn't reach much."

"Looks like you were doing a pretty good job at what you *could* reach."

Odds and ends of Murray's gear had been pulled from her sled bag and were scattered around her, being rapidly buried by the blowing snow.

"Yeah, well . . . seemed good to do something."

Her speech had slowed even more. She grimaced, and Jessie could hear her teeth chattering.

Hypothermia setting in, Jessie thought, knowing time was critical. Have to get her warmer.

Pulling gear from the sled bag, she located Murray's cold-weather sleeping bag, unrolled and laid half of it under as much of the woman's body as she could, wrapping the rest over her, tucking it in.

"Can't have you freeze while I get this thing off you, can we?"

"Thanks. I was . . . getting . . . pretty cold."

Quickly Jessie began to pull out and toss everything still remaining in the overturned sled.

When the bag was empty—all the equipment and food piled into the snow—Jessie threw her weight against the sled and found it, if not easy to lift, at least possible. As fast as she could, she cleared the snow away on the downhill side, then, unfastening Murray's team of dogs, slowly, carefully worked at lifting and moving the sled into that space a foot or two at a time. Gradually, with Murray helping a little to hold it away from her legs, it was worked clear of her lower body.

The injured driver lay where she had been flattened into the drift by the weight of the sled, right leg twisted over the left, but Jessie had no way of knowing how bad the break was under the heavy bib-overall snowmachine pants the woman was wearing. There was no sign of blood on the fabric, but, just the same, she cautiously unzipped that pants leg and carefully investigated for a compound fracture, which, to her great relief, she did not find.

"Not as bad as it could be, Gail," she told her friend encouragingly. "We'll have you out of here and back to somewhere warm and safe in no time. Now let's get you into this sleeping bag, so you'll stay warmer while I get set to give you a ride down the hill."

Leaving the pile of gear, she called Murray's team of dogs from their rest in the snow and, fighting the wind and flying snow, untangled the gang line and got them lined up in the right order on the downhill end of the sled that was still on its side, and hooked the gang line to a stanchion. With the team pulling, and the sled in motion, it was a little easier to tip it back onto its runners again. She moved the dogs to the front of it, where they belonged, and let them help turn it around till it was headed downhill.

"Hey, good . . . going," Murray told her, as she was helped to an upright position and half carried, hopping feebly on her good leg, to her sled, where Jessie had put back anything that had been in the bag that could help cushion Murray's ride down the hill and keep her as warm as possible—extra clothing, dog jackets, a blue plastic tarp. The rest she had ignored as retrievable later, or not. It was unimportant and extra weight to carry. In her own sled there was enough food to last the two teams until they reached Forty Mile.

As carefully as possible, padding it with a piece of foam that had been used for packing around some of the gear, she fastened Murray's injured leg to the handle of the ax she had carried, the best splint she could devise.

Have to pass this one on to Ned Bishop, she thought in amusement. He can tell Charlie and use it the next time a musher questions the rationale behind making an ax required equipment.

Retrieving the thermos of hot peppermint tea from her own sled bag, she made Murray drink as much as she would, then left it in the second sled with her.

At the last minute, she went to the injured musher's team, took two of the dogs off the gang line, and put them into the bag with Gail for warmth—sheer animal body heat that would undoubtedly be more effective than tea. The two snuggled down close beside their musher and she smiled.

Turning her own team around, Jessie fastened Murray's dogs to the back of her sled and prepared to go back the way she had come, one team and sled after the other. First she went back to fasten the bag completely around the hurt musher.

There was no choice. She would have to be taken back to the unofficial Forty Mile checkpoint, where they could contact the Yukon Quest officials in Dawson for medical assistance, which would probably come in the form of a helicopter.

"I'm . . . sorry to . . . interrupt your race . . . this way," Murray said sleepily.

"Oh, hell, it's only a race, Gail, and there are lots of races. I didn't really want to get to the top of this sucker . . . ah . . . anyway . . . Oh, damn."

Totally focused on helping an injured fellow musher in trouble, Jessie had completely dismissed anything but what must be accomplished in this crisis. Now it suddenly occurred to her that there was, and still remained, a reason unrelated to the race that had made her anxious to attain the summit—the delivery of Debbie Todd's ransom.

Mentally she swore again, pausing briefly in her effort to snap up the sled bag and give Murray all its enclosing protection.

What the hell was she going to do now?

"What's wrong?" the other musher asked from her prone position in the sled, where, for the first time in a long, cold time, she was somewhat sheltered from the blasts of the wind and snow. "What is it, Jessie?"

Jessie was thinking hard, trying to analyze the problem and see her way through it to some kind of solution. She was faced with an impossible situation—a completely horrible choice that was no choice—and there was no good answer.

She plainly could not leave Gail Murray—injured, hypothermic, frostbitten—alone in the storm on American Summit, ransom or no ransom. Murray could die.

But if she didn't deliver the money the kidnappers had demanded, it was perfectly possible that Debbie could die. They had already killed one person, Rick Roney's handler, B. J. Lowery. Why should they hesitate to get rid of another? They wouldn't care that there were extenuating circumstances—solid life-and-death reasons that Jessie had to go *down,* instead of *up,* the mountain. They would only care that they didn't get what they had demanded.

Oh, God, she thought, what can I do?

If only Ryan were behind, instead of ahead of her. He already knew about the abduction of Debbie Todd. She could have told him the rest and counted on his discretion as well as his help. But there was, of course, no way of reaching him—he was already going down the other side of the summit toward Eagle.

Damn, and double damn.

"What's wrong?" Murray asked again, now struggling to lift her head and shoulders to get a look at Jessie's face.

"It's nothing, Gail," she lied firmly, and closed the sled bag around her. "Just a snap that wouldn't work right. Okay? Don't worry, and don't you dare go to sleep. You hear me, Gail? Stay awake and as warm as you can, and I'll get you down from here. That's a promise."

But what could she do about Debbie? She had almost reached the top. Someone could be waiting for her somewhere up there and now she wouldn't show. But Gail Murray was real, right now, and Jessie's help was essential to her immediate survival. The only thing she could do was take events as they came, in order, whatever the result with its accompanying burden of guilt. Where was it written that making this kind of choice had to be fair? She didn't have to like it—she just had to do it.

She had made her choice.

"Let's go, Tank," she called to her leader, and they started back down the impossible hill, through the whirling whiteout, in wind that angrily threatened to blow them off the mountain.

Whatever she did, she was wrong before she even started.

Jessie's heart was a lump in her throat.

CHAPTER NINETEEN

"It is clear and cold, and there is no wind. When daylight comes we can see a long ways off. And it is very quiet. We can hear no sound but the beat of our hearts, and in the silence that is a very loud sound."
— Jack London, "The Sun-Dog Trail"

WHILE JESSIE WAS GRAPPLING WITH HER TORTUROUS DECISION on American Summit, her friends in Dawson were anxiously waiting for time to pass, expecting that she should soon be on the downhill side of the mountain, on her way into Eagle, and that they wouldn't have many more hours to endure before hearing from her about the ransom drop.

Caswell had informed the Alaska State Troopers in Fairbanks of the abduction of Debbie Todd, carefully making them aware of the consequences of any leaks of information. They had agreed to send a trooper to Tetlin Junction to establish a roadblock, from which they would watch for anything suspicious where the summer road from Dawson joined the Alaska Highway. With luck, it would be worth the trouble of a trooper spending long hours in a camper on the back of a truck, with a generator running to keep from freezing. Any vehicle carrying snowmachines, a young woman, or a dog would be looked at with particular care.

Of course, as Delafosse and Caswell had agreed, this

might be fruitless, for there was no way of knowing where the ransom would be handed over. It was a long way from Dawson City to Eagle, and there were hundreds of places Jessie could be contacted. The summit, however, was the most isolated and led to a direct route west into Alaska for anyone on a snowmachine. The last few miles before Tetlin Junction would be open for people who lived along it, and Delafosse thought the summit was the most likely spot for the ransom transfer to take place.

Late in the afternoon of the day after their meeting, a call came through from the small forensics lab in Whitehorse.

"We checked everything for possible fingerprints," the technician told Delafosse, "and found partials from three individuals.

"One set is smaller and more detailed than the rest. It came off one of the candy bar wrappers and is a complete set, both hands, as if someone had spread it out and held it down with all ten fingers. If the woman you're looking for was trying to leave prints to let someone know she'd been there, these would be the ones.

"Another set of partials, which we got from the underside of the gas can handle, is interesting for another reason. It's the right hand—didn't get a thumb, but the index finger and one next to it are good ones. The next, the ring finger, is about half missing on the pinkie side. Not just partial—missing. There is no pinkie print at all. In two examples this pattern shows, so we think that whoever made the prints may be missing that little finger and part of the ring finger as well. You're looking for a three-fingered man—well, almost three fingers—on the right hand."

"Interesting," Del agreed. "Anything else? You said three people."

"Yes, but only partials on the third. There's just enough so we know there was another person, not enough to really do any good. Oh, the sandwich bag also had the woman's prints on it, partials only, if it was the woman—the same smaller ones, anyway."

"Any luck on the burned letters?"

"The burned ones were made with the pen your guys found. It was also used to print the first note, but not the second one. Handwriting matches, as far as we can tell. There wasn't much left to compare on those scraps."

"So, the writer may have lost the pen in the cabin and used another for the next note. He might have been practicing with the burned scraps, or made a mistake."

"Right-o. And you can tell Michael he was right, the sandwich was ham and cheddar—with mustard—dark German variety. You want the brand?"

Delafosse chuckled and told them that if he found it necessary, he'd get back to them on that.

Turning to Cas, who had been trying to track a one-sided conversation, he filled in the details.

"So . . ." Cas said slowly, thinking hard, "we could presume that Debbie was probably in that location, at least for a short time."

"I think we can say that. It's a good assumption. There's some other assumptions that can be made as well, and a couple of considerations I didn't want to talk over with the whole group, especially Leland."

"Yeah, I've got one or two of those myself—like the transportation of her team to where it was found near the highway."

"From the tracks in the snow, they didn't drive the sled to that spot. It was unloaded—both dogs and sled—from a truck, which means they had to have a truck that would carry both. Now, it could have been an open truck, but that would be unusual, and, with a lot of people involved in mushing traveling that road—and we've asked a good number—we haven't found anyone who saw anything like that. I would guess they moved that team and sled on a truck with a dog box—a rig no one would notice as odd."

"Right." Caswell nodded agreement and took it a step further. "It would also make sense that anyone who had access to that kind of vehicle had some kind of connection to sled dog racing—a musher, or handler."

"You've got it in one. I think this is all connected to the race and someone—more than one someone—involved in it."

They looked at each other, frowning.

Caswell swore. "There's too many people, scattered from here to Fairbanks, to even begin to question them all."

"We could narrow it down some if we knew who was where at what times, but it would take days, and half of those we'd need to talk to are in transit, either on the race route or heading west on the highway. But there's another thing that bothers me. That dog of Leland's—Royal? The one that was missing from Debbie Todd's team, when they found it?"

"Yeah?"

"Why the hell would they have taken *just one dog?*"

"Leland said it was a very valuable leader—worth a lot."

"But they haven't mentioned it at all—just the woman. You'd think they'd have raised their ransom demand to account for it, wouldn't you?"

"Maybe. Maybe it was some kind of a problem—got protective of the woman, or something—and they killed it. It's easier to shoot a dog and get rid of it somewhere it'd never turn up. I still can't quite understand why they left Lowery's body so close to that team, knowing it would be found—that it had to be."

"I'd guess that killing wasn't planned and they didn't want to take the time to move it. He must have stopped to help them with unloading the team, or saw something he questioned and wanted to know what was going on— he may have recognized them, if they are connected. Most of these mushers know each other—sled dog racing's a pretty small world."

"Couldn't that missing dog have escaped in the transfer? He could have run off into the woods and been impossible to catch. They wouldn't have wasted time on it. He couldn't identify anyone."

"Possible. Someone may yet pick him up running loose."

"Del?" Claire appeared from the kitchen, where she was concentrating on dinner for the three. "I'm out of cream. Will you make a run to get some? I need to watch the pie."

"Sure. I'm sorry, hon—that pie was my job."

"That's okay, you've got other things to take care of. You had everything together to make it, so I just went ahead. The crust won't be as good as yours, but it'll be edible."

She smiled at Cas's interest in their division of duties.

"Del's a much better baker than I am. He had a mother who won prizes for her pies."

"What kind?"

"This one? Apple. That okay with you?"

"Better than okay. My favorite."

"It'll be better with cream."

"I'm gone," Del said, stomping his feet into boots at the door. "You want to come, Cas?"

"Naw. I'll stay here and make sure the fire doesn't go out—and soak up the scent of apples and cinnamon."

It was after midnight and half the pie, along with dinner, was only a memory, when the phone rang sharply in the Delafosse residence.

Used to wake-up calls, Del caught it on the third ring.

"Hello?"

"Inspector Delafosse?"

"Yes. Who's this."

"My name's Jim Ryan and I'm calling from Eagle."

"Racer? I think Jessie Arnold mentioned your name."

"Right. She's an old friend. I understand that you know something about Debbie Todd's disappearance?"

"Who told you that?"

"Ned Bishop gave me your name."

"He there in Eagle?"

"Yeah. He came in earlier today."

"Okay. What can I do for you?"

"Well . . . look, I left Dawson ahead of Jessie—she's still behind me on the summit. I just got in over here. She told me what she knew about Debbie from Jake Leland, before we got into Dawson—we were running together. On the way here, I got to thinking about something that happened in Pelly Crossing and began to wonder if it could be connected to this kidnap thing."

"What's that, Ryan?"

"When Jessie was ready to leave Pelly, the vet found that two of her dogs had chips that didn't agree with the numbers they had on the list. He—and Ned—made her leave the dogs before she could go on."

"Chips? What kind of chips?"

"Computer chips. Identity chips that're read with a scanner—sort of like the zebra labels on stuff at the grocery store. They have numbers that are unique to each dog, so they can tell that the dogs in your team are the same ones you started with."

"Okay. How does that—"

"It was weird, because the numbers of the chips in Sunny and Wart—that's the dogs Jessie left—had numbers that said one of them, Sunny, was one of Leland's dogs that he had loaned to Debbie for this race. A dog named Royal."

"Royal? The dog that was missing from Todd's team when they found it?"

"Yes. Confusing, isn't it? What I don't understand is how those dogs of Jessie's could pass screening at two checkpoints before Pelly, then suddenly come up with some other numbers, especially one listed to another dog. It doesn't add up. Those chips are inserted under the skin, between the shoulders. They can't be switched. So those bad chips were the same ones Sunny and Wart had had from the start of the race—before that, since they were put in a couple of weeks *before* the race. Understand?"

"I think so. How big are those things?"

"Small. Tiny. The size of . . . say, a pencil lead."

"And couldn't be extracted?"

"Not without cutting the skin to find them. They move sometimes, if they're not placed just right, but are supposed to be permanent."

"And you think this is connected? How?"

"I have no idea. I just thought it was a piece of information somebody ought to know.

"Have you heard anything about Jessie? She was acting kind of funny when I last saw her along the Yukon. We stopped together for a rest, but she insisted that she wanted to run alone. We often run together."

"Not yet. You were ahead of her?"

"Yes."

"Well, then, she should be coming into Eagle soon. Maybe you'll see her there."

"I hope so. I'm kind of keeping an eye on her in case she needs help. Listen, Inspector. Just tell me one thing. Is Jessie carrying a ransom for Debbie Todd?"

"What gave you that idea?"

"Nothing . . . oh, everything. It was just a thought that would explain a couple of things—her running by herself, not wanting me to wait for her. I'm no dummy—I can piece things together. Is she?"

"Ryan, I can't talk about this. Just keep a lookout for Jessie, and tell her I said to call me immediately, if you see her."

"Okay. I will."

"Thanks for calling about those chips."

"Sorry it's so late."

"That's all right."

"What difference could a confusion over a couple of identification chips make?" Del wondered out loud at breakfast, after filling Caswell in on Ryan's phone call in the wee hours. "How could it be connected?"

Caswell shook his head and shrugged, his attention focused primarily on demolishing a stack of sourdough pancakes with homemade syrup.

Claire, her red hair pinned onto the top of her head, Celtic blue eyes turned to her husband, laid down her fork, took a sip of her coffee, and frowned thoughtfully.

"You say she had to leave two dogs in Pelly Crossing?"

"That's what Ryan said."

"But they let her continue the race, obviously. She made it here." Claire paused to pour them all more coffee.

"That's right," said Del.

"Well, what was the result of leaving two dogs? It must have slowed her down some. Less power to pull her sled."

"That's right. Maybe someone wanted her to slow down, you mean?" asked Del.

"Yes, or thought it would take her out of the race completely—some illegality. I don't know what the rules are."

"Hmm, possible. But why? If they had her in mind to take the ransom—and the first note had her name in it—they wouldn't have wanted her out of it."

"Well, then, maybe a slow-down was the reason. But how could they confuse the chips? If Ryan is correct, she went through the first two scans with no trouble and the chips were the same in all three cases." Claire pushed her chair back.

"Maybe it's not connected at all," Cas suggested. "It may be a complete coincidence—just a mistake, as Ryan speculated."

"Also possible. But it's almost too much, that dog having the number of Leland's Royal," said Del.

"I think you need to figure out *who* would want Jessie either to slow down or be taken out of the race," Claire said. "If it's a coincidence, then someone besides whoever took Debbie Todd had a reason to give Jessie trouble. Maybe they wanted to be sure she didn't win."

It sounded much more ominous than that to Caswell, but, as usual, he wanted to think it over thoroughly before coming to any conclusions.

"I think we need more information," he said, lifting another forkful of pancake mouthward. "There's a whole bunch of pieces that don't fit this puzzle. And isn't it about time we heard from Jessie?"

CHAPTER TWENTY

". . . I looked about me; saw . . . the grub sacks . . . the frosty breaths of the dogs circling on the edge of the light; and, above, a great streamer of the aurora bridging the zenith from southeast to northwest. I shivered."
—Jack London, "A Relic of the Pliocene"

EVEN DRIVING ONE STRING OF DOGS AND LEADING ANOTHER, it took Jessie less than half the time to go back down from American Summit than it had taken to go up, though it was still slow going through the whirlwind of snow that continued its relentless assault upon the mountain, eradicating any suggestion of a trail.

Periodically, she would halt the tandem teams for a short rest, and go back to be sure that Gail Murray was all right and still awake in the sheltering sled bag. Plowing through the drifts was rough going, however, so she remained conscious partly as a result of the bumps and jolts.

Murray still could not feel her feet, which worried Jessie considerably, though the pain that could have resulted from such a ride without the numbness would not have been at all pleasant. Jessie hoped that moving the injured musher onto the sled and dragging her downhill was not further damaging a spinal injury she had no way of identifying. That there was little alternative was small comfort to her fears. All she could do was hope the lack of sensation was due to cold, for the loss of a toe or two, even a

210

foot, to frostbite would be any active person's choice over paralysis. At least the rest of Gail was sheltered, even a little warmer, thanks to her canine companions, and her verbal responses more alert and coherent.

They had reached a point where Jessie could begin to make out the tree line, when she thought she saw something moving on the hillside below. A few minutes later she was sure. Another musher was headed up the hill in her direction, working as hard on the steep slope as she had not so long before. They had practically met each other in the obscuring storm, however, before she could make out the identity of the team and driver, catching a glimpse of Lynn Ehlers's friendly, weathered face and dark beard, though it was now as white as it would be when he was eighty, blown full of snow.

Their teams met and she pulled her sled just past his so they were even and stopped.

"Jessie. What the hell happened?" he asked in concern, assessing the situation and quickly making the obvious assumption of misadventure. Only mushers in trouble needed to be transported. "Who is it?"

"Gail Murray. Her sled fell over on her. She's got a broken leg and . . . who knows what else. She can't feel her feet—she's also hypothermic from lying in the snow for the better part of an hour up there on a switchback."

"Jesus! How'd it ha— Oh, hell, it doesn't matter how. We've got to get her down, fast—back to Forty Mile, I'd guess. Right?"

Jessie almost wept in her relief and appreciation of his immediate assumption that it was *we* and not *you*.

Mushers, she thought—and not for the first time—were some of the best and most caring people on earth. It simply would not have occurred to him—like most who ran the wilderness trails with all their perilous possibilities for disaster—to consider anything short of providing an injured musher with all the help he could muster.

Stepping off his sled runners, he was about to see what could be done when he took another look at Jessie's face and saw that the tears in her eyes were not only the result of the wind.

"Hey," he said, with a grin that accentuated the weathered creases around his eyes, and laid a heavily mittened hand on her arm. "It'll be okay, you know, Jess."

She smiled ruefully back at him and shrugged her shoulders in slight embarrassment and distraction. Jess? No one but Alex Jensen called her Jess.

"Yeah. Thanks, Lynn. You don't know how glad I am to see you."

"Well, good. Then I'm glad I'm here. Let's see how we can work this out. How about if I turn around and run behind you until we get out of the worst of this bastard storm. Then we could trade off the lead and make an endurance run."

She drove ahead to give him room to swing his team around without their having to struggle any farther up the hill. As she waited and was impressed with how expertly he handled his dogs, she thought again of the mission that she had interrupted and the choice she had made in turning back down the mountain. Could this be a window of opportunity to complete her mission? Probably not. It wouldn't be fair to leave him alone to finish the rescue she had already begun, but . . . He knew nothing about it. How could she explain?

Stepping off the sled, she walked back to check on Gail Murray. Sensing that an abatement of the elements was close ahead, the dogs pulling the second sled were still on their feet, ready to go. They gave her curious looks as she passed them. Hey, they seemed to say, let's get going and out of this awful weather.

Murray was awake and alert, hypothermia on the retreat.

"What's going on?" she asked. "Why'd we stop?"

"We've got company," Jessie told her encouragingly. "Lynn Ehlers just showed up and he's going to help me get you back to Forty Mile."

"Great. Listen. I'm not complaining, but I've got a little feeling back in this bad leg. It's not real comfortable, but

I can handle it for now. I can't swear about later, though, if it keeps coming to life. You got anything for pain in your kit? We left mine up on the hill.''

"Yeah, I sure do. Never travel without it—you just never know. I'll get some for you."

When Jessie came back, Lynn had introduced himself to Gail and was telling her that it would be no big deal getting her back down the Forty Mile River to the Yukon.

"It'll take a while, but you'll be just fine."

"Thanks." She smiled a little in response to his optimistic good cheer. "How's my team doing, Jessie?"

"Just great. Here, swallow these." She handed Murray a couple of capsules and opened the thermos of tea.

She was glad that some sensation had returned to Murray's leg, though she thought it might be more painful than Gail was admitting and might cause her some real discomfort on the uneven parts of the trail. It relieved some of Jessie's own worries about spinal injury, but there was still the possibility of frostbite to consider. If Gail's feet were frozen, it would hurt like hell when they began to come to life.

"Let's get going," Ehlers suggested. "We're burning daylight."

Closing Murray back into her close shelter, they went back to their sleds and continued down the hill and into the trees, which at first were thinly scattered on the slope, but quickly became a forest that broke most of the force of the wind. The snow, however, continued to fall and drift in the intermittent gusts.

As soon as they came to a spot that was more sheltered and level, they stopped to rearrange themselves, build a fire, and feed and water both the teams Jessie had brought off the mountain. Lynn decided to snack his, having fed them before starting uphill.

"They'll get a good feeding next time we stop," he decided.

Sensing a break, all the dogs ate and drank well, then

lay down and curled up in heat-conserving circles for a snooze.

"We'll have to give them short rests," Ehlers commented, when they had finished the chores and were satisfying their own appetites close to the fire. "We ought to get going as quickly as we can. Long runs and shorter-than-ordinary rests should be okay."

"They've certainly earned more," Jessie told him. "I'm really proud of my guys, but you're right. This has to be a speedy run."

"You've got a good-looking team. All veterans?"

"Yes, this year they are. Even Pete, who's getting up there. He's run six years for me. Five Iditarods in a row."

Within the sled in which she lay now motionless, Murray had eaten a little soup, then almost immediately had drifted off to sleep. Jessie thought that this would be all right, now that she was no longer so cold she could hardly talk. She was going to need all the rest she could get on the trip to the big river, especially if it turned out she was in any real pain.

Staring into the fire, Jessie was once again torn between the two commitments she had made, though neither had anything to do with the race. *She* was the one who had promised to get Gail Murray back to Forty Mile, not Lynn Ehlers. She was also the one who had agreed to be responsible for getting the ransom money to the top of American Summit, or wherever the kidnappers decided to contact her. Once again it had come to a choice.

Could she explain some of the problem to Ehlers without telling him all of it? In these circumstances it wouldn't be fair to ask him for something so important without telling him the reasons for the request. Could she ask him at all? Would he think she was copping out on—

"Jess? What's on your mind?" he asked in a quiet voice, and she looked up to find him watching her with a concerned and questioning expression. "You've got a frown that says something's bothering you—a lot. Given the situation, I think we're pretty well set here. What's worrying you so much?''

She hesitated, surprised out of her own reverie.

He waited.

"It's not so easy, Lynn. There's more to this than you know."

"Better tell me—have it all out, before we go ahead with this."

"Well . . . that's just it. I'm not . . . Oh, hell. I need to go back up there, soon."

"Why?"

"You already know that Debbie Todd's missing and they haven't found her. What you don't know is . . .''

Jessie gave in and once again told an outsider everything, including what they knew about the disappearance and B. J. Lowery's murder, Jake's and the Yukon Quest's money-gathering and concern for secrecy, even her own contact with Delafosse, and why she needed to be where the kidnappers could find her to collect the ransom she carried.

When she finished, he sat for a minute, staring at her in astonishment, with the odd hint of a grin twitching the corners of his mouth.

"Good God, woman. I heard in Forty Mile about you pulling John Noble out of that hole in the ice. Is there anything that could go wrong with this race that you haven't got caught up in—or anything you can't do?"

Shaken from the anxious consideration of her alternatives by his view of what had happened to her over the last few days, Jessie could suddenly see a sort of twisted humor in all she'd been through. Once she did, she couldn't stop the release of tension that started as a chortle and ended up a belly laugh that bent her double as she rolled back on the sled on which she was perched. Her laughter set his going, and it was several minutes before either one was again capable of coherent speech.

"Oh, wow. I needed that," she told him, gasping for air.

"Guess so. Me, too. Now . . . what do you want to do?''

She stopped, startled by his question.

Most men simply assumed that they should take charge of a situation, went ahead and did so. Actually, it was more the way they thought—in terms of action rather than consideration. Solving problems was something to *do*. It had always irritated her to be so easily and without question cut out of a determination by this assumption. It had made her stubbornly insist on her right to make decisions, and she realized that she had been instinctively ready to do so again. But Ehlers had not reacted as she had almost subconsciously expected he would. He had not short-circuited the procedure, but was waiting for her to be part of the process.

What do you want to do? Such a simple question—such an enormous relief to feel she didn't have to fight for her interests.

"What do I want to do? I want to help you take Gail down. I want to go back up that hill. I want to be twins, is what I want, Lynn. Dammit."

"That I can't help with. But it seems to me you'd better get going back up there. Look at it from a practical point of view, Jessie. You are the only one who can carry that money—the one they designated and will expect, right? I *can* take Gail back to Forty Mile, but I *can't* carry the ransom. Doesn't that make the decision for us?"

It clearly did.

What seemed a very long time later, in the deepening dark, the light from Jessie's headlamp illuminated a snow-covered heap that was the equipment she had removed from Gail Murray's sled bag on the downside of the second switchback of American Summit.

Through the fading light, she and her team had once again made the nightmare uphill climb through the blizzard, which continued its remorseless, unmerciful assault on them. Knowing what to expect had made no difference in the difficulty of the seemingly perpetual ascent. If anything, it was worse, as tired muscles were required to repeat what had already strained them to a point of depletion.

The only relief came in the last mile or two, when the snow gradually stopped falling and the wind hushed its howling to a mere moan. Jessie had looked up to see a couple of stars hesitantly peeking through a break in the overcast. Slowly the break had widened, and through it she could also see a hint of moonlight along the edge of the clouds.

Stopping the team just above the switchback, she now thrashed her way through the drifts and started to dig the snow away from the pile of gear, to locate the food Murray had carried for her dogs.

Before leaving Lynn Ehlers to make the run back to Forty Mile alone, Jessie had given him most of her own dog food, knowing she could pick up Murray's on her way to the summit. Though mushers seldom feed their dogs exactly the same things, whatever formula it turned out to be would be edible, and hungry dogs wouldn't care. It seemed the best way to ensure that all were fed enough to make safe passage.

Now, as she brushed at the snow, she was confused to find the pile covered with less than she had expected. Only a thin layer covered most of it, and the pile was scattered as though it had been dug through—searched.

Someone's been here, she realized, and worried suddenly that the food she needed would be gone. But it was there and nothing seemed to be missing—not that it mattered much, except for the food, though it was unsettling. No one had passed them on their way down the hill, or after they had met Ehlers. To search through this pile, someone would have to have come from above.

It was not hard to make the mental leap to assuming who it might have been. When she hadn't showed up as anticipated, someone waiting for her might have come down, found this location, and searched the equipment to see if it was hers—and if, by chance, the ransom had been left along with the rest. It made perfect sense. Who else would be traveling back along the trail? Not a sled driver, certainly.

Well, whoever it had been, they had not found what they were looking for, obviously, because she still carried the scarlet-taped package of money in her own sled.

Loading Murray's dog food into her sled bag, along with the other musher's first-aid kit to replace her own, also gone with Murray and Ehlers, Jessie started the team on up the slope, which soon was not quite so steep. The wind dropped even more, and as the country leveled slightly, she could see that the hill undulated away ahead of them. Though the storm had obliterated the trail, there was a marker or two in the depressions between drifts, and the faint suggestion of a track beside them. Another, deeper suggestion was visible off to one side.

Stopping the sled, Jessie waded across to it, curious, and carefully brushed and blew away some of the light unpacked snow. Only a little way beneath the surface was the unmistakable track of a snowmachine, compressed by the weight of the vehicle that had made it. It overlapped another—someone had come and gone back over the same trail, confirming her earlier assessment of the equipment search. If she was reading this correctly, somewhere up ahead was someone not connected with the race—someone waiting for her to appear with the ransom she had been instructed to carry.

Feeling the pocket of her parka to assure herself the handgun was still there, she went back to the team and got them started again, heading west, watching carefully for any sign of company on the crest.

CHAPTER TWENTY-ONE

*"The snow spread away, level as the great harvest plains,
and here and there about us mighty mountains shoved their
white heads among the stars. And midway on that strange
plain which should have been a valley, the earth and the
snow fell away, straight down toward the heart of the
world. . . . We stood on the dizzy edge that we might see
a way to get down. And on one side, and one side only,
the wall had fallen away till it was like the slope of the
decks in a topsail breeze . . . 'It is the mouth of hell,' he
said; 'let us go down.' And we went down."*
—Jack London, "An Odyssey of the North"

JESSIE HEARD THE ENGINE OF THE SNOWMACHINE BEFORE SHE
saw it coming toward her through the veil of snow propelled by the wind across the summit. What came first
into view was not the machine, but only the form of the
driver, for the machine itself was hidden below it in the
fog of flying white.

Stopping the team, she waited, watching, as the whining
apparition approached and gradually became clearly visible—a dark rider on an even darker conveyance. By-
passing the string of dogs, the figure pulled up beside her,
did not turn off the engine, but set it to idle and sat for a
minute looking at her without speaking. She directed the
light from her headlamp at him and stared back, in sus-
pense, aware that her breathing had quickened and her
heart rate increased.

219

He wore a heavily insulated black coverall, boots, and gloves made for snowmachine travel in extreme weather. A black helmet with a darkly tinted faceplate hid his features and made him as anonymous as he was ominous and threatening. There was absolutely nothing that might aid her in identifying him, now or later.

Swinging a leg over the saddle of the snowmachine, he came up to her and stopped. As she watched, he removed one glove. Under it, he wore another glove, thinner, less insulated. Deliberately, he took a handgun from one pocket and, pointing it in her direction, spoke for the first time.

"The package," he demanded, in a voice slightly muffled by the helmet and the wind. "And don't do anything dumb."

"Where's Debbie Todd?"

"Not here. You'll find out later, after we get the money. But if we don't get it, you'll never know."

Jessie gave in. She hadn't really expected Debbie to be there anyway.

"Right. It's in the sled."

She stepped from the runners of her sled and walked around the opposite side to open the sled bag.

He followed, either in anticipation of what he was about to be given, or because he wanted to stay close, not trusting her.

Opening the bag, she took out the red-taped package of money and, without a word, held it out.

"Put it on the Ski-doo."

Imperious son of a bitch, she thought, as she moved back around her sled and crossed to the idling snowmachine. Probably doesn't want to have to hold anything but that gun.

He opened a compartment under the saddle and gestured to it.

She dropped in the package and stepped back from the machine.

"Now, put your gun in there with it."

"What gun?"

"Don't be stupid," he told her. "I know you've got one somewhere—probably on you. Put it in there."

Slowly, Jessie reached into her parka pocket, took out the handgun by the barrel, and laid it in the compartment with the package of money. Now her only protection was gone.

If it gets used in Alaska, it won't be me that uses it, she thought in discouragement.

How could he possibly have known? Delafosse was the only one— No, that was wrong. Several people could have known, and the only way this person could have known for certain was if one of them had told him. Who? She started to make a mental list, but was interrupted.

"Get on."

"What?"

"You heard me. Get on the snowmachine."

"I've got a team to drive to Eagle. I can't leave—"

His hand steadied the gun directed at her chest.

"I said—*get on*."

Reluctantly, she got on.

"Now you're going to drive this thing and I'm going to ride behind you. And don't forget that now I'm the only one with a gun. Right? Move up."

Although she moved as directed, Jessie again protested.

"What about my dogs? I can't just abandon them."

"Somebody'll find 'em. If they don't, it's not important."

"But why take me? What good will it do? I'm no good to you. Just tell me where to find—"

"This time you won't be telling anyone anything— about where you handed over the money, or which direction I went when I left, will you? You shouldn't have gone to that Canadian cop, Jessie. You didn't follow instructions."

How did he know about Delafosse? Had there been someone watching her, who saw her slip out of the hotel, even with all the care she had taken? Could the two she had gone out the door with have been only pretending to be drunk? She doubted it—they had smelled intoxicated and being drunk was hard to fake convincingly. Who, then? How the hell did he know, and how much did he know? Had someone seen Fitzgerald bring the firearm to Don Graham? It had been disguised, not out in the open. Could they have guessed? Maybe it was Graham himself? Not Don, she thought. Could Fitzgerald have mentioned it? Surely not—with Delafosse to warn him. Who else knew that she had it? Bishop? Ryan? None of them seemed even remote possibilities. She trusted them. But there must have been a slip somewhere.

She stared at the snowmachiner, knowing he wouldn't tell her.

So, he wanted to keep her from reporting on the delivery of the ransom? Somehow Jessie didn't think that was the whole story. Where did he intend to take her? Was she becoming a second hostage? Why would they need a second? Could it be because they no longer had the first? Unanticipated, this turn of events frightened her, but there was nothing she could think of to do about it, or any way to get word back to anyone.

He slid onto the seat behind her and the sudden contact with his body made her cringe away from him. He slid away a little and she felt the hard barrel of the gun pressed into her back.

"You know how to drive this?"

"Yes."

"Then turn it around and get us going, the way I came."

Scared because her secrets were known, and worried about leaving her team, Jessie did as she was told, aware of the firearm solidly pressing against her spine. She hated leaving her team unattended and uncared for on this barren, inhospitable plateau. They *were* important, and such inconsideration for animals that depended on food and care from their drivers filled her with helpless anger. Left by themselves, they would curl up and sleep. He was right that, eventually, some other racer would probably find

them there on the trail to Eagle. But it could be long hours
before that happened, especially if any closely following
mushers turned back with Lynn Ehlers to help take Gail
Murray to Forty Mile, as he had assured her they would.
She hoped the team would not have moved by then.

Before they were out of sight, she looked back and saw
Tank standing in his lead position, staring after her as if
trying to figure out what was happening. He would expect
her back soon. She seldom left them without a word or
some attention, definitely not for long, and not on a noisy
snowmachine. She wondered what he was thinking, what
he would do.

"Watch where you're driving and speed it up," her
captor told her abruptly, poking her with the gun barrel.
Even through her parka, it seemed cold and intimidating.

She turned back to her reluctant assignment, hoping
for . . . what? This was a turn of events none of them
had anticipated or could have planned for. What the hell
was going to happen now?

The break in the overcast was as temporary as it had
been sudden—a mere pause for the wind to gather its
breath. Soon there were no stars to be seen, snow began
to fall again, and the wind picked back up to its previous
intensity, whipping snow and ice from the ground, obscuring the high plateau of the summit. A few shapes loomed
low out of the cloud of blowing white, trees twisted into
fantastical shapes from years of trying to survive in the
power of the wind. They appeared almost alive and tortured, as if they would move in writhing contortions the
minute Jessie wasn't looking at them directly.

It became more difficult to see and she drove carefully,
getting used to the unfamiliar machine. It had been a couple of years since she'd driven a snowmachine and she
had never liked them. Compared to the peaceful, quiet
running of a sled dog team, they were annoyingly noisy
and seemed to whip through the drifts so fast there was
little chance to look around at anything but what was coming up next. It took almost all her concentration, as the

weather deteriorated, just to keep going back over the suggestion of the track the machine had left in coming to meet her. The rest was concerned with the gun she felt jabbing at her back whenever they hit a bump. She could only hope it would not discharge if the man riding behind her accidentally tightened his finger on the trigger. If it weren't for that threat, she might have tried to accelerate suddenly, or tip them over in a drift and hope she could get away.

"Get it going," he told her once. Otherwise, he was silent, though she asked him several questions, trying for some kind of information. Where was Debbie? When and where would she be released? How far were they going? She got no answers.

When she increased their speed a little, he put his left arm around her waist to hold on, as he continued to hold his gun ready in the other hand. She hated the feel of it and his closeness behind her on the machine, felt the muscles in her back tighten as she leaned as far from him as she could. Her shoulders began to ache with the strain.

Eventually, they came to a place where the trail markers indicated that Yukon Quest racers should turn right and follow the Taylor Highway, deeply drifted closed for the winter, as it ran steeply downhill for the last fifty miles into Eagle, another community situated on the banks of the Yukon River.

"Take a left," her captor instructed her, and she could see the hint of a track that went to the west on the Taylor, on its way to Tetlin Junction far away and below in the Alaskan Interior, on the other side of miles of mountains and mining country.

"Where are we going?" she asked.

"You don't need to know," he said, and refused to answer any other questions. "Slow down for a minute."

The hand that held the gun must have been getting too cold to function, for, as soon as she slowed the machine, he removed his arm from her waist and changed hands, putting the heavy glove back on his right hand and removing the other so he could manage the gun. The right arm then slid around her.

"Go," he demanded, and she obeyed, still detesting his presence behind her and his touch, even through his thick clothing and hers.

There was something about him that seemed familiar—made her uneasy—something about his voice. She wished he would speak again, so she could carefully listen.

"Where are we going?" she asked again, but the only answer was another angry jab from the gun barrel that made her shudder and crank up their speed, though she didn't dare go too fast in the storm.

The snowmachine headlight was almost worse than none, reflecting back from the curtain of windblown snow. Going toward Eagle would eventually have brought a lessening of the wind, at least. Now, crossing a ridge, they seemed to be close to disaster as the gale threatened mercilessly to blow them off and down the steep western side.

At last they came to a junction with the Top of the World Highway that ran through to Dawson. Jessie had heard about this road from a friend who had crossed it during summer months and spoke in awe of its incredible vistas. She remembered that the friend also told tales of the notorious western descent of the Taylor Highway that was nothing but a narrow gravel road with switchbacks that clung to the almost vertical hillsides, and knew before her abductor told her that this was where he would want her to go.

Almost immediately they were rounding sharp curves filled with drifts. To the left was nothing but a dizzying cliff that fell away, to be lost below somewhere beyond her sight. The only relief was that, as they went farther down, the wind had lost a little of its force and gave her a better chance to see ahead.

More than an hour later, they finally reached a lower elevation where the road ran down the bottom of a long valley between the tall hills. Once, in the headlight's beam, Jessie caught a glimpse of some abandoned mining equipment, an antique grader, and a shed or two, covered with snow, tucked away on a piece of land that had once been cleared, but now was full of the small spruce that were reclaiming it, growing up around what had once been someone's dream of riches. Mining on a small scale still went on in this country, and some were able to find enough gold to exist, if not grow wealthy. No one traveled here during the winter, though.

Somewhere along this road was a small community called Chicken. The story of its name—true, but reminiscent of many northern tall tales—was that the residents had wanted to name it Ptarmigan, for the Alaskan state bird, but could find no one who could spell it, so they settled for Chicken.

She realized that in her fear of the unidentified man behind her on the snowmachine and their unknown destination, along with apprehension about what would happen when they got there—wherever *there* was—she was mentally escaping by considering the country that they passed. She wondered what was happening to her team back on the summit, and prayed that someone would find them and take them down to Eagle. They would be hungry soon, and she wouldn't be there to feed them. Tank and the rest would not understand that.

As they rounded a bend in the drifted road, a rolling vista of snow-covered hills spread out before them.

"Stop," the voice behind her barked suddenly. "Get off and step away from the machine."

Swinging a leg across the saddle, she did so, her heart in her throat, close to panic. What could he possibly want in this desolate place? Why get off? Would he shoot her now? She stood staring blindly at a dark, snow-covered spruce near the track, feeling totally helpless and stupid with fear, heart pounding, knees weak.

At the sudden sound of the engine revving up, she whirled and saw that the machine was in motion. Already ten feet beyond where she stood in snow to her knees, he was rapidly moving away from her, still heading west. She distinctly heard him laughing gleefully over the increasing roar of the engine.

"Hey. What the hell? You can't just leave me here."

God, what a predicament. She wanted to be away from him—but not here—not abandoned . . . here.

He could, and clearly intended to do just that, for he didn't even look back at her shout. He wasn't going to shoot her. There was a much easier and less personal way of killing her, wasn't there? Just leaving her there, far from anywhere, in dangerous below-zero temperatures, with no food or means to keep warm, other than the clothes she wore, would do the trick nicely.

"You bastard," Jessie yelled after the dark, sinister figure on the machine that was rapidly disappearing into the wall of blowing white. But he did not so much as glance behind him. Almost as if he had never existed, he was gone, swallowed up by the fog of snow, over the brow of a hill.

For a few minutes she could hear the whine of the snowmachine rise and fall, before that sound also vanished into the night. Left standing, aghast and horrified, in the dark, she was almost overwhelmed by the abruptness of the vast silence of the wilderness that surrounded her. The small sounds of snow carried on the wind rattled faintly against her parka hood and icy crystals blew into her face to mix with tears of frustration and anger at this unbelievable turn of events.

She had not yet begun to feel the anxiety or dread over just how easily this snowbound landscape could be the last place she would ever know.

CHAPTER TWENTY-TWO

*"The snow had covered the trail, and there was no sign
that men had ever come or gone that way . . . Then the
woman began to fall."*
    —Jack London, "The Sun-Dog Trail"

ALONE IN THE SNOW AND THE DARK, JESSIE HAD FEW OPTIONS.
She knew that people in severe cold can quickly surrender
their body heat, lose any desire to move, and those who
move little or not at all grow sleepy and eventually lie
down to die. Without shelter, the only way to keep warm
at all was to keep moving.

A body cools first from the extremities in preservation
of the most critical parts of the body, those organs most
necessary to life. Therefore, the fingers, hands and feet,
nose and cheeks, freeze first, while the blood is drawn
into the trunk to protect the heart, the lungs, and the other
systems essential to circulation, respiration, digestion. To
keep the body warm and blood flowing normally requires
that the body exert itself.

Jessie was dressed warmly, in preparation for extreme
cold. A musher riding the back of a sled does not expend
as much energy as one pumping, pushing, or running behind it. Since sled dog drivers ride their sleds much of the
time, they have learned what clothing to wear to keep
themselves comfortable in extremely low temperatures.
She knew that, stranded, without her team and sled, with

no prospect of shelter, if she could walk and keep walking, she would not freeze. But motion burns calories, which, in the cold, require almost constant replenishment. Without food, without rest, a person can only go so far. Would Jessie be able to travel far enough?

She was not entirely without resources, for in one large pocket that she had sewn into the inner lining of her parka, she always carried a small amount of emergency supplies zipped into a plastic bag that she never touched. This included fire-making supplies—a handful of matches, some heavy waxed paper that could be torn into strips and a slim bar of petroleum-soaked wood fiber—some painkillers, a small amount of duct tape, an ace bandage, half a dozen Snickers bars, six peppermint tea bags, a plastic bottle that would hold two cups of liquid, several disposable chemical hand warmers, and a coiled wire saw. In another pocket she had a Swiss army knife fat with blades and tools that she used mostly in repairing her sled and harness for the dogs, and an extra pair of wool socks.

Furious at being left to die in the snow, she spent the first few adrenaline-filled minutes coming to terms with the shocking reality of her situation, then, practicality taking over, began to take inventory of her assets and make important decisions.

The plastic bottle she immediately filled with snow and tucked inside her parka, between her wool sweater and the thermal underwear she had on next to her skin. If she was going to stay in motion to avoid freezing, she would soon need water to drink, or risk dehydration in the effort. The snow in the bottle would melt and be reduced to a minimal amount of liquid, but it could be refilled and the process continued as long as her body was warm. Snow would also have melted in her mouth, but she knew that eating snow to satisfy thirst resulted in an unacceptable sacrifice of body heat, cooling her body core from the stomach out.

She had not eaten since just before leaving Lynn Ehlers at the tree line on the other side of American Summit, so she took out one of the Snickers bars and ate it quickly, before it could freeze in the cold. Frozen candy bars were certainly edible, but also stole body heat, and sometimes teeth. She knew a musher who had previously run more than half the Quest with a tooth broken on a frozen power bar, hoping it wouldn't cause him an agony too great to continue.

As she chewed the sugary combination of caramel, nuts, and chocolate, she determinedly started walking in the direction the snowmachine had gone. It would do no good to leave the track or try to go back over the mountain to find her team. She and her abductor had traveled much too far on the snowmachine to retrace their path on foot, and anyway she would never be able to struggle back to the summit in the storm that was still raging. It was bad enough where she was.

Somewhere, sometime, she would need rest, for not only had she made the exhausting climb to the top of the summit, she had made it twice. The tension and stress of rescuing Murray and of driving the snowmachine with a gun in her back had also taken their toll on her energy, as had the poor sleep at the stop with Ryan on the Yukon. Before long Jessie could feel the leaden-boots syndrome beginning, as she labored through the soft, deep snow.

Periodically she stopped to catch her breath, to drink what had melted in the bottle, and refill it with snow. In a treeless space at the crest of a hill the wind had all but blown away the track of the snowmachine. The farther she went, the more time it had to fill in behind the man who drove much faster than Jessie could walk. She continued in the direction that seemed most obvious, but the trees closed in around her, and soon there was nothing that looked remotely like either a track or a roadbed under the enormous expanse of white. Everything was white—the trees, the sky, the ground, the very air around her.

What the hell did I do to deserve this? she wondered. I must have done something really awful to somebody sometime without knowing it. Again, she thought of her team, stranded back on the summit. She hoped that Ehlers had found help in getting Gail Murray back down to Forty Mile. It wouldn't be long until they would be arriving there and could summon medical assistance. Jessie wished she were with them and out of this cold hell.

Maybe I could find a spruce with branches that come to the ground, she thought. I could crawl into the space under it where the snow couldn't reach and maybe find enough dead wood to build a fire.

It wouldn't last long. Then what?

Well . . . I'd be warmer.

Yeah, and no closer to any real shelter . . . still lost where no one knows where you are . . . even you.

Right. Better keep going—somewhere.

Back in Dawson they must be working on something. Delafosse was no slouch. Soon they would realize she was late getting into Eagle and go looking—she hoped. Still, they might find her team, if that hadn't already been done by some other racer, but they would have no idea where to look for her. Her abductor had planned viciously and well. She was one solitary, very small figure in a landscape so huge and white it might as well have been erased from consideration. They could hunt for weeks and never locate her, the track of her passage rubbed out by the wind and heavily falling snow.

Oh, that's depressing. Think about something else. You can't just give up.

I know. I won't. I certainly *won't*. This makes me furious. If I can beat them by surviving, you better believe I *will*.

She knew what Alex would be quoting right now, Frost—an appropriate name:

And miles to go before I sleep,
And miles to . . .

Without so much as a flicker, her headlamp suddenly went out, the batteries dead. No amount of shaking could bring it back to even a minute of hesitant life, and the extra batteries were on her sled. She thrust it into the outside pocket that had held the handgun, and went on.

In the dark, she felt disoriented and directionless. Starting down a hill, she fell over something under the snow, a fallen tree trunk, perhaps, and got up, knowing she was completely on the wrong course. Thinking for a minute, she turned ninety degrees from the direction she had been headed and walked away from it, hoping to find the track again. With no success in one direction, she followed her tracks back to where she had made the abrupt turn and walked the same distance in the other direction. That was just as fruitless, and again she returned to where she had started.

With the dark white snow blowing around her like a mist that partially obscured the ground, every hill, depression, and gully looked the same. She couldn't even tell which direction was west anymore, with the flat whiteness giving her no clues. There was nothing helpful—no stars or moon, no shadows, very little light.

Stumbling through snow almost to her hips, she realized that she had somehow left and completely lost the trail. Dazed, she searched around her again, yet saw nothing but white everywhere. She tried to put out the spark of panic that grew in her mind, but no trace of a trail appeared and fear blew the spark into a burning coal.

Well, she thought, I'm really lost. Got to stop looking for the track of that damned machine. He may have run a few circles just to confuse me anyway. I could go back and try to find the place where I messed up, but I'd better just figure out which direction seems the best and go that way. I can't stop moving, so maybe it doesn't matter so much *where* I move, as long as I don't quit. Can't quit.

It seemed there was a small separation between the few trees she could make out ahead of her, a hint of what might once have been a trail, or a trapper's track. So she went walking along it, and refilling the water bottle, as time dragged on. At some point, she ate another candy bar, hoping to give her flagging energy a boost, and it helped for a little while, but not long. Soon she began to stumble more often and knew that in not too long she was going to be in real trouble. It seemed she had been moving forward forever.

When she had walked until she was drained, Jessie began to fall. Snow covered her clothing, and her feet and hands, even in their well insulated protection, had begun to grow numb with cold. She wiggled her fingers and toes to encourage circulation.

Staggering to the crest of a small rise, she found herself looking down a long hill into a valley that was mostly obscured with swirling white. The wind blew dry curtains of snow over the edge of the hill that scoured away at her face with icy grains, then deposited them on the leeward slope. Coming and going in clouds, the snow obscured everything along the ground. As it subsided and thinned slightly, a long ways away, she thought she glimpsed some kind of dark structure, low to the ground—a cabin? Maybe. A hallucination? Maybe. Whatever it was, it seemed impossibly far away, as it disappeared into the drifting paleness—a rock outcropping, probably—just a dream spun of exhaustion, desperation, and desire.

She stood in the wind's gusts, staring stupidly at the place where it had been, disbelieving it, unable to make herself start toward it. But there was nothing else and at least it was something to aim for. Maybe it was real. There might be someone . . .

"Help," she tried to cry out, but only a ravenlike croak emerged from her dry, tired throat. "Help." Only a little louder than a whisper, it would never be heard unless she was much closer—most likely not even then.

With a burst of determination and fear, she thrust herself forward over the snowy crest and was suddenly up to her waist in a drift the wind had piled below the rise. Half buried in it, she thrashed and struggled, trying to force her body forward, miring herself in the process and sinking even deeper. With a gasp of frustration, she lost her balance and fell over into the powder, which swallowed her.

For a long minute she lay still. It felt so good to lie down. She curled into a heat-conserving ball, closed her eyes, and let her breathing steady. She felt warmer, but so very tired.

I could sleep, she thought. If I could rest for just a little while . . . then I would be able to get up and make it down the hill . . . later.

CHAPTER TWENTY-THREE

*"He was older than the days he had seen and the breaths
he had drawn. He linked the past with the present, and
the eternity behind him throbbed through him in a mighty
rhythm to which he swayed as the tides and seasons
swayed. He [was] . . . a broad-breasted dog, white-fanged
and long-furred; but behind him were the shades of all
manner of dogs, half-wolves and wild wolves, urgent and
prompting, tasting the savor of the meat he ate, thirsting for
the water he drank, scenting the wind with him, listening
with him and telling him the sounds made by the wildlife
in the forest, dictating his moods, directing his actions, lying
down to sleep with him when he lay down, and dreaming
with him and beyond him and becoming themselves the
stuff of his dreams."*
—Jack London, The Call of the Wild

AT THE TOP OF AMERICAN SUMMIT, JESSIE'S LEAD DOG,
Tank, woke suddenly from his sleep in the snow and raised
his head, listening.

For a long time after Jessie had taken something from
the sled and gone away on the iron dog that roared and
whined and smelled unpleasant, he had stood looking after
her into the curtain of snow, puzzled. Though there were
times that she depended on his judgment, it was usually
not his place to question her actions, but her abrupt departure had been as unexpected as it was unusual, and he
didn't quite know what to make of it or what to do. So

he did nothing, but waited, anticipating that she would soon reappear to tell him where she wanted him to lead the rest of the team.

Eventually, when she did not return, he thought that perhaps she had meant the team to rest, though this was not a comfortable place to sleep and she had given them nothing to eat. He grew tired of standing and was cold, for the wind had blown his fur full of snow and its icy crystals had frozen again in the hair around his eyes and nose.

The other dogs had dug themselves into the snow and lay curled in balls of fur that were rapidly drifting over, forming warmer pockets that contained their body heat and let them sleep more snugly. Making a small sound of resignation in his throat, half whine, he dug his own depression, turned around in it several times, and lay down nose to tail, where he was soon snoozing, though more lightly than the rest.

Now, in the dark, something woke him.

Raising his head, Tank poked his nose through the drift that had formed over him, and a small avalanche fell away from his inquisitive muzzle. The wind was still howling across the open plateau of the summit, drowning out all except the nearest sounds. He listened carefully, but heard nothing else. He was aware of the other dogs resting comfortably in their small caves beneath the surface of the snow, heard one stirring, shifting position slightly. The world was a whirl of flying white, difficult to see through and growing colder.

Something was wrong. Jessie had not come back and they had been resting there by the sled for quite some time, longer than she would generally leave them to fend for themselves. Where was she? Did she need him? Somehow he felt she might need him. Could she be waiting for him to bring the team to wherever she was? She had not called—or if she had, he had not heard her. But maybe that was what had broken his uneasy sleep. Had it been Jessie's voice that demanded his attention?

He stood up, turned his back to the force of the wind, tucked his tail between his legs, and thought hard.

Jessie had trained him to come with the team when she called or gestured—made sure that he knew how to bring the team by himself, without her guidance, if necessary. Sometimes she had stood on the opposite bank of a creek filled with ice and water, or walked a long ways ahead until she was hidden behind trees and brush, and called him to come. When she did this it was up to him to pick the best route through or around the obstacle, whatever it was—find her track, swim, if necessary—to bring the rest through to her. Then she always praised him, made him proud of his success.

Was this another test? If it was, it was past time to go and find her.

Shaking his coat thoroughly, he moved away from his resting spot, pulling the gang line along behind him, tightening it and the tug line that connected Pete's harness to it, disturbing the older dog, bringing him and his running mate to their feet. Time to go?

Dog by dog, the process continued as Tank moved purposely ahead in the direction Jessie had gone, until all were awake, up, and in their places along the now-taut line that connected them to the sled. They stood, yawning and shaking themselves to rid their coats of snow and ice, rested and ready to go again. But where was their driver?

If Jessie was not present, all the dogs recognized Tank as their leader. If he indicated they should pull, they did, for they counted on him to know when it was time. Now he moved, so they followed behind him, breaking the sled runners loose from where they had lightly frozen into the icy surface, pulling the sled slowly at first, then faster, until they were moving together at their usual ground-covering trot.

Tank was following the feel and scent of the trail on which Jessie had disappeared. He caught the scent of several teams that had passed this way ahead of him, along with the offensive smell of the iron dog. This was the way. There were hints of Jessie's familiar scent as well, so he knew he was on the right track.

The team was silent, for sled dogs seldom bark when

they run. Swiftly, they ran through the dark, like shadows, like a ghost team, without the usual beam from the driver's head lamp. Cleanly, efficiently, they towed the heavy sled behind them, moving in well practiced concert, a live machine, capable of long hours at this speed of travel.

They slowed once, when Tank found that the trail divided and hesitated momentarily. One track went to the right and it smelled of other dog teams pulling sleds. The other held only the smell of the iron dog, the noisy metal thing that Jessie had ridden into the dark. But it told him that she had gone that way, so that was the direction in which he turned, swinging the rest of his teammates with him, and they were off again.

The snow grew deeper, packed only in the narrower track of the iron dog, but it was sufficient to their needs and they continued to follow it. It grew crooked, winding around the sides of hills, over icy places where water had frozen under it and Tank could hear the scraping of the sled as it passed over the solid slickness. The way remained quite smooth, for, though he could not know it, under the iron dog track, beneath the snow, lay a gravel road used only in the summer. This enabled them to pull the heavy sled on a level surface, which kept it from overbalancing, as it might have on a more uneven track.

He had been hungry for a long while and thought that, when he found Jessie, she would feed him, give him something to drink, also. That was an encouraging idea that made him increase their speed slightly, as the steep hills gave way to flatter ground and the trail, with its olfactory hints of her, began to pass between trees.

Her scent was growing stronger. Soon, now, he was sure he would find her waiting for him with dinner and approval for his ability and talent in following the difficult trail without direct guidance—the test she had set him.

Soon. He would find her, soon.

At five in the morning in Dawson, the lights were still burning in the Delafosse cabin and no one was asleep.

Claire sat in one of the chairs by the fire, periodically poking at it nervously. Del had just taken several empty glasses and coffee cups to the kitchen and returned with the rest of the apple pie on three plates.

"It's long past time for her to have made it into Eagle," Caswell stated in irritation and worry, as he paced the floor, unable to be still. "Why haven't we heard? Something must be wrong."

"I know, and I don't like it." Delafosse set the pie on the hearth, crossed to the telephone, and reached for the receiver. "Enough waiting. I'm going to call Eagle."

Before he could lift it, the instrument rang demandingly under his hand.

"Delafosse."

In growing concern, Cas watched him.

"How long ago? How bad is it? Yes. You've already contacted them? Yes. Who brought her in? Did he say anything about meeting Jessie Arnold? Get him on the line, will you?"

Another space of silent attention.

"Yes . . . hello? Yes. Is this Ehlers? What happened up there? Really an accident? You're sure?"

Claire got up from her chair and came to stand beside Cas, also listening intently.

"She told you what was going on, then? Yes, I do understand. Yes. What time? No, she hasn't reached Eagle—at least she hasn't called. That's true. No. We don't know."

A pause, then, "You're sure? Okay, but take it easy, and look carefully to see if there's anything to give us a clue also at what . . . Yes. I'll wait for it. Thanks."

Shaking his head, he finally hung up the phone and turned to Cas and Claire, who were both waiting, tense and anxious.

"That was Forty Mile. Half an hour ago a musher named Ehlers brought another, Gail Murray, down from the summit with a broken leg and a certain amount of hypothermia from exposure. She may have frozen a few toes, but seems okay otherwise.

"That was Ehlers I talked to last. He said that he met Jessie coming back down from pretty close to the top with Murray, working both their teams. She had found Murray pinned under the hurt woman's sled that had tipped over on a switchback. Ehlers volunteered to take over and bring her down. He says Jessie turned around and went right back up there. Says she told him she had something important to do but he hasn't told the race officials that she was going to deliver the ransom. She told him to get hold of me and let me know she was running behind schedule."

"She's still behind schedule," Cas calculated. "That accounts for part of the time, but she still should have reached Eagle by now."

"That's what Ehlers thinks, too. He's going to get some sleep, then head back up there. He's hours behind and it's blowing a real son-of-a-bitch blizzard on top, but maybe he can find out something. Or maybe she'll make it into the Eagle checkpoint ahead of him."

"Who is this Ehlers guy? Any possibility that—"

"I don't know, but I sure do intend to find out—and fast. Let's go down to the Quest office and get some information. Claire, why don't you go on to bed. We'll be back soon."

"Not a chance, you closet chauvinist. You think I could sleep now? I'm going, too."

The temper that went along with the red hair had made its first appearance, soliciting a grin from Cas.

"Guess you asked for that one, Del."

"Guess I did at that. Sorry, Claire."

John Noble—who had arrived in Forty Mile ahead of Jessie, wet and chilled, and left behind her—made it through to Eagle. When two more racers reached Eagle without seeing any trace of her or her team on the mountain, those waiting in Dawson knew that something had gone terribly wrong on American Summit.

They immediately headed for Eagle.

CHAPTER TWENTY-FOUR

"When the frost grows lusty at sixty below, men cannot long remain without fire or excessive exercise, and live."
—Jack London, "A Daughter of the Aurora"

THERE WAS A SOFT PILLOW AND SHE WAS WARM AND DRY IN her own big brass bed—safe . . . and warm. If she opened her eyes she would be able to see the log walls of her home cabin and the row of mustache mugs that belonged to Alex on a shelf across the room. He must be awake and already up, for she seemed to smell coffee brewing and hear the sizzle of bacon in the big cast-iron frying pan.

Ah, well . . . time to get up if she wanted her two eggs over-easy to really *be* over-easy. Alex always overcooked them. He liked his eggs fried hard enough so there was no runny yellow yolk to wipe from the plate with the last crust of toast. What a waste.

Jessie opened her eyes—and was blind.

There was nothing but black before her.

It isn't really dark when you close your eyes, she thought. If you look carefully you can see colors behind your eyelids, lines and swirls, shimmering spots. It's only completely dark when you open your eyes and there is absolutely no light at all. Closing her eyes again, she compared the two, thoughtfully.

It was cold. Had she left the window open too far again? No. It was her feet that were cold. She assessed the situation, opened her eyes to the blackness once more, and realized that her whole body was cold—terribly cold. What the hell was going on? Where was she?

Outside. You're outside.

How could I be outside? It's the middle of the winter.

A race. You were running a race.

What race?

A race on the river.

The Yukon Quest, she remembered suddenly.

And you got lost.

Well, I'll go back to sleep for a little while and think about it later.

You'll freeze.

How could I freeze? I'm warm.

No, you're not. You're outside in the snow. You're cold. Too cold. Don't go back to sleep.

She sat up, the snow fell away from her, and it was true. Suddenly there was . . . not light, but . . . less dark. Wind and snow were hitting her face, but she could hardly feel it.

I fell down, she recalled clearly, and it buried me. I've got to get up. I *will* freeze if I don't.

Staggering to her feet, she began wearily to fight her way out of the deep drift into which she had floundered. Carefully this time, she worked hard at getting out on the downhill side. Soon the snow released her, came only to her thighs and, relieved, she found she could move through it.

Was a cabin—somewhere? I thought I saw something before I fell. How long did I lie there? Too long.

Stomping her numb feet and swinging her arms to hit her wooden hands together to encourage circulation, she stood trying to see around her. Looking back, she could make out the rise from which she had fallen and figured out in which direction she had been looking before that. If there had been a cabin—a shelter of any kind—if her eyes weren't playing tricks on her, it had been off to the left a little and had seemed a long ways away. Tucking her hands into her armpits, she started moving in that direction. It was as good as any other.

You must not lie down again, she told herself. Whatever happens, you *must not lie down*.

Right.

There was a grove of trees, tall birch, bare bones without leaves, to her right, and a long open slope, partially obscured by blowing snow, out ahead. Keeping near the trees, where the snow seemed a little less deep, she wallowed and reeled through it, going down along that slope.

It was all she could do to keep putting one foot in front of the other. Once again she fell, and forced herself up immediately, as she felt the desire to lie there sweep over her in frightening waves. For a long, long time she struggled on through the whiteness of the world around her, and began to feel slightly warm again. Was it really warmth created by action, or that seductive pseudo-warmth of lowered body temperature, lack of energy—freezing? She dared not assume either.

The slope finally ended in a stand of snow-draped willow. It had the shape of a creek—hidden under the drifts, lined with willow brush. Looking up, she found she could see a dark squarish shape beyond it.

There *was* a cabin. It wasn't the hallucination she had feared and refused to let into her mind. It was really *there*.

Summoning the last of her strength, she found a space between the willows and dropped down onto the creek, crossed it, feeling the hard ice beneath the snow, and forced her way back up onto the opposite bank.

Where was the door? There had to be a door.

Rounding a corner of the cabin, she found she had walked out of the deep snow in which she had become accustomed to walking and onto a surface that was packed. A vehicle had driven there, almost up to the door she could now see next to a window. There was a dim light in the window. Someone was *there?* The man on the snowmachine?

Fear of him left her mind—wasn't important—didn't

matter. Only attaining the shelter of the log structure mattered. There was nothing else.

Jessie moved to the door, pulled off one of her heavy mittens to open it, walked in, and closed it by falling back against it.

Warm. It had to be warm, for there was no snow inside, but she was so cold she could not feel it. Gradually she sank down into a heap on the plank floor, closed her eyes, and lay there, gasping for breath.

"Jessie? Jessie Arnold? Oh, God. Is it really you, Jessie?"

There was a voice and someone was kneeling beside her on the floor, shaking her shoulder.

"Jessie. Wake up, Jessie. Where did you come from? How did you find me?"

Slowly, Jessie became aware of her surroundings and the woman who kept calling her name frantically—and sniffling.

"Let me alone."

The shaking continued.

"*Please*, Jessie."

Raising her head a little from the floor, Jessie peered at the shape of the head, silhouetted in the dull light from a fire that burned feebly across the room and drew her attention like a magnet.

"*Debbie?*"

"Yes. How did you ever figure out where I am? *I* don't even know where I am."

Jessie's teeth chattered and her whole body was shaking.

"Look . . . I'm really . . . cold. Let me get warm . . . okay?"

Rolling over, she made it to her hands and knees and crawled across the uneven surface of the plank floor to where a tiny fire burned in an old fireplace made of river stone. A barrel stove would have been more efficient at holding the heat, but even this diminutive flame was a small heaven of warmth and light. Probably better that she didn't warm up too fast anyway.

Stripping off the other mitten and the gloves that still covered her hands, she lay down by it and held both palms out toward the warm glow.

"My feet. Can you . . . get my boots off?"

Tears still running down her face, Debbie worked at the laces and pulled them off.

"Oh, Jessie. I'm so glad to see you. I was so scared. I thought I'd just die here—all by myself."

"Not if I can help it, you won't. But I can hardly believe I stumbled onto you by accident."

Jessie's wool socks were damp. She moved her feet in them closer to the fire, but not too close, and lay soaking in the small heat it generated. If her hands or feet were at all frozen, dry heat was one of the worst things for them.

She waited, expecting their recovery to be painful, but just two fingers began to throb a little as they warmed— the rest felt stiff and cramped, but she began to be able to move them. Relieved, she pulled off her socks and checked her feet. The heavy, insulated boots had done their job well—no frostbite was apparent.

"I think I made it just in time. Can you put on some more . . . wood?"

"There's only a few sticks left," Debbie told her. "I think we'd better save it."

"What do you mean? If they were using this place to keep you, there must be wood."

"No. There wasn't much and they burned most of it in big fires before they left."

"Who is *they*? Who were they, Debbie?"

"I don't know, except for one that I saw when I wasn't supposed to, and I didn't recognize him. They kept me blindfolded and tied up all the time—until just before they left. That's when I saw that one guy—for just a second, as he went out the door."

"What did he look like?"

"Oh, sort of tall and nice looking—maybe thirty-something. He had on a snowmachine suit—all black. I didn't know him."

"How many were there?"

"Two—but they talked about at least two more. From the sound of his voice the other one was older, but the younger one was in charge. They didn't seem to like each other much."

"What gave you that idea?"

"Oh, just the way they talked. You know. The older one didn't like the other one bossing him around. He didn't like staying here while the other one was gone, either. There wasn't much he did like—he was mean."

This younger man might be the one who had picked her up on the summit, Jessie thought. So, Debbie could recognize him.

"How long was the younger one gone?"

"I don't know. A long time. They packed up and left right after he came back."

"How long ago did they leave? Are they coming back?"

"Hours ago. I don't think so. They took everything with them on the snowmachines."

"They had two?"

"Yeah. They must have brought me here on one of them while I was still knocked out from a shot they gave me. I woke up here a couple of days ago. They've been gone for hours now. They laughed about how I wouldn't be found till spring."

"*Jesus*. Why are you still here? Didn't you think about trying to walk out?"

The young woman held out her bare hands and pointed to her feet, clad only in wool socks, like Jessie's. Though she wore her parka and the rest of her outdoor racing clothes, the bright mittens that Jessie had noticed in their meeting before Braeburn were absent, along with their idiot string.

"How could I leave?" Debbie asked, bitterly. "They took my mittens—and my boots."

Jessie stared at her in astonishment and horror.

With little wood, the purposeful theft of the mittens and boots was a death sentence, for without them there was no way the young woman could have left the cabin, even to collect anything to burn, without freezing her feet and hands. They had clearly intended that she should stay here—permanently.

"I assume they fed you while they were here. Did they leave you any food?"

"They fed me some sandwiches and junk food. But no, they didn't leave anything. Took it all with them. Said I wouldn't need it—that . . ." She swallowed hard and began to cry silently. "That . . . it would just prolong . . . the inevitable."

"Dear God. What—"

"Could we not talk about it, please? I just can't."

She sneezed, wiped her eyes and nose with a grimy tissue she dug out of one pocket, took a deep breath, and changed the subject.

"Jessie . . . how's Jake? What's happening with him . . . and my mom? I know they got asked for a lot of money to get me back. And the young one was excited about having got it when he came back. Do you know anything about my team and sled? Did they . . . hurt my dogs?"

Jessie hesitated, not wanting to worry the young woman more than necessary, feeling sick at how she had been treated—afraid to ask more at the moment. She wanted to reassure Debbie, but saw no reason to go into detail.

"Your dogs and sled are fine. Someone found them and brought them into the checkpoint. Your parents paid the money, with help from some other people. I carried it to one of the kidnappers on a snowmachine. Jake's okay, Debbie. He and your mom are really worried about you, of course, and doing everything they can to get you back. Your mom came to Dawson when she heard. A lot of people are looking for you."

"I'll bet she blamed him for letting me go in the race, didn't she?"

A small lie: "I don't know, Deb. But it'll be all right. We'll get out of here somehow." A quick change of subject. "Look, I've got a lot more questions about how they grabbed you in the first place and other things, but right now we need more wood."

"Where do we get that? I've burned everything I could find or pry loose—a couple of planks from the floor, an old wooden box . . ."

"You may not be able to go outside, but I've still got *my* boots. I've also got a wire saw that I can use to cut dead wood from some of the trees. We'll stay warm, at least, as soon as my hands and feet are a little better. But, honestly, I don't know how we can travel anywhere with you in stockinged feet."

Debbie gave her a long silent look, fear creeping back into her eyes, before she spoke, bravely.

"You could go, Jessie. Maybe you could get me some wood—lots of wood—then go by yourself—find someone to come back for me. But . . . you might not make it. I don't know where we are."

More tears of frustration, anger, and fear ran down her face to drip off her chin.

"I've got a pretty good idea," Jessie told her. "But before we think about it, I'll go after wood."

"Wood will keep us warm for a while, but without food we'll both die here. You'd really better go."

Gutsy, Jessie thought. Really courageous for such a young person in these circumstances.

"Or you could go," she told Debbie. "My boots would fit you, too, I bet, and you aren't as tired as I am. I walked here halfway from the summit, after that son of a bitch dumped me off the snowmachine and left me. I didn't know you were here. I just got lucky, that's all—we both did."

"He left you, too?"

"Yes, the bastard. But let's talk about what to do after I play woodsman, okay? I'll also fill my water bottle with snow, so it can melt us some water to drink."

Debbie slumped in discouragement that suddenly appeared, as she thought about their situation and her courage ebbed.

"But we haven't got anything else—nothing to eat. We have nothing. Do you think we're going to die?"

Jessie grinned at her, remembering what was left of her emergency supplies.

"Hey, Deb. We're not alone, at least. We have each other, and we'll soon have heat and water. And what you don't know is that we've got more than that."

She took the plastic bag from the inside pocket of her parka.

"Look. We have *four* Snickers bars. We're rich."

CHAPTER TWENTY-FIVE

"It is very easy for a hungry man to freeze."
—Jack London, "The Sun-Dog Trail"

A SIZABLE FIRE WAS BURNING IN THE STONE FIREPLACE OF the old log cabin, and a substantial pile of branches, twigs, and broken bits of dead wood that Jessie had dragged in from outside was drying across the small room, dripping melting snow into pools of dampness that soaked into the dry planks of the floor. They had used the wire saw, attaching two sticks for handles through the loops at either end, and, stretching it taut between them, pulled it back and forth so that the sharp metal cord chewed into the wood, making pieces of reasonable size. They elected to burn some of the larger branches, one at a time, by laying one end in the blaze and moving it farther into the fire as it was consumed, conserving the energy it would have required to cut it.

In front of this luxurious blaze, the two women, warm enough to open their parkas, sat on the floor by the hearth chewing small bites from half a Snickers bar each.

"All right," Jessie agreed, reluctant at the thought of returning to the frozen world outside. "I'm willing to go and try to make it out to somewhere, find someone, if you are sure you can stay here alone. But I'll have to get some rest first and it will be best to wait till it gets light, because it's easier to get lost in the dark. I've been lost once and it turned out okay, but it might not have, and I'd rather give myself the best chance I can. Those snowmachines have left tracks that can probably be followed out to the road, though it's miles to Tetlin Junction, I'd guess.''

''You won't want to follow them in that direction. They were going to go east, up to the summit, then to Eagle, I think—maybe Dawson. From the way they talked, they hadn't completely made up their minds. It seemed to depend on the weather, or someone—something—else. I couldn't ever really tell.''

''That's strange. You'd think they'd want to get as far as possible from the race and people who will be looking for anything suspicious. Your parents are in Dawson with the race officials—who know about this, by the way—and the RCMP inspector, who's working hard on it. They may think these guys are gone, but they won't take any chances with anyone who comes into town from American Summit.''

''Well, maybe so, but that's what they said.''

''Exactly what did they say?''

''The younger one mentioned someone in Dawson they were supposed to contact, but he didn't want to. They argued about where to go, Eagle or Dawson. The younger one wanted to go to Eagle because no one would expect them there. The other one said they would be less obvious if they slipped in with all the people in Dawson. But the other guy said there was no reason to share the money, if they could get away with it before the others could do anything about it—so he wanted to stay away from Dawson, because of that other person.''

''Did they mention a name?''

''Yes, but I didn't recognize it and now I can't remember what it was.''

''Any other clue to his identity?''

''No . . . well, they said no one would ever suspect him. Whatever that means.''

''It means it may be someone who's involved with the

race in some way. Someone who would be expected to be there—wouldn't seem questionable.''

Jessie remembered wondering how the snowmachine driver had known she had a gun, when most racers wouldn't have them because of Canada's handgun laws. Once again, she ran through her mental list of possible suspects and came up as empty of any real idea as before. Who could it be? She was too tired to think.

"I'm going to try to sleep for a couple of hours, Debbie. When I wake up it should be light and I'll make a try at walking out of here. You should sleep, too—save your energy.''

They added wood to the fire, lay down by it, and were soon asleep. In her exhaustion, Jessie dreamed no dreams at first, but Debbie whimpered and muttered in her sleep several times, reliving the nightmare reality of her last few days of captivity. Awake, she knew she was, if not completely safe, at least out of the hands of her abductors. Asleep, she wasn't so sure.

She could hear dogs barking. Then, out of the woods next to her snug log house in Knik, Jessie watched Tank bring the team into the dog yard. Sunny was running in his usual place, as was Wart. She hadn't lost them after all. Tank saw her and stopped the team. Then he barked. What was wrong to inspire him to bark? What was he trying to tell her? Then the whole team began to bark and howl. It became a cacophony of howls and *ki-yai* yips.

A piece of wood in the fire fell with a thump, waking her to half-consciousness and concern. More wood. Get up, Jessie, and put some more on the fire.

She opened her eyes and realized that she could still faintly hear the canine chorale from her dream. Sitting up, she listened, expecting it to fade as she woke completely. It didn't.

"Debbie." She reached to shove at one of the feet of the still-sleeping younger woman. "Hey, Deb. Wake up.''

"Aw-w . . . what? I'm awake.''

"Listen. Do you hear dogs? What the hell is that?"
They sat for a minute, listening intently.
"That *is* dogs! It *is*."
"Could it be wolves?" Debbie asked.
"Not a chance. If I didn't know better . . ."
Getting to her feet, Jessie headed for the cabin door and threw it open.

Outside, the snow had stopped and it was growing light enough to distinguish shapes against the stark white of the ground.

The sounds were louder now. Definitely dogs.

Stomping on the boots she had left near the door, she went out to the corner of the cabin and looked in the direction from which the howls and barks were coming— between the willows she had stumbled through last night to reach the structure.

Tangled in a snarl of line and harness, below the bank, on the ice that had silenced the voice of the creek's gurgling water, was her own team, struggling to get out, the heavy sled tipped over and lying on its side next to them.

"I don't *believe* this," she said, glancing back at Debbie, who had followed her to the door. "Those are *my* guys. Somehow they've followed me and found us. I absolutely *do not believe* this."

But it was true, and as soon as she had zipped her parka and donned her mittens, she hurried to unscramble the knot they had fallen into in their attempt to cross the creek.

Tank greeted her with a wide doggy grin. The Darryls licked her ears as she hugged them both at once, and Pete responded to an affectionate head-rubbing with a yip of hello. The rest were vocal, but Bliss was ecstatic, leaping to set both front feet against Jessie's hip to be petted, a thing not usually encouraged. Jessie did not reprimand her, understanding the feeling of delight so strongly herself that it brought tears to her eyes.

"Oh, you beautiful mutts. Such good, *good* dogs you are. Good puppies to come so far and so well." Sinking to her knees, she took her leader's head between her hands and kissed him directly between the eyes, caressed his ears. "Tank, I *love* you. You are the very, very best leader ever. How smart you are and what a good job you've done. Good, good dogs, all of you."

Swiftly, she untangled their traces and got them lined up in order on the bank. With their pulling and her pushing, they managed to right the sled and pull it out of the creek bed to a position next to the cabin door.

Debbie still hovered in the half-open door, smiling widely.

"Are they *really* yours? How did they get here?"

"The only way they could have is to have followed my track from the summit. It's incredible. They came all that long way by themselves, without getting stuck or tipping the sled over. I don't know how—it's hardly possible—but they clearly did it."

"What great dogs."

"You've got that right. Now we have food, Debbie. And not only that. I have an extra pair of boots in the bag—I always travel with them, just in case. But the first thing I have to do is water these guys and feed them the very best meal I can come up with." Jessie was so relieved and overwhelmed that she heard herself pouring it out in words and couldn't seem to stop. "Don't build up the fire again, will you? It'll be too warm and I'm going to bring them inside for breakfast and a good rest. They've earned it. How do you feel about sausage and pancakes before we plan how to get out of here?"

"I feel just fine about them. Have you got any more of that peppermint tea?"

Turning, Jessie gave Debbie a warm smile, and slowed down a little to appreciate the importance of such a simple request after all the younger woman had been through.

"I do, indeed."

Just after noon, as the two women headed uphill for American Summit, the sun showed up between the clouds that were rapidly dissipating, and sent long beams of glowing gold between the trees. It reflected from the soft, powdery snow in sparkles that seemed a celebration of their deliverance.

The world through which they passed was drifted high with clean white so deep that it could easily become traps for the unwary, but it also covered anything ugly or unsightly. It was not perfect—there were still answers to be found for the many questions in Jessie's mind—but it seemed particularly sweet, as she drove her thankfully recovered team, and appreciated the quiet windless sunshine, though the temperature read several degrees under forty below on her thermometer.

Tank led his teammates steadily forward, casting a look back every now and then, checking to be sure she was still riding the runners on the back of the sled, where she should be. Debbie Todd rode in the sled, her feet warm in Jessie's extra boots, hands in similarly loaned mittens, over a pair of wool socks. Like the dogs, she and Jessie were both well fed and filled with new energy generated by rest, food, and their relief at the unexpected, extraordinary solution to the situation they now agreed had been more desperate than either of them wanted to admit or dwell on.

Jessie listened contentedly to the soft, familiar *shush* of the sled runners on the snow, feeling there should be some kind of musical accompaniment. Huge orchestral swells with lots of strings and trumpets would have been appropriate. She couldn't seem to stop smiling.

Curious, and a little anxious to know exactly where the snowmachine riders had gone, Jessie followed the tracks that were just visible under a layer of snow that had been deposited before the storm abated. As Debbie had predicted, it was clear that they had not decided to disappear onto the highways of Alaska, but, upon reaching the road that would have taken them there, had turned and gone back up instead, toward the summit and either Eagle or Dawson. Not wanting to run into them accidentally, both women watched carefully, and were glad that, in the clear sun-filled air, it was not difficult to see a reasonable distance ahead.

Even with Debbie's extra weight in the sled, the dogs pulled easily and well, keeping up an enthusiastic, steady pace that drew them to the summit faster than Jessie had hoped. There the wind had died and it was possible to see practically forever over the rolling plateau with its twisted trees that no longer looked half alive, but merely wind-tortured into their strange unearthly misshapes.

The team carried them back up along the snowbound Taylor Highway which Jessie had been forced to cross in the opposite direction the day before, and finally brought them to where the Yukon Quest race route joined it for the downhill run to Eagle. In all that way, they saw no one. Now Jessie stopped the sled to give the team a rest, as well as to examine the junction to see if there were any sign of which direction the two men on snowmachines had gone. There were marks of all kinds in the snow—those of sleds and the feet of dogs, and a confusing number of snowmachine tracks.

Debbie had climbed out of the sled, stretched to relieve a few kinks from bouncing over the irregularities of the trail, and gone forward to pet the dogs, when she suddenly straightened, her attention drawn to a distant rise in the direction of Forty Mile.

"Jessie," she called, with a hint of tension in her voice. "Hey, look, there's someone coming."

Jessie stood up from her careful scrutiny of the tracks, and shaded her eyes with one mittened hand to see, momentarily concerned. What she saw soon relieved her anxiety.

Coming up the trail, too far away to identify, was a team of sled dogs, their driver pumping hard with one foot, then the other, from the rear runners of the sled.

They waited and watched as the racer drew slowly closer, raised one hand, and waved, long before he was close enough to communicate vocally.

"It's Lynn Ehlers," Jessie said with a smile, when he

was near enough to recognize. "He's coming back up from taking Gail Murray to Forty Mile."

"Forty Mile? Why?"

By the time Jessie had filled Debbie in on the accident Murray had suffered on the summit, Ehlers had covered the remaining distance and pulled up next to them, grinning broadly.

"You *found* her. Terrific. Good going, Jess."

"Yes, well . . . not exactly through super sleuthing," Jessie told him. "I just . . . stumbled into the same place. We sort of saved each other, with the help of my team."

"Where? What happened?"

"Let me make a fire and get some food going for these wonderful, intelligent, talented, fantastic dogs of mine, and I'll tell you."

"Sounds like they've been exceptionally good at something."

"You couldn't guess the half of it. There has *never* been a team like this one."

"Aw—all you Alaskan mushers are inclined to see things larger than life. Has to come from living in such a big place—the water, the air—something."

She laughed. "Maybe. Whatever it is, I love it. This wild, wonderful country is the best place I can even imagine. I'm afraid I'm hooked—couldn't live anywhere else."

CHAPTER TWENTY-SIX

"You've thrust the soul from a living man's body . . . the hand of all mankind is against you, and there is no place you may lay your head."
    —Jack London, "Which Make Men Remember"

THE REMAINING FIFTY MILES TO EAGLE TOOK THE TWO TEAMS just over ten hours, including time for one extended rest break. They came down to the small community on the banks of the Yukon River just after midnight on the steep plowed road that was the last of the Taylor Highway, glided through town toward the checkpoint next to the old schoolhouse, and were rewarded by the reverberating clamor of the bell that was rung to announce the arrival of each and every racer.

People began to appear on the street, pouring from doorways to run alongside the sleds.

"Welcome to Eagle."

"Who is it?"

"God—it's Jessie Arnold . . ."

". . . Ehlers . . . "

". . . in the sled . . . Jake's girl . . ."

Ned Bishop was dumbstruck when she pulled up at the checkpoint. So startled to see her that it seemed all he could do to remember his job.

"Holy shit—*Jessie*. Where the hell have you been? We've been worried sick—everyone looking everywhere

258

for you—and Debbie Todd. Half the snowmachines from here to Dawson have been up on the summit. They found nothing but a buried pile of equipment and stuff—''

"Gail Murray's."

"How'd you find her? The planes were going out today—a helicopter coming from Whitehorse."

Realizing Jessie had no way of giving him answers through the storm of his questions, Bishop finally stopped trying to ask and tell everything at once.

Jessie stomped in the snow hook and stepped from the runners to give Debbie a hand out of the sled.

"I noticed the tracks of a lot of traffic back up there," she told him, grinning. "You wouldn't believe me if I told you all about where we've been and how we came back. But I will, if you'll check me in first."

"You going to finish?"

"Why not? I'm a little behind, but I've made it this far. It's gotta get better from here. Right?"

He just nodded, his mouth hanging open as if he would never understand the way mushers operated, and almost automatically began his usual checklist of the items required of a Yukon Quest racer.

"Deb? *Debbie.*"

Calling her name, Leland fought his way through the growing crowd of spectators to reach his stepdaughter. All but knocking her from her feet with the enormity of his hug, he rocked her back and forth in his arms, tears streaming unabashedly down his face. "Oh, God, Deborah, we were so worried."

"Hey, Jake," she said, her arms tight around his neck. "It's okay. I'm fine—*really.* Where's Mom?"

"Jessie?"

She turned from enjoying the enthusiastic Todd-Leland reunion to find Inspector Delafosse beside her, with Cas.

"Hi," she said. "Sorry I couldn't—"

"Hi, yourself," Del told her. "No need for sorrys now. Looks like you did well enough without us."

"Not till those bastards are caught. I think . . ." She paused as he directed a nod to the space behind her.

"Somebody else here to say hello," Del said.

Already knowing, she whirled and there was . . .

"*Alex*. However did you . . . ?"

But she didn't care, as she was swept into a giant, now-I'm-home embrace of her own.

"The snowmachine came out of the trees and onto the lake, right at me—"

"Mandana Lake?" Jake asked.

"Yes, about two-thirds of the way across."

Jessie had already told the rescue tale and Debbie was telling the assembled group about her abduction. Sitting next to Jake Leland, she assessed the faces at the table in the schoolhouse, around which everyone in Eagle who had been involved in the situation, even in a small way, had gathered: Delafosse, Cas, Jessie and Alex, Ned Bishop, Ryan—who had been about to leave when Jessie showed up at the Eagle checkpoint—and Lynn Ehlers.

"Let her tell it all, Jake," Delafosse suggested. "Then we can ask questions and fill in the gaps, if there are any. Go ahead, Debbie."

"Well, the snowmachine came right at me. The man riding it had on an all-black snowmachine suit and a dark helmet that I couldn't see his face through. It scared me. I had a run-in with another machine a while back and I don't like those things at all. I was watching him pretty close and expecting him to turn and stay away from my team—I was obviously on the trail and all—but he just kept coming. I stopped the team and got off, ran up by the dogs, and was waving, thinking that for some weird reason he hadn't seen me. He ran right up to us, then he started making circles around my team and sled, getting closer and closer. The dogs were all nervous and I was scared. Finally I got back on and drove off, hoping he wouldn't be really stupid and run into a team in motion.

I hoped he was just being obnoxious—you know?—and would go away.

"But he kept right behind me, even when I went up off the lake ice and into the trees. Then, after a while, there was another snowmachine coming toward me on the trail with two people on it. With one coming behind me and one in front, I stopped again. They stopped, too, and got off their machines. That's when the one guy—the one behind me—took out a gun and made me get on his machine and drive."

"That's just what he did to me on the summit," Jessie said.

Debbie nodded. "Yeah, it had to be the same guy, Jessie. We went a long way in the dark until we finally stopped at a place where there were some old cabins."

"Minto?" Caswell muttered to Delafosse, who nodded.

"There were just the two of us on the snowmachine," Debbie continued. "The other two went somewhere else with my team, I think. Jessie says they left it by the highway—and that they killed somebody's handler?"

"They did," Delafosse confirmed. "We've got your team in Whitehorse, Debbie. It's fine."

"They didn't get Royal. I let him go when I stopped the second time. I was afraid they'd hurt my dogs, but he was the only one I could cut loose. He took off when they tried to catch him. You haven't found him?"

"As a matter of fact, they found him in Carmacks yesterday," Jake told her. "He came in by himself. A musher found him sleeping with his team when he went to feed them. He's okay, just a little thin."

"Oh, thank goodness. Well, after we got to . . ."

"Minto," Delafosse reminded her.

"Yeah, after we were there awhile, the other two showed up in a truck—I heard it, but didn't see it. Up till then, I couldn't see their faces because they had helmets on. Before the one with me took his off, he blindfolded me and told me not to look, or they'd have to kill me. Sometime later they gave me a sandwich, a candy bar, and some water. Then they gave me a shot of some kind and I don't remember anything else till I woke up in the cabin on the other side of the summit, where you found me, Jessie.''

"So you don't know how long it was between the time they gave you the shot and when you woke up in that cabin?" Delafosse asked.

"No, but it must have been a long time, because I was really hungry. I felt awfully sick after I woke up, then I thought I'd starve. They fed me sandwiches—balogna and mustard. Yuck, I'll never eat another one—ever. And water, they gave me water. Then they argued with each other, and the younger one was gone for a long time. He finally came back all happy with the money and they took my mittens and boots, and left.''

"How many of them?"

"Two, but there were more that they talked about—another two, I think. It was hard to tell sometimes. I kept going back to sleep, and then I just let them think I was asleep for a while, but it was so uncomfortable tied up.''

"They tied you?"

"Yeah—well, I was tied when I woke up the first time in the cabin.''

Delafosse glanced at Leland before his next question.

"Did they hurt you, Debbie? Sorry, but I have to ask. Did they . . . harm you?"

She blushed and shook her head, but answered strongly. "No. The older one mentioned it once—like *why not*, what would it matter *anyway?*—but the other one told him to forget it, so he didn't do anything. I was panicked. That's when I thought they were going to shoot me, but they just made sure I couldn't leave, and went away.''

"Left her there to starve and freeze to death," Leland exploded. "What kind of bastards would do that?"

"It is permanently engraved on my awareness, Jake," Delafosse told him. "And I promise you we'll get them, somehow. Right now we need more information. They kept you blindfolded the whole time?"

"Yes, except right as the younger one went out the door the last time. I thought he had gone, and pulled off the blindfold just as he went out and he hadn't put on the helmet yet, so I got a pretty good look at him, but only for a second."

"Would you know him if you saw him again?"

"I sure would."

"Tell us what he looked like."

"He was thirty-some, maybe thirty-five. Quite a lot older than me, but younger than you, Jake."

"What else?"

"He was kind of tall and really good-looking. I'd have thought he was a nice person, if I hadn't known better."

"Good-looking how? Who would he remind you of—maybe not exactly, but in kind of looks?"

"Oh, sort of like—this is going to sound dumb—but he reminded me of the angel on our Christmas tree. Kind of thin-faced, even features, kind of . . . pretty. You know what I mean? Great teeth. I saw his teeth—white and straight. Kind of blond/brown hair—pretty short. I didn't see his eyes except from the side."

"Some angel," Leland growled. "Devil, maybe."

"How about the other one—the older one?"

"I didn't ever see him."

Alex had been completely silent, feeling that he should let Delafosse run the questioning. Now he couldn't resist a question.

"You heard him, though, Debbie. Would you recognize his voice if you heard it again?"

"Ah, yes . . . I think so. He sounded grumpy."

"Low or high voice?"

"Low. Kind of like he smoked a lot."

"Did either of them say anything that would give you any idea of where they lived, or what kind of work they did?" Delafosse asked.

"No . . . well, they knew about driving dogs and the Quest. The older one was angry because he wasn't racing in it."

Something rang a bell in Jessie's mind. Where had she heard that before? Braeburn. The guy in the restaurant in Braeburn.

" 'Hoo-Doo' Wilson," she said suddenly.

"What?" Delafosse, along with the others, turned to look at her.

"Cal Wilson. They call him 'Hoo-Doo.' I don't know why. Anyone remember him from racing years ago?"

Ryan nodded. "Don't know him, but I've heard of him—seen a picture. He ran the Iditarod a few times early on, didn't he?"

Everyone else looked perplexed.

"Right. I heard him complaining in Braeburn about how the races weren't fair, too expensive, and somebody ought to do something about it. That was Monday, the day after the race started."

"Same day they took Debbie," Cas calculated.

"Anyone else see this guy anywhere on the race?" Delafosse asked.

"They wouldn't know what he looks like," Alex reminded him.

"But he's here," Ryan said. "Or he was a while ago. I saw him in the Trading Company Cafe. At least I think it was him."

"So—they came here. I sort of thought they would have gone to Dawson." Jessie straightened attentively.

"I heard him ask about snowmachine repairs," Ryan said with a sly grin.

"You mean one of these bastards that took my daughter is here in town?" Leland roared.

"Come back here and sit down, Jake," Delafosse told him. "It looks like he may be—if he *is* involved—but let's not go about this wrong. We'll have to prove it somehow. Debbie, you said you'd know his voice?"

"I think so."

"Well, if we can find him, let's find out." Leland immediately got to his feet again, headed for the door.

"No, Jake," Delafosse commanded. "I don't want any

trouble and you'd be inclined—with good reason—to punch him out before we could get answers. Besides, if he sees you, he'll know what's what, and may refuse to answer anything. You stay here with Debbie. She's going to need some support in seeing this guy again."

Jessie was glad he had noticed the apprehension growing on the young woman's face, and settled back in her chair.

"If we find him, we'll bring him back here for questioning. Debbie, I want you and Jake to go with Jessie into the next room where you can hear but he won't see you. If you know his voice—are sure it's him—let Jessie come in to tell us, okay?"

"Sure." But Debbie looked decidedly uneasy.

While the rest waited, Del, Cas, and Alex went to see if they could find "Hoo-Doo" Wilson, taking Ryan along to pick him out. It wasn't long before Lynn Ehlers, who'd been keeping watch from a window, saw them coming back up the street with Wilson in tow. Debbie, Jake, and Jessie left the room as Delafosse had instructed.

"I don't understand what the hell you want from me," Wilson was complaining, as they ushered him inside. "I'm just watching the race—and trying to get my snowmachine fixed."

Delafosse waved a hand at a chair on the side of the table that would put the man's back to the door into the adjoining room.

"Sit down, Wilson. We just have a few questions—need a little help on something."

"Who's that?" He pointed at Ehlers, who had returned to his seat at the table. Ned Bishop was absent, having been called outside to check in another incoming Quest racer.

"Meet Lynn Ehlers from Minnesota—one of the mushers in this race."

"All the way from Minnesota? Must have cost you a bundle. Think you got your money's worth?"

He got an ironic half-smile from Ehlers, and a short answer. "I think so, yes."

"Sit down," Delafosse reminded him.

Grudgingly, Wilson sat.

"When did you arrive in Eagle?"

"This afternoon. What's it to you?"

"Where did you come from?"

"Dawson. Why?"

"Down the river, or over the summit?"

"Ah . . . the river." Wilson frowned and moved restlessly in his chair. "If you've got some reason for this, you'd better tell me what's going on, or I'm gone."

Delafosse looked up to see Jessie standing in the doorway, nodding confirmation that Debbie had recognized Wilson's voice. He smiled slightly, leaned back in his chair, and gave the man a long critical look before responding in a tone that showed him to be all RCMP inspector, a tone that grew sharper as he continued.

"I don't think you came from Dawson, Mr. Wilson. I think you came from the other side of the summit on your snowmachine—the Alaskan side. I think you came with another, younger man, and that the two of you left Debbie Todd alone in an abandoned cabin below the summit, with no food or water, without the means to keep herself from freezing—"

"Hey. What the hell? I never . . . You got the wrong guy here and—" Wilson tried to interrupt, but was overridden by Delafosse's steady flow of accusations.

"—and all this happened because you and your friends kidnapped her from Mandana Lake, took her first to Minto, where you mistreated her, drugged her, transported her across the summit, and finally left her to die. In between you killed B. J. Lowery, who saw something he wasn't meant to, and left his body near where you left Debbie's dogs, by the highway. Then one of you got a large amount of ransom money from Jessie Arnold and left *her* out in the middle of a storm with no transportation or hope of making it to safety. *You* are in *deep* trouble, Wilson."

As Delafosse paused to take a breath, Wilson once again began to whine his denials and sputter hollow-sounding alibis.

"Not me. I was in Dawson. You can ask . . . I never had anything to do with . . . You can't—"

"Might as well give it up, Wilson. It's not gonna wash," Caswell commented dryly.

"It's over," Delafosse said. "You were part of it and we can prove it. Show us your hands."

"What?"

"You heard me. Show us your hands."

As Jessie had noticed in Braeburn, he had no little finger on his right hand. From the doorway, she could now see that part of the ring finger was missing as well, but didn't understand its significance yet.

Delafosse nodded and made a beckoning gesture to Jessie.

"Aw . . . that don't prove nothing," Wilson insisted.

"It will," Delafosse told him. "We have your prints on the gas can you forgot in Minto."

"You can't, because I wasn't . . ."

His voice choked to a halt as Debbie walked across the room to stand at the head of the table, where he could see her plainly.

"Yes," she said, indignation and fury in her voice, "I'm here, you bastard. I'd know that voice anywhere. How could I ever forget? You scared me half to death, then left me to die—alone."

Recovered from her first apprehension, she confronted him like a young Valkyrie, wisps of her auburn hair fairly cracking with static that matched her voice.

At her stance and statement, "Hoo-Doo" Wilson lost it and began to give up his contradictory claims of innocence. Instead, he frantically began to blame his pretty young partner for everything—betrayed him easily and willingly in a vain attempt to present himself as a blameless dupe.

"Franz Hildebrand was tossed out of racing back in

1984 for doping his dogs,'' Ryan volunteered, hearing the name of the ringleader. ''He said then that he'd get even.''

''I saw him at the start in Whitehorse,'' Jake said, suddenly remembering. ''Wondered at the time why he was there. He's kept clear of races ever since the incident with drugs that got him barred. Tall, thin guy in a green, patched parka. You're right, Debbie, he does look otherwordly—face of an angel, eyes like a cat, and the heart of a stone predator.''

Debbie stared at him, appalled. ''I *did* see him before,'' she said. ''I'd forgotten—I only saw him from the front. He came and talked to me in Braeburn, just before I left. I didn't . . . know.''

There were just a few tears mixed with her anger.

''It's all right, baby. We'll get him,'' Leland assured her.

''Where is he?'' Delafosse demanded of Wilson.

''He took off down the river with the money. Fixed my snowmachine so it wouldn't run and sneaked out on me, headed for Circle this morning. Rotten bastard.''

''It's clear enough to fly,'' Cas said. ''We can catch him before he gets there, or be waiting for him.''

''I'll be going with you for that one,'' Alex told him. ''It's in Alaska—where it's going to be a satisfaction to do my job—in more ways than one.''

''Hey, *this* is Alaska,'' Delafosse suddenly realized, and turned to Jensen and Caswell. ''I've been treating this like it was my case, and that stopped at the border. I apologize.''

''Go ahead, Del,'' Alex seriously encouraged with a grin. ''It's been your case from the start. Don't worry about it. You're doing our work for us.''

''Okay, if you say so.'' Delafosse chuckled and turned back to Wilson.

''And who else was in on it? We know there are a couple of others. One that was with you when you abducted Debbie, and at least one more that has been giving you information from the checkpoints. Who are they?''

"That vet—Spenser. He mixed up the numbers of the chips, so two of Arnold's dogs were disqualified—we wanted to slow her down some."

"Bob Spenser?" Jessie's astonishment stopped the questioning momentarily. "That's incredible. Why would he do that?"

"Franz had something on him—he was caught somewhere in the Lower Forty-eight with an underage girl. Made the papers and cost him a teaching position."

"He's taken care of my dogs for years."

"Don't worry, he's not interested in dogs," Wilson couldn't resist saying with a nasty grin.

"I didn't mean that, you filthy old man."

"Who else?" Delafosse interrupted, yanking Wilson's attention back into his groveling recitation. "Who else was helping—passing on information? Someone told you Jessie had a gun. Who was it?"

As Wilson spat out the name of the last accomplice, the room grew silent with shock, disbelief, and a deep sense of anger.

CHAPTER TWENTY-SEVEN

"I am not a tree, born to stand in one place always and know not what there be over the next hill; for I am . . . made to go here and there and to journey and quest up and down the length and breadth of the world."
—Jack London, "Li Wan, the Fair"

"SO FRANZ HILDEBRAND DREAMED THIS ALL UP. *AMAZING*," Jessie said with a sigh, as Alex walked her back to where she had bedded down her team for their rest. "If he'd turned around as I went out of Braeburn, I'd have recognized him. All I saw was his back, as he was talking to Debbie. And I think I saw him one other time, too far away to see his face, but I remember that green parka—on the bluff of the Takhini River, first day out. I could be wrong, but I think so."

Wilson was safely secured, even from Jake Leland, who had finally agreed that he wasn't worth the effort of thrashing, except in court, where he would eventually wind up along with the others.

The group had agreed to say nothing of the results of their meeting until the other three kidnappers had been collected—all Alaskans, all now on the Alaskan side of the border. No one wanted to lose them or have them warned, so they all agreed to be silent and let the law do its work.

"We're going to have some real cooperating and coordinating to do with Canada,'' Alex said, as they walked through Eagle. ''But, with Del's help, I think it'll get settled in our courts.''

''Couldn't they be tried in both countries?'' Jessie asked.

''Anything's possible, but I doubt anyone will take the trouble, if they get what they deserve. Anyway, we've got to get the rest of them first. Cas and I will get a hop to Fairbanks with one of the Yukon Quest pilots, then pick up an official van, drive to Circle, and arrest Hildebrand as he comes off the river.''

''Dr. Spenser's already left for Circle. He'll be there checking the teams as they come through.''

''I think we'll let him slide until we can get the last two at the same time. He won't suspect that we know anything about his part in this, or be going anywhere fast.''

''I'd like to be there,'' Jessie said.

''You probably will be by then.''

''Now I can finish this race—somewhere in the middle of the pack and not as well as I intended—and take my mutts home. Debbie's going to run with me—so are Ryan and Lynn Ehlers. We all know we're too late to place, so we thought we'd just enjoy it together.''

''Leland's going to let her go? I thought her dogs were in Whitehorse.''

''*Let her?* He'd have a hard time stopping her, though he may have some trouble convincing her mother. She may be his step*daughter,* but she refuses to be a *child.* All this has made her grow up a lot—the hard way—but she's decided that the best way to get over it is to get right back on the horse that threw her, and I agree. Jake's realized it, I think. He's agreed to have her dogs flown in from Whitehorse. She won't be an official racer—for that she would have to go back to Mandana Lake, where she left the trail—but she doesn't care. She's going to be a really good racer soon, Alex. I'm proud of her, and I'll be glad to spend some time with her.''

"I can understand that, all right. She really laid into Wilson. Surprised even herself, I think."

They walked a ways in silence. She pulled off a mitten, took his hand, and tucked them together into the pocket of his parka.

"Hey, trooper. Did I tell you I'm glad to have you home? I was never so glad to see you—well, maybe once, on the Iditarod that time just outside of Nome."

He stopped and turned to face her, light from the windows of a house they were passing shining on his smiling face, glinting from an ice crystal or two that clung to his handlebar mustache.

"I've been wanting to talk to you about that."

"I know. When you heard I was in trouble, you just dropped everything in Idaho and came flying back up here, didn't you? And you've got to go back, right?"

"Right. But that's not all, Jess."

He reached for her shoulders, drew her close, and held her in the circle of his arms.

"I've got something—"

"I *knew* it," she interrupted. "You're going back down there to stay, aren't you? I had a feeling in Pelly Crossing that—"

"Sh-h-h. I've got something to ask you."

"*Alex.*"

"I said, hush. Let me talk now. This isn't a competition."

She waited, meeting the serious intent in his eyes with a wary stillness of voice and body.

"I'm through tiptoeing around about this, Jessie. Will you please marry me?"

Her silence continued, but she gave a small exhalation and looked down, unseeing, at the middle of his chest.

"Well? Will you?"

She looked up again. "Alex . . ." she began softly.

"Think, Jessie," he cautioned. "Don't just react. Think. This is the time for it."

"I'm thinking," she assured him. "But you *are* going to stay down there, aren't you? I have to know."

He nodded slowly. "Yes. They've offered me the sheriff's job, and I've accepted—for a lot of reasons. And, yes, I want you to come with me. But it's more than that, Jess. You know it is. You've known for a long time. I want a home and a family—even if that's just the two of us and a lot of dogs. But I want it settled, secure—permanent. It's past time, and I want us to get married. I love you, Jess."

"And I love you—more than I've ever loved anybody."

Something in Jessie's chest began a dull throbbing ache. She couldn't seem to get past what she could identify as disappointment—and a certain amount of enervating anger at his solitary decision. She took one step away from him.

"You've accepted it, but you never even told me about it."

"I had to make a decision. You were already in Whitehorse and so totally focused on the race that when I got you on the phone I knew I couldn't go into it. I told Cas I was going to take it."

"I had a feeling he knew something he wasn't saying."

"I told him not to tell you. It wasn't his place—it was mine. Look, Jess. Yes, I've committed to this sheriff's job in Salmon. I can't walk away from it now. It's two years of my life—promised. I never thought that you would feel so . . . this way."

"But you decided without me, committed without even asking me—without finding out how *I* felt."

She heard herself saying it and knew it was wrong—that she was making it the issue to avoid answering his proposal. He knew it, too, and turned away to face the river, discouraged.

"Is that the point? Are you going to turn being angry at me into a reason to say no? I'm sorry. You're right, I should have asked you. I made a mistake. Please don't punish us both for it. That shouldn't be the point."

"But I feel like you've done an end run on me and I haven't had time to consider any of it. I'm damned if I do, and damned if I don't. No matter how I feel, or what I do, we'll both lose somehow.''

"I don't want to lose you, Jessie."

"And I don't want to be lost. I know what being lost feels like."

In an agony of conflict, she knew that much. She didn't want to be lost. The rest would have to wait until she had examined it, considered every possible result.

"Don't ask me to make a decision right now. If you do . . . I don't see how I can say yes. Don't force me.''

"*Force you?*" Stung, he turned back to her, upset and frustrated.

"Didn't you hear me? I said I wanted to marry you, share the rest of my life with you. Not drag you off by the hair to someplace you'd hate, like a Viking raider. You've never even seen my Idaho. How can it be so easy for you?''

"*Easy?* Not just going ahead and taking a chance— saying yes—is the hardest thing I can ever remember doing.''

"Maybe that's what you should do, for once. But it doesn't seem like it's hard for you. You seem to just accept it as impossible without fighting.''

She thought about that for a minute, looking out at the solid shapes of the ice blocks on the Yukon.

"I think," she said slowly, "that women think differently. We're more practical in the long haul. Maybe we *do* accept what we perceive as inevitable more easily, but that doesn't mean we don't agonize over it—don't die inside. This is terribly painful for me, Alex. Don't misunderstand that. But, if it isn't going to work out for us, I'd rather it were quick and clean, than long, drawn-out, and crippling.''

"You sound as though I'm making some kind of demand that you have to resist. I'm not, you know. I'm trying to share something I love with someone I love.''

"Well, maybe I *do* feel that, in a way. I don't take well to demands—but you're not really the demanding sort, are you? I know you love it there, Alex. But that doesn't mean I will. Do you see? I love you. You know I do. I'd give almost anything for you—to you. But I won't give you less than my best, and I don't know if my best can include Idaho. Can you understand? I don't know what I would do there—who I would be. I have to know that, before I can promise you without telling us both a lie."

He was enormously hurt and disappointed. She could see it written in his eyes, in every line of his body. His voice sounded hollow in the cold air.

"So, you're saying no."

"I'm *not* saying that, Alex. I'm saying let me think about it a little longer. I've got a race to finish. While I do that, let me consider it—give it some time. Then, when it's over, let's go back to Knik, where we live, where things are more normal, and talk about it, okay?"

He shook his head. "I can't stay that long. I've got to fly back in four days."

She thought about that. "You'll be coming to Circle and Central. I'll come in, but don't expect too much there. I'll be exhausted by then and trying to get mentally ready for the last big summit that comes just after Central. Will you meet me in Angel Creek? That's just outside of Fairbanks on the Chena Hot Springs Road. I'll have an eight-hour layover there before making the last run through North Pole to the finish line. Meet me there and we'll work out an answer. Keep an open mind, and so will I. That'll be time at least to have given it some more thought."

Jessie, Debbie, Ryan, and Lynn left Eagle together the next morning as the sun came up to shine on the ice of the wide Yukon River. They settled easily into the long, steady, 180-mile run to Circle, taking turns in the lead position, stopping for regular rests, passing other mushers, but being passed by none, for they were well behind any of those whose racing ability, quality of dogs, and speed could have bested the four. They knew they would not

win the race—would not even place in the top few—but
were content that what they had already accomplished was
worth more to each of them than prize money.

Most of the time they were on the river, but a few times
the trail left it to portage through woods and several icy
lakes, and when they stopped to rest they usually pulled
off to camp in the woods, or next to a driftwood pile
frozen into the edge of the highway of ice.

They ran north through another jumble of ice blocks
and cracks where the river had frozen restlessly in the fall,
thawing and breaking apart to refreeze again into a paralyzed wasteland of natural ice sculpture. Forty miles out
they stopped for a middle-of-the-night rest at a two-story
trapper cabin at Trout Creek, and Jessie felt for the first
time since early in the race a sense of peace and wonder
at the silent display of northern lights that twisted ribbons
of color across the sky over her head.

She stood alone on the riverbank and let go of most of
the tension she had accumulated for the duration of Debbie's abduction and their attempts to get her back safely.
Part of it, she knew, was almost not making it out of the
wilderness herself, coming close to freezing in the snow.
It fueled her appreciation of all she observed and experienced, the people she valued, and she thought it probably
would for a long time. It made her want to hold fast to
what she had, instead of taking it for granted as she had
done in the past. Yet even as she admired and treasured
what she had, still she turned her attention to whatever
was coming next, for it might be lovely, as well.

What was she to do about Alex and his proposal? She
was not ready to analyze her feelings just yet, she decided,
wouldn't force it, but would let it float until the answer
naturally came to the surface of her mind.

"Nice night."

She looked over her shoulder to find Lynn Ehlers standing a little behind her, looking at the colors of the night.
The three-quarter moon floated in the nets of the aurora
like a silver seashell from some cosmic beach.

"Hmmm," she agreed, and there was comfortable stillness between them for a few long minutes. In the trees behind them, she could hear Debbie crooning to her dogs as she checked them before catching some sleep for herself. Someone opened the cabin door to toss a panful of wash water onto the snow and, in the light that fell through a window, Jessie could see steaming rising from the spot where it had landed and now froze.

"You know, Lynn, I never really said thank you for helping me with Gail Murray on the summit, for taking her to Forty Mile in my place. If you hadn't . . . well, you gave up your best chance in the race to do that, and you hardly know any of us—Gail not at all."

"It wasn't a big thing, Jess. If you race, you come to expect that bad things can happen and you may need to be part of them sometime or other. Honestly—I was honored that you trusted me. You really don't know me, either, but you told me what you needed anyway, and why."

"Well," she told him with a smile, "there are people I've raced with for years that I wouldn't have told. You get so you can read people pretty well. Anyway, thanks."

Another silence. This time a listening one.

"Ryan said something earlier today that led me to think that you and that trooper who showed up yesterday are an item. Is that true, Jess?"

She hesitated. "Oh, Lynn. Right now—I just don't know. We have been. But things are a bit mixed right now. Until we get it sorted out, I'd have to say, yes. We're trying to be."

"Okay. That's fine. I just wondered. But, as a friend, would you mind if I called once in a while after this is all over?"

"Of course not. I hope you will."

They walked back to the trapper cabin and left the night to its own dark hues.

CHAPTER TWENTY-EIGHT

"Silent, inexorable, not to be shaken off, he took [it] as the fate which waited at the last turn . . . [He] believed in those rare, illuminating moments, when the intelligence flung from it time and space, to rise naked through eternity and read the facts of life from the open book of chance."
    —Jack London, "Which Make Men Remember"

WELL BEFORE DAYLIGHT THE NEXT MORNING, THE FOUR MUSH-ers were on their way again, rested and ready for what the day might bring. At this point, at a tall cliff, the Yukon widened where the Nation River came in to join it and help in giving the frozen surface the impression of wide, slow-moving waters. The wind picked up, blowing any residue of snow from the glare ice, on which the toenails of the dogs made scrabbling sounds, but gained little purchase, and the runners scraped as the sleds and mushers swung back and forth at the back end of the gang lines. It slowed the group's speed slightly, but they were making good time and did not mind. They were not running so much to compete anymore as to finally arrive at the finish line.

They were not tired or ready for a rest, but made a traditional stop at Biederman's cabin. This was out of respect for Charlie Biederman, who in 1934–35 was the youngest mail sled driver in Alaska. At age fifteen, he had made the Upper Yukon's last mail run with a team of dogs in 1935, just as the airplane took over. In fact, carrying the "government mail" by dog sled on the river highway between Dawson City and Circle had been a Biederman family tradition from the early days. The sled Charlie used when he started driving had been on display in the National Postal Museum at the Smithsonian since 1995, just before he died in Fairbanks, waiting for the Yukon Quest winner for that year to cross the finish line, which Canadian musher Frank Turner did twenty hours later.

Ryan had suggested that they stop only briefly, but they found that people had come in from trapline cabins all around the area to watch the mushers come through on the Quest. So it was an hour of greetings, congratulations, questions, hot food, and drink, before they could be on their way north to a longer rest at Slavin, where the park rangers provided a spacious shelter in a two-story cabin on the left-hand riverbank.

Through the dark, they ran together after Slavin, trading places in their train of four, stopping frequently to make coffee and warm themselves, snack their dogs. It was one of the most pleasant runs Jessie had ever made in a major race. The pressure of winning had been lifted away and, though they did not run slowly, all being good drivers with top quality teams, they did not push themselves, either. It was, to her, as good as the best of training runs, when she would come home through the wilderness country that she loved, tired and pleased with her efforts and the performance of her dogs, glad to have gone and glad to be back—satisfied in a way that added to her personal account in the accomplishment bank. Running with four other people who felt this was a warm way of realizing what couldn't be articulated.

She thought of Alex, briefly. If I wasn't a musher . . .

There was much laughter and easy conversation, sharing of food and ideas, naps and wake-up calls. Ehlers was made an honorary Alaskan by the acclaim of the other three, which was formalized in scratches with the awl from Jessie's Swiss army knife onto a scrap of birch bark picked up somewhere by Ryan, and presented with great fanfare and hilarity. He promised to come back, if not the next year, then at least very soon. From the bemused expression she saw several times on his face, she thought he would, for it was clear that he had been infected by the lure of the far north and its people.

It was a long, flat run through the night, and they were all tired and ready for a long rest when they came to the first of a group of small islands and sloughs that told them they were almost to Circle. Before the Klondike gold rush, this settlement had been the largest in the area; it had been named Circle because the early miners thought they were *on* the Arctic Circle.

Debbie was in the lead when they crossed from the last little island to a big channel, went up the bank, and were suddenly at the checkpoint.

Leland was there with Debbie's mom, who flew to her daughter, to assure herself that all was well. He just grinned, the same proud expression Jessie remembered seeing at the start in Whitehorse, mixed with a touch of humor, and let them be women together without him. But when his glance met Jessie's and his lips formed the words *thank you,* she knew how much he meant it.

The four racers were directed to spaces near a big log cabin with white frame windows, the Alaskan flag pinned to the wall, along with a large WELCOME TO CIRCLE banner. They pulled their dogs in next to each other to begin the check-in process and went about finding straw for the dogs and the supplies they had shipped to this location.

Billy Steward all but flew to reach Jessie first and, losing all his teenage self-consciousness, wound his long arms around her in a huge hug of welcome before he realized what he had done, started to draw back, realized he didn't care, and hugged her again.

"Hey, Jessie. We've been waiting and waiting. How was it? Did you make up any time? Are you very tired? I wish we could help you here, like we did in Dawson."

Linda Caswell, her eyes dancing in her attempt to keep

from laughing and embarrassing him, was next, and her embrace was less exuberant, but no less warm.

"You made it. We're awfully proud of you. Billy doesn't know everything about Debbie and all, but Cas told me," she whispered in Jessie's ear.

"Here's your bale of straw," Don Graham sang out in his bass voice, pulling up with it and her supplies on a sled behind a snowmachine. "They told me it was okay to bring it this far, but you'll have to take it off to be legal."

"Thanks, Don," Jessie told him, conflicted, as she turned next to Alex and Cas, who were smiling from a position next to the dogs. Alex was down on one knee, accepting affectionate greetings from Tank, who, Jessie knew, had felt his long absence. Cas gave her a very straight, serious look and a slight nod, as Bob Spenser, the vet, came with an assistant to test her dogs, and she knew what was about to happen.

Out of the dark came two more troopers, who stood on either side of Spenser.

"Robert Spenser?" Caswell asked.

The vet looked at him, surprised by the official tone. "Yes." Then, catching sight of the men beside him, his competent expression crumpled and he dropped his clipboard. "Oh, God—no."

"You are under arrest," Cas told him. "Anything you say may be used against you . . ." He continued the Miranda warning, as one of the other troopers handcuffed the broken man. They led him off in the direction of a van that Jessie could see parked next to the checkpoint building.

There was a confused buzz of questions and comments from the people who had gathered to watch the racers come in and found themselves witness to something unexpected. The mushers themselves, and all those gathered around them, were unusually quiet, all except one knowing that it wasn't finished—that there was one more person to be called to account for Debbie's abduction, B. J. Lowery's killing, and the attempted murder of both Debbie and Jessie. In that uncomfortable silence, Jessie noticed that Alex had moved around her sled to stand with the trooper who had not gone with Spenser to the van.

"Don Graham?" Caswell asked quietly.

The big man gave him a startled look. "What?"

"You are under arrest—"

"Oh, shit. What for? I never had anything to do with—"

"Don't, Don," Jessie said suddenly, and took a step forward. "Please, don't. Wilson told us all about it in Eagle."

He stopped what he had been about to say and looked down at her, his face unreadably sad.

"I never meant to have you involved, or hurt, Jessie. I was only interested in the money."

"I believe that," she told him. "That's why it was so hard to understand and accept."

"I tried to stop you from running this race."

She thought about that for a moment.

"You mean the stanchion that broke?"

"Yes, that, your two missing dogs in Knik, and the sick ones in Whitehorse. I'm sorry, Jessie."

"You messed with my *dogs?*" She gave him a long, disappointed look and turned away.

Caswell read him the warning while Jensen restrained him.

Large and strong as he was, he could have put up quite a struggle, maybe succeeded in getting away or injuring someone, but he let them do their job without a fight or a further complaint.

"Well," he said with a hint of bravado when they had both finished, and even managed a rueful grin, "I guess I did it to myself. You never play, you never lose. It started out worth the chance."

"Franz Hildebrand?"

"Yesterday," Cas told her. "We spotted him on the river yesterday morning from the plane, and were waiting for him when he got here. He had all the money, just like

Wilson said. Leland got him right in one—face of an angel on a stone predator.''

"No trouble?''

"Well, he did have trouble getting up the riverbank when that piece of cable Alex and I were carrying took him off his snowmachine. Accidentally, of course.''

"Of course. Good grief, you two. I should have known there'd be something.''

"He just got a little banged up and didn't have a chance to use his gun. We got lucky, I'd say.''

"Somehow his bruises don't half bother me. I can't figure out why.''

Alex and Cas grinned at each other like a couple of small schoolboys, instead of the Alaska State Troopers they were.

Jessie ran the rest of the race alone, at her request, knowing she must now try to confront herself with Alex's proposal.

Ryan insisted on her going out first, behind Debbie and Ehlers by half an hour, but, from times past, she knew he would only follow, unless she wanted company. She hadn't known that he was aware that something was worrying her, and also had a confession of his own.

"I've felt badly ever since I went ahead of you over American Summit, when I knew there was something going on,'' he said.

"That wasn't your fault, Jim. I told you to go—we had to do it that way, no matter what came of it later.''

"That doesn't make me feel less guilty.''

"Oh, give it a rest, Ryan,'' she teased, to dilute the appreciation she knew he recognized. "Let your new wife give you the guilties. I refuse to be responsible.''

"I'll just stay away from both of you for the moment, thanks. But if you get to longing for a chat—or can't make it over Eagle Summit with that scrap team you've got—''

"Scrap team, my . . . This team will run the legs off yours.''

"We'll see. We'll just see, when we come to where performance really counts."

And performance soon counted.

They ran to Central, where Crabb's Corner made them welcome with a break that included some of the best food on the race in a cafe so full of wonderful, enthusiastic people that it felt like the end of the race and was exceptionally hard to leave. Here they were met by a tangle of media that had now heard the basics of the kidnapping and ransom plot and were anxious for any statement they could get from Jessie. They crowded around her with their cameras and questions until she escaped back to her team and the trail.

Eagle Summit was not, as its name suggested, near the community of Eagle, but sat glowering over a deep valley to the west of the Central, fine dry snow streaming from its crest like the sail of a giant ship. It was the last major obstacle in the race to Fairbanks.

When Jessie reached it, the wind was blowing its usual whiteout on the summit, making it as much, or more, of a struggle than American Summit had been. The steep climb seemed more threatening and foreboding as the trail went up and up, till at a few points it seemed the dogs must fall back onto the sled. Wading through drifts that reached to her waist one minute, down to what was almost bare, rocky ground the next, she pushed and shoved the sled and encouraged Tank and the team to their best efforts.

Once again, they went on and on, a seemingly never-ending nightmare. But finally coming out on top, where the trail eased to a run across another barren, treeless space that gave her a floating feeling, she found the thin sunlight made the ice crystals dance in the air around her, and two sun dogs hung their concentrated rainbows in the sky.

At the unofficial checkpoint at Mile 101 on the Steese Highway, which led to Fairbanks and allowed spectators to reach the communities of Circle and Central, she rested the dogs beside a small frozen lake. The wind continued to whip snow over the glare ice in streams and ribbons that made the dogs curl themselves up in their usual protective balls, once they had had sufficient food and water.

Ryan caught up, and they shared sandwiches pressed on them for the trail in Central, then Jessie snoozed—or closed her eyes in her sleeping bag on the sled and gave the impression of snoozing.

In actuality, she was trying to concentrate on her feelings about Alex, marriage, and Idaho. What kept interrupting her attempts at serious decision making were images of the race she was about to finish and the wide territory of the Yukon through which she had passed.

In her mind, ravens again rode wind currents over the Takhini River, the Chain of Lakes strung themselves out like beads along the string of the race route, great blocks of ice forced the trail into twists on the Yukon, and the barren landscape of the Klondike mining country rolled away over miles of mountaintops.

She recalled the look of ghostly moonlight reflected from river ice, filling its frozen passage with silver between canyon walls. The image of tortured trees on American Summit gave way to a memory of beams of sunlight that made a ladder across the trail she had run on the way back from her close brush with mortality in the frozen dark. She could almost have reached out and laid her hand on the steam she remembered rising as it froze in the light from a cabin window.

And there were the faces and voices of so many friends and valued acquaintances: Billy's enthusiasm, and the Caswells' support. Delafosse and Claire had been so ready with help, Ryan with companionship, Lynn Ehlers with easy friendship—Leland, Bishop, Murray . . . John Noble, dripping his thanks. And Debbie Todd, with whom she now had a bond that would endure.

With a sigh, Jessie released her concentration and let these impressions flood into her mind, realizing that they were, after all, a part of the equation that confronted her.

CHAPTER TWENTY-NINE

"Slipping back the hood of her parka, she bared her neck and rose to her feet. There she paused and took a long look about her, at the rimming forest, at the faint stars in the sky, at the camp, at the snow-shoes in the snow—a last long comprehensive look at life. A light breeze stirred her hair from the side, and for the space of one deep breath she turned her head and followed it around until she met it full-faced."

—Jack London, "Keesh, the Son of Keesh"

HAVING CROSSED OVER HILLS AND LONG VALLEYS, ROSEBUD Summit, a screaming downhill run, and a tangle of creeks and overflow, Jessie ran the last easy four miles of broken trail into Angel Creek, ready for a mandatory eight-hour rest. The parking lot around the small lodge building was a mass of vehicles and people who had driven out from Fairbanks and its surrounding communities to watch the racers in the middle of the pack come through.

Checking in, she found that Debbie Todd, who had arrived just half an hour before, had saved a space for her.

"Could we run the last part together, do you think?" the young woman had asked her, and Jessie was glad to agree.

"If you don't mind waiting for me an extra half hour, I'd like that."

Food was heating for the dogs, and she was pulling booties off their feet, when Linda Caswell and Billy found her.

"Cas and Alex got caught in town," Linda told her. "There was a bunch of paperwork and arrangements for . . . well, you know. But they'll show up soon."

Billy stood silently watching Jessie work, his hands in his pockets, and she knew he itched to help, but there was something else. She let him come to it in his own time.

"Jessie?" he said.

She glanced up to find a painful frown on his face and waited for his question.

"Why did Don do that?"

What could she tell him? The boy had followed big, bluff Graham around like a young dog follows his leader, admiring, learning, trusting. There was no explanation that Jessie could possibly attempt that would cushion the shock of his betrayal—heal even a fraction of the pain she was seeing and hearing in Billy. It made her sad and angry.

"Sometimes people make mistakes, Billy," she reminded him. "We won't ever really understand why— maybe he doesn't understand, either. But he's not a totally bad person because of one mistake—even if it was a big one."

"I *hate* him."

"No—you don't. You hate what he did. So do I. But don't hate him. Remember the good things. Can you try to do that?"

"I don't know. Maybe later—not right now."

"Later will be fine. Take your time."

She got up and gave him back the hug he had given her in Circle, then sent him off to see if the vet was anywhere handy to look at a questionable abrasion on Bliss's foot.

Jessie had eaten, rested, and sorted out everything from her sled that she would not need in order to lighten it for a fast run to the finish line. All the extra equipment and supplies would go in her truck with Linda and Billy. Graham had asked Cas to drive his truck back to Knik. The dogs were hitched and ready, and there was less than half an hour left before she could check out and get back on the trail, when Alex Jensen came walking across the lot to find her sitting on her half-empty sled bag, sipping a cup of peppermint tea.

"Hello, you," he called. "How's it going? Sorry about the delay in Fairbanks."

"That's okay."

She patted a spot beside her on the sled and he lowered himself onto it.

"How's Don? Bob Spenser?" she asked.

"Locked up along with Hildebrand and Wilson, but okay, considering."

"I still have trouble believing those two could have let themselves get mixed up in all this."

"They didn't know it was going to turn so ugly, I think."

"Me, too."

There was a long pause, as each of them searched for a way to get to what they really needed to talk about.

"Jess," Alex finally said, "I want you to know that I'm sorry I didn't turn down the job, rather than make my own decision about it. I should have waited till I *could* talk to you about it."

Sometimes people make mistakes, she remembered telling Billy, and that one mistake didn't make them bad people.

"You did what you felt you had to do," she told Alex. "It doesn't matter now. I'm over being mad about it, okay?"

"Okay."

He waited, knowing there was more.

"I already knew—in Pelly Crossing—that you weren't coming back—not to stay," she said.

"You said that."

"I've been thinking about a lot of things in the last three days. You're right that I've never seen Idaho, don't know it at all, but . . ."

"I've been thinking, too. Couldn't you come down this spring for an extended sort of visit before you decide? We could write and phone till then."

"A long-distance relationship?"

"Well . . . yes, for a while. If you really don't want to live there, we could write and commute until I could come back."

"That's two years."

"Yes."

She wondered at his optimism, quiet for a minute or two in the dark beyond the lights of the Angel Creek Lodge.

"Hey, Jessie," Debbie called out, beginning to move her team toward the checkpoint.

She got to her feet. "I'll be just a minute here, Deb."

"Jess?"

Turning so she could watch his face to read his response more directly, she replied.

"We could try, but you know it won't work. We'll start out determined to work it out, somehow. We'll see each other once or twice a year, write letters, misunderstand a lot, get frustrated at the distance and telephone calls that don't get answered, or miss each other. Then, gradually, apathy and other interests will replace the hurt feelings and we'll realize we haven't really talked for weeks—the letters will get farther apart in the mail. I can't honestly say I think it will be different, can you?"

"I don't know."

"The other critical thing I know is that I'd have to give up racing if I moved to Idaho. The last three days have told me I'm not willing do that, Alex. It's what I do."

"Why should you give it up? There are races in places besides Alaska—the Rocky Mountain Stage Stop . . . the Minnesota Bear Grease."

"That's only two. Here there are dozens. It happens here—centers here."

"You could come back for them."

"I wouldn't—couldn't. It would cost the earth. We couldn't afford it. From Idaho, I'd have to ship dogs and sled, besides equipment and gear. I'd have huge travel expenses for every race I entered."

"Farther than Whitehorse from Knik? Wyoming isn't far away."

"That's only one race."

"You've always said you don't run dogs just for the races."

"I don't. I love just being out there—the solitude, this country, my mutts. But the races are things to measure myself against. They give it all focus."

"There *are* other things, Jessie."

"I know there are. But not for me—not now. You love it here, too. Would you give up law enforcement?"

He thought about that, carefully examining his reaction to the unexpected question of equity, and she saw the negative answer in his eyes as he ruefully shook his head and answered honestly.

"No, but it's not that simple. I don't have to give it up to be here, or there. And where I am doesn't change the way I feel about you. But I've already promised. . . ."

Without me, you promised, she couldn't help thinking. *You,* not—*we.*

"I love you, Jessie. We can work it out. Please . . . don't say no. Think about it. Give it some time. You can do that much, can't you."

"I don't think so, Alex. I've never been good at dividing myself—can't live in two pieces. *This* is my life. How can I leave it? How can you?"

"How can I not, Jess?"

There are always choices, she thought. But that's not quite right, or fair, either.

"I know, and I'm sorry."

There seemed to be nothing else to say.

With an ache like something broken under her breastbone and in her throat, she looked at him with long and conscious care, wanting to remember *everything*—the shape of his face, the pain in his eyes—all the reasons.

"Take . . . good care, then, trooper," she said in a voice that stumbled. "I love you."

His lips moved in a thin smile, full of regret, and he nodded, once.

She pulled the snow hook, Tank started the team, and they went out of Angel Camp to finish their race.

Author's Note

LIKE MANY GREAT CONCEPTS, THE IDEA FOR A RACE FROM Fairbanks to Whitehorse was born in a bar.

At first this was only the inspiration for the enthusiastic conversational flight of fancy of a small group of men gathered around a table at the Bullseye one night outside Fairbanks, Alaska, following the Bullseye–Angel Creek sled dog race in April 1983. They wished the race could be longer—to Whitehorse, perhaps, or . . . what the hell, why not all the way to Skagway, Washington, Oregon . . . ?

By the time their dream race had reached California it was time to head home, which they did, dismissing the idea of a race to Whitehorse as beer-splashed fantasy. That is, all but two of them did. The appealing idea kept drifting back into the minds of Leroy Shank and Roger Williams.

Shank, a three-time Iditarod racer, felt there should be an alternative to the famous Anchorage-to-Nome race, which he thought had outgrown its origins and no longer successfully represented the Alaskan pioneer spirit. Williams was no musher, but had spent three days at the Whitehorse McBride Museum, and felt that Yukoners and

Alaskans shared similar identities based on their mutual
history and background.

So, with nothing but enthusiasm and an idea that
wouldn't go away, they began to create a race that not
only would follow the historic routes established during
the gold rush, but would offer the same racing opportunities to a trapper with only a few dogs to run his lines as
it would to a professional musher with hundreds of dogs
and the sponsorship of corporations—a race that would
require the racer to use not only distance racing savvy but
bush survival skills as well.

Though the logistics were staggering, organization and
preparations all but overwhelming, the first race, run from
Fairbanks to Whitehorse in 1984, was an instant success. It
was named the Yukon Quest in recognition of its historical
foundations and its challenge to those who run it.

Actually, it is two completely different races, for every
other year the starting line is drawn in Whitehorse and the
mushers run the opposite direction, altering the challenges
and strategy of the route.

The Yukon Quest's reputation as the toughest sled dog
race seems justified, if debated by mushers who have raced
in the Iditarod as well. Longer distances between fewer
checkpoints certainly encourages self-sufficiency in its participants, who must run its length with only one sled. Attri-
tion is high; one-third of the mushers who leave the
starting gate scratch from the race and never cross the
finish line. But for those who cross that line, the personal
satisfaction of a challenge accepted and met is a validation
that needs no other reward.

Care must be taken, however. One man, Frank Turner
from Whitehorse, has run each and every Quest since the
first in 1984. He won the race in 1995, establishing a
record time (in either direction) of ten days, sixteen hours,
and twenty minutes. Turner is proof that sled dog racing
is addictive, and the Yukon Quest a challenge that many
cannot resist measuring themselves and their teams
against—again and again.

"And there sat Arthur on the dais-throne,
And those that had gone out upon the Quest,
Wasted and worn . . . stood before the King."
         —Alfred, Lord Tennyson,
         "The Holy Grail," Idylls of the King

Thanks and appreciation to:

My editor, Trish Grader, who has a real talent and sure instinct for what works—and what doesn't.

Yukon Quest committees in Fairbanks and Whitehorse for their generous assistance and support.

All the mushers, race officials, veterinarians, volunteers, sled builders, trainers, media folks, and spectators on both sides of the border, for their forbearance in answering dozens of questions.

Leroy Shank—who, with Roger Williams, dreamed up and believed in the Quest in the first place, then, against all odds, found ways to put the trail under it—for his trust and the sharing of his precious records and recordings of the race and its beginnings.

Frank Turner, the only musher to have run every single Yukon Quest since the beginning, and winner of the 1995 race, for a tour of his kennel and his considerable insights on the race and its running.

Anne Turner, mainstay of Frank's dedicated support crew, for patience and friendly assistance.

Bruce Lee, Winner of the 1998 Yukon Quest Sled Dog Race, for so generously sharing his experiences and memories of the Trail of '98.

Crabb's Corner in Central for their warm reception, shelter, and great food.

Circle Hot Springs for a long soak in their wonderful outdoor pool, in temperatures that froze rising steam on the surrounding trees till they looked as if they'd been flocked.

The friendly, helpful people of Whitehorse and Dawson City, Canada.

Toby Talbot, for half a lifetime of friendship and hospitality, and for collecting and sending me every scrap of Fairbanks newsprint that even suggested the words *Yukon* or *Quest.*

The Alaska Dog Mushers Association for support and information.

Vanessa Summers for the sharing of her considerable talent in creating the maps that grace my books.

For More Exciting Novels
by Award-Winning Authors

Sue Henry
Termination Dust
Sleeping Lady

Marcia Muller
Deceptions
Time of the Wolves
The Cavalier in White
There Hangs the Knife
Dark Star
The Tree of Death
The Legend of the Slain Soldiers
Merrill-Go-Round

Bill Pronzini & Marcia Muller
The Lighthouse
Beyond the Grave
Duo
Double

John Lutz
Death by Jury
Dancer's Debt
Diamond Eyes
Nightlines

Max Allan Collins
Murder by the Numbers
Butchers Dozen
Bullet Proof

Visit us at www.speakingvolumes.us

OCT 1 9 2018

9 781628 152616